HULAGU'S WEB

The Presidential Pursuit of Senator Katherine Laforge

David J. Hearne

HULAGU'S WEB
The Presidential Pursuit of Senator Katherine Laforge

Copyright © 2008 by David J. Hearne

Published by Subterfuge Publishing
PO Box 8008
Lumberton, Texas 77657
www.subterfugepublishing.com

Cover Design by:
Angela Farley

www.hulagusweb.com

ISBN 9780975597699

Library of Congress Control Number: 2008910963

Printed in the United States of America

To my wife Stacie for her support, tolerance and love.

Acknowledgments

Numerous people played a role in the writing of Hulagu's Web, directly or indirectly. On the political horizon, I must acknowledge Ron Paul for his courage of seeking true political change and Nick Lampson for trying to melt party lines and actually represent his constituents. All the military men and women who put their life on the line so the rest of us can take life for granted. I salute you, and hope my portrayal of your life in Iraq does you justice.

I am grateful to Ben Lee who provided a great deal of editorial support, research, and creative ideas to help with the completion of this book.

I would also like to acknowledge Mark and Jennifer Wulf, Pamela Truax, my wife, and Carol Crosby who helped edit the manuscript.

I want to thank Danny Lantrip, Keith Reese and the Sundancer crew from Houston, Mississippi. They introduced me to solar car racing and were the champions of the Dell-Winston Solar Car Challenge.

Among the many I should acknowledge are those true pioneers in the new era of renewable energy. Innovators like Kris Delorme of Turtle Mountain Community College, Gwen Holdmann for her research in Absorption chilling, Michael Briggs University of New Hampshire and expert in production of biodiesel from algae, Cliff Etheredge and David Etheredge Roscoe Wind Council, Judy Treichel- Executive Director of the NV Nuclear Waste Task Force, Glen Kertz president and CEO of Valcent Products, Kent Batman - President of Hardin Fuels Inc..

Finally I need to recognize those associates and friends of mine who inspired me or kept me going: Robert Verde, Art Williams, Jannie Venter, Daoying Ma, Mayank Vadher, Chris Kyle, Joel Russell, Jason Whitney, Jason Huebel, Representative Mike Hamilton, and again my good friend Mark Wulf.

Contents

PART ONE

New Hampshire Primary 2004

As the Chief squinted through the swirling snow, the large bus emerged from the gloom of that dark January morning. It sat quietly on the wrong side of Route 12 stalled in the snow bank. The steam from its cooling engine merged with the falling snow to darken the night even more. The tires on the exit side were shredded, and the large bus rested on its rims, causing it to lean precariously toward the road. Narrow beams of light streamed out of the bullet holes on the exit side of the bus, spotlighting the flakes of falling snow and the eerie, deserted road. The bus's still blazing headlights illuminated the snowdrifts and a bloody body, which was shrouded in a thin layer of glistening snow. As Chief Richardson moved closer to the bus, he could hear moans coming from inside the vehicle and smell the acrid odor of cordite. On the cold steps of the bus, his flashlight revealed a frozen patch of red slush and small red icicles that had formed from the blood dripping down the steps.

The memory of January 25 is indelibly etched deep in my mind. Even before the inevitable blare of the alarm went off that morning, I lay there in that state of half sleep and half awake, enjoying the warmth of the bed and my wife nestled close to me. I only had a scant four hours of sleep, and I wanted to savor every second of it. The wafting aroma of fresh coffee was an ominous sign that my last seconds of sleep were few before the alarm would come alive. I grabbed the top of the blankets and pulled them up to my cold nose just as WKNE FM invaded the quietness of the morning by blasting out the morning news. I opened an eye and glimpsed out into the still dark morning. All night long the howling wind had swept over the house, swirling the snow up through the branches of the pine tree outside my bedroom window. Little swirls of fresh snowflakes still danced about on my frozen windowpanes as the wind painted the snow over the town. The glowing red numbers on the radio read five A.M., which gave me about an hour to shave, shower, dress and eat before I was due at Charlestown's town hall. I fought back that powerful temptation to just lay there bathed in the warmth of my wife's body snuggled warmly against me, but somehow found the strength to toss off the heavy blankets. I felt the chilly air hit my naked body and shivered as Stacie instinctively grabbed the blankets, and without opening her eyes pulled them tightly around her body. It was then that the WKNE announcer's voice penetrated my consciousness, and his words shocked me into full reality.

"Police at the scene confirm that Presidential candidate Senator Katherine Laforge's campaign bus was involved in a serious accident. The accident, three miles north of Walpole, NH on route 12 appears to be the result of an assassination attempt on Senator Laforge. At least four members of her campaign staff are reported dead. The condition of the Senator is not currently known. The Senator was on her way to Charlestown, NH to reveal her Iraq Reconstruction Plan at a 7 A.M. televised Town hall forum. If the reports are accurate, then this will be one more in a series of assassination attempts against Senator Laforge in the last two years. Stay tuned to 103.7 FM for the latest developments on this late breaking story."

I felt stunned, almost nauseous, as I grasped the gravity of the news. I had just left her company only seven hours earlier. She had invited my wife and I to her campaign bus to celebrate her high standings in the Presidential race, and reminisce about our childhood in Charlestown, NH. Yesterday's polls had her on top, so the meeting was very upbeat. It just seemed unfathomable that this report could be true. She had been one of my best childhood friends, and I was dumbfounded, but thrilled to hear that she had become a Texas Senator. I had often thought of her and relived the memories of the things we did as kids, but after leaving school, we did not see each other very often.

Still contemplating the Radio News, I walked into the bathroom to shave. I turned on the hot water and just stood there studying my reflection in the mirror, as the mist from the steam slowly erased my image. It was somewhat symbolic of a ghostly face that would inexplicably emerge later that day from the mist of the snow and make me question my sanity. I did not know it then, but this brisk wintry dawn would herald in the final leg of a journey that had started innocently many years ago. Today I would experience life's madness as the paths I had traveled converged cataclysmically with those of others in life's vast web.

It was two years ago in the summer of 2002 that gave birth to this maelstrom that ripped into my life on this cold January morning. It started when I received a letter announcing a class reunion with the special guest of honor being my old classmate Katherine Hanna Laforge, now the honorable Senator Laforge of Texas. I read the letter over a couple of times and vowed to attend the event. I had never been to a class reunion, nor had I seen hardly any of my former classmates, since I marched down the aisle to Edgar's pomp and circumstance clad in cap and gown.

The last twenty years I had worked as a Project Manager for NARA (National Archives and Records Administration) in Washington D.C. Stacie and I had lived comfortably in a nice house in Oxon Hill, Maryland, about fifteen miles from my office at Capitol Hill. My job was not an exciting occupation like the life of a CIA or FBI agent, but it was challenging and offered many privileged views of secret decisions and actions taken behind closed government doors. In short, I was a glorified historian of our government's policies and events. Over the years, my research had accumulated many interesting stories that I parked deep within my memory required by law to keep secretly to myself. Often, these discoveries were quite exciting, making my job very interesting. However, my career came to a screeching halt in the winter of 1999 when I was mugged at a mall. My hospitalization and rehabilitation from the injuries forced me to take an early retirement from my profession. I was left with no major permanent damage except occasional headaches that I manage with medication. We sold our house in Oxon Hill and moved back to Charlestown looking for that peace and security offered by small New England communities. The fact is, I dreaded my retirement. At the same time I accepted it as a positive thing that gave Stacie and I the time to fulfill some of our lifelong dreams.

Being free to go to this Class Reunion was the first real positive benefit I could contribute to my retirement. I actually looked forward to this event and a month later, July 14, 2002, Stacie, and I were sitting in the Walpole, NH Country club listening to music from the sixties. In front of me were twenty of my former classmates that had metamorphosed from their youthful faces and attractive bodies that I remembered into strangers with caved in cheeks, protruding bellies, sagging breasts and wrinkled faces. I could feel each studying my transformation with the same shock and bewilderment as we all listened to the Shirelles belting out "Mama Said." But even through this erosion process we all had endured over the years, most of us were still recognizable as the Billy, Judy, Vince, or Steven of yesterday.

Just attending a class reunion denotes your unspoken acceptance to be judged by your peers in a "living progress report." The big question on everyone's mind is where do they stand in the new pecking order of the old class. I knew nothing of their lives, and they likely knew nothing of mine. With the constant wailing of songs from our youth like Roy Orbison's haunting, but beautiful song "Crying" and the magic of a couple of cocktails, we were soon all telling jokes of our past and reminiscing about those days long gone by. Another drink or two later found each of us inexplicably divulging who, and what we were now and the progress report started to take shape.

Our class was basically like most others. We had those who had stayed emotionally and intellectually the same, but just aged physically. They still thought Chubby Checker's "The Twist" was still popular on the radio. And of course, we had those who were financially successful and those who still worked for minimum wage. There were those who changed in ways we never would have fathomed, and then those like Senator Laforge who reached the top of the mountain we all once had sworn to climb. She was the shimmering star for our class, and it seemed very bizarre to refer to her as Senator. She was really Kat to all of us, and her position in the real world made us feel a bit uncomfortable when talking with her.

As a kid, she had lived next door to me, and we had played together every day. She was the ultimate tomboy then and played only with us boys. She played army men, cowboys and Indians, went camping with us, handled frogs and snakes, and was basically my best friend. But then Mother Nature started changing Kat, and suddenly we were not allowed to play the same with her any longer. Now my best friend used makeup, perfume and dressed in the latest skirts or dresses. Her parents started involving her in more traditional women activities, and our friendship quickly changed. Older boys started to take notice of her, and it was hard for us to be around her without angering her latest suitors. In high school I asked her out on a date, but felt so awkward trying to be romantic that I never asked again. I think she was equally uncomfortable dating her old frog catching buddy, and was glad I gave up so quickly. We remained friends and she shared with me every detail of her life, including her most intimate dating adventures. As a senior she was probably the prettiest girl in class, and, of course, very popular with the guys. However, none of our classmates got to date her because she started going steady with a boy from College. Even though we were all a bit jealous, we did think that was really cool. For her it was probably very good, because she was able to stay focused on schoolwork and still be considered "very in" to all of us. We would all study together, and some weekends she would enlist me to drive her to Dartmouth to visit her boyfriend. Just as high school graduation rolled around, her senior romance fizzled. I don't think she really cared, as she was off to Stanford University. While in college, we corresponded back and forth for a few months, but the letters became less frequent and then virtually stopped. Regardless, my interest in Kat continued, and over the years I eagerly followed her political ascension, watching in awe, as my childhood friend became Senator Laforge. Often, I found myself excitingly watching C-Span and other news programs, just to catch a glimpse of Kat debating world issues with other political leaders. The infrequent letters I occasionally did receive from her, always excited me and became treasured mementoes.

Kat was still very attractive after all these years, and I had my suspicions that a bit of her beauty and youth had been augmented by modern medical advances. She was definitely the most stunning woman at our reunion. She lost no time mingling with us and playing politics. Kat told us how glad she was to be here among her old friends. She spoke of how often she had thought of us and how homesick she had been for Charlestown and the Monadnock Valley. Her sentiments did not appear that genuine since Kat had not seen most of us for over a quarter of a century. My relationship with her was different because we occasionally did meet since we both worked in Washington. Regardless, we all were genuinely glad to see her again and to all be together. Our entire class would have been labeled by most as a bit dysfunctional, because few of us seemed to keep in contact with one another.

Tonight we were all searching for those nostalgic magic moments of long past. For most of us there was really nothing significant that had happened between the time we were celebrating and this moment we were now sharing. One thing we all agreed upon was that Senator Laforge was now legitimately rich, famous and powerful, and to the utter disbelief of most of us, was also hinting at running for President of the United States. She was one of us, so her success felt like something we all could celebrate. The funny thing about Kat was that she never tried to be popular, but was anyway. She showed traits of a politician in high school by being that individual who could be friends with those of the "In Crowd", and then with those students who others ostracized. She was always studious and was voted at graduation as the "Most likely to be a librarian."

Most of the night we all sat around talking and joking in large groups. Finally, four of us, Senator Laforge, Tom Hester, Vince Hand and myself broke away from the others and reminisced privately of some of our old exploits. We had been a very close group of kids and shared many adventures. We were very proud of what Kat had accomplished and wanted to hear more about life inside the capital beltway. Just as Dee Clark hit one of those unforgettable high notes in his song, "Raindrops", we commandeered a table in the corner of the banquet room that afforded us some privacy for a few minutes. Kat ordered us all a new round of drinks, and we sat there with the candle flickering shadows across our faces. After a few minutes of raucous banal between all of us, Kat bent over the table and quietly said, "I need to confess that I did not really come here just to reminisce about high school. I came here hoping that I would reconnect with my three best old buddies and charm you into wanting to rekindle our friendships. I am drastically short of people I can talk to and trust in my life. And I really need some trusted confidents in my inner circle that are not influenced by party hacks or political job pressures."

I think we were all surprised with her candor. "You want to employ us?" I asked.

You could see Kat's smile and her eyes twinkle in the candle's light. "No, not quite, at least not openly. I just want us to be friends like we once were, when I knew you guys would welcome my calls anytime day or night. Running for President is going to be a lonely, confusing harsh time for me, and like I said before, I need trusted friends I can talk to and confide in. Of course, I have my wonderful husband Ira whom I love and share most everything with, but he is afraid of being candid with me about my views and the realities of what I am involved in. I need trusted friends like you that I can divulge things to and know that it goes no further. Having politically untainted friends in my corner is very important to the success of my Presidential run and for my own political protection." She paused and took a sip of her daiquiri and then continued, "You will probably read a lot about me in the next few months, some good and some bad. I need to warn you that some things that we discuss might even put you in harm's way. Washington can be an ugly place as I am sure you are aware of. Anyway, I want you to think about what it might mean to your life, your plans, and your privacy in associating with me as I run for President. Hell, you might not even support me at all as a Presidential candidate, and that is certainly understandable after all the mean things I did to you when we were kids."

Vince interrupted her by proposing a toast, "To the next President of the US, our old friend Kat."

We all drank to that and Tom interjected, "This will be a first for a Kennedy loving head-in-his-ass Democrat like Vince to vote for a Republican President…wow!"

Kat smiled at Vince. "Ignore Tom's crassness and thank you, I really appreciated your toast."

She sat back and glancing at each of us said, "I don't want your answers now. I want each of you to think about it for a while. I will call each of you within the next few days to see if you would like to get together to let me talk your ears off about my platform, and how I envision you helping me in this Presidential race. If the thought of this is at all uncomfortable to you, then your answer is easy. It should be a definite "no." But if I charmed you or interested you at all, I promise you a few exciting months that we all will share together."

After she outlined her simple needs, we all sat stone silent. Kat then broke our silence once more.

"If any of you do decide that this is of interest to you, please understand that our relationship will be a sacred covenant. Breaking it could result in dire consequences for all concerned. You cannot discuss my request with any one, not even your wives." She smiled at each of us and said, "Okay, let's have fun again and toast to renewed friendships."

With a click of glasses the conversation ended, and we all blended back into the reunion talking about old cars, strange diseases, divorces, kids and how great music used to be.

My mind was racing. All I wanted to do was to hold Stacie and forget about Kat and our little discussion. Moments like these reminded me of how important Stacie is to my sanity, and how lucky and strange it is that we are together. In the background, Blue Moon by the Marcel's was playing, and the words just seemed to say it for me.

Blue Moon, you saw me standing alone
Without a dream in my heart
Without a love of my own

Blue Moon, you knew just what I was there for
You heard me saying a prayer for
Someone I really could care for

And then there suddenly appeared before me
The only one my arms will ever hold
I heard somebody whisper, 'Please adore me'
And when I looked, the moon had turned to gold

Stacie and I had our last dance and said the compulsory "Good Byes" to everyone. I noticed then that Kat had already left as her limousine and entourage were gone from the parking lot.

As we headed north on Route 12, we knew we were back to the present as WYRY played Lee Greenwood singing, "God Bless The U.S.A." I found myself emotionally pumped up from my meeting with Senator Laforge, and found conversation difficult with Stacie. This triggered an automatic fear in her that something was wrong, or that I was melancholy from meeting with all my old classmates. I wanted to tell her what Senator Laforge had discussed with me, but I was not really sure what it all meant, or if she would even call as she had promised. I was not sure if talking to Stacie about this would expose her to danger. I decided to give her a very condensed version. I told her that the Senator wanted to stay in contact, and that she invited me to call her anytime, day or night. Stacie was into the political scene, so she appreciated this future relationship with the Senator. I had just finished giving her a run down on Kat, Vince and Tom, when my cell phone rang. It was Senator Laforge. "Hello, are you surprised, I called you so soon?"

"Yes, but glad you did."

Kat responded back, "Are you interested in talking more about our new friendship?"

"Yes", I hesitantly said.

"Great, well let's meet at the Miss Bellows Falls Diner tomorrow at 2:00 PM., would that be a convenient time for you?"

"Hell, I am retired. Anytime is convenient."

The Senator chuckled and said, "Good, remember our meeting is private, just between you and I."

"I haven't forgotten."

"It was great seeing you again, and I will be thinking about you and your family tonight. See you tomorrow!"

The call ended, so I folded my cell phone, and placed it back into my shirt pocket.

Stacie turned to me and gave me, her what-did-she-say stare. Under her withering look, I told her the truth that we were going to meet the next day at the Miss Bellows Falls Diner. Somehow she knew that she was not invited, and blessed the meeting by telling me that she was happy that I would get to see an old friend again. Astonishingly enough, she dropped the subject and just cuddled up against me as we drove home.

While driving along Route 12, which wound its way alongside the Connecticut River, I found myself engrossed in a Radio talk show. The host was engaging his listeners in a spirited debate on the problem the UN faced with weapon checks in Iraq. A lady called in and expressed her disgust with Bush because he talked tough on Iraq, but didn't do anything to back it up. She commented on how Clinton did not allow Saddam to snub us. She said she was glad he bombed the crap out of Iraq in 98, because Saddam would not allow the UN to search for Weapons of Mass Destruction (WMD). The next caller wanted to know what world she was from, because he felt it was obvious that Clinton bombed Iraq to divert attention or complicate the vote on impeaching him that day on Dec. 16, 1998, which did not eliminate the problem.

I was glad the program was lively because I was fighting falling asleep and needed something controversial to listen to as I drove home. Stacie had already fallen asleep in the passenger seat.

The commentator expanded on Clinton's attack explaining 'Operation Desert Fox' as a way to thwart Saddam's ability to threaten his neighbors with nuclear, chemical or biological weapons. He paraphrased Clinton as saying he recognized other countries had weapons of mass destruction, but Hussein was in a different category because he had used such weapons against his own people, both Kurds and Iranians. The radio host explained that Clinton's 100-hour attack on Iraq consisted of firing four hundred fifteen, 1.5 million dollar cruise missiles and 600 laser guided bombs at pre-selected targets associated with Iraq's WMD programs.

The show's host cited President Clinton's argument that the attack was necessary, because without a strong inspection system in place, Iraq could rebuild its chemical, biological and nuclear programs in months, not years.

Another person called in stating Clinton was no better than Saddam, because he authorized the slaughter of his own people at Waco, Texas and eighty-two people were killed because of allegations that Koresh had produced illegal weapons, sawed off shotguns or whatever. The talk show host disconnected the caller. I am not sure why because certainly the massacre did happen, and Clinton was President at the time. The Host ignored the caller's comments and instead interjected a quote from Clinton's speech regarding the reason he launched the attack on Iraq in Ninety Eight. "If we turn our backs on his defiance (Saddam), the credibility of U.S. power as a check against Saddam will be destroyed." I wanted to call in myself and bring up the point that 'Operation Desert Fox' did not succeed, because now we have a third administration faced with the same old festering Iraq problem.

Before I could dial my phone, a nervous listener from Boston called in and went into his unique theory for the many problems in the Middle East. He said that 1998 marked the third manifestation of 666, ushering in a new coming of the demonic evil of Sorat, the true Antichrist. The caller claimed he was a priest and wanted all to know that in the next few years' great evil will happen to test our faith. The announcer chided the caller about being a little extreme, but the Priest pressed on with a dire warning that this demon's goal is to strip humans of their souls, egos and all goodness. He said, "Sorat's evil will be spread by his infernal army of soulless followers willing to give their life for his pleasure of subjecting mankind to horror of the ultimate magnitude." The host thanked him for his views and let out a big sigh of relief as he disconnected the caller.

The show was entertaining, but I still found myself thinking about my meeting with Senator Laforge the next day. I hoped my excitement over the Sunday afternoon meeting would not bring on one of my dreaded headaches. Kat's chance of being a major contender for the presidency seemed such a remote possibility to me. I wondered how sincere she was in her expectations of winning the presidency from an incumbent. The truth was I had no idea of what I was about to embark upon. In fact had I known, it all would have been inconceivable to me that night.

A year and a half has passed since that hot July summer night. I had been standing transfixed in front of the bathroom mirror for a minute or so, watching the moisture on the glass, getting lost deep in my many thoughts of the past. My face slowly took shape again in the mirror, and I leaned forward, resting my arms on the sink, studying my salt and pepper hair stuck in matted clumps to my head. The bathroom door behind me opened and Stacie entered. She put her arms around me, kissed the back of my neck and silently comforted me. It was obvious to me that she had heard the news, and was not sure of what to say to me about Senator Laforge. Her silence and gentleness were more than enough.

PART TWO

Miss Bellows Falls

I pulled my naked self away from the mirror and Stacie's encircling arms, and stepped into the shower. My eyes were now moist from the raw emotions raging deep inside of me, and I wanted the water to wash away the evidence. The steaming pulsating shower hit my back and immediately started to relax me. I leaned towards the shower's back wall and closed my eyes, letting the blanket of cascading hot water sooth my body and mind. The drone of the shower blanked out the bedroom's radio still blasting out news of the snowy crime scene on Route 12. I felt Stacie kiss my wet shoulder and her soft hands move across my back, as she tried to hurry me up, so we could leave sooner. She closed the shower door and my thoughts jumped back to speculating on the attack of Kat's campaign bus earlier that January morning. As the stream of warm water calmed me, my memories of my meeting with Katherine back in July of 2001 floated back into my consciousness. I remembered the excitement I felt the day after the class reunion, and how the morning dragged on until 1:10 PM when I finally climbed into my car and drove to Bellows Falls.

* * * *

The Miss Bellows Falls Diner stands on the west side of Rockingham Street. The thirty foot long diner was a favorite place that we use to frequent as teenagers. Meeting here was certainly a little nostalgic for Katherine, but you could also find privacy here. The Diner had a distinctive barrel roof and porcelain enameled metal sheathing, the latter having a polychrome color scheme. The Miss Bellows Falls diner retained its original appearance over the last 50 years in spite of adding all types of modern conveniences.

I arrived about thirty minutes early to make sure I was on time for this meeting. I parked my car on the south side of the Diner and walked to the big chrome door of the entrance vestibule. Fortunately, most people were sitting at the counter leaving three booths open. The booths were oak with a red Formica topped table. They were designed for four people and had a metal clothes post attached to its aisle end. I selected a table in the far corner of the diner, which offered a clear view of everyone coming and going. I indicated that I would have company and ordered a cup of coffee and a piece of apple pie. I had not been here for quite some time and the elegance of the polychrome enameled metal panels gracing the walls and the long Formica topped counter still excited my passion for the past.

As I sat back to wait for Kat, the diner's old jukebox entertained me with a new country tune by the Jamie Talbert Band. Before the song ended, my waitress was back at my table with my coffee and a hot piece of apple pie topped with a slice of Vermont Cheddar cheese. A coffee stained newspaper that had been left behind on the counter caught my eye, and I confiscated it. The headlines read, "President Mohammad Khatami – tells Bush to stop insulting Iran" and below that was a story about "Four Boston police officers hospitalized after scuffle." A more cheery story was a review about the movie "Road to Perdition" with Tom Hanks. I started to read the article, just as I noticed a sedan pull up with a man and woman in it. The man was dressed in a nice suit and Kat was in a blouse and jeans, carrying a very elegant briefcase. Katherine was coming in alone.

She waved to me for a second as she stood in the vestibule and then walked the twenty-five feet or so to my booth. She gracefully slid into it and placed her briefcase on the adjacent seat. Katherine told the waitress who came over that six others were joining us, and she wanted to order their food now, and save the table right behind us for them. The waitress took the large order and agreed to reserve the table behind us for them. Kat told her to just set out everyone's diet cokes, but hold their food until they arrive. Before I had a chance to embarrass myself by asking about who the others were she winked at me and said, "This buys us a bit more privacy. And the citizens of Texas want to buy you lunch so order whatever you want." She was good at making things work her way.

Her ploy was just in time because as the waitress left our table, a couple walked into the diner. The guy was a tall seedy character wearing a black leather vest and worn jeans. His muscular arms displayed a multitude of tattoos. At his side was a sparsely clad lady with a very sexual demeanor. They walked directly towards the tables that Kat had just reserved.

"I'm sorry, sir, but those seats are taken," the waitress exclaimed, as the couple prepared to sit in the booth behind Kat.

"Taken? What do you mean? A joint like this don't need no reservations," the man angrily retorted.

The waitress nervously responded, "Um, sir, those seats are reserved for the rest of this couple's party, and they have already ordered their food." The waitress nodded towards the Senator.

The burly man glared at the waitress and grabbed his lady friend by the arm and swung her around. He did not reply back to the waitress, but shot a piercing look at me as he sauntered over to the counter just a few steps from our booth.

I watched them as they took seats at the counter. The minor incident for some reason made the hairs on my arm stand up and a shiver ripple through my spine. On the back of his vest was the name of some motorcycle group, which was unreadable to me without my glasses. I reached for them just as Kat snapped her fingers in front of my face. I smiled at her and apologized for being so easily distracted, but those two were peculiar.

I stayed focused on Katherine now and told her how very honored I felt to be someone she still trusted and would consider as her friend and confidant. She smiled impishly and said "friends are a hard commodity to find anymore." She said she was even happier than I at having my friendship back in her life. Once Katherine got her burgers and fries, and I had my liver and onions, she started talking quietly about the importance of our friendship. She again stressed that I should realize the seriousness of having an association with her, even a distant one, as she prepared to run for President. She portrayed our relationship as a covenant between two individuals and reminded me that once a part of a covenant, it is often difficult to walk away.

If I did become involved, it could interfere in my life immensely and expose me to an invasion of my privacy and possibly place me in danger over some of the information, she might divulge. At this point, whatever she said just enticed me more to get involved. Adventure had eluded me for years and just being associated with a candidate for the presidency was exciting. Once more, I emphatically told her, "Yes, I want to be involved."

Katherine smiled and said, "Okay, great, then let's have one more understanding. You do not discuss what I tell you with anyone, not even Tom or Vince. In fact, it is best for you not to talk about me at all with them, unless I specifically tell you to mention something to them. I will tell them myself that you decided against my offer, okay?"

Again I nodded an agreement and spat out another, "okay."

"Great so let's get down to business. I need to bring you up to date on my campaign, what I am involved in right now, and how you can help. First, did you catch the news about Iraq today?"

"No, not really. I was just glancing at the newspaper when you arrived."

"The news is reporting that Syria is violating the U.N. embargo and delivering to Saddam, refurbished T-55 tank engines, replacement parts for T-72 tanks, military trucks and even an anti-aircraft cannon."

I looked at Katherine and asked her. "And what should that mean to me?"

"Good question. I think it means you can count on seeing another war happening soon."

"I take it, you don't believe the sanctions are going to work?"

"Absolutely not." She replied. "Saddam has no problem finding willing countries to supply him with weapons or spare parts for his military equipment. Look at it this way, if Syria, the sitting President of the U.N. Security Council, finds it perfectly ok to provide its old arch enemy with weapons and spare parts, why shouldn't other countries?"

"Very good point!"

"Many countries do it not only for the money, but because they want other nations to fight their grudges against us. It is a crazy world. During the eighties, France, Russia, and our own Reagan Administration supplied Iraq with weapons to fight Iran. Israel was also supplying weapons to Iran to fuel the fires even more. We all made money from the arms deals and had our battle with Iran fought for us by Iraqis. Saddam served basically then as our proxy fighting Iran."

"I am sure you are right that others would like to see us in a similar situation."

"Most certainly, we now have our nemesis that celebrates any problems we may encounter. The Palestinians danced in the street after 9/11, and I feel certain that some officials in European countries privately gloated over the tragedy. We are tolerated, but despised by many governments. As a Senator, I have come to learn that jealousy is as rampant between governments as it is between people. Our military power and money are what insulates us from their hate and ability to destroy us."

"So, if you are elected President will you have a different strategy to end the crisis with Iraq?"

"The problem won't wait until I am elected. I am convinced that war with Iraq is a near certainty. However, I do have a plan that I hope will remove some of the reasons we have for war with Iraq, or if all goes well, even prevent it."

"What is your plan?"

"I cannot divulge it all to you, but I will tell you some of it today. Unfortunately, I have to hold back some of the plans. Actually, not all of it is even known by me. Regardless, you will know way before the general public gets wind of it."

"Kat, am I going to wish I had never got involved with this?"

The Senator raised her hand and interrupted me. "You will never be involved in anything that might hurt you. You might toss and turn some nights wondering what the hell is happening, but I won't drag you into any situation that could expose you to any type of harm. I need you to be my liaison to the public and to be a trusted friend that I can count on when I need advice or perhaps a favor."

"Okay Kat! I trust you and like I said before that twenty odd boring years at NARA makes it hard to turn down anything that hints of excitement."

Katherine smiled at me and continued. "Good, so let's continue with the business at hand. Let me tell you what I will face if I win the Presidential

election this time. The 9/11 attacks on the World Trade Center, the Pentagon and Flight 93 is our Pearl Harbor of the new century. Those attacks
ushered in a new insidious war for us to fight. And, I am telling you, that this
new war is as serious to our country as the Second World War was sixty
years ago. This time, we are faced with a war that we just might lose."

Kat paused, looked at me seriously and said, "As successful as we were
militarily in Afghanistan in routing out the Taliban government and al-
Qa'eda, the terrorist movement was far from defeated. In fact, it has
spread out more into an even larger global organization. Actions like 9/11
are viewed by many Muslim extremists as a huge recruitment event and
more of a reason to join the militants. We are facing a worldwide terrorist
movement funded and supported clandestinely by countries and extreme
Islamic figureheads. This is guerilla warfare on a global basis. They are
cunning and are as dangerous to our country as Hitler was in the WWII.
They can defeat us."

"You really believe that? We have the best military in the world, for
sure."

"They don't need a huge army to wage war. They only have to evoke
fear in our people and divide the American public. The political climate here
is so divisive that if there is a war, and the leaders of these terrorist organizations adopt the same tactics that Ho Chi Minh used against us in the
Vietnam War, this conflict will be won psychologically and never hardly
fought on the battlefield. We will fight ourselves. Our myopic and power
hungry representatives will lose the war for us regardless of how well our
soldiers fight or how many battles they win."

Katherine dug around in her brief case and pulled out a folder. She
glanced back at me and said, "A lot is going on in the Middle East. We have
an undeclared war on our hands that is very hard to define to the American
public. We have always been a country that stood for religious freedom,
but that one tenet of our government is almost untenable now with the
attacks that Bin Ladin has brought to our doorsteps. Back on Feb 23, 1998
when President Clinton was busy refuting his sexual relations with Paula
Jones, the Arabic Newspaper, 'Al-Quds al-Arabi,' published an ominous
declaration of the 'World Islamic Front for Jihad' against the Jews and us,

the Crusaders. The declaration was signed by Islamic militants like bin Ladin and others from Egypt, Pakistan and Bangladesh. In short, it calls upon all Muslims to kill us wherever we are. It tells them to kill anyone who is American, Christian, or Jew. Their fatwah, or ruling, is to kill Americans and their allies – both civilians and military. They make it an individual duty for every Muslim to comply with this ruling, if they are true to their faith and want to be blessed by God. In essence, it was a religious declaration of war against our country and people, but at that time it was not taken seriously by the Clinton administration."

Katherine handed me a paper, which was a copy of the declaration. She pointed to a yellow highlighted paragraph that she wanted me to read and said, "This is their call to all Muslims to attack us."

The paragraph read: "We -- with God's help -- call on every Muslim who believes in God and wishes to be rewarded to comply with God's order to kill the Americans and plunder their money wherever, and whenever they find it. We also call on Muslim ulema, leaders, youths, and soldiers to launch the raid on Satan's U.S. troops and the devil's supporters allying with them, and to displace those who are behind them so that they may learn a lesson."

I looked up at Katherine and said, "This is unbelievable. They claim it's God's order to kill Americans. I had never heard about this at NARA. Is this declaration still a concern?"

"Most definitely it is still a concern!" She said, "You never heard about it because there was never an answer from our administration regarding this religious declaration of war. But as I said, when this fatwah was issued, Clinton was embroiled in one of his sexual scandals and did not have the time to really get involved with this threat. But there are over a billion Muslims, so we are talking about a potentially lethal situation if only a small percentage of them were to follow the instructions of this fatwah. After the 9/11 attacks, we did go to battle with a secular entity that we loosely defined as terrorist. But in reality, the terrorists we are battling are all Islamic."

Kat pulled out another paper and placed it in front of me. It contained a picture of an odd looking beast that looked much like a dragon, but had many heads. "Do you know what this is?" She asked.

I looked at it and then back at her and responded hesitantly, "Some my-thological dragon, I guess."

"It is a Hydra, the beast that Hercules tried to kill. Each time he cut off one of its heads, two more grew back. These Islamic radical organizations view themselves as living hydras. As we destroy heads of their organization, more appear to continue the evil. In the Bible, the mouths of the hydra represented the gateway to hell. I often feel that the hate and barbaric brutality preached and practiced by those who head these organizations could only come from Lucifer himself."

"I cannot agree with you more. Their acts are vile, senseless and disgust-ing. It infuriates me to think of all those who died on 9/11 for some obscure bull shit radical religious reasons that no one still understands. Excuse the language, but it just infuriates me."

Kat shook her head in disgust and continued. "You can see, we have a big problem. While radical Islamic clerics preach total intolerance to anyone who is not a devout follower and sanction killing and enslaving their adversaries like in Sudan, we are shackled by our constitutional principles to tolerate all religions, regardless of how insidious their views. As politicians, we have to tip toe around when discussing this war on terrorism in order to avoid characterizing the enemy as Islamic. We also have to use the generic label of terrorist to avoid the media attacking us of being anti Islamic."

"You think that they will attack us again within our borders?" I asked Katherine.

"It is very easy for them to strike virtually anytime they want within our country. We have over eight million Muslims living in America now. In fact, Islam is the fastest-growing religion in America. We have had a large immigration of Muslims, and a great number of African-Americans have adopted Islam. With followers in the millions, Islamist enjoy a large pool of souls to find converts to their radicalism. They certainly can and have found willing partners to attack us from within our borders."

I was astounded and I replied to Katherine, "I never realized that we had that many Muslims in the states. It is going to be very difficult for you to win this election if you are open about your feelings and beliefs."

"Well, these are more than feelings. These are facts that we have to face. Remember, John Walker Lindh was an American Muslim convert, who just pleaded guilty to aiding and fighting for the Taliban. This guy was from a nice Bay area middle class family. You have to ask yourself, how did he get indoctrinated so easily? We just have to hope that, we can avoid radicalism invading the great Mosques within America and turning more Muslims against non-Muslims. With their conception of God wishing all non-Muslims killed, it makes it extremely hard to deal with radical Islamists like those that were convicted of killing Daniel Pearl. Ahmed Omar Saeed Sheikh is a hero in Pakistan for killing and beheading Mr. Pearl."

"I have read about it. It is really sick that in today's civilization, any religion would sanction such barbaric acts. This is the type of horror and savagery that went on centuries ago. I cannot fathom this kind of hate, and I find it hard to have any respect for anyone associated with a religion that promotes this type of barbaric act. These are acts of the Devil not acts of any God."

Senator Laforge looked at me for a couple of seconds and then leaned closer to me.

"You have to be careful with what you say about issues like this, or you will find yourself accused of promoting hate towards Muslims. Many Muslims don't advocate this type of barbarism, but are afraid to speak out against it."

"Yes, I guess you are right, but it infuriates me that we cannot openly state our feeling about those who want to destroy us. It is really disgusting. This Ahmed, or Omar or whatever his damn name is, is an animal. This guy actually filmed the murder, and holds Pearl's severed head up in a video that they released, bragging about their barbarism."

"I understand your anger, and I must admit it also consumes me sometimes. That is one big reason, why I am campaigning for President. I feel I can make a difference in this struggle. Let me finish telling you about my Iraq plans."

"Okay, it just makes me sick that anyone supports scum like that. When I was driving home last night, I listened to a talk show with some crackpot talking about his theory on this demon, 'Sorat.' He claimed that he is here among us to destroy all humanity with the help of his followers who thrive on killing. Maybe he was not that far off, especially if we have people who are so full of hate and enjoy killing as much as these terrorists claim."

"You have to try and not let it affect you so much, because that is what they want it to do. Now take a couple deep breaths while I go over my stand and views on Iraq. Understand that these are strictly my own views of why we must be in Iraq." Katherine said quietly. "We need to have an entrance into the Middle East to help rebuild an Arabic nation that can be leader in the region. We also need to help it solve problems of human life, by creating technologies of production like farming, and technologies of social order, like cities and law. We want to bring stability to the region and gain a great ally. For me it is not about oil, but for many others politicians it is. It is about bringing modernity to their doorsteps. It is about allowing them to taste freedom and a better way of life. This is what we have to do to keep them from changing our way of life. This whole struggle is a war to save civilization, as we know it."

"So when will this war start?" I asked Katherine.

"We won't have a ground war with Iraq soon, because Turkey's fragile government was just crippled on July 8th when Prime Minister Bulent Ecevit's closest aid, Deputy Prime Minister Husamettin Ozkan, quit. Two other Ministers and fifteen Legislators all stepped down, which basically dismantled Ecevit's administration. Turkey is our primary logistical ally in the region. So, until the chaos in Ankara is resolved, we will be forced to find a new ally or postpone any serious military action against Iraq."

"I read a couple of days ago that Jordan was considering allowing us to use bases for preparation of a possible military attack against Iraq."

Katherine looked at me and smiled. "If what you read were true, it would mark a complete reversal of Jordan's previous stand regarding our use of Jordanian territory to launch an attack against Iraq. I don't think Jordan would feel safe exposing itself to the potential problems that could result from being openly aligned with us. Jordan is a very small country in that region. I really think there will be no war until next year. We will spend the next few months in preparation for war and enlisting other countries to work with us."

Katherine took a sip of her soda, paused for a second and then said, "I am sure that the President would like to go in now and be done with this war. Avoid all the debates, protest and drama by everyone wanting to keep the status quo. But unfortunately, it is not going to happen that easily. We are going to play the UN game and try to align some of our so-called allies to work with us. I have my doubts that we can persuade those against this action to change their minds. If we cannot, we are pretty much alone on this action."

"There are already protests. I watched one on the news taking place in San Francisco. I am sure these are nothing compared to what will probably occur later. You are right, we are going to have some epic arguments between appeasers and warriors on this war."

Katherine's face looked serious and she said, "I don't want to come off too cocky, but my election committee has a very serious meeting planned for me with Saddam, which will enhance my candidacy, and hopefully, prevent a lot of bloodshed."

"You are going to have a face to face meeting with Hussein?"

"That is the plan, but all details are not yet ironed out. If all goes well, I can assure you the meeting will be headline news in a few months. Hopefully, a real solution to the Iraq dilemma will be the result of my negotiations. The meeting is very important to me. It will either be my entree into the West Wing, or the end of my campaign. It is a totally secret operation that only a few of my most trusted associates know about. I would hope you could use your knowledge and contacts in NARA to smell out if anyone else has knowledge of these plans. You know how to research transcripts and reports without being obvious, I assume. Just try and see if any abnormal interest is being paid to my travels, actions, P2OG mentioning or with an operation called, 'Hulagu'?"

"What is 'P2OG'? I asked.

"P2OG is a rumored new policy created by the Pentagon's Defense Science Board (DSB) to give the ability to fight terrorist with clandestine black ops and covert missions. The policy allows the CIA or Military elements to launch these operations. Some of my colleagues claim P2OG is just some Meme purposely contrived to keep terrorist off guard. But, others like myself, believe it is a real policy and that covert operations will be carried out under it. Do you remember the old book on Hulagu, I used to bore you guys with?" Katherine questioned.

"Absolutely, I remember that book." I responded.

Katherine said, "Saddam Hussein and I, sort of share one obsession, as we are both history buffs and have an affinity for the story of Hulagu. Saddam refers to us as the 'new Hulagu,' that his country has to face."

She had named the operation after a Mongol warrior that, as kids, we had heard about from an old dilapidated book. When we were kids, Kat had a fixation on this book and would hide it in our underground clubhouse behind my house. The book was a grisly story illustrated by dark images from wood engravings depicting Hulagu's soldiers slaughtering the soldiers of Baghdad hundreds of years ago. Maybe it was her way of showing us that she was one of the guys. While Tom, Vince and myself were all peeking at the panty section in the Sears and Roebuck catalogue, yesterday's version of today's Victoria secrets catalogue. Kat was hung up on history. All of us, except Kat would consider it a lucky day when we would acquire a National Geographic magazine that actually showed naked breasts of women from some African tribe. However, Katherine was different, and found old history books with yellowing pages, her pleasure. This favorite book she would illuminate with her trusty Space Cadet flashlight and read to us the gritty story of Hulagu. I included part of the story here because of Kat's obsession for it, and that it is probably the genesis of the events, of which we all became a part.

Katherine would skip to Chapter 2 of "Hulagu the Warrior," and tell us all to shut up as she read in her most serious scary voice.

"The last impact of the horsemen blasted the entire wall inward. The ancient stonewall crumbled with a muffled roar raining stones and dust onto the people below. Through the holes shrouded with the swirling dust clouds, horses with their mounted warriors burst forth like angry hornets into the courtyard of the city. The horses trampled over the fallen and wounded buried beneath the debris of the wall. Those still standing or protruding from the pile of rocks were put quickly to the sword. Severed heads and body parts were trampled and pulverized as the invading horsemen poured through the breach in the wall. With their snorting steeds, the horsemen gathered together near the hole, glaring at the trapped people in front of them. With practiced precision they drew their bows and methodically unleashed a shower of arrows into the crowd of screaming men, women and children pleading for their life. The arrows found their marks dropping people in the trapped crowd. Slowly, the horsemen moved towards the crowd unleashing more arrows at them. Those trapped, with the arrows still quivering in their bodies, fell to the ground into pools of blood from their dead comrades. Finally, the few standing knelt down among the dead and dying begging the horsemen for their life."

Katherine would stop for a moment and take a drink of soda. We all wished she would stop reading this scary shit, but none of us would dare tell her. With a little nervous giggle, she would ask us, "what do you think they do next?" Without waiting for an answer, she would launch back into the next scene.

"The horsemen dismounted and with swords drawn, moved forward among the corpses littering the ground. They menacingly edged towards the remaining living women, children and men. The soldier's faces glistened with sweat and their swords and shields were splattered with the blood of their victims. The cowering women and children heaved and shook with the fear of the horror that surrounded them. As the first woman looked up at the invader, the glitter of the flashing metal was the last sight that she saw. And then the battle was just a cacophony of crying, screams and the gurgling sounds of the dying mingled with the distinct sounds of the swords, ripping into the necks and slicing through the bones and sinews of the few that had not yet been put to death."

"Blood was everywhere. On the floors of homes and splattered on stonewalls and pooled under bodies littering the streets. Even the Tigris River became a swollen trough of blood fed by the slaughter of thousands in the city of Baghdad by the marauding hordes of Mongols lead by the scourge of God, Hulagu Khan. Hulagu was the grandson of Genghis Khan and his cruelty and love of killing was unsurpassed. It is said that the Tigris River ran red with the blood of the massacred for over 30 days as the Mongols systematically moved through the city killing everything and everyone they could find. Thousands were beheaded, burned, put to the sword, or disemboweled. Women and girls were raped; many of them were then mutilated and murdered. Some claim that up to two million Muslims were slaughtered at this time. The streets of the city of 'Peace' as called by Arabs were littered with the rotting corpses of the dead and the air was putrid with the stench of death. The smell was so powerful that even the invading Mongols had to keep away for several days. The slaughter in Baghdad was so thorough and brutal that the atrocities are seared into Muslim's memories forever."

The waitress came back to our table and wanted to know if we needed refills, and if our friends were still on their way. Katherine assured her that they were, and took the waitress up on new drinks. As she stepped away from our table Kat asked her if they served the soda Moxie? The waitress gave Kat a sad look and said, "No, but it is available at the local stores."

I smiled at Katherine as I wiped grilled onions off my lips. I remembered vividly her story of Hulagu. I also remembered drinking bottles of Moxie when I was a kid. Katherine flipped out her cell phone and called her aide who was still waiting in her car, and asked him to cruise around town to the local grocery stores to see if he could buy a case or two of M O X I E. Her sedan backed out of the parking place and merged into the Rockingham street traffic.

Katherine smiled at me and said, "I wanted to keep him busy, and I really do want to introduce Moxie to friends back in Texas and Washington. Most of the country has never tasted it."

Katherine returned to her views on Iraq. "I think making Iraq a friendlier country to the US will deter worldwide terrorism in the long run. Many will disagree with me, but we have to help make things better for these people who have been taught to hate us. We have to give them a reason to like us. The youth in these fanatical tribes and clans in Iraq love our technology, music, big cars, and modernization. This stuff is as mesmerizing to them, as it is to our kids. The youth of Iraq should be our target. The radical Islamists target them to use for their cause as Mujahideen or suicide bombers, so we must offer them an alternative, something better. If we do not we will end up with millions of walking suicide bombers in our midst."

"So, it is not a quick fix in Iraq you have in store?"

"No, but it will be a very new beginning without all the bloodshed that our present direction ensures. Right now we have an elusive enemy that is as difficult to fight as my chance of winning the Power Ball. Many here in the states do not even admit that terrorism exists or poses a threat. It is like the mentality of someone with cancer when they refuse to accept that they have it. We cannot win an insidious war by avoiding the battles. Fighting a virtually invisible enemy is very difficult. They are so secretive that the names of their members are hidden, even from other associates. It will be a damn hard job. And, Islamic terrorists are even a threat to individuals like Saddam Hussein. So, making peace with Iraq will free up more resources to fight them, and perhaps even align another ally in fighting these maniacal barbarians."

"If our plans succeed, I will announce my candidacy, and I will be in a very powerful position to win the election. I also have one more major plank in my platform that is equally as controversial and will surely make me many enemies."

She let me hang for a minute as she took a long drink and slowly put the glass back down. "So what is this other thing?" I asked.

"I want to get rid of the Federal Income tax and replace the whole cumbersome system with a National Sales Tax modeled after the one proposed by the National Retail Sales Tax Alliance. This will help millions of Americans and make paying taxes effortless. The government will receive taxes from anybody who spends a dime in our country. It will eliminate tons of regulations and everyone will be easily taxed. Aliens, drug dealers, visiting foreigners, prostitutes, gamblers, and basically anyone spending money will be taxed accordingly. A higher sales tax will be levied against luxury items and rebates given to those who are living on social security or under a certain income level. It will cost us much less to maintain and be fairer to all. However, lawyers, accountants and IRS agents will hate it."

"How much will that add to everything we buy?" I asked.

"It probably will be around fourteen to 17 percent. At first glance that might sound high to you, but remember, no federal tax will be taken out of your pay, so your check will be much higher. Once we determine how much money we can save by eliminating the cost of existing compliance issues, we can adjust the rate. Right now it is estimated that $300,000,000 is spent by the IRS for purely collection expenses and compliance issues. That is a tremendous waste of tax paper's money."

"Well, if you win, it will be like a revolution here in America," I remarked.

"Oh yes, this will be a major change. It is not the first time it has been proposed, but it will be the first time it becomes part of an election campaign. A lot of congressmen support it. Big names like John Linder, Billy Tauzin, Collin Peterson, Max Baucus, Dr. Alan Keyes and a host of others sponsor the Fair Tax proposal. But I am not going to be able to make this work if I fail in my Iraq mission."

"You will do great!" I offered.

"Please don't patronize me. I won't stand a chance in hell to win this election if I cannot demonstrate I am as tough as a man when dealing with tyrants like Saddam. It is a perception thing. With our war on terrorism and this decade old standoff with Iraq, I have to show I am a leader strong enough to deal with national security issues."

"Seriously Kat, I am not patronizing you. When we were kids you were the toughest of all of us. We all looked up to you, and we still do. Look at you, a Senator from Texas, and that in itself demands respect. People will see you as a force that has to be taken seriously."

"I hope you are right. I will be up against a pretty strong incumbent for the primary. And if I win that, I will be up against some very seasoned tough Democrats. I need to get the women's vote, and believe it or not, they are the hardest votes for me to win. The majority of women vote for men. They vote for the handsome guy, or it is just some old patriarchal culture ingrained into our female subconscious. I still have some very high hurdles to jump."

"You think women have a little of the Stepford Wives syndrome when it comes to voting?"

Kat smiled and retorted, "Not just a little, a whole lot. Unfortunately, women the world over easily succumb to the idea that they are inferior. Look at what happened in Afghanistan and even now in the Sudan. You have women who are treated no better than farm animals in those countries, yet they make no real effort to change their position in life. Many will even tell you that it is the way it is supposed to be, and that they are content living as chattel. It is maddening to me."

I didn't really know what to say to all of that and for a moment there was an uncomfortable silence between us.

Kat broke the silence, "Dealing with Saddam is a huge challenge to me. This guy has outlasted three of our Presidents in this stand off so far. I think anyone with any knowledge of him would agree that he is cunning, charismatic, and megalomaniacal. He is a legendary figure, regardless of the evil we see in him. Without him, Iraq would probably still be a hellhole of warring tribes, clans, and feuding religions. Iraq had been in a virtual coma since Hulagu's beating centuries ago, and I have to give Hussein credit for reviving it. With his Stalin like brutality and iron determination, he pulled these dark age feuding factions together again and turned Iraq into the center of the Arab World. He amassed a huge army to retain control and protect his people from the next Hulagu."

"I take it, he considers us the next Hulagu?"

"Absolutely, Saddam refers to the United States as the 'new Hulagu.' He also makes sure that all are reminded of the many biblical experts who believe Iraq was the location of the fabled Garden of Eden, the birthplace of Adam and Eve. That is why he refers to Iraq as the 'mother of civilization.' A famous quote from one of his speeches is: "It is the mother of civilization of Iraq, which Hulagu of this age wants to attack. So, tell him in a clear, loud voice, 'Oh, evil, cease your evil doings against the mother of civilization.'"

Once more our cute waitress interrupted us, and convinced me to try another dessert. Kat decided on the same.

Katherine had another observation she wanted to share with me. She told me the story of Gilgamesh, the fabled king of Uruk Iraq who ruled that city approximately 4700 years ago. He was said to have had a dream that was described in Tablet 4 of the story of Gilgamesh, and it went as follows:

The skies roared with thunder and the earth heaved,
Then came darkness and a stillness like death.
Lightening smashed the ground and fires blazed out;

Death flooded from the skies.
When the heat died and the fires went out,
The plains had turned to ash.

"Gilgamesh's friend Enkidu would often interpret these dreams. This particular interpretation is missing from the ancient tablets. Most believe that Enkidu, like most political hacks, would have put a positive spin on this dream for his boss like he did on the other dreams, but was this dream perhaps more?"

Katherine leaned over the red Formica table with a mouth full of apple pie and asked me seriously. "Was this the vision of today's modern warfare at the gates of the cradle of civilization? Is this the Hulagu of Saddam Hussein speeches? Or is Saddam Hussein the incarnation of Hulagu's spirit, which has arisen again to continue the slaughter of the Iraqis?"

She leaned back into her seat, and I could sense that Senator Laforge was looking at me for some sort of reaction to her last question. I looked at her and said. "Hell Katherine, I have no idea. I certainly do not understand what Hulagu of old has to do with today at all. It sounds to me like just another way to complicate, or to legitimize or to give some brutal tyrant a reason to be who he has demonstrated himself to be."

Out of the diner window, I could see Katherine's sedan returning to the parking lot and resuming its old position again.

Katherine asked the waitress for the bill and to make those other hamburgers 'to go'. She locked her eyes on mine and said, "You are basically right. Hulagu of the past has little to do with today, but we do have a new Hulagu that Saddam Hussein will soon meet, and the new Hulagu will be the savior of Iraq."

Katherine reached down, grabbed her cup and finished her coffee.

I was not sure what she meant by her last statement, but I could sense we were about to end our meeting. I asked, "What do you want me to do for you?"

Senator Laforge replied, "You have already started doing it. Just being my friend and someone I can safely confide in. I am beginning to know so much about things. For my own safety, I want others to know what I know.

I want others to be aware. So, what we are doing now is basically all I really need you to do for me. Hopefully, I can repay you big in the future for this favor. In the meantime, I want you to have this as a reminder of our conversation."

She handed me a small plastic container displaying an old worn coin of some sort. On the case was a label that read "Ilkhanids, Hulagu 654-663 AH."

She said, "This is a 700 year old coin. It is not worth much today, but keep it and someday it may become very valuable. You know I am still a big coin collector, and I thought a Hulagu coin would be very appropriate for our conversation today."

I thanked her for the gift and told her that I thought I understood what she wanted, and I was glad to be there for her. We shook hands and Kat told me that she would like us to leave separately. She motioned to the waitress to bring me one more cup of coffee, and left a $20 tip on the table.

Our meeting was over.

I still had little idea of what, if anything, I was involved in, but had enjoyed the conversation with my old friend, Kat. I had the feeling that the reason for our visit was something like the old Czech proverb that stated: 'Do not protect yourself by a fence, but rather by your friends.'

I looked out the window and watched Kat drive away. The motorcycle guy and his lady friend were paying up and heading out also. I looked at his arm covered with tattoos, and suddenly he turned his head towards me, as if he had felt my stare. I glanced away from him and locked my eyes on the paper in front of me, but I could still feel his eyes glaring at me. A rush of adrenaline surged through me as I avoided looking at him. Then I heard the sound of the motorcycle, as it roared down Rockingham in the same direction Kat had just taken. With all the thoughts that were churning in my head from talking with Kat, I was probably thinking a bit schizoid, but a weird unease from his presence lingered within me as I sat there toying with my Hulagu coin.

* * * *

The sound of Stacie's voice ended my interlude into the past. The shower door opened and she stepped into the steamy cubicle.

"I hope you do not mind sharing the shower, but you are using up all the hot water." She said through the thick moist air.

I felt her cool firm breast press refreshingly up against my back as I welcomed her, "Please join me, honey, I need some distraction."

Her hands reached up to my hair, and I felt her squirt shampoo on it. She ran her fingers lightly through the shampoo in my wet hair, working it up to a thick lather.

With a soft sponge from the shower rack, she began to spread shower gel over my shoulders and down my back all the way to my buttocks.

A swirl of heat ignited in the pit of my stomach, as I felt Stacie's small pink tongue flickering down the small of my back. A rush of hot water crashed over my head as she lovingly slid her hands around my waist. I was now completely distracted.

"Men never do evil so completely and cheerfully
as when they do it from religious conviction."
~ Blaise Pascal

PART THREE

The Accident

*Prophet, make war on the unbelievers and the hypocrites and
deal rigorously with them. Hell shall be their Home: an evil fate.*
~ at-Taubah 9:73

With steaming cups of coffee in hand, Stacie, and I walked through the attached barn to our unheated garage. My breath fogged in the chilly January air as I pressed the red button on the garage door remote. The morning quiet was broken by the sounds of ice and snow popping off the garage door as it noisily retreated into the ceiling. I was dressed in a warm parka, but still shivered as the icy morning air hit my face. Outside the wind blew and snow floated lazily to the ground. It was a light snow flurry, much less than had fallen during the night, but it still added to the three inches of fresh snow covering the driveway. A foot high mound of snow and slush deposited earlier by a snowplow sealed the exit. Beyond the driveway, headlights pierced the darkness, and I heard the crunch of tires on snow as a car passed slowly in front of our house. Other people were already up, heading to the town hall.

I opened the car door and mentally prepared myself for the harsh coldness of the leather seat. Quickly, I dropped myself behind the steering wheel. My teeth began to chatter from the hard cold inside the car. I pumped the gas, turned the key and a plume of condensation enveloped the rear of the vehicle. The windshield was iced up from the slush left on it from the previous night's visit with Senator Laforge, so I switched on the defroster. We both sat in the car as the motor slowly warmed up. I reclined in the driver's seat, and hugged myself for warmth while Stacie huddled next to me, with a scarf over her nose, already red from the cold.

When the car idled smoothly, I turned on the headlights and prepared for that lunge into our snowy driveway. Twin jets of water sprayed onto the dirty windshield as the wipers slapped the grime and ice away from my view. Peering through the streaked and fogged windshield, I searched for headlights on the road in front of our house. Convinced that no cars were approaching, I gunned the engine to make sure it would not stall. Then, pressing down on the gas pedal, I gripped my steering wheel and propelled the car out onto the driveway. The momentum of the car let me easily maneuver down the driveway and burst through the foot tall barrier of snow at its end. As the front wheels cleared the pile, I spun the wheel to the right turning us onto the road. This was always the point where Stacie would yell that she would never ride with me again.

We drove over the railroad tracks, and just as we passed the old Elm's Hotel building, we could see the headlights of the traffic moving aimlessly along Main Street in our little town of 4000. Cars were driving around the block, some with their windshields almost opaque from frozen slush. Senator Laforge's visit had attracted many flatlanders and news agencies. In fact, Main Street swarmed with the media army. Vans and satellite trucks from CNN, FOX, ABC, CBS and NBC were all parked along the street. This morning, the eyes and ears of the world were focused on Charlestown, NH.

As we neared Main Street, the weather came on the radio. "Residents of Keen New Hampshire awoke to ten degrees below zero weather. The cold snap was brought on by a fast-moving storm that blanketed the East Coast last evening with up to five inches of snow. The storm closed airports and some area roads. This nor'easter storm - drifted northward along the coast after forming when moist air from the Atlantic collided with the cold air over New England. The storm system will affect Maine later this morning. A chance of more snow, sleet or freezing rain is forecasted for across the region for Monday and Tuesday."

"Late breaking news: New Hampshire State Police have closed the section of Route 12 where Senator Laforge's Campaign Bus was found stalled in a snow bank. All traffic going north or south between Walpole and

Charlestown, New Hampshire is being rerouted to Route 5 on the west side of the Connecticut river. Chief Richardson from the Charlestown Fire Department stated that multiple bodies have been found at the grizzly scene. Bodies have been found in the bus and in the snow surrounding the bus. The campaign bus had been hit multiple times by bullets and possibly explosives. It is still unknown who is responsible for this brazen attack or the reason behind it. Stay tuned for further updates."

The warmth from the car heater wrapped me in a soothing embrace as the chill numbness of my ears, nose, and cheeks began to recede. As I drove down Main Street searching for a parking space, I recalled the previous accident that Senator Laforge had endured. Since then, she had told me many of the details from that September evening in Iraq. There have been many renditions of the events of that night, but I believe my version is the most accurate.

* * * *

Kat had confessed to me how elated she felt when her face-to-face meeting with Saddam finally started to become a reality. As the secret diplomatic and security issues were pursued by her close's associates, Kat grappled with trying to learn everything she could about Saddam and Iraq to insure her mission's success. Her ability to win the presidency rested squarely on the outcome of her meeting with Saddam Hussein.

I had become much more involved with Kat's operation. She had discovered my innate ability to reduce a myriad of historical fragments into a logical comprehensive perspective. She liked my work because it was stripped of the pervasive bias accompanying most contemporary news. Kat's mission soon became my obsession, and I set up an office in my house that became headquarters for research, at least to me. I framed the Hulagu Coin that Kat had given me and hung it on the wall. On the adjacent wall, I hung a picture of a Hydra to remind me of the evil I was involved in fighting. I hoped that these things would give me the inspiration needed to help her succeed in her mission. Deep into the morning the smell of fresh coffee and the sound of baroque music emanated from my sanctuary, as I read books and trolled the web for information, on whatever I was researching.

To get the research material back to Kat, I set up an innocent Web site that began to swell with the results of my studies. I named it, "Hulagu's Web," sort of a play on Kat's fascination for Hulagu's influence in Iraq, and my craving to infuse Kat's clandestine mission and my work with more of a feeling of intrigue. My site, www.HulagusWeb.com, provided an easy way to openly communicate with Kat, but without anyone realizing its real purpose. It appeared as just another innocuous site dealing with Iraq, Saddam, Islamist or terrorist activities to any web surfers who chanced upon it.

The first task that Kat asked me to handle was an overview of Iraq's religious makeup. I immediately immersed myself in the job and went about finding everything I could regarding religion in Iraq. My first draft on Iraq's religious landscape included statistics, facts, and examples that were representative of the bigger picture. I made it clear that ninety five percent of the population adhered to some form of Islam. Within this shared religion, an age-old deadly battle raged between two Islamic sects, the Sunnis and Shiite's. The divisiveness between these elements was sinister, destructive, and deadly as demonstrated by the numerous killings of members of one sect by members of the other.

I harbored a natural reluctance to make any statement to Kat that could be construed as a disparaging attack upon a world religion, but I concluded the darkness surrounding Islam should not be ignored. I felt the tenets of this religion had become so mutated by the religious dogma and hatred spewed by its spiritual leaders that it had reverted from an inspirational power of good into a deadly pernicious psychosis. Militancy appeared to be unbridled in Islam, and it had permeated to the highest level of their hierarchy. An example exemplifying this was the Shiite revered spiritual leader, Ayatollah Khomeini statement, "The purest joy in Islam is to kill and be killed for Allah."

Another important excerpt that I felt Kat should be made aware of came from a respected Islamic scholar, Ibn Kathir who was born in 701AH. He was a favorite of Sunni Muslims, the Islamic sect, which Saddam Hussein was a member. Ibn Kathir stated that, "Allah says that the man is the leader over the woman and is the one who disciplines her if she does wrong. 'Because Allah has made one of them excel the other', this is because men are better than women, and a man is better than a woman. Therefore, prophet-hood and great kingship were confined to men, as the Prophet said, 'A people that choose a woman as their leader will not succeed.'" I felt, if Saddam Hussein believed this Islamic doctrine, he would most likely want Kat to become President because Allah would doom her leadership.

One other item that I felt Kat should be aware of was a passage in Hadith 3:885 regarding the Islamic story of a Bedouin who came to Allah's messenger and said, "O Allah's Messenger! I ask you by Allah to judge my case according to Allah's Laws." His opponent, who was more learned than he, said, "Yes, judge between us according to Allah's Laws, and allow me to speak." Allah's Messenger said, "Speak." He said, "My son was working as a laborer for this man, and he committed illegal sexual intercourse with his wife. The people told me that it was obligatory that my son should be stoned to death, so in lieu of that I ransomed my son by paying one hundred sheep and a slave-girl. Then I asked the religious scholars about it. They informed me that my son must be lashed one hundred times, and be exiled for one year, and the wife of this (man) must be stoned to death." Allah's Messenger said, "By Him in whose hands my soul is, I shall judge between you according to Allah's Laws. The slave-girl and the sheep are to be returned to you, your son is to receive a hundred lashes and be exiled for one year. You, Unais go to the wife of this man, and if she confesses her guilt, stone her to death." Unais went to the woman next morning, and she confessed. Allah's Messenger ordered that she be stoned to death.

Kat had worked in the Senate on bills for women's rights and specifically measures condemning any nation sanctioning stoning to death of its citizens for illegal sex or homosexuality. I had obtained a video of an actual stoning and linked it into "HulagusWeb.com" I wanted Kat to be totally aware of the reality of these barbaric customs and the general danger she faced if her mission went awry. She would be dancing with the devil when she visited Hussein, and I hoped she knew she should take the lead.

One thing I had often pondered while working at NARA was how a single individual gains mass submission of an entire population. No one could wield this type of power held by tyrants if we were not somehow predisposed to accepting subjugation by another. It must be some human flaw or social malaise that allows this to happen. There could not be Saddams, Pol Pots, Hitlers, Attila the Huns or similar scourges of humanity if we as a society were a bit more responsible and less sheep like. What I was now involved in made me feel a bit closer to being someone who was not simply an ant of society.

My position in life now was to provide research to help make changes in the world, not to simply archive the past as I had done for so many years. Kat now depended on me to help with her research on many issues. Problems like WMD issues, Kurdish resistance fighters, terrorist activities in Iraq, Saddam's life history, United Nation policies, political issues regarding Iraq here in the states and anything else with significance to her upcoming mission.

Finally, the last few days before Kat's planned meeting with Hussein, the focus of our research shifted to his life history. I had a small phone conversation with Kat a day or so before her trip, and I could sense the nervousness in her voice. There was impatience and even a bit of apprehension discernible in her voice.

Saddam Hussein fits the mold for a Middle East ruler. He was one man holding the concentration of power and not bound by any constitutional framework. Right from the inception of his regime he exhibited cunning and steadfast determination to become the supreme leader of Iraq. His ruthlessness had assured his rule of the country since 1979. Saddam's humble background, amazing willpower, focus, and ability to achieve his dreams endeared him to those of his Clan. They felt there was no stopping him, in terms of what Iraq is all about, and its position in the whole world. Saddam shaped a secular government for the first time in modern Iraqi history. It was a ruthless government, albeit, but one able to achieve success in forging a national community out of a country dominated with diverse social elements. This is a land where brutality is the norm. Any leader in the Middle East trying to maintain secularization, modernization and the promotion of a worldly education realizes Muslim fundamentalists will constantly oppose him.

Saddam handled his religious distracters with the same iron fisted determination that his neighbor, Hafez Assad, had applied in Syria. President Assad maintained his power by being ruthless and killing anyone or any groups opposing him. He totally annihilated 20,000 Muslim guerrillas, in the town of Hama, who referred to him as "an enemy of Allah." From that day on, Islamic fundamentalists used caution with any mention of Assad or the Batth party in their venomous diatribes.

I hoped Kat understood that if her actions diminished Saddam's hold on Iraq, it could expose the people of Iraq to the fundamentalist Islamic revival vision of a global culture under Sharia, which is the Islamic solution to all world problems. Sharia (Islamic law) promotes an implacably hostile view towards the secular world. It seeks a political effort imposed by religious laws to implement their tenants of veiling women, mutilation of thieves, execution of adulterers and anyone renouncing the Islamic religion. Fifteen hundred years ago their Islamic prophet, Muhammad, on his death bed is said to have commanded, "Behold! God sent me with a sword just before the Hour, and placed my daily sustenance beneath the shadow of my spear, and humiliation and contempt upon those who oppose me." This is the Islamic apocalyptic call to all believers to wage war through the world to convert non-believer to the "True faith" or kill them.

One of the most important transformations of religions in modern time was to abandon their narcissistic, self-perceptions and to love and be tolerant of those of other faiths. But now, this instilled tolerance practiced by these religions traps its believers into trying to accept and rationalize the zealous hatred held against them by the inflexible Islamic fundamentalist dogma.

The day had finally arrived and Senator Laforge found herself viewing Baghdad as it appeared on the horizon. Her plane circled over Baghdad as it waited for permission to land at Saddam International Airport. This Airport had lived in a virtual twilight zone for ten years. It had sat there with deserted terminals, empty duty-free shops and an air traffic control tower, which controlled nothing.

It was now modernized, and the refurbished passenger terminal had brand new lounges and even duty-free shops. French celebrities, opposed to the UN sanctions, had been the first to break the sanctions and fly into

Iraq's airport. The airport's use was still primarily for humanitarian or diplomatic purposes.

The Senator's arrival was met by a large welcoming party. Heading the group was Qusay Hussein, the President's youngest son. He was there on Saddam's request to act as Kat's escort to the meeting place and to assure her safety. A security force of armed Fedayeen guards surrounded Kat, and watched her every move while protecting her from anyone wishing her harm. In addition to Qusay and this element of the Fedayeen, the welcoming party consisted of trained actors rattling off lines riddled with pathos about sanctions. Saddam Hussein had cast the welcoming party with the most dignified, stoical looking Iraqis and the cutest doe-eyed children to help alter her perception of Iraq. It was as if he wanted her to self-flagellate herself for not doing more to help lift the debilitating UN sanctions. Any guilt she might have felt was quickly diminished as she viewed how Hussein used the current resources coming into his country. It was obvious that lifting sanctions would scarcely help Iraq's poor. In among the wretched squalor of Baghdad's bursting shantytowns, Saddam's palaces (all 65 of them) glisten smugly like giant jewels.

Finally, just as the sun was setting, Senator Laforge and her entourage left the Airport for the final leg of their journey to the undisclosed meeting place with Saddam Hussein. As their caravan of cars and armour vehicles left the Airport, the sky began to churn with angry dark clouds. At first, it was only large raindrops splattering on the pavement making tiny ringlets in the dust on the hot road, but then the clouds burst, the sky flashed and the storm awoke the night. The ferocity of the pouring rain sounded like a muffled drumbeat on the roof of the Senator's limousine. As the rain poured down faster, thunder echoed its vengeance through the dark night. The rain beat hard on the street and the trees shook from the wind. The anger of the storm sent shock waves of lightning flashing like strobe lights through the dark.

Nature's light-show painted patterns of flickering shadows on the faces of Qusay Hussein's Fedayeen body guards who sat directly across from Kat. They looked much more westernized than she had imagined of men from a Muslim nation. Their hair was cut in slicked back western styles, and they sported well shaped waxed mustaches. They resembled gangsters from a 1940's B movie, not elite bodyguards for the heir apparent of Saddam Hussein.

Lightning flooded the gloom with light, and then the darkness would again overtake the night and their faces would fade into the blackness. As they drove along the avenue, Senator Laforge had found herself focusing on this phenomenon instead of listening to Qusay's interpreter. The storm seemed to heighten her tenseness, her stomach cramped and goosebumps seemed to sprout from her skin. She felt her arm tremble and hoped that Qusay or his bodyguards did not see her uneasiness. Senator Laforge snapped back to Qusay's words that were fading from her memory and asked him to please repeat the previous question.

The buildings that streaked by were plastered with large threatening images of a stern-faced Saddam, standing against an inferno-like red backdrop. The strobe light illumination of flashing lightning and the rain streaking the posters made his appearance as ominous as the sinister clouds sweeping over the city.

Deadly lightning etched itself across the skies and illuminated the glistening armored vehicle, which rumbled ahead of the limousine. The storm was stronger now and the thunderclaps were sharp, as lightning continued to pierce the sky and illuminate the Baghdad skyline. The rain and wind whipped the antenna on the armored vehicle. The antenna bent to the might of the wind and vibrated from the pounding of the rain. Another huge sheet of lightning spread across the Iraqi sky; it was a beautiful pyrotechnic show. Suddenly, after another thunderclap, the back of the armor vehicle pulsated with a shimmering bolt of lightning, which smashed through its hull. A huge spray of sparks followed by black smoke shot up from the vehicle as it came to an instant halt. The limo driver slammed on his breaks, and the limousine started to skid towards the smoking pile of rubble. Senator Laforge braced herself for the collision, and the car tore into the twisted smoking wreck with a loud roar. Kat's body shot off the seat and catapulted into the harden glass of the privacy partition. Her head spilt open like a ripe watermelon dropped on the ground. Blood poured down her face and onto her twisted body. Then the sounds of thunder and rain faded away into semidarkness and a few seconds later she floated into a coma.

Three Fedayeen members ran splashing through the puddling water to the smoking limousine. Moans and yells could be heard coming from the vehicles. The armored vehicle was billowing smoke and the smell of burned oil was strong. The limousine had flipped over twice and its weight had caved in its roof. The roof now looked like a wrecking ball had been dropped on it. Two of its doors had been ripped open from the impact of the accident. The passengers were heaped upon one another; some dead, some dying, some slightly injured and some unhurt, but all tightly gripped in the menacing wreckage and menaced by the jagged steel and leaking gas. One stunned bodyguard wiggled from his imprisonment and was led away from the wreck by a Fedayeen. On the initial impact, Qusay Hussein had been ejected from the limo and was spared from being crushed as it tumbled about. Two Fedayeens bent down into the doorway of the smoldering car and yanked on the Senator's arm to pull her free. The lower part of her body was concealed under a piece of one of the limousine's seats. The collapsed roof of the limousine pressed down hard on the piece of the seat locking the Senator tightly in place. A Fedayeen guard reached under the seat and cut through her belt and sliced open the side of Senator Laforge's dress. As they renewed their attempt to pull her from the wreckage, they felt her body slip from its pinned position and heard her unconsciously lose control of her bodily functions due to the tremendous tugging on her body over the other wreckage. As her legs moved into view, they could see red lines being carved in them from the springs or pieces of steel that had slammed into her leg and were now slicing through her skin and muscles. The combined smell of gas, smoke and feces wafted from the Senator's prison, but the Fedayeens were too busy to notice. They saw her foot slide from under the seat, and they quickly balanced her among them and moved swiftly away from the wreckage. As they rushed to safety, the slickness of rain and blood on her body made them struggle to maintain their grip on her. As one Fedayeen guard regained his grip on her arm, the expandable band on the Senator's watch gave way, and it fell to the ground, sinking to the bottom of a puddle. No one noticed, or cared, and they kept rushing back toward the other limousines at the rear of the caravan. Deep inside the watch, a drop of water found its way and a tiny blue spark momentarily flickered, snaking across the circuitry. Just as the damaged watch stopped ticking the limousines' wreckage exploded into a huge fireball scattering its pieces through the air and lifting the armored vehicle and hurling it into the nearby building. People close by tumbled around like leaves blowing in the wind. The Senator was heaved through the air and on to a vehicle ten feet in front of her. Her left arm snapped as it bent behind her from the impact of her body smashing into the vehicle. She laid sprawled on the hood of the vehicle blood spreading over her face. It trickled down her cheek, paused for a moment, then plunged from her chin to the wet road below.

In the distance, sirens could be heard blaring into the rain and smoke filled night air. The faint glimmer of the flashing red and blue lights, were now visible. The smoke billowing around the wreckage and bodies was so thick, that it blocked out the bright flashes of lightning still illuminating the sleeping city of Baghdad. The sounds of the sirens grew louder and some of the injured tried to rise. Burning wreckage and smoldering body parts lay scattered over the road and sidewalk. The arrival of the wailing ambulances plunging through the darkness, smoke and rain were welcomed as saviors. Men leapt from the trucks and ran to the first person they saw needing help. The flames were still burning, as the medics searching for survivors scurried between the wounded and dead. One medic knelt by a sprawled soldier adverting his eyes from the man's pleading looks as he tried in vain to dam the flow of blood. He felt death conquer the soldier and closed the man's glazed eyes.

The night was still punctuated with thunder rumbling above, and streaks of lightning raking the sky. The steady downpour of rain soaked the cast of wounded and dead, in this horrific tragedy. It was a night of bearing witness to fleeing souls, the termination of glimmering hopes, and the anguished sting of friends departed. Many souls retired that tragic night. The blowing winds, and the sirens of the ambulances seemed to morph into a soul piercing lament that even the rumbling thunder could not hide.

When the medics spotted the Senator's battered body, it still hung over the hood of the car. She was breathing, but unconscious. It was obvious that this woman with a cross dangling from a gold chain around her neck, was not a Muslim. The medic was about to leave this infidel, but had to fight his religious beliefs because he heard Qusay Hussein shouting at him to save the

Senator. He hoped Allah would be merciful on him because he knew the wrath of Qusay Hussein was far more imminent. He knew what the Koran says about infidels 'The unbelievers among the People of the Book and the pagans shall burn forever in the fire of Hell. They are the vilest of all creatures.' But he clearly understood that Qusay Hussein wanted the infidel (the vilest of all creatures) to live, and it was his job now to save lives and not help to fulfill prophecy. And most of all, he knew that his life was contingent upon the survival of this unbeliever.

As the medics lifted the Senator onto the stretcher, an injured Qusay Hussein hobbled over to them ranting of the importance of saving this woman's life. With Qusay's prompting, they quickly moved the unconscious body to a waiting ambulance and loaded it on board. Qusay pushed aside a medic and entered the ambulance along with his wounded bodyguard.

As the doors slammed closed, the ambulance instantaneously roared onto the road. Onlookers rushed about to clear the path of the wailing sirens and flashing lights. Qusay looked down on the Senator and could see her tortured breathing.

With the wail of the siren seeping into her dulled mind, she drifted further into her memories and the world inside her tormented dreams. Her mind started to replay the sights and sounds of the last few hours. Like a mist-filled dream, the visions of the day drifted through her consciousness playing deep inside her brain. She recalled the chartered jet flying low over the barren Iraqi landscape, which was spotted by twisted hulks of deserted cars, trucks, and military vehicles. She had never been to Iraq before this important clandestine trip. Like a movie, her mind replayed the views she had enjoyed earlier that morning as she flew over the Iraqi border from Syria. She could see again the rugged view of the terrain below. This region was sparsely inhabited by pastoral nomads and was covered with a wide, stony plain scattered with rare sandy stretches. Wadis or watercourses crisscrossed the terrain. This land was so desolate and uninviting, that according to many Iraqis, even a rattlesnake felt lonely living there. The sirens of the ambulance metamorphosed into the hiss from the jet of the air conditioning above her seat in the small-chartered jet. She looked out the window of her mind and could see the Iraq desert below brimming with rubble. She envisioned she was flying, over a huge rubbish dump that the two wars and endless poverty had created. For miles upon miles, the land below was scattered with junk and collapsed buildings from the wars fought on this desert.

Thunder rattled again and its reverberations echoed through her sleeping mind. Her dreams grew darker and she envisioned, she was at home in Houston at a park and groups of people were gathered in a circle jeering at a woman who was buried in the ground up to her waist. Her mind swooped in closer to the woman buried to her waist. Terror ripped through her mind. She saw herself as that woman. Kat wanted to help her, to shield her, but all she could do was helplessly view this horrific scene. She saw the crowd push a man who was stumbling and pleading into the circle. She heard the taunting shrieks of the crowd yelling at him to cast the first stone. Her eyes filled with terror as she recognized this man as her husband, Ira. She was locked in her nightmare and could not hide from its horror. She saw herself pleading for mercy. But her pleas, just excited the boisterous leering crowd even more, and their frenzy of yelling became louder, and completely drowned out her voice. Her eyes were full of terror and tears streaked from them. The men and women were yelling at her "Fornicator", "Whore", and "Adulterer."

A prophet appeared and faced the crowd announcing that no stone should be thrown that should kill with a first or second blow, or so small as a pebble as to do no injury to the condemned. He smiled, blessed the crowd and moved back towards the circle's edge. Reaching it, he turned towards Kat and his face suddenly mutated grotesquely into the face of Sorat. For a long moment, he stood there smiling smugly at Kat, and then his booming voice rang out and commanded his dominions to commence the stoning. Like humans void of soul or mind, they jeered and yelled as they went about selecting their most jagged stones. Kat's husband faded from her view. Then suddenly the first stone smashed into her, splitting open the skin on her left breast. She heard herself shriek in pain. As the stones mutilated her, her screams and the crowd's jeers were drowned out by the hideous sounds of Sorat laughing uncontrollably and his booming voice yelling, "God is great." Another stone smashed into her head from the back, as the crowd grew bolder and louder with yells and shouts. Men rushed to the edge of the circle and spat at her as they heaved their stones at her face. A fist size rock smashed into the back of her head spraying blood across the ground and exciting the crowd even more. The blood made them bolder and their yells and shouts intensified. Now her face was pulverized from the stoning. The blood soaked her hair and splattered on the ground all around her. A spray of blood and spit now accompanied her cries of pain. Both her eyes had been ruptured and her teeth smashed. Thick dark blood oozed from her broken jaw. Her left breast was totally stripped of its flesh, and its nipple hung solely from a piece of skin. Blood streamed down her chest making glistening red spots on the ground. The gore pleased Sorat, and he gleefully watched the proceedings to ensure that no one used a stone of the wrong size.

In Kat's dream, she saw a vision of herself raising her head and pleading for mercy from the thunderous crowd around her. A large woman, with a string of spittle flying from her mouth screeched, "God is great," as an answer to Kat's plea. Then the woman followed her chant, with a large stone violently hurled at Kat's fractured skull. The impact jerked her head backward and this woman who looked like Kat fell silent. Her agony had finally ceased. She had found her peace. The crowd was still in a frenzy and continued to stone and spit at her, until Sorat transformed himself back into the image of a holy prophet and told them to stop. He blessed them and thanked them for doing Allah's bidding and they all shouted, "God is great."

The roar of their chanting got louder as her mind reeled from this vision from hell and her breathing strained. She made guttural sounds, and the medic adjusted the oxygen flow of the resuscitator. The ambulance was only a few miles from Ibn Sina Hospital. The same hospital used by Saddam Hussein. The oxygen seemed to calm her mind and the scene of horror and the maddening chanting drifted away.

Her agitation seemed to subside in the solitude of the new dreams that formed in her brain.

The ambulance sped down the street escorted by Iraqi police vehicles blasting the way towards the hospital.

The driver was expressionless, focusing only on his life and death task of driving. The wind had been so strong that it would shake the ambulance as it sped down the road and in some places along the road it had toppled trees.

Like the churning clouds outside, Kat's brain was swirling with new memories invading her consciousness. Memories of her husband, daughter and her three cats flickered like a family slide show in the theater in her head. All of it was so real that at some times she could even hear their voices as they wished her well. She took warmth from these sights, and they seemed to calm her soul. Her family was the foundation of her life. Most of the time she had led an idyllic American dream existence. But today, her life was hallucinations and dreams. Darkness full of voices, some real and some not. The shadows of this ceaseless night morphed into all she had seen and known. While she lay still and peaceful, flashes of demons and angels rattled her consciousness with confusing memories that were like umbilical tendrils hooked to the world outside her mind. But she stayed locked in its solitary, alone, somewhere between life and death.

The ambulances rushed into the docking bay at the hospital. The wailing sirens died as the ambulance doors abruptly slammed open. All around there were rushing people, the craze of a loud and chaotic emergency.

The ambulance crew lowered the Senator's stretcher gently to the ground. Now the horror of her condition was painfully obvious. She was covered in blood from a multitude of cuts and lacerations. The medics had put a neck brace on her. She was barely breathing on her own. A sickly pale pallor had consumed her face, and she looked near dead. A rushing mass of doctors, nurses and Fedayeens moved towards the stretcher containing the Senator, who was escorted by the medics and Qusay Hussein.

* * * *

I did not know this entire story on the morning of January 25 2004, when Senator Laforge was scheduled to hold her meeting at our town hall. Since then much of the mysteries unfolded as Tom, Vince and myself sorted through the events since the meeting with Senator Laforge at our class reunion in 2002.

Allah's Messenger said: There is a remedy for every malady, and when the remedy is applied to the disease it is cured with the permission of Allah, the Exalted and Glorious.

PART FOUR

After the Accident

We had not envisioned that the street would be so packed with vehicles so early in the morning. On the north end of Main Street, we finally spotted a parking place cut into the snow bank. Ironically it was about the same distance to the town hall as it would have been from our home. The Town Hall was a three or four minute walk from this location. As I backed into the parking space, the crunching sound of snow almost blocked out a special radio news update. With the engine still running, we sat in total silence listening to every spoken word. I sucked in a lung full of air and tried to contain my emotions. It was more grim news. The announcer confirmed that one of the bodies found in the bus was Senator Laforge's husband. Stacie eyes filled with tears, and she started sobbing. The announcer stated that Ira, the Senator's husband had been shot four times; three in the head and once in his back. Most likely, he had died instantly. I reached over to console Stacie. She really had not known Ira well, but having spent the previous evening with them, made this much more personal.

This was our first encounter with losing a friend to murder. A whole array of emotions was descending upon me. I felt anger, helplessness, grief and at the same time unbelieving that such a horrible act could have happened to someone I had come to know and been so involved with for the last year and a half.

Ira's murder made life feel inconsequential. The world continued on its unshaken path complete with falling snow and people walking, chatting and laughing and unmoved or unaware of the Grim Reaper's early morning visit.

The cold tears on Stacie's cheek moistened my face bringing on a panoply of overpowering emotions. I felt grief, and a sense of loss at the realization of life's fragility.

Stacie wiped her tears away trying to control herself, and I bit my lip hard to control my tears.

Stacie asked in a near whisper, "What should we do now?"

I just sat there quietly at first and then told her, "We should still go to the town hall and see what if anything is happening there. Maybe we will hear something more about Kat. I hate it when they spoon feed us the news."

She dabbed her eyes and I tried to dry her face off, so the tears would not freeze on her cheeks. We slid out of the car and walked in silence towards the Town Hall. As we approached it, neighbors cheerfully greeted us probably unaware of the latest news. I spotted Tom Hestler so we walked over to him and asked if he had heard that Ira was murdered.

Tom's shocked look, answered the question.

Stacie reached out, hugged him and shed a few more tears. Tom asked me what had happened, so I went over the previous reports. The cold and the snow seemed trifle now as we discussed Ira's murder, worried about Kat and tried to make some sense of what was happening.

Tom reminded us of how less than two years ago, Ira stood by Kat as she recovered from her accident in a Baghdad Iraqi hospital. For both of them, it had been a truly a tenuous period. When that accident was first reported, it devastated and depressed me. We had all worked so hard to make her secret trip to Iraq a political success, and then that terrible accident seemed to destroy all we had worked towards. There was no escape from hearing about it either. The headlines of every media outlet in the world trumpeted the accident or assassination attempt. CNN, FOX, MSNBC, CBS and ABC were constantly reporting, "Breaking news of the injured American Senator from Texas recovering in an Iraqi Hospital."

Reuters had been the first to report the incident of the Senator's automobile accident in Baghdad, but with very few facts. "Senator Laforge injured in Iraq." Screamed the headlines that morning.

After the accident, Ira kept us all well informed of Kat's medical status. In fact, the morning after the incident, he held an impromptu news briefing at their home in Houston. Outside their home, hundreds of people waited around for more than four hours to hear Ira's briefing. The weather in Texas had been very wet the previous few days. So wet that the President had declared parts of Texas a disaster area due to the flooding from the torrential rains. But luckily, that morning of November 6, it was clear, dry and warm. Kat's supporters did not have to brave the rain, only the press Corps that milled about jockeying and bullying for the best positions in front.

The news briefing had been promised for 10 AM (CST) and precisely at that time Ira's front door opened and two of the Senator's aides ushered him to a make shift podium. He looked terribly distraught, but maintained control of himself as he welcomed the reporters and his wife's many supporters.

Ira stood there, gazing out at all of them and started reading from his prepared statement:

"Good morning, ladies and gentlemen. I am here to give you as much information as we know about my wife's current situation. Yesterday, my wife Senator Laforge was admitted to Ibn Sina Hospital in Baghdad, Iraq suffering from a concussion, broken arm and various other injuries. Her caring physician, Dr al-Janabi, said my wife would remain hospitalized for a few more days. He added however, that my wife was out of danger and would continue to improve."

A cheer went up from the crowd and people started chanting, "Get well Kat."

Ira waited for the noise to subside and then continued with this briefing.

"Thank you for your concern and love for my wife. Let me continue. I was told that in her current medical condition, she is also showing signs of elevated blood pressure and treatment is being done at Ibn Sina Hospital to avoid any bleeding complications."

"The Senator has undergone what was described as an extensive examination of her multiple injuries, and will have to remain immobile for some days. They want to insure that the gains made so far in her recovery continue. The Senator will receive limited visitations to allow needed rest and a faster recovery. She is currently on medication and will undergo treatment at the hospital as she continues to recuperate. The doctors are very optimistic about her complete recovery."

Another roar of approval forced Ira to stop and wait for quiet.

Ira waived his hands for quiet and then said, "I want to quickly dispel any notion that my wife is dead or is a prisoner in Iraq. As many of you have already heard, this was not just a simple car accident. It seems, from the preliminary examination of the wreckage, that this was an attempted assassination of Mr. Qusay Hussein or of my wife. A bomb was apparently placed in the limousine that both my wife and Mr. Hussein were riding in. Numerous men were brutally killed in this attack, but my wife, Qusay Hussein and a few others were spared death."

Tears welled up in Ira's eyes, and he paused for a moment to recover his composure.

"Excuse me!" he continued, "But our priority now, besides the quick recovery of my wife, is to exert the utmost efforts to identify the person or group responsible for this attempt on my wife's life. Senior officers from the Fedayeen headquarters in Baghdad, Iraq spent hours examining the scene and assured us that there would be no cover up. Although some reports have been aired by Al-Jazeera News that this attempted assassination was the work of a splinter faction of Kurds, no opposition groups have made claim to this attack. The spokesman from Qusay Hussein's office also has denied that there is any proof of the Kurd's involvement in this attack. Essentially we do not know at this time who is responsible for this terrible incident. Any new revelations as to the perpetrator of this horrible act will be reported to you as it unfolds."

Ira paused for a moment and looked out at the forest of cameras staring at him and then locked his eyes on his wife's adoring supporters and said.

"I know all of you are wondering why my wife was in Iraq? Her trip was kept as a total secret, so no one could jeopardize it. She had hoped as a Presidential candidate to establish some sort of trust and good will between Saddam Hussein and herself. With this trust she felt she could mold a peace plan that would prevent hundreds of our men and women from dying in the deserts and streets of Iraq."

"This is not the first time in history a Presidential hopeful has sought a peaceful resolution with a foreign adversary. Former President Reagan is said to have worked out an agreement with Iran to free the 52 American Embassy hostages, if and when he was elected over the incumbent Carter. The day of President Reagan's inauguration, Iran agreed to accept $8 billion in frozen assets and a promise by the United States to lift trade sanctions in exchange for the release of the 52 Americans. They were released a few hours after Reagan took office. Well, my wife hoped to accomplish something similar. She felt that if she was elected as President, her presence on the international scene would defuse some of the animosity between our two countries. She was willing to offer Saddam Hussein certain minor concessions and promises, if he would agree to disarmament, immediately after my wife's inauguration. Many of you will criticize my wife for doing this, but her intentions were honorable. She desired to save American lives and to resolve this bitter conflict between two great nations. She was on her way to Saddam Hussein's Presidential palace accompanied by his son, Qusay Hussein, and bodyguards when a bomb exploded in the vicinity of her limousine. By the grace of god, my wife had just been removed from the vehicle, because of an automobile accident that happened seconds before the bomb detonated. At the present, this is all I know about my wife's situation. As more information is received, it will be reported. I hope all of you will pray for her tonight and wish her a speedy recovery."

"Now if you have any questions, I will attempt to answer them."

"Sir, we have been told that the Senator is actually in a coma. Is that true?"

"Yes, she is in a coma, but we anticipate her to recover from that very soon."

A reporter from CNN immediately got Ira's attention and asked, "Will you be visiting your wife in Baghdad soon?"

"No I will not. I think under the circumstance that I should wait for my wife to recover and be returned to us. Some of her aides will be joining her there. We have a daughter who needs to have one of us here to comfort her during this crisis."

Ira's eyes started to get blurry from the tears welling up. He stopped for a second and dried his eyes and said, "Ladies and Gentlemen, I think I will have to end this briefing now. I want to thank you for your attention and your concern. Thank you all and have a good day."

Ira was led away from the podium among the roar of the reporters clamoring for more, and the well wishers yelling, "God Bless Senator Laforge."

The rest of the morning self-proclaimed experts in car accidents, Iraqi culture, Saddam Hussein's life and even Senator Laforge's life monopolized the talk shows.

On CNN, a brain specialist was asked about future problems that Senator Laforge might experience from her head injury. His response created a new concern for the Senator's office and Ira to challenge. The Doctor implied that a common effect of brain injury is behavior problems. The most common of which involves a diminished ability to interact appropriately with other people. This was not the type of prognosis that would enhance the Senator's bid for the presidency. The Doctor went on to predict that other less frequent problems would probably include aggression, property destruction, verbal abusiveness and tantrums. Now for many Presidents the majority of the last four symptoms are common natural traits of their personality, so the Senator's aides joked that Kat's head injury really made her that much more Presidential. If anyone continued to listen to the Doctor's summation of the problems, they would have heard that if these injuries were addressed immediately after the damage, the symptoms could be very much diminished or eliminated. And even more important he concluded, "Not all head-injured people develop these problems."

The Senator's accident became the major news story on TV and in newspapers. Many political factions were praising Senator Laforge as the most peace seeking Senator. Peace rallies in the US had individuals marching around with signs that pictured Kat Laforge and Saddam Hussein cheek-to-cheek and read "Peace comes from understanding your neighbor."

Saddam capitalized on this event and used the publicity to promote and enhance his image as a benevolent leader. Qusay Hussein made it a true photo opportunity. The Iraqi Information Minister included pictures of

Qusay standing or sitting near the comatose Senator, with virtually every news release of the Senator's condition.

To counter the constant U.S. government demand to release the Senator to their care, Saddam Hussein argued convincingly that the Senator was a guest in his country and her welfare was his responsibility. Even more important was that Kat's condition was too grave to allow moving her to another location.

Saddam campaigned to provide the most advanced medical attention available. He enlisted a renowned Chinese doctor who was famed for pioneering and successfully using skin regeneration technology by stem cell culturing in the treatment of deep burn victims. Other specialist involved in the creation of man-made tissues or organs, known as neo-organs were also invited to Baghdad to assist in the Senator's recovery. The physicians needed cell regeneration methods to restore cells that had suddenly died due to the shock to the system, or other complications from her accident. The US government also sent doctors to help with the Senator's care. Saddam's biggest concern was the real possibility that the Senator might die in Iraq, and he would be held accountable for her death by denying her proper care. However, if she survived, it would create major positive publicity for him, and his regime.

While Senator Laforge's coma continued, numerous celebrities capitalized on the public's curiosity and Iraqi's desire to keep the limelight on the situation. Her bed became a magnet to many of the media whores. The TV constantly showed footage of individuals standing by her bed like a Reverend who claimed he would get the Senator home, and a foul looking Michigan movie producer who vented his hatred for the evil of America while wishing the Senator a speedy recovery. Some luminaries were actually there to put pressure on the Iraqi government to send the Senator home. But, the majority of them came simply for the publicity it provided them. Throughout the world, however, people did pray and support the Senator's unfinished peace work that she had come thousands of miles to accomplish.

The Iraqi Information Ministry relished the cast of characters that entered into the media frenzy. He ordered, with Saddam's blessings total celebrity treatment for any visiting American icon that was known for their anti US government views. The Minister also made sure that every visit was announced to the media, so their views would be broadcast worldwide.

President Hussein immensely enjoyed the insults and anti government comments provided by the American visitors. Not only did they help his cause in the Arab world, but since they were American celebrities, their fans would also listen to them. He and his Iraqi Informational Minister, Mohammed Saeed al-Sahhaf, joked often about how these naïve Americans were the most effective and inexpensive PR people for the Baath Party. And best of all, America was completely impotent with its own stupid laws to stop its vocal radical fringe groups from assisting al-Sahhaf propaganda needs.

The Senator had become such hot propaganda property that great care was placed on her appearance. Nurses changed her bandages prior to each visitor and everything in her room remained perfectly arranged. The room had large windows to provide natural lighting for cameramen filming the visits. The nurses followed a checklist of medical and appearance requirements prior to the visits. Two attractive nurses dressed in immaculate uniforms were assigned to take care of her and one was present in the room at all times to observe her and provide answers to any questions about the Senator's health. Being monitored by two nurses was part show and part Saddam Hussein's genuine concern for the Senator's well being. Hessa al-Nasere, was appointed head nurse and was given the responsibility to represent Iraq as a peace loving country to all news people that she encountered. She was fluent in English, attractive and came from a very respected Baath Party family.

On the third week of the Senator's coma, as the normal checks were being performed, a nurse viewing the Senator's (ICP) Intracranial Pressure Monitor suddenly noticed she had eye movement. She turned to call for another nurse and when she turned back, Kat's eyes were wide open and appeared to be following her movement. She moved her hand back and forth in front of Kat's eyes causing them to blink, but then Kat closed them once again. This was the first real sign of Kat's recovery. As the two nurses checked her nasogastric tube and her caloric supplement, they noticed Kat's head twitch to the left. Their eyes lit up knowing that these were good signs of recovery. They rang for a doctor while continuing to adjust the IV sugar/saline solution that had helped Kat's dehydration problem. An American doctor named Benoit, was the first to step into the room and seemed shocked that the Senator was showing these signs of recovery. Dr al-Janabi arrived next and seemed immensely happy when he learned what the nurses had seen. The doctor turned up the volume of the American music playing in the room. This was a part of their Coma Stimulation program for the Senator. They felt that the music would make her feel more at home and stimulate more of her senses to prompt her out of the coma. The doctors stood there for about five minutes waiting for more signs, but finally gave up and went back to their previous work.

President Hussein made the Senator's recovery a very personal thing and spoke of her as his friend and a friend of the Iraqi people. He awarded medals to the Fedayeen, who helped save the Senator, and proclaimed their families as heroes of Iraq. As part of a good will campaign, friends of the Senator were openly invited to Iraq. I was tempted to go, but decided to decline. Actually, no one accepted, but the gesture was reported on all news outlets. The news reported the reason that all declined was pressure from Washington. In war protest in some left wing bastions, the Senator's image became a part of the symbols of peace displayed on banners and signs.

Another few days went by without any visible sign of recovery. But the doctors patiently, and confidently continued their treatments using every means available to maintain her comfort and to assist her recovery. The Senator's concussion remained serious enough that they had to relieve some of the pressure on the brain by draining some of the fluid. The INTRAPARENCHIMAL WAY (CAMIRO) was the Intracranial Pressure Monitor method used to maintain the pressure of the cerebrospinal fluid surrounding the brain and spinal cord. That morning they relieved the pressure again, and the Senator actually responded by moving and speaking the slurred words that sounded like, "Ira, Ira." Her eyes blinked open and she attempted to move her right arm. Her left arm felt heavy from a cast. The doctors spoke to her and asked Kat if she heard them. She moved her head and looked at them, but did not respond. She did yawn, stretch and then again closed her eyes.

Once again, Senator Laforge slipped deep into a terrifying night of sleep. In the twilight of her dream, a large glass panel materialized in front of her. As it took shape, it seemed like a large window with her image reflected off of it. Her body began to shake with fear. The feeling of desperation surged through her mind as she recognized this vision. Her eyelids fluttered trying to pull herself out of the dream, but the darkness held its vice like grip on her consciousness. Her buried fears seemed to float from deep within her mind to the center of her dream, filling her with terror. And then her own face emerged trance like from behind her reflection in the glass. It wasn't another reflection, but her own face gazing at her and following her every move. Silently, she screamed, but not a sound came from her mouth. And there she remained, frozen in fear between wakefulness and the replaying of this nightmare. She felt she should recognize the scene before her, but her thoughts were scattered and chaotic. Her likeness seemed to spiral downward into a dense, pitch blackness that made her heart freeze in mortal terror. She saw her reflection turn red, and she felt that she was dying, but no one would heed her yells or pleads for help, not even the woman wearing her face who sat outside the glass watching her every move. She felt like she was being consumed from within and shook uncontrollably. The glass panel began to dissolve along with the images of herself and then Kat's forehead broke out in sweat. She jerked violently about in her bed and then awoke suddenly with her eyes wide open, trembling from the nightmare. As she lay in her bed and gazed around the room the terror slowly ebbed away from her consciousness. She could see images around her that looked like people, but they were hazy, and she could not form the words to ask for help. She closed her eyes and slowly sank back into her sleep.

One rule the Information Ministry had set for the nurses was to insure that none of the actions or presence of a visitor agitated the Senator in any visible way. The agitation occurs as a result of the frustration and inability of a semi-aware comatose patient to communicate or express them self. At the bedside of the Senator, an antiwar activist escorted by some Iraqi children was filming a commercial of his heartfelt feelings of the horror that the US was about to unleash on Iraq. The Senator started to rhythmically scream and thrash about and then suddenly opened her eyes and looked straight at this person beside her bed. The nurses looked at the monitor and noticed that Kat was showing very good signs of awareness. The Senator still staring at the group by her bed, waved her right hand at the entourage to leave and labored hard at pronouncing, "go" to them. Immediately, the nurses ushered the entourage out and called for the doctors.

The Senator's eyes peeking out from her bandaged head followed every move of her nurses. Twenty-seven days had slowly ticked by and finally she seemed to be coming out of the coma. In a broken and almost incomprehensible voice she asked for her husband "Ira."

As Kat's eyes focused on her room, she noticed the crowd of unknown faces staring at her from the backdrop of flowers and cards surrounding her bed. She heard the soft voice of a doctor greeting her with a "Hello Senator."

She glanced at the Doctor speaking to her, but did not recognize him. "Who are you?" She tried to ask, but only a raspy whisper came out.

The doctor introduced himself "I'm Doctor Benoit from Bethesda Naval Hospital. The President requested that I be here to assist in your treatments. The President sends you his warmest regards and hopes that you have a very speedy recovery."

Senator Laforge felt a new wave of panic as she tried to put together her situation. She knew she was in Iraq, and she knew she had been in an accident. "What day is it?" She rasped.

Doctor Benoit told her it was Monday Dec 2nd. "You have been with us a few weeks now, but all is going well."

Kat could not believe she had been unconscious for that long. She wanted to talk to Ira because she felt he could help her understand what was going on. She felt afraid. As Senator Laforge's consciousness slowly returned, she started feeling even more confused. The President would be very disturbed with her mission to Iraq to see Saddam Hussein. Why was an American doctor here in Iraq? Was the doctor here really to help or was he here to perhaps create an international crisis?

An Iraq Doctor introduced himself and told Senator Laforge how thrilled he and his staff were to see her conscious. "You had us very concerned for a couple of weeks. But you are a fighter Senator and our

President Hussein and all of us are so happy to see that you are recovering. As soon as you feel up to it, President Hussein still wants to meet with you. But now you should rest." A glimpse of a smile flashed across the doctor's bearded face as he firmly grasped Kat's good hand. He rubbed her hand, said something in Arabic, and then he and his staff left the room. The Senator was alone again with only the two attractive nurses hovering over her and smiling.

She tried to stay conscious, but quickly felt herself falling back into darkness again. Her mind replaced reality with a new vision of herself sitting in a room with a man directly in front of her, who looked much likeSaddam Hussein. They would talk and laugh for a while, but then the discussions would turn serious. This man would lean over towards her and mumble incomprehensible words. And then fear raced through her as the man stood up and turned away from her while talking loudly to unseen men. Silence replaced his voice. There was total silence now and then this man turned back around toward Senator Laforge. As she gazed at this man in front of her, the unseen figures moved into view surrounding him. They were shadowy figures, dressed in military uniforms, and they seemed to move closer to her. A dull roar unheard by her ears reverberated through her mind replacing the previous silence. Suddenly, the walls of the room became crimson red. They appeared to turn into liquid and then collapse like walls of red water. The roaring red liquid swirled around her, and then she felt a terrific heat. Suddenly, fire erupted from everywhere inside the room. A hand reached out to pull her back from the fire, and she grabbed it tightly. Her frightened eyes opened, and she was greeted by her two guardian Angel nurses hovering above her. One was holding her right hand trying to soothe her. She gazed at them trying to form a "thank you." She was not sure if they understood her words, but she knew she was communicating in some way because they smiled warmly at her.

Now she was awake and her mind raced with questions like; why was Ira missing from her bedside? Why are her long time friend and best Aide Paul not here? She focused on a new face appearing above her and tried to remember the man's name. It was Doctor Benoit. "Good morning Senator,

I hope you are feeling better this morning, so we can chat for a few minutes about your progress and how we can get you better."

The Senator nodded her head and attempted to utter a simple "Okay"

Dr Benoint continued, "You have been in a coma for about 27 days. We are grateful that you have pulled through. You had us scared at first. Initially, it wasn't clear whether you would even survive. You have to expect that some of your memories might sometime be confusing. Senator, brain damage is a thief, and you will probably be unable to remember parts of the last month. Actually, you are probably suffering from retrograde amnesia, and now that you have regained consciousness, we are moving forward on the road to recovery."

Senator Laforge's lips moved in the white maze of bandages covering her face, and she weakly said, "Thank you Doctor. I am still in a state of confusion."

Dr Benoit questioned, "Do you remember the accident and the events immediately preceding it?"

Senator Laforge hesitated, and then quietly said, "No, I do not really remember that much at all. I am not sure what is real and what were nightmares and dreams I experienced in my coma."

Dr Benoit said, "Well one thing that is very real is that the President wants me to tell you that he is counting on you to serve your country, and to try and do the right things by remembering who you are and what you as the Senator have learned about situations like this. America is counting on you. Don't let us down."

The Senator did not really understand what all that was supposed to mean, if anything. She did feel honored that the President was thinking of her and still talking to her. The Senator asked Dr. Benoit if her husband had been notified of her recovery.

Dr Benoit replied, "Yes he has, and we have a letter for you from Ira. If you would allow me, I will read it to you."

"Yes go ahead" the beaming Senator replied.

Dear Kat,

I know you are probably very confused by your ordeal, but I hope you can under-stand why I cannot be with you at your bedside. You have had a terrible accident and things are just coming back to you. Try to understand why I cannot be there and trust Dr. Benoit to help you have a speedy recovery. You have done a great job, and it is time for you to come home. As soon as they release you, we will all be together again to help you put this crisis behind us.

Love always,

Ira

The Senator listened to the words and a deep feeling of depression descended over her. Ira was always much more loving in his letters than this. This was not even a letter, it was a short note. Did he not love her any longer? Something was being unsaid in this letter. Ira had always stood by her in every situation that she had been in, both good and bad. Something was just not right for him not to be here and for him not to say more about himself or how badly he was missing Kat.

Dr Benoit could sense her depression and offered, "Senator, you are in a foreign country and in a very odd situation, so try to understand that it is natural for you to feel mentally confused and occasionally depressed. However, things will get better. Senator, most victims of car accidents suffer from post-traumatic stress disorder (PTSD), which includes physical, cognitive and emotional symptoms. I am going to work with you and use some techniques, specifically adapted to treat car accident trauma. These techniques should help you recognize and trust the innate healing wisdom of your body to hasten your recovery. However, I have to warn you that you are going to experience more headaches, irritability, mental confusion, lack of mental acuity, and temporary memory loss while getting better. Physically, you are still facing days that you will experience flu-like symptoms, but these are expected, and we can control them. Your biggest problem will probably be with your short-term memory, but that will continue to improve each day. So hang in there."

"You and I are going to attempt to mentally, walk through each of the activities that happened to you before your accident. Prodding your memory in this way may enable you to recall what happened to you and give you full recollection as to why you are now here. Initially, the left side of your body was paralyzed."

"But very soon you should be able to stand and walk unaided around the hospital. Your left arm will be noticeably weak for awhile. Your muscles that atrophied during your coma will improve quickly with daily physical therapy."

"In the immediate future, I am going to spend much of our time with your speech therapy, physical therapy, and mental gymnastics to help you relearn things and recover your memory as much as possible. By us proceeding slowly with this treatment plan, moving from events prior to your accident and understanding where you are now we will gradually work toward the center and transform this terrible experience from fragmented images to your total awareness of what happened. Once we are there, you will have total continuity of your memories, and be able to place this traumatic event in your past where it belongs. We do not want to leave gaps in your memory. We want you to remember everything."

Thousands of miles away, Ira had become very busy preparing News Releases about the prognosis of his wife. Her campaign had been derailed by the event, and he hoped that, he would be able to repair some of the damage. Ira had been in constant contact with the Senator's campaign committee chairman trying to assure him that the cause was not in vain.

As Ira was writing notes for his daily news briefing, his cell phone rang. He hoped it would not be media hounds who had discovered his private cell number. The caller ID displayed 'Unknown,' which infuriated Ira. He closed the cover in disgust, letting the caller get his voice mail and then returned to his notes.

The reports of the Senator's retrograde amnesia were very detrimental to Kat's run for the presidency and Ira wanted to find information that would refute that this condition would have any effect on Kat's duties as President. The phone rang again. He flipped his cell open and again the caller id displayed no number. Concerned that it might be his daughter calling, he pressed the call button and his most irritated voice said, "Hello?" It was not his daughter. A woman's voice said "hello Ira." Ira's voice froze for a second. And then the caller asked. "Are you there?"

The voice was unmistakably that of Senator Laforge's.

Ira blurted out, "Oh my God Hello!"

Her reply was quick. "I have missed you so much Ira. I think about you and Lyndsey every day."

In a soft voice, Ira responded, "I pray every day that you will be released and come home. You are always in our thoughts."

"Ira, I need your support right now more than ever."

Ira stood silent for a moment as a well-manicured hand reached up to the cell phone, removed his grasp and purposely closed it.

Two soft arms wrapped their self around his waist, and he felt lips kiss the back of his neck. Ira's eyes were solemn and wide with what seemed like horrific fear. Ira pushed the arms away and turned around, facing the woman who had embraced him. His heart swelled from the raging emotions he felt as he tried to catch his breath. The call had reached into his soul and Ira asked God to help him find solace and strength to continue on. Ira squeezed his eyes shut forcing a couple of tears to dampen his cheek, and then hugged his wife. The Senator looked up into Ira's eyes as she tried to think of the words to say that would comfort him. There were none, but she pressed her lips against his damp cheek and kissed him. Even she was trembling now as they both embraced.

She knew he was scared, and her heart raced with her own fear of what had happened. No matter how irrational it all seemed, this was her new reality and she and Ira would have to find a way through it.

With an almost trembling voice Ira asked her "How much longer do you think this will go on?"

Kat squeezed Ira's hand and quietly said, "I just do not know!" Now, there were tears running down her cheeks and there was nothing Ira could do to stop them.

In a darkened hospital room in Ibn Sina Hospital in Baghdad, Iraq another woman sat on her bed with a phone receiver in her hand, rocking back and forth, and trying to contain her swirling emotions of having finally heard her husband's voice and words after surviving this terrible ordeal. She could still hear him saying, "I pray every day that you will be released and come home. You are always in our thoughts."

* * * *

I did not know before that cold January morning in 2004 that two Senator Laforges existed. This startling revelation came about as Tom, Vince and myself broke our solemn pledges that frantic morning as we shared with each other all we knew about Senator Laforge. The prospect that she was dead compelled us to break our oath of silence. We had sworn that we would not share anything Kat had said with anyone or discuss it among ourselves, but the events of this morning seemed to invalidate that pledge. The evil that erupted this morning made us all feel compelled to divulge our knowledge to each other. Perhaps some of what we knew would help solve why this attack had happened. As Tom, Vince and myself began to discuss what we knew, it became very apparent that we were talking of different incarnations of the Senator.

> *If you pledge an oath for something and a better alternative comes*
> *your way, break the oath and atone for it and do what is better.*
> ~ Bukhari, Kitabu'l-Iman wa'l-Nudhur, No. 6622

PART FIVE

ComDefC1

Large menacing icicles hung from the cornice of the old brick and granite town hall. Their deadly pointed tips shimmered forty feet above in the bright beams of the spotlights that swept across the façade. Dark ice sprinkled with fresh snow cloaked the rusticated brick pilasters rising two stories from the granite foundation. The town hall had served little purpose for quite some time, but in the last few weeks, workers had wiped away the film of grime, cobwebs, and dust obscuring its stately magnificence. Now, a new radiant look emanated from her thick brick walls, despite the cold and snow. The 1872 landmark seemed to gleam in the dark cold morning with its new mission. It used to be the place where the town would show movies, sponsor dances for teenagers, host shows for the area craftsmen and of course hold New England town meetings. The building's prominence over the years and all the memories and dreams that it shared with those in Charlestown made it the perfect choice for a campaign stop. This morning it would reclaim its eminence even if only for a moment in time.

In front of the town hall, a large gathering of people milled about in the frozen slush. The crowd was clusters of groups huddled together for warmth and companionship with their breath plumed out around them like misty blank cartoon speech balloons. The noses of the early arrivers were red and raw from the chilling cold wind and snow. Drifting in on the wind was the distinct smell of smoke from a wood burning stove or fireplace. The tantalizing aromatic trace of fresh brewed coffee floated along with it to tease the senses. Across the street from the town hall, a group of children played on the frozen, wind-crusted snow throwing snowballs at each other and laughing as they enjoyed nature's beauty. Mixed with their laughter was the constant clamor of people coughing and the murmur of voices. On the east side of the hall, huddled a group of young protesters waving their signs, chanting their little jingles and taunting those that dared approach them. Their signs declared Laforge an enemy of the poor, a liar and a destroyer of the economy. One sign read, "Laforge robs the poor. Vote for Dean, he's not mean." Some townspeople were very angry that these individuals had the nerve or stupidity to even appear here in Laforge's hometown on this terrible morning.

Sunrise wouldn't occur for about forty-five more minutes, but the crowd was well illuminated by the lights from the town hall, near-by homes and streetlights.

From within the town hall, the morning came alive with the celestial sounds of the Keene State College choir. The doors were finally about to open. The choir's hypnotic harmonics drifted tantalizingly out into the milling people. The music's mesmerizing arrangements subdued the clamor of the crowd with its beauty and feelings. The town hall's doors swung open and like a mass of lemmings we all tried to trudge toward the inviting light streaming from its entrance.

When we entered the building, Vince Hand joined us. This was the first time we were together since the 2002 high school reunion. After a few cursory hugs and handshakes, we all headed to the auditorium on the bottom floor. TV sets had been hastily mounted in the auditorium to show any breaking reports about the attack on Laforge and her entourage. New information had been temporarily stifled by the police and investigators who had cordoned off the crime scene on Route 12 from reporters and camera crews until all bodies and evidence were collected and documented. The morning TV shows still focused on the Laforge story filled with the constant rehash of the morning events, commentary on Ira Laforge's murder and what Senator Katherine Laforge stood for. A good number of police and armed security guards milled about the crowd observing everyone and chatting on their little phones. Booths had been set up to sell souvenirs and books about Senator Laforge and other political luminaries. Even more important was the concessions stands that were selling hot coffee and pastries. The aroma of fresh brewed coffee was exciting and soothing to our frozen noses and helped us forget the discomfort of the rest of our face, fingers, and feet as they slowly thawed out.

With fresh cups of coffee warming our hands, we grabbed a table near a radiator and sat down to discuss the changing events. I was glad we were inside out of the cold with half an hour yet to go before any of the impromptu tribute for Senator Laforge would begin. I think all of us were convinced that the Senator was dead or mortally wounded by that time. The news had not mentioned her specifically as being dead, but nor had they stated the opposite. You could just feel that something evil had happened – a strange warmth, an unsettling flitting presence like the flick of a feather brushing across the back of your neck. Everything seemed like a sign to me, even the snowflakes falling on the adjacent window that melted instantly into little beads of moisture had to mean something.

As I watched the beads of condensation turn into a tiny trickle of water, I noticed how oddly our images trembled as reflections in the large window. They were like wavering apparitions in a fog. Perhaps I was witnessing that wispy tenuous point where perceived reality merges into the world of dreams or even into another dimension.

The constant waiting with little information on the events of the morning was taking a toll on me. The voices of my friends, the roar of the crowd in the hall, and the perpetual derisive chanting of protesters outside were muted by the loudness of the thoughts that now consumed my mind.

Ira's murder and the probability of Katherine's death made me more conscious of the transience and short length of life. I envisioned Ira's final moments, to have been like a video that God suddenly put on fast forward, hurling him to the end of his mortality until there was only the quiet hiss, like a tape makes when it ends with its snowy blank screen of nothing. Life is such an energetic race of futility.

A feeling of helplessness and bitterness raged inside of me   . We are told that death is simply a transition from one spiritual form to another, but that morning I doubted it. I probably looked like I was in some sort of trance. But even in that cacophony of noises playing in my head, I could still discern the voices of my friends talking to me and trying to snap me out of it.

I looked at them wide-eyed and gathered my thoughts. My conscious thoughts were the desire to talk about everything that I knew about this situation. The sound of my own voice startled me as I impulsively blurted out, "I know something that probably no one else here knows about Katherine."

I wanted to tell them about my trip to Texas. I had kept most of the details of the trip a secret from everyone, even my wife for over a year. But on that terrible morning, I felt the need to share it with them. It was something they definitely should know.

Vince and Tom looked at me inquisitively, and before they could ask me anything, my wife said, "What is it, you think we need to know? Tell us, don't hold it back."

I reminded them of my trip a year and a half ago to Houston, Texas. The trip occurred about a month after the death of my father and at a time I was still trying to settle his estate. My father had owned a small coin collection, which I now found impossible to liquidate at any reasonable price in the Charlestown area. Senator Laforge had invited me to her home in Houston to help me sell this coin collection. Katherine was an avid coin collector and owned a collection worth around three million dollars. She had acquired her coins over her entire life, and for the last decade with the assistance of a numismatist named Mike Fuljenz. She had read about Mike, the President of Universal Coin and Bullion, in some articles published in Coin World and sought him out to assist in her collection of rare Type Two Double Eagles.

She had become enamored with collecting coins when she read about the Howard Bedford, one million two hundred thousand dollar coin collection that was assembled over a seven year period at a cost of about $13,000.

Mike had told Katherine about other collections, such as the Garrett family collection of gold coins that sold for more than 25 million dollars, and the Eliasberg collection that sold for $11,000,000 in 1982. Fuljenz stories and her weakness for history hooked her, and she aggressively went about collecting rare gold, platinum and silver coins.

Mike took the Senator under his tutelage, and helped her to become a savvy coin collector. He steered her towards the best and rarest coins and constantly searched for the most exotic finds in the coin world. Over the years her trust for him grew to the point where the Senator maintained a bailment agreement with Fuljenz and gave him the right to buy and sell her coins at his discretion.

Senator Laforge planned to introduce me to Fuljenz, and since they were close associates, she guaranteed that I would get preferential treatment.

Katherine had scheduled my introduction to Mr. Fuljenz at a restaurant called Tuffy's Eatery in Mauriceville, Texas. When we arrived at the restaurant, located 70 miles east of Houston, the proprietor, Mike Hamilton was waiting to welcome us. Mr. Hamilton was not only a restaurant proprietor, but also the local Texas legislator for his county, and a staunch supporter of Senator Laforge. Always the politician, Katherine and Mike Hamilton immediately delved into discussions about H.R. bill this and H.R. bill that. I listened in amazement as Katherine discussed one Senate bill that big names in both parties favored. It was called the SCNT (Somatic Cell Nuclear Transfer) bills, and it had been introduced by Republicans Alan Specter and Orin Hatch, and Democrats Dianne Feinstein and Edward Kennedy. This was a bill to prohibit human cloning while still preserving important areas of medical research, including stem cell research. Katherine said that those opposing the bill felt that Congress was trying to define a sub class of unborn humans who are simply legislated to be used as research material and then destroyed before they can become full term. Just as the conversation started getting interesting, a man with a well-manicured beard walked up to our table and flashed a big smile at Katherine. It was her good friend Mike Fuljenz.

Mike was a gregarious guy who was very animated in his conversations. He sat down with us, and after Katherine introduced us to each other, he told me that she had informed him of the death of my father. He offered his sincere condolence. Mr. Hamilton exchanged greetings with Fuljenz and then excused himself, to return to his work of hosting the large lunch hour crowd.

I asked Mr. Fuljenz how long he had been involved in the coin business, and he said practically all his life. He gave me a quick overview of his company, Universal Coin and Bullion, that he had molded over the last decade. He had turned his dream into a world-class operation that now held the respect of the numismatic community. Fuljenz and his company had become an icon in the precious metal world, as collectors and investors treated his market predictions as gospel.

Mr. Fuljenz told me it was an honor to have the Senator recommend his services. He assured me that whatever coins my father had acquired, he would offer me the best prices possible. His demeanor and wealth of knowledge in the precious metal market made me feel comfortable that I had finally found someone to help me liquidate my father's collection.

I was surprised when Katherine glanced at her watch, and coyly asked Fuljenz if he would take me back to his office and give me an appraisal of my father's collection, while she took care of some other business. To her relief, Fuljenz seemed more than happy to accommodate her and entertain me for the afternoon. She told Mike she would send a car or personally pick me up around 5:00 PM.

The lunch meeting was over and we all got up to go our separate ways. Mike Hamilton was still at the front door greeting the lunch crowd, but took the time to say good-bye to us. The exchange lasted only a couple moments, but as we started to walk away, we discovered that Katherine had already vanished. Mr. Hamilton winked at me and simply said, "She is gone to take care of some of her business. Don't worry about her, she will catch up with you later." I looked at Mr. Fuljenz quizzically, and he continued, " Time for us to get back to Beaumont."

Mike Fuljenz showed me to his car and thirty minutes later I was in his conference room watching him categorize my father's coin collection. He made little piles of coins from the collection and added up a few numbers on a notepad. Suddenly, his deep voice blurted out, "How does $85,000 sound for your collection?"

I looked at him to see if he was serious and waited for a scintilla of a second before I quietly said, "Great, thank you!"

While I was basking in my good fortune, Senator Laforge was speeding along Highway 69 towards Lumberton, TX. Her destination was a ten-minute jaunt north of Beaumont. She had driven this route on Highway 69 to Cooks Lake Rd. a hundred times. The final leg of her clandestine journey always gave her an eerie feeling of foreboding as she drove down the narrow road shaded by low hanging branches.

Cooks Lake Road was alive with the sounds of the bordering swamp. Her destination was in sharp contrast to its surroundings. Almost exactly two miles down the road on the left, a small house was visible from the road and Senator Laforge turned into the dirt road leading to it. Blending in with the trees bordering the approach were CCTV security cameras mounted on poles. They were perpetually scrutinizing every movement, she made as she drove down the short road. Their whirling sounds as they tracked you, blended in with the cacophony of spring peepers, cricket frogs, cicadas, other insects and birds of the nearby swamp.

The house was unassuming and set back over a hundred feet into the densely forested yard. It had the appearance of a folksy starter home that intentionally understated its true size, with the bulk of the complex hidden underground. It was made to blend into the landscape of this Texas road. Four large mastiffs sat menacingly drooling and panting in front of the building. A large man with a shaven head stood guard at the doorway. He was dressed in a tee shirt and jeans with a pistol strapped to his side. The Senator smiled at him and greeted him with a hearty "Hello Tony" Tony opened the door and let the Senator into the poorly furnished house, and nodded for her to proceed into the next room.

The room had one door on the opposite wall with a small box on the side of the door in which the Senator inserted her thumb. She waited a few seconds for the fingerprint scanner to recognize her print and then the door quietly swung open. It was a massive 4-inch solid steel door that was covered on one side with cheap paneling to camouflage it. As she stepped through the door, it automatically began to close in a quiet, smooth and steady arc.

Ten feet ahead of Katherine an armed guard sat at a table playing cards. He flashed the Senator a smile and greeted her with a thick Southeast Texas drawl. The Senator smiled back and asked him how was his solitaire game. She did not wait for an answer, but went ahead with inserting her security card into the lock. She heard the audible click and grabbed the handle to pull the door open and stepped into the freight elevator.

Outside it was a hundred degrees, but now as she rode to the laboratory five floors below, she felt the coolness, and it relaxed her. The laboratory door was straight ahead of her as she got off the elevator. Katherine quickly strolled over to it and looked up at the eye scanner mounted above the door. She stared at it, unblinking as her iris was interrogated and checked for a match in its database of iris patterns.

A green bulb flickered noiselessly above the steel door sliding silently into the wall. As it inched open, light from the brightness of the laboratory flooded the gloom of the dark hallway. Inside was a labyrinth of cubicles and rooms alive with the work of the best physicist, scientist and computer programmers that the CIA could hire for this clandestine mission.

The Senator always felt goose bumps on her arms as she entered through these doors. It might have been caused by the 65-degree coolness, but more likely it was from the excitement she felt for the work being done there.

Katherine knew what she was about to see and even was in control of when the vision would start. She had found it an emotional, mind-altering experience to watch a living likeness of herself materialize in front of her own eyes. She said at first it felt like an eerie dream or a drug induced hallucination as this replicate of yourself appears. But it is not a dream because you awake from them, and hallucinations are illusions you do not expect, and these visions were expected.

Before going into politics, she had been very much interested in physics. If she had not become Senator Laforge, she would have most likely became the physicist Laforge. Somehow these two career desires had merged, and now she was being exposed to the most remarkable science, since the work on the atomic bomb. Her first few exposures to the cloning experiments were extremely frightening and emotionally disturbing. The Senator would struggle with her own sense of reality and how to cope with what inevitably would appear before her in the glass observation booth. Each time as she was preparing for total molecular analysis and memory recording, she would feel highly agitated and nauseous. The biosensors attached to her body and her molecular imaging on the observation screens would reveal the confusion and reactions to her fears.

When the bays of electron guns started glowing red, beads of sweat would appear on her forehead. This moment would mark the point when the transformation of her biodata and molecular mapping was about to begin. The flooding of specifications, the trillions and trillions of details were spewed from the computer by a massive optical vortex that delivered the data at light speed. The control panel in front of her would turn into a blur of blinking green and red lights culminating with the distinct hiss of the electron guns firing in perfect unison. Then inside the glass observation booth in front of her, her mirror image would materialize. At that precise instant, ComDefC1 (Combat Defensive Clone) code named Hulagu would share the same fears and anxieties that Katherine had just experienced seconds earlier and even its facial expressions would parrot those of the Senator's at the time her bio scan was performed.

Albert Einstein is quoted as saying, "Only a life lived for others is a life worthwhile." The Senator had burned this saying into her mind, and she hoped that Hulagu would use this shared memory to understand its destiny. Life's call to die demands tremendous courage to accept, and she knew that Hulagu still feared death, just as she did, because they both shared the same consciousness and personal biography that live within her.

As odd as it may seem, the Senator felt the deepest compassion and respect for Hulagu and its destined sacrifice. Although they both shared the same memories and secrets of Katherine's past, from this moment on, each of their futures would be unique.

Hulagu and Kat both knew what their immediate future held, and the psychological chaos that ComDefC1 would be experiencing as it resisted the inevitable, but at the same time acquiesced to it. Definitely, it was a far greater emotion than most of us could ever imagine.

The creation of each version of ComDefC1 was a precisely planned variation of the accuracy of the unique position, velocity and spin of each particle making up the individual being cloned.

The twentieth century Quantum Physicist, Werner Heisenberg, had discovered that certain pairs of measurements have an intrinsic uncertainty associated with them. When we attempt to measure anything at the subatomic level we are constrained by these laws. The very act of measuring depends upon light, which itself is a stream of photons. These photons have enough momentum and mass that when striking a particle being measured, its course or velocity is altered. Another obstacle to overcome in the process of quantum cloning was the calculation of the spin of each particle making up the individual being duplicated.

In 1922, Otto Stern and Walther Gerlach discovered that atomic particles possess an intrinsic angular momentum, or spin, and that this spin is quantized (that is, it can only have certain discrete values). The "Spin" of every particle being copied was calculated and stored along with all of the other biodata of the person being cloned.

At first, the Heisenberg uncertainty principle seemed to be a major obstacle to the cloning project. But they soon realized that the accuracy and the method of calculating the various properties of each particle of the person being cloned would actually allow them to more accurately control the degree and speed of apoptosis in the clone.

Apoptosis is cell suicide, which is orchestrated by T cells. They are normally associated with the immune system and are responsible for detecting foreign invaders. The goal of the physicist was to create clones that would only live a predetermine time and then die in what would appear as a natural death. They wanted the death of each clone to mimic nature's natural disruption of cellular function or tissue destruction. The clone would die from a heart attack, stroke, or some other common condition resulting from the destruction or deterioration of critical cells of major organs.

Katherine had sat transfixed as she watched ComDefC1 gain its consciousness and recognize its situation. The Senator's concentration was shattered by the voice of Dr. Sawtelle saying, "Hello" to Hulagu. Its head turned and looked at Dr. Sawtelle and responded back with a simple hello. It was Katherine's voice heard coming from the speakers of the observation booth. Air washed lightly in and out of Hulagu's lungs. It was the first breaths of air that its lungs had ever experienced. Its likeness and matters were so much like Katherine's that even her modesty was reflected in its actions. The overhead monitors exhibiting ComdefC1's biosensor readings clearly displayed its nervousness to its nakedness. This at first seemed to trouble ComDefC1 more than its realization of its transient existence.

Dr. Sawtelle asked Hulagu if it felt it would have any problems following the program that it had been taught through the Senator's mind. The Senator had trained her own mind to accept that her thoughts, experiences, and fears would all be shared by Hulagu. ComDefC1 glanced at Katherine strapped into a control chair directly in front of the observation booth and gave her a smile and nod of agreement.

At first, ComDefC1 was asked to see if it had any problems with mobility. Hulagu walked to the glass separating itself from the observers and then proceeded to stretch itself in various ways. ComDefC1 said it felt nothing odd about its physical being or its ability to move about. On the Senator's computer console the observation cameras scanned every inch of Hulagu's naked body. Doctor Randall directed Hulagu to sit in the examination chair. The chair was complete with additional monitoring devices designed to measure normal human vital signs and the degree of decay or instability the clone was experiencing.

Hulagu sat down on the chair and strapped the various devices to itself and the monitors came alive with the new stats. Its blood pressure and heart beat rate was comparable to Katherine stats, which were also displayed on the screen. Both sets of stats were monitored in unison to help detect abnormalities in Hulagu's vital signs.

Dr. Sawtelle continued on with the program by requesting that Com-DefC1 provide details of its remembered past.

ComDefC1's memory was vivid with the visions of what the Senator had done in the past 58 years. It talked of remembering its mother and its childhood and finally talked about the recent pass, about the feelings of love for Ira and Kat's children. The development of ComDefC1's autonoetic awareness was very important. It provided the ability to subjectively recollect experiences from memory, introspectively applying them to current thoughts and emotions to predict a future outcome.

Memory, in a very real sense, is reality. What the brain's limbic system decides to 'see' and store away becomes the life we have lived. It is the smells, the music, the pain, the loves, the places you have been and all the experiences recorded by the brain. Memory is the core of what we accept as reality. ComDefC1 remembered companions who had enriched Kat's life, family, folks at the office, neighbors, friends, and even people of whom Senator Laforge haven't talked to in years. ComDefC1's memories disturbed the Senator emotionally and she felt more connected to it then ever. She felt sorry that its existence would be so temporary.

Dr. Randall continued testing ComDefC1's noetic awareness by talking about things and facts that were not present, but should be readily available in its mind to retrieve, visualize and understand their significance. Its anoetic awareness was also tested and graded by presenting situations that would cause ComDefC1 to react to certain stimuli. The success of these innate responses would define how human it would appear to others.

They went about discussing the mission as the Senator had trained herself to perform and how Hulagu would participate in it. They discussed Hulagu's understanding of its inevitable demise, and that it should consider itself as an extension of the Senator. Doctor Randall asked ComDefC1 if it felt fear or problems controlling its emotions. Hulagu responded with the fact that it dreaded its own destruction. Hulagu said that it was hard for it to imagine that it was not real and did not have a past greater then the past few minutes in the glass observation booth.

A table laden with food rose through a hole in the floor. Dr Randall asked Hulagu to drink the glass of water on the table. Hulagu obliged and as it drank the water, all watched its vital signs. A spike in its blood pressure stats suddenly appeared on the monitor and Hulagu stared straight through the glass wall into the Senator's eyes. It had also felt the change in its body and desperation could be seen in its eyes.

Dr Randall and Dr Sawtelle began to console Hulagu. The monitors focused in on a lesion that opened magically down the left side of its back. Hulagu blurted out that it was in pain, and that it was afraid of what it was experiencing. The Senator felt so connected to ComDefC1 that she wanted to do something to protect and help it with the obvious pain it was experiencing. Dr Sawtelle told ComDefC1 to use all its remembered experiences and training to help it accept this phase of its existence. Its temperature shot to 104 degrees and you could hear it gasping for air. Its body shuttered and bloody saliva bubbles appeared from its nose. The pores around the lesions started to bleed profusely and scarlet patches of skin appeared upon its body and face.

This was so macabre, the Senator was actually witnessing the throes of her own death, hearing the exhalation of her last breaths, and hearing the sound of her last heartbeat. She was seeing how death would inevitably embrace her. For Katherine, this was the most disturbing sight of all to see - your likeness, still alive, but dying slowly and desperately in front of your very own eyes, without a prayer of survival.

Katherine had never even experienced a relative going through the throes of dying, so seeing herself die in front of her own eyes was most disturbing.

Hulagu's body began to tremble in anticipation of imminent death. Its face turned red, spittle dripped from its mouth, its stomach heaved, and Hulagu's bladder and bowels emptied simultaneously filling the receptacle beneath the examination chair. Hulagu didn't feel it happening as it kicked spastically and jerked in its restrains. The monitors showed that its mucous membranes were also hemorrhaging. Its skin turned purple and Hulagu's mortality ended, and it returned to the darkness it came from.

Hulagu had lived barely an hour, but its physical death, the end of its life in bodily form had somehow been considered a success by the physicist in their quest to control life and death. A cheer filled the laboratory when Sawtelle announced that ComDefC1 death occurred again within the intended time frame.

But for Katherine, its death was not a cause of celebration, but simply the acceptance of the amalgamation of her existence and Hulagus. To her, its demise was just an intermission in a series of resurrections with her phantom.

Kat wondered, if heaven existed, would its doors open for Hulagu, would an Angel of Death welcome it and did Hulagu share her soul?

It is ironic that in the Islamic faith it is destined that non-believers will not die. Like Hulagu, they will not be allowed to die, but will be locked in a revolving existence of life and death over and over. They say that:

"Death will come from all angles, yet they will not die. Therein they will neither die nor live. Every time they seek to get away, they will be driven back. Their skins will be burnt off then replaced with fresh skins. Their abode will be the Fire - the torment of the Fire that they used to deny. And it will be everlasting."

* * * *

As I concluded the chronicle of my trip to Texas, a gust of wind, sounding like giant wasps, whined through the icicles and window frame next to where we sat. It's ferocity caused me to tremor, or perhaps I shook due to the thoughts surging through my mind. Even with the chill hanging over the town hall, beads of sweat appeared on my brow betraying the calmness my voice attempted to convey. I felt like I had just betrayed a friend and opened Pandora's box to the world. I hoped I could reconcile this ill feeling of exposing this secret intrusion into nature and God's domain.

I could tell from the expressions on the faces of my friends and Stacie that they were as dumbstruck as I had been, when I first learned of these experiments.

Tom was the first to comment. Is this for real?

A thud sounded as a snowball hit the window next to where we were sitting. The snowball burst into a spray like a dandelion gone to seed with the wispy flakes scattering harmlessly in the wind. The protesters were not receiving the attention they wanted and were now becoming more brazen and annoying. Outside, the glow of dawn spread across the ashen sky and soft snow continued to float lazily about.

Inside, at my table, harsh words floated about as my friends, and I tried to reconcile feelings with the events that I had just revealed to them.

PART SIX

Total Recovery

The shattering of the large window above our table stunned us. It exploded inward, filling the air with sparkling bits of glass and powdery snow that spread across the floor like a flood of confetti. The pointed shards of cold glass bounced harmlessly off the thick cloth of our heavy coats, but Vince was not as fortunate. A pointed shard punctured his right leg and glistened in the grey dawn light. It grotesquely protruded from his blue jeans turning dark with blood. Vince's anguished moan was almost inaudible against the howl of the wind howling through the broken window.

The drone of voices in the auditorium faded, leaving only the distinct tinkling of glass shards, the sound of the choir singing and the wailing of the wind. The shattering window terrified everyone in the room. We all sat dazed for a moment as police rushed about.

No one at our table dared move for fear of being cut by the shards of glass lying everywhere. A woman sitting at the adjacent table had also been slightly injured. Her son, sitting next to her, was cut somewhere in the head. A trickle of blood snaked down his stoic face, as he sat quietly, not crying. It was a miracle that more people had not been hurt.

The police swooped in around our tables as someone yelled for the paramedics. Vince dazed, looked down at the shard protruding from his leg and carefully brushed away small pieces of glass surrounding it with a paper plate. His leg quivered as he tried to hold it rigid. He feared the shard breaking off deep in his leg would cause more damage.

The police looked out the broken window and saw some protestors sprinting away from the building. The vast windowpane had been hammered and smashed by ice-laden snowballs thrown by the protesters intent on disrupting the event. An officer shouted at them to order them to stop, but they gave no heed, responding only by gesturing obscenely back at the police. Three officers outside took up the chase. Inside the auditorium other police and security guards helped us move from our seats, avoiding the broken glass while a lone paramedic knelt beside Vince examining his wound.

Senator Laforge had been a magnet for protest movements everywhere she campaigned. She told me that at most campaign stops, protestors arrived early and inundated the landscape with their posters, banners and rhetoric. They blocked entrances to buildings where she was scheduled and intimidated those who came to hear her views. The Senator's biggest concerns were towns, with populations of two or three thousand. The onslaught of these groups would completely bankrupt their police budgets. New England, famous for its proclivity to participate in the democratic process, now found its convention challenged by the sheer cost of controlling protestors drawn by the Presidential hopefuls. The mayors and councilmen of small towns were distressed over the exorbitant cost their citizens could incur. The potential financial burden and damage to their towns made them hesitant to invite candidates out of lock step with the demagoguery of these hordes. The Senator often referred to these swarms as the Brown shirts of the 21st-century. The lofty idealism of the protestors' rhetoric was lost by their mob-like cruelty unleashed on those that thought differently.

More than ever before, this primary seemed awash with these protests. Senator Laforge was disliked or feared by numerous groups. Her views on Iraq and foreign policy infuriated the self-proclaimed peace activist. Her out spoken views on the war on terrorism and the war declared on us by Islamic radicals collided with the dictocrats of the politically correct ideology. Her brazened campaign to replace Federal Income Tax with a Federal Sales Tax scared and angered many lawyers, accountants and long time IRS employees. And the oil rich feared her plans to free us from OPEC's shackles. It was this last group more than any other that felt she must be stopped not mater what the cost. Her platform was a maelstrom of frightening changes that to some represented a mini revolution; a terrifying socioeconomic change that embroiled hard liners on each side of the political spectrum.

With her views and the large powerful following she enjoyed, organized protest was inevitable. Her diverse critics and staunch antagonists coalesced into a group whose actions blurred between civil disobedience and a mini organized terrorist movement. The movement swelled with an array of discontents blending their causes and joining ranks to strike out against the Senator's ideas. The old adage, "Sticks and stones will break your bones, but words will never hurt you" stood juxtaposed to the reality of violence and death that ensues so often from the clash of the squirming intractable memes locked in our group psyches. Senator Laforge knew well that simple words and the ideas they express could blossom into the carnage that plagues mankind.

The medic handling Vince had cut away the pant leg around the pro-truding shard. As the medic manipulated the piece of fabric from the shard, Vince's leg quivered and the piece of glass popped out of his flesh like a large sliver. The blood oozed from the wound as the medic hurriedly cared for it.

The town hall was now in a total turmoil. People gathered around win-dows watching and cheering the police as they arrested some of the protes-tors. Upstairs the choir had tried to maintain calm by continuing their program. I was very distressed at this new interruption, but the newscasters were turning this into the story of the hour. WTCB's reporters and camera crews were on the scene filming the turmoil in the town hall. Outside, another TV crew was covering the police arresting the protestors who had broken the window.

Vince refused to be taken to the hospital for observation and just asked to have his pant leg taped back on. The medic refused to do it, but gave him the tape, so he could do it, himself. The nice thing about living in a small town is that you can wear about anything and get away with it. Most people sympathized with Vince's situation and knew he wanted to be left to his own device. We found a new empty table on the opposite side of the auditorium.

Vince hobbled over to join us and plopped down in the vacant chair . I knew he was in some pain, but he refused to let it interfere with his desire to be a part of this event.

A concession ran by a group called the GTRW from the Senator's state of Texas brought us fresh cups of coffee and pastries gratis. The woman in charge was an attractive buxom lady with dark hair. She personally came over and planted a friendly kiss on Vince's cheek for his bravery.

Vince's poker face broke out into a broad smile, and he blushed at the attention bestowed upon him from such an attractive lady. Between the effects of the Darvocet and the kiss, Vince seemed oblivious to the cold and snowflakes that blew in through the broken window being temporarily sealed with a tablecloth.

While police and maintenance personnel went about returning calm to the auditorium, we returned our focus to the reason we were here in the first place.

I was very interested in what Vince or Tom might know, but my inquisitiveness was met with only awkward silence that seemed eternal. I think all of us were waiting for the other to speak, but the issue of breaking our oath of silence still prevailed.

Human frailty and rampant curiosity finally won out, and Tom opened the conversation again, saying, "You know what you told us may answer a lot of questions that I had about some calls I received from someone I thought was Katherine, convalescing in Baghdad. I think our pledge of secrecy needs to change. I think we all should talk this out, but what we say should go no further than the four of us, unless we all agree otherwise. Is everyone in agreement?"

Hell, I was ecstatic and lifting my coffee, I said, "I'll drink to that."

Everyone jumped at his suggestion and new promises were hastily made among us. Stacie was as inquisitive as I, and her eyes revealed the excitement she felt as we all speculated over the last few years of Katherine's life.

We sat, sipping our free coffee, compelled to unravel more of this puzzle surrounding the Senator's trip to Iraq.

Now Vince also opened up and said he had more details that seem to paint an even more bizarre picture of what happened on the Senator's first trip to Iraq. Vince disclosed that he had discussions with an old friend of ours who was residing in South Africa and had related bizarre tales to him about the Senator. Vince had pretty much dismissed them because they did not make sense to him at that time. However, it had planted doubt in his mind because our friend Wilson was not a man who would embellish a story. Our acquaintance with Wilson dated back to our junior year in high school, when he was a fresh air kid living with the Laforge family. He was an avid baseball player and shared many other interests with us. Unlike many relationships, he maintained his friendship with us over the last few decades. With what Tom knew and what Vince related from these conversations with Wilson, a clearer picture emerged of Katherine's murky trip to Iraq.

Tom claimed he had spoken often with the Senator, after her first contact with Ira. She told Tom how upset she was with Ira, and asked if there was any news or rumors in the States of which she should be aware.

Tom knew that after the Senator hung the phone up from her short conversation with Ira, she became very emotional. A torrent of emotions flooded her mind. She was angry, sad, confused, lonely, afraid, and desperate. Her eyes had filled with tears, and she had felt the blood pounding in her head. Katherine did not want anyone to see the concern and sadness in her eyes when she hung up the phone. She lowered her head back to her pillow and stared at the ceiling above. Katherine laid in complete silence with her eyes closed contemplating her feelings for Ira. Why did he not want to talk to her? Why did he not call or write to her more than that one single letter? Katherine was sure he heard her and for some odd reason did not want to talk to her. All of this had made her feel very alone and confused. She did not want to be depressed because it might slow down her recovery. Katherine wanted to talk to her husband and have him tell her that he loved her and missed her and mean it. She decided to call again. She dialed his number and it just rang and then the voice mail came on. She hung up, but then thought that she should try again. Perhaps Ira did not have time to answer the phone. Katherine dialed the number one more time and waited. Someone picked up and said hello! It was him. Kat said, "Ira, please talk to me." No one spoke for what seemed like an eternity, and then she heard Ira. "Are you alone?" He whispered.

"Yes!" Kat replied.

Suddenly, a new voice was talking to her on the phone. It was a woman's voice, and it sounded familiar.

"I need to speak to Ira." Katherine demanded.

The woman asked, "Is this my friend Hulagu?"

"No, this is Katherine, Ira's wife. Let me speak to him."

"I am sorry he is not available." The woman's voice coolly said.

Then the voice spoke once more "Hulagu, it is not wise for you to call here." And then the phone disconnected.

Who in the hell was this woman? Why would she not let her speak to Ira? Who is this bitch that's answering for Ira? She could not believe that he was with another woman. This just could not be true. That bastard! Ira was her world and now when she is trying to get her life together and get back on her feet, she has to go through losing him. Her life seemed to become much worse, and she could not focus on what was going on. Katherine just felt such bitterness toward Ira for not having the decency to talk to her. She wanted to destroy this woman who was with her husband, while she was in an Iraq hospital. She wanted to jump out of bed and beat the shit out of her. She also knew that this was a private matter, and she should not allow her emotions to show.

The nurses entered her room again and their expression made it evident that they knew she was distraught. The head nurse, Hessa, came up to her and grabbed her hand asking her if she was all right? Her concern felt genuine and Katherine appreciated the warmth and interest Hessa showed towards her. The nurse looked into her eyes and asked if she was homesick? Katherine shook her head, yes, and squeezed her hand back. She looked up at Hessa and asked if she would try and find her something to help her sleep. Glancing quickly at Kat's chart, Hessa, crinkled her nose and replied that she was sure she could help. While she went for a pill, the Senator's mind searched for any memory that would help her figure out who the woman's voice was on the phone. This person sounded so familiar. Why would someone answer Ira's phone and not let her talk to him? Why was this woman calling her Hulagu? Who the hell is Hulagu?

The nurse returned to Kat's bedside. Kat turned her head and looked up at Hessa just as Hessa held out her hand holding the sleeping pills. She held a glass of water out for Kat to wash the pills down. Hessa sat down in the chair beside Kat's bed and simply held Kat's hand for a few seconds. Kat gazed at Hessa in appreciation, as her eyes got heavier. She heard Hessa in the background saying in her lyrical voice, "I am so glad that I have the honor of taking care of you. I hope we become good friends." Kat did not reply because the pills took hold of her mind, and then her worries faded away into the deep respite of her sleep.

The Senator looked peaceful again with her mind closed from all the problems she was facing. Hessa carefully placed Kat's hand back on her chest and got up out of the chair to resume her work. The Senator enjoyed her repose for about 90 minutes, and then her eyes started to rapidly move about in her sleep. Blood pumped into her cerebral arteries and her REM sleep stage took hold. Kat had been able to block out dreams lately, but this night, her subconscious screamed out and visions bubbled up to her consciousness. The night had capped a day, packed with an enormous number of problems. The mental and emotional stimulation triggered and fed a vicious cycle of dreams.

Locked in her sleep, she was at the mercy of fearsome creatures that lurked in the darkness of her subconscious. From those shadows the curtains of her nightmare slowly slid open, presenting scenes from frightening memories. At first there was just a kaleidoscope of jumbled visions with a drone of voices constantly chanting, 'mission, mission, mission, you must do your mission.' She couldn't remember exactly how the dream had gone, but she had vague memories of walking into a hotel surrounded by numerous men that were prodding her forward. She remembered a paralyzing fear accompanying that constant chanting of 'mission, mission, mission, you must do your mission.' Maybe that was coming from her head and not from the people around her. Strange sights and a cacophony of voices replaced that quavering din. Now faceless mouths were uttering, "Welcome to Syria, welcome Senator to our hotel, welcome to Syria, welcome to Damascus."' All the while a blanket of men seemed to move her forward away from the smiling mouths to a looming sinister door and then the old din of words returned. "Mission. Mission, mission, you must do your mission." She was stuck in some slow motion scene, unable to move, or scream.

Other memories percolated up from the depth of her mind. Men in smocks loomed over her and a hypodermic needle danced in the air and then slowly descended. "It won't hurt," a stoic face with black eyes muttered. Then she was lost within a dream's dream world and her body shuttered and convulsed to the myriad of events that raced across the cobweb of neurons deep within her brain. Somewhere among those memories were the secrets of her being. The horrors of these subconscious scenes were overloading her consciousness with fear and anxiety and strange sounds gurgled from her.

Another kaleidoscope of images washed over her. Among them was a scene of a long latex balloon wiggling in mist with disembodied hands stretching and examining it. Smiling mouths filled a background wavering in and out of view. Something metallic, shining like silver attached itself to the balloon and then both suddenly dissolved into nothing. Another disembodied hand appeared dangling a long white snake looking object. On its side were words that appeared to rise from it and grow larger. This vision made her body visibly shake, and she cried out into the darkness. On the side of the object glowed the word "Semtex". It shimmered and pulsated and then rippled across its entire length as it floated away.

Words echoed about, "They can't see it. They can't smell it. It is in you now. You are ready." Fear froze her as those words reverberated in her mind. "It is in you now. Deep in you now. Seventy-two hour. Your mission. Your mission. Your mission."

She could recall that she reached to stop something, to stop them, but all she grabbed was a foggy, misty haze. Her stomach roiled with that memory, and suddenly she vomited pulling herself out of the nightmare. Her skin glistened with sweat, and strings of vomit hung from her chin and nose, but she was awake and alive. And now those haunting visions evaporated into nothing.

The night exploded with the sound of sirens and the distant chattering of anti aircraft on the outskirts of Baghdad. Senator Laforge awoke with a jolt, as a strange feeling crept through her consciousness. She sat up in bed, oblivious to the vomit and watched the barrage of anti aircraft guns from the safety of her hospital bed. As the tracers sliced through the sky, like the lightening on the night of the accident, something awoke deep in her mind illuminating it with the same brilliance as the bright flashes from the explosions on the out skirts of Baghdad.

Parts of her dream bubbled to the surface of her consciousness, and she suddenly remembered who she was. She felt awakened, with sights and thoughts surging to the surface, as the synapses deep in her brain flickered crazily, unloading their hidden secrets into her consciousness. Like tiny explosions, the memories of her accident blasted into her mind. The confusion in her mind was quickly replaced with a myriad of questions and emotions. Her consciousness reeled with the reality of who she really was.

The darkness of her confusion gave way to a new dawn. She relived the fear she felt as she was tossed about in the limousine and the shock of Qusay's 300-pound bodyguard smashing into her stomach as the vehicle tumbled about. The impact of this large man was so powerful that it ejected the semtex from her like a ribbon of toothpaste being shot from a tube. The rope of semtex flung about within the passenger's compartment like a three foot long deadly snake. She remembered being dragged from the limousine by frantic Fedayeen guards, and the tremendous confusion outside, as they rushed her to safety. Then the limousine exploded, blasting her with debris and the tremendous heat of the detonation.

The fan's cool air chilled her as she sat on crisp white sheets, staring into the dark night. She felt total awe of what was appearing in her mind. She was not Senator Laforge. She was ComdefC1. She was a clone.

But why was she still alive? She remembered she was to think of herself as a 3D apparition, a specter, or an extension of the "real" Senator. In fact she had witnessed her destruction many times over, as they had experimented with various permutations of her creation. Her memories and thoughts were like a veritable howling maelstrom in her brain. She remembered that she was given only a 72-hour window of time to accomplish her mission. Within 72 hours from the time, she landed in Baghdad, she was to assassinate Saddam Hussein and any others that were around him, when she detonated the semtex hidden deep within her. She was a walking time bomb, much like the insane religious fanatics that strap explosives to them selves and kill unsuspecting women and children. ComDefC1 was the

CIA's ultimate Manchurian Candidate, an assassin with unprecedented cunning and deadliness.

Another barrage of anti aircraft guns could be seen lighting up the sky. The noise and the flashes brought ComDefC1 back to her immediate reality. She wiped perspiration from her forehead as she sat there trying to figure out this situation. For a moment all other thoughts drained away, leaving her only to ponder her precarious, yet miraculous existence. The quiet darkness of her room soothed her like a soft comforting blanket. It wrapped her up protecting her from the despair that surrounded her. The solitude made her dilemma seem less real and terrifying than it really was. In the dark she pressed her lips tightly together as she searched her mind for answers.

Her thoughts slowly fell into place. She was confident that if she continued this masquerade as the Senator, and the charade of having amnesia, the CIA would be forced to leave her alone. If they tried to eliminate her, they risked exposing the entire cloning project, and ruin the Senator's career and her chance of being President. ComDefC1 speculated that the CIA would observe her closely and try to keep her alive for their benefit. She had no doubts that they wanted her released and returned to the United States. Out of the public eye, they would then destroy her or lock her up forever in some laboratory.

With a deep sign, ComDefC1 rubbed her palms across the clean sheets, savoring the sensation. She had been alive for over a month, and she knew the CIA and the Senator must be in a state of sheer panic. The celebrity status bestowed on ComDefC1, as the Senator, made her a major liability to the CIA and prevented Katherine Laforge from exposing herself to anyone who was not a part of this operation. The accident ended the mission, and left the Central Intelligence Agency in a- very difficult situation.

Since ComDefC1 and the Senator shared the same DNA it was unlikely that medically, or scientifically she could be exposed as an imposter, but her existence would be considered a threat, by the Agency. She realized her only hope of survival hinged on being perceived as the Senator at all times.

The Senator's staff had unwittingly promoted this subterfuge with their story that Senator Katherine Laforge had risked her life and career to bring a peaceful solution to the problems between Iraq and the USA. It was reported that she had gone to Iraq to have a face-to-face visit with Saddam Hussein, and broker some sort of a peace accord, which would be implemented when and if she was elected President of the United States. The news also talked about her facing a $1,000,000 fine plus up to 12 years imprisonment, for her noble attempt to help the USA avoid war. What they did not mention was that no one had ever been prosecuted under this statue.

As she sat in her bed, dawn arrived. Slanting sunlight cut through the morning mist, casting its shadows on the window's lace curtains. It was like a shimmering heavenly light sprinkling golden glitter all around the hospital room. This morning was her entry into this fairyland of the real world around her. The soft breeze from the ceiling fan gave her comfort in her solitude. This was a new morning, a true dawn to her new life. She was shedding her fatalistic view of inevitable death. The winds of change had gripped her, and for now it had erased her sadness and depression.

Her new mission was to prevent the knowledge of her recovery from those around her. Her awareness of being alive was ever so intense as she thought of this miracle she was experiencing, and every little thing around her became special and precious. In the morning silence, she tried to contemplate her future while listening in wonder to her heart beating life through her body. She felt awe for her good fortune and felt a oneness with the universe, which she was now a part of.

I cheated death these last few weeks, she mused. By all rights, I should have died but by some strange coincidence, I survived. Perhaps it was the blood transfusions, or the tissue transfers, or maybe a clone simply repairs its minuscule flaws and lives on.

She found she had no answer – only that her life was truly a great gift. ComDefC1 knew she should have vanished like vapor in the wind. Now, with the new lease on life, she felt an overpowering desire to escape the Senator's identity. She had accepted the one inevitable, that the Senator's memories and knowledge deep in the folds of her brain would guide and form much of her future decisions. The Senator would always be within her, slowly fading, but yet still omnipresent. She realized that all she was, is, and will be, would always be shared by this ghost of the Senator living deep within her mind and soul. Often in her solitude, she would hear the Senator talking to her as if she truly lived within her.

This new stage of her existence was like a rebirth for ComDefC1. Her old self had faded away, and she had metamorphosed into this new being that recognized and cherished her survival. Many take the miracle of life for granted, but she treasured this gift and vowed she would do anything she could to survive. She was fully aware that survival relied on her ability to deceive, and take control of all situations. She had to plan for all possible contingencies and learn to respond to events and perils quickly.

The alarm radio switched on and the Voice of Iraq blasted out rock from the speakers. The FM station VOI was owned by Uday Hussein and ironically played American and British rock music. It was the most popular rock station in Iraq. ComDefC1 reached over and turned it down. She was still very much consumed by her thoughts and wanted to think more about all of this before the nurses visited her this morning. One more thing had changed this morning, she was suddenly aware of her interest in Dr. al-Janabi. She knew she had always looked forward to seeing him, but now it was abruptly clear she had amorous feeling for Ibrahim. His loving gestures and signs of support in her adverse circumstances made her feel that he also had real feelings for her. She experienced a sense of vulnerability. These feelings for Ibrahim made her feel somewhat uncomfortable. ComDefC1 was also concerned, that she was perhaps emotionally confused and did not want to lose her self-esteem by surrendering to feelings that were brought on by the situation. Regardless, she looked forward to seeing Ibrahim this morning.

There was the sound of approaching footsteps, and Dr.Ibrahim al-Janabi opened the door. Ibrahim could see Kat was very much awake and appeared much happier than usual, and asked her "How do you feel this morning?"

She felt confused and weakly greeted Ibrahim. ComDefC1 realized that her behavior was not that of the Senator, and quickly tried to pull herself together. She hesitated a few seconds to compose herself and think of an appropriate reply. "I feel good this morning," she blurted out, "and I look forward to my physical therapy."

Ibrahim smiled, and sensed Kat's peculiar demeanor. "I must make my rounds, but I will be back to help you with your therapy."

At the Nurse's station, Dr. al-Janabi reported the Senator's condition. Lounging at the desk was Dr. Benoit, whose eyes lit up when he heard the news.

ComDefC1 was surprised to see Hessa enter her room escorting a very excited looking Dr. Benoit. Kat had often wondered about Dr. Benoit. Was he there to look out for her interests or was he there to report on her to the CIA? ComDefC1 knew that Senator Laforge had never met him before because there was no recollection of Dr. Benoit in her memories. Com-DefC1 realized immediately that she must be cautious with every word and action in front of Dr. Benoit. She was glad that the radio was still on and some Iraqi announcer was bantering away, because she could hear her heart pounding in her ears as she gazed at Dr Benoit when he asked her, "how are you feeling today?"

ComDefC1 met the Doctor's gaze and calmly replied, "Good enough to want to get back to my work soon. I need to find out what is going on with my campaign and be able to catch up with my mail, and any legislation that I should be aware of."

Dr. Benoit blinked with surprise and replied, "You should not be con-cerned about those issues now, only focus on getting better so you can get on with your life."

ComDefC1 retorted back, "I would be ashamed to go back until after I took care of the primary reason I came here, which was to talk to Saddam Hussein. I owe this to my supporters."

Dr. Benoit looked strangely at her and said in a measured voice, "Sena-tor, are you sure that is what you want to do?"

"Hell yes, that is what I must do after getting my ass blown up," Com-DefC1 answered caustically, "I need to bring back something from this trip. Don't you agree?"

Dr. Benoit simply nodded in agreement and added, "Well, Senator, I guess you do feel like your old self again!"

Was his reply sarcasm or some sort of probe into her intentions? Com-DefC1 was not sure but she was not going to give on this. She would be the

Senator, in every way that she felt bubbling up from within her. What would the Senator have done, was the question she constantly asked herself?

Benoit picked up the Senator's chart hanging at the end of the bed and started chatting with Hessa about it. ComDefC1 heard a torrent of Arabic whispers being exchanged, and she barked to Dr. Benoit and Hessa to be polite and speak English in her presence. Benoit sheepishly smiled and apologized for his rudeness. "I was just trying to see how you are recovering and healing from the accident."

Hessa added that she would not talk in Arabic any longer with others, if they can speak English.

ComDefC1's comments must have bothered the Doctor, or it was the medical charts he had read, because he abruptly turned to her, told her he was glad for her progress, and hoped that things would continue this way, so they could all soon go home. He came back over to the bed and shook ComDefC1's good hand and said, "Senator, I'm sorry I offended you, and I want you to know that I am here to help you, in any way I can, to get you back up on your feet."

ComDefC1 pumped Benoit's hand and said, "Of course, I understand." As the doctor left the room, ComDefC1 made a mental note to ask Hessa to restrict Dr. Benoit's access to her unless Dr. al-Janabi accompanied him. She did not trust him to administer any drugs to her or treat her in any way. She felt sure that Dr. Benoit was strictly there to serve the interest of the CIA. She doubted that the doctor's motive was anything other than being an assassin's assassin, and ComDefC1 did not want that to happen. Her encounter with this Doctor from Walter Reed Hospital fed into her feeling of paranoia. This man appeared to be her biggest threat.

The morning dragged and ComDefC1 looked forward to her therapy later that afternoon. As soon as ComDefC1's casts and bandages were removed, the real work had begun. She had learned how to stretch her muscles again, ride a stationary bicycle and walk on a treadmill. Part of the therapy was simple things, like the therapist applying ice packs to her leg and arm to reduce the pain and swelling.

Ibn Sina hospital also used a machine that sent a mild electrical current to the muscles in her arms and legs through pads applied to the skin. The electrical stimulation reduced the pain and swelling and helped relieve her stiffness. Every other day ComDefC1 got to work out in a heated swimming pool. Using the water to support her body made it easier to move. Once a week, they would give her a whirlpool bath followed by a complete massage, and today ComDefC1 was going to experience ultrasound as part of her treatments.

That night she felt sadness and loneliness consuming her again. So much had happened in the last 24 hours that she had not thought about the reality of what she was, but now it hit her. Her world was a silent kingdom of her own. Realizing that even her memories were not hers, but those of Senator Laforge made her feel acutely lonely, because she felt her mind had nothing in it that belonged to her. All of the happiness and love that she had felt earlier now ebbed away as the reality of what she was ate away at her.

Most people could take solace in thoughts of their childhood or some period of their life, but not ComDefC1. She realized that every thought of a friend or an event was really just a mirage of the past. She felt her life was now dark and meaningless. She felt so lonely because she had no one to talk to that, she could divulge her feelings or secrets to. Even if she could establish a relationship with Dr. al-Janabi, she could never divulge to him what she really was. The human desire to talk to someone about her anguish engulfed her. Loneliness is a psychological need that must be satisfied.

ComDefC1 wanted some sense of identity. Who was she now? She knew she had to take control of herself quickly, or she would end up delusional. She knew she was in what seemed like an inescapable situation that was totally isolating. There was a feeling of despair, and not knowing how much more of this painful loneliness she could take. How agonizing this was! A living prison cell, an inescapable reality, she felt this need for companionship, but everywhere she turned there was none. Nothing out there was like her. She was truly alone in this universe. The loneliness so deep inside of her seemed to have a life and personality of its own. It was like a demon that left her scared, angry and hating.

She desperately looked forward to seeing Dr. al-Janabi in the morning. She knew that just his presence would sooth and calm her. ComDefC1 realized she had to work on separating herself from all that was stored in her mind. The philosopher Descartes made the often-repeated statement that, "I think, therefore, I am." ComDefC1 wanted to change that. What she wanted was to be a new person unchained to the identity locked inside her mind. She knew that her thoughts were from her conditioned mind. This was a mind, which judged the future from all the experiences and cultural baggage it had absorbed to help shape each of its new thoughts. She had to learn when to listen to these voices of the Senator, in a very impartial way, and to use these memories to shape thoughts that would be her own unique thoughts.

Part of having your own identity is having a name, that you feel defines you, and ComDefC1 had thought a lot about that. Stored in her mind, were memories of the story of Frankenstein. She had easily identified with the monster from Shelly's story. The monster had the same beginning; straight out of the laboratory created from necessity and expediency. Both of them yearned for a companion in life and Dr. Frankenstein wanted his monster to die and be out of his life just as the CIA and Senator Laforge most likely wanted. It did not take long for ComDefC1 to decide that Shelly would be her last name.

Her Catholic background provided her with a handful of Biblical names to ponder over. She wanted a first name that spoke of her existence, one like Anastasia that meant 'Resurrection' or Joanna a Hebrew name for 'God is gracious'. She tried both of them with Shelly but neither sounded right and then she remembered the name 'Zoe' meaning eternal life. In the New Testament, Zoe was used numerous times to indicate eternal life. It was a name that she liked and in a tiny whisper, she said, "I am Zoe Shelly." It sounded right and oddly enough related to her existence because as she recalled from the Bible, Zoe or eternal life is the whole future of the redeemed, and the final glory and reward to which the children of God enter.

These two names merged together were the roots of her new identity. She could not use this name now, but she could work at creating this person in her mind and on paper. "I shall be … Zoe," she told herself. She silently whispered it again, "Zoe Shelly," she smiled to herself and then happily collapsed across the bed.

Zoe's life was now consumed with, waiting, plotting, pretending and hoping for better tomorrows. Her mind was constantly whirling with plans for her survival. Each moment of every day she steadfastly became more and more acquainted with everything she could about her surroundings, guard schedules, staff changes, common sounds from the hall and where she was located in Baghdad. This was the type of information necessary for her to acquire to successfully accomplish an escape from this hospital confinement. And the escape had to happen before they released her to the American contingent constantly demanding her freedom.

She knew she was in the Ibn Sina hospital in an exclusive district of Baghdad. The building was a three-story hospital on Haifa Street right down the street from the Presidential and government offices. It was used only by the members of Saddam's regime and privileged others.

Ibn Sina hospital was considered the best-equipped medical facility in Iraq. It had burn treatment capabilities and an excellent surgery staff complete with the latest equipment. Nothing was too good for this hospital, because it was responsible for caring for all of Saddam Hussein's family. The hospital was a secure haven protected by the Fourth Platoon from the Fifth Battalion of Saddam's Special Republican Guard's First Brigade. These soldiers were equipped with BKC-RBK Kalashnikovs and under the direct command of Qusay Hussein. Saddam Hussein had given his youngest son, Qusay, control of both the Special Intelligence Agency and the Special Republican Guard.

Zoe had been convalescing in the same room that she was initially admitted to. Oddly, it was the same room that in August of 2002 Abu Nidal had died in. Abu Nidal, born as Sabri al-Banna, was a Palestinian terrorist and trusted confidant of Saddam. He was a much-feared Palestinian murderer, who had built his own small army of thugs that shared with him his lust for killing. His list of patrons included the most brutal and megalomaniacal of Middle Eastern dictators. Saddam had been perhaps his longest ally and loyal sponsor. Libyan dictator Col Gaddafi established strong ties with him until 1998. For a short time, he had also provided services for President Assad, but that was short lived because of the actions he had taken for Saddam Hussein against Syria during the Iran/Iraq war. President Reagan had placed him on the most wanted list of international thugs and terrorists. He maintained that position until President Clinton replaced him with Osama bin Laden.

Like Zoe, Abu Nidal received a VIP welcome, and was treated at the Ibn Sina Hospital within 100 yards of Saddam's office at the Presidential Palace. His cause of death was shrouded in mystery. The official version was that he committed suicide, but most believe Nidal was murdered by Saddam following some sort of a disagreement.

A chill passed through her when she realized the strange coincidence that they both were assassins, and that Nidal's life ended in the same hospital room. Even more bizarre was the fact that directly adjacent to her room was the perpetually reserved hospital room for Saddam's eldest son, Uday.

This was the same hospital where Uday Hussein recuperated after he was nearly shot to death Dec. 12 1996 by unknown assailants in the plush Mansour district. Three or four gunmen in jogging suits and helmets surrounded him while he was stopped in his expensive armored car. They tossed hand grenades at his car, shattering its windshield and then at point-blank range, fired automatic rifles at Uday, hitting him numerous times. His injuries included a ruptured bladder and stomach, and damage to his leg and spine that left him with constant pain and a permanent limp. The Islamic Dawa Party, an Iran-based Iraqi opposition group, took credit for the assassination attempt, but Saddam never proved this. Uday Hussein was 32 when the attack occured in the Mansour's shopping boulevard where he had spent much of his hard-drinking brutal nightlife or raping, killing and maiming people.

As her days in the hospital slowly ebbed by, her escape plan continued to evolve and mature. A major necessity for a successful escape was to enlist at least one trusted Iraqi ally. Her target became Dr.Ibrahim al-Janabi . He possessed a position in the hospital to assist in her escape, and she was becoming very much infatuated with him. She made it abundantly clear to Ibrahim, that her husband was having an affair with another woman. Zoe claimed Ira had not visited her since her accident because of his illicit relationship. Her amorous feelings for Ibrahim were genuine, and she began to show more interest in him every time he visited her. She baited him with questions of what he would do if war came to Iraq and told him how she could help him establish himself in America as a doctor. She engaged him in conversation at every chance meeting, she had with him. If he was checking her temperature, she would look deep into his eyes and worship him with her glaze. Ibrahim began to reciprocate and he would caress her hands and press his finger against her lips, and she would give it a kiss. She found herself seeing his handsome bearded face, whenever she closed her eyes and even remembering the scent of his cologne. She felt a bit foolish as she fantasized about how far the relationship could go, but she also felt that anything now was possible. The adoration she showed in her eyes for Ibrahim was real, because she credited him with giving her the gift of life. He had become a God to her.

Along with her amorous advances on the doctor, she busied herself with activities that would keep her adversaries believing she still thought she was Senator Katherine Laforge. She had purposely become very demanding of the Senator's staff in the states and constantly inundated them with request to provide her with reports and research results on platform issues.

One report forwarded to her as she continued her charade, was a study from the U.S. Department of Energy titled, "Aquatic Species Program Biodiesel from Algae." The research had been prompted by the 1973 OPEC embargo that caused gas prices to jump four hundred percent at the pumps. The study detailed activities that the government had taken on tests at a highly restricted area in Roswell, New Mexico. These tests exhibited that certain strains of algae growing in ponds could be converted into biodiesel. The experiments demonstrated that a one-acre pond could annually yield ten thousand gallons of biodiesel. She read the reports over several times. This was an amazing discovery.

She knew that the government helped subsidize farmers to grow soybeans that produce only forty gallons of biodiesel per acre per year. Why would a solution that produced nine thousand nine hundred and sixty gallons more per acre be secreted away from the public? The confusing part was this solution to our energy crisis had been available since the 1970's, but no party or administration chose to implement the plan to decrease our reliance for OPEC oil. She wondered if Senator Laforge was aware of this report? The question of, why it was not being used, continued to bother her. She decided that publicizing this study and fighting to implement its solution would be something Katherine would have done. She could not see how big oil could swing so much power to silence the government from using this solution to free us from OPEC's clutches. It would certainly make us a more secure nation and end our need to have our soldiers die to insure foreign oil reaches our shores. But it would end the record breaking billion dollar profits made by the oil giants as they steadily increased their prices for gasoline at the pump. Political campaigns on both sides of the aisle are funded by big Oil. If a politician wants a contribution from the petrol industry, he will do best to accept their lobbyist advice above science, logic, and certainly over their constituent's needs. She also realized that rational arguments are of little concern to politicians seeking election money from big oil.

Zoe fired off a request to the Senator's staff for more information on producing biodiesel from algae. For some odd reason, Zoe felt Senator Laforge would appreciate her efforts as moving in a direction that would create more popularity for her in the upcoming Presidential campaign. She looked forward to discovering more about biodiesel and if any action at all is being taken to implement algae production.

* * * *

The shrill screech of the intercom abruptly interrupted our discussion. A quick series of annoying hisses admitted from the speakers, and then the deep voice of Father Grudziński floated out into the auditorium. Tapping the mike he asked: "If I could please have your attention." His plea for quiet was repeated throughout the auditorium by others and suddenly the din subsided. A tall, imposing figure, Father Grudziński was well liked by the people of Charlestown. He was attired in serious black, clerical garb with sharply creased and pleated pants and the customary Roman collar framing his handsome face.

Father Grudziński began; "Good Morning and thank you all for venturing out on this very cold morning. We have all gathered here to find solace among friends as we struggle to accept the violent acts of a few men earlier this morning. I have been asked by associates of Senator Laforge to say a few words about this incident. Our town of Charlestown is a good place, with good people, but today a terrible tragedy broke the heart of our community. Here, even in our little town, we learn we are not immune from senseless violent acts that plague our society. Ira Laforge, and four aides to Senator Laforge whose names have been withheld have been taken from us. Four of the alleged perpetrators were also found dead at the site of this terrible crime. And we are still unable to give you any additional information about Senator Laforge's condition. Police are still withholding this information. This violent act will mark our community for years to come. It is a wound that will take time to heal in our hearts. The Good Lord allowed me, to be here to try to offer some solace to those whose lives are now forever changed by the events that unfolded earlier this morning."

His words of comfort flowed effortlessly as he glided across the floor with the wireless microphone locked in his hand. His words, the intensity of the moment and the light streaming through the frost covered windows awakened the magical, mystical sense of the sublime. It was a feeling I used to get as a young man when light beamed through the stained glass windows filling the church with a rainbow of many hues.

Father Grudzińsk asked everyone to join him in singing the hymn "Eternal Father Strong to Save." Slightly off key, he started the hymn, and was immediately joined by the Keene State College Choir. The people sitting at their tables joined in.

Eternal Father, strong to save,
Whose arm hath bound the restless wave,
Who biddest the mighty ocean deep
It's own appointed limits keep;
Oh, hear us when we cry to Thee,
For those in peril on the sea!

The somberness, and poignancy of the scene were intense. Tears streamed down many cheeks during the hymn. Father Grudzińsk had picked the same hymn sung as President Kennedy's body was carried up the steps of the U.S. Capitol to lie in state. As the last verse of the hymn ended, Father Grudzińsk looked out amongst us and called all of us all to bow our heads.

"Lord, You visit us with trouble this day. We are all deeply saddened. We thank You for your presence at this time of need, and we ask You to help protect us all from harm. We humbly ask Your blessing for those who perished in this terrible act and for their families and friends who grieve for those lost."

"We pray for the families and survivors of all those whose loved ones were taken. God we pray for the eternal rest for those who died and commend these souls to the care and mercy of God. We ask for pardon for the souls of those who were responsible for these acts of transgression against God's law of love and our worldly laws. Amen."

A chorus of Amen's echoed back from our tables and then the Keene State College Choir filled the auditorium with the words of "The Lord is my Shepherd"

THE LORD is my shepherd; I shall not want.
He maketh me to lie down in green pastures; he leadeth me beside the still waters.
He restoreth my soul: he leadeth me in the paths of righteousness for his name's sake.
Yea, though I walk through the valley of the shadow of death, I will fear no evil: for thou art with me; thy rod and thy staff they comfort me.

This room of humanity was lost to the events and moved by the hymn. All felt the reality of what had happened and tears streamed down from many eyes. Some recited their own private prayers and others sat totally quiet staring at the choir. The shining eyes, the quivering lips, and the somber faces moved me deeply. Oddly, I felt caught up in a strong wave of spiritual exaltation. I was one with the rest of the mass of humanity mourning the loss of friends.

Father Grudzińsk changed the mood a bit and asked the choir to sing, "Just a closer walk with thee," a hymn with almost an upbeat sound to it.

While they sang, he moved about the room and announced that if anyone wanted to talk to him, he would be available to help them in this time of sadness. As he moved by a muted TV, which hung from the ceiling, I swallowed hard. A news bulletin scrolled across the bottom of the screen that read, "Senator Laforge missing from attack site….."

PART SEVEN

Escape Plans

The snow had started to fall heavily again, and it whipped angrily at the large windows in the town hall. A murmur rippled through the auditorium as the audience speculated why Senator Laforge was not found at the crime scene. The most popular explanation was that she was kidnapped. Yet, no one had contacted authorities with any demands related to her disappearance and no one had claimed responsibility for the attack. Another scenario was that she had escaped the carnage and was hiding in the surrounding woods. If that was the case, she needed to be found soon because the freezing temperature and fresh snow flurries could freeze her. Others speculated that she might have been taken from the bus and her body disposed of at some other location, perhaps in the Connecticut River. At that time, I lacked any real theory myself. I just knew I would like her found or some conclusion to the mystery of her disappearance.

Another concern had crept into my mind that cold morning. It was a very selfish one, but it was real, and it increased the anxiety I was already experiencing over the attack on Katherine. I worried that I would no longer be in the fray of events. My work with Senator Laforge had become so much of my life, that without it, I feared my life would be without purpose. My research and perseverance had provided her with the powerful alternative energy report that became the foundation of her energy platform. This work was an extension of who I was and without it, I feared I would mentally wither away.

During the last few years, I had slowly lost my innocence. The high-minded attitude I once held had been replaced by a great deal of cynicism. I wanted to be left more and more to myself. I enjoyed my days and nights of intense research in diverse areas, and I liked the fact that Senator Laforge wanted facts and not a spin to everything I reported. I was learning that problems do not always have perfect solutions. I wanted to experience that cathartic moment where the complex was revealed to me in total clarity and the answers would be simple and logical. I was learning that change could be so gradual that in one's lifetime it is often imperceptible.

The anxiety and fear had triggered one of my dreaded headaches. It was time for medication before I got nauseous and dizzy. I hated the medication probably as much as the headaches. Often it would bring about random mental images and cloud the lens of my consciousness to where myself seemed to peer through an opaque glass. I slyly swallowed a pill with a mouth full of coffee. At these times, I would close my eyes, and I would silently utter every vile invective, I had ever heard until the feeling subsided.

Vince watched me with my eyes closed and his fingers drumming on the table. His previous smile had evaporated and was replaced with a look of exasperation.

Finally, he ventured, "You okay?"

I peered at him through a haze of condensation that had formed on my glasses. "Yes I am fine." I replied.

"Well it makes me nervous with you sitting there with your eyes closed. Hell, I don't know if you are alive or dead when you do that!"

"Sorry, it is just a minor headache I was nursing. It is about gone now."

At an adjacent table, a mammoth man with his buttocks spilling off his chair was also staring at me.

"You want to hear more about Kat's Iraq visit?" Vince inquired.

"Absolutely", I replied coming out of my mental fog.

"Well, I am not sure how accurate all of this is because some is just ru-mored stuff, I heard and some is from conversations I had with her when she was trying to figure out what was going on back here in the states." Vince offered.

"I know she was having a hell of a time trying to recover from the accident.

* * * *

"Her body was healing, through the best of care given Senator Laforge by the Ibn Sina Hospital staff. Zoe knew she was experiencing a measure of the captor-prisoner syndrome, where isolated victims form emotional attachments with their abductors. But in her case she felt it was only natural, since there was no one else in her life. Just those who she felt wanted her dead like Dr. Benoit and his group of cronies waiting to snuff out her life.

Her face hardened as she thought about her emptiness. But when she pictured Dr. Ibrahim al-Janabi, tall, slim, bearded, with his dark eyes blazing with warmth, she melted a bit and her lips soften. Zoe felt drawn to him and made no effort to quell this budding emotion. Her attachment to Ibrahim was even more important emotionally because of the alienation she felt from Ira. She knew it would sound crazy to others that his rejection stung her so badly, since she was simply his wife's clone. But it did hurt. The feelings were as powerful as those phantom feelings that plague people who lose an arm or a leg. They still feel it itching or aching, but it is physically not there. More than anything, she missed him because she had lived as Katherine and loved him as deeply as Katherine.

She conversed in her mind with herself. "My emotions, my memories are as real and as poignant as hers," she declared. She blinked back unwelcome tears as she thought this.

Her thoughts spiraled back to the beginning, the CIA, Katherine, and she fought back dark anger. They had played God, she silently fumed. "I was not supposed to outlive the 72-hour window they gave ComDefC1," she thought, but she had. Her miraculous life was perhaps God's will to punish those who played in his arena.

I have become a Trojan Horse, she mused darkly, in a way the ancient Greeks never anticipated.

But her thoughts delved deeper, sifting ancient lore for a closer, more fitting parallel. And found it. In feudal Japan a living warrior who failed to commit suicide upon the death of his master was a warrior without honor. He made his own way outside accepted societal constraints. In Zoe's situation her master, the CIA, was not dead, but she felt they did want her dead. She was an aberration, a loose cannon the Company could not afford.

Zoe felt cold, her heart ice. Ronin she may be, yet she could not disassociate herself from the essence of her own identity. She understood intuitively that her true self was governed by the principles, the ideals and the emotions of Katherine Laforge. They had all been cloned into her along with bones, muscles and skin. And short of death Zoe could no more turn her back on those principles, than she could stop thinking and feeling. Caring was synonymous with love, and she cared deeply. Emotionally Zoe was Katherine in every sense, especially where it involved love of country, love of ideals, love of family and posterity.

Pushing herself up, Zoe cradled her head in her hands. "Somehow I must find room for me in here," she told herself. As she agonized, a snippet of a poem, 'But Now,' written by American poet Cynthia Proctor came into her thoughts....

> *"But now,*
> *My life not ended, though changed in many ways*
> *Feel gentle wings that guide me*
> *Still grace, with love,*
> *My days."*

Zoe longed desperately for the guidance of gentle wings. Suddenly, the door opening brought her back to the moment. The head nurse pushed through the doorway, clothes draped across her arms. On her heels followed two others who surrounded Zoe.

"You must dress quickly," the woman urged, her tone quivering with excitement. "Our Leader calls for you."

They garbed her in the traditional Iraqi woman dress, leaving off the conventional head-covering because their patient was a Westerner. When Zoe met their critical approval, they assisted her into a wheelchair, and then wheeled it into the corridor.

"By coming here, to the hospital, he honors you," the head nurse stressed. "Be most respectful," she cautioned sternly, "but most of all, when he speaks, you must never, never, never contradict him."

They wheeled her only a short distance down the hall, to the room reserved for the Iraqi President. When they wheeled her through the doorway,

Zoe found the room's décor remarkably austere, but what furnishings Saddam Hussein permitted were in fine taste. A big man, Iraq's President pushed from the couch to his feet, waved the nurses from the room, and then regarded her in open appraisal.

For this visit he had abandoned his military uniform for a stark black Western suit, white shirt, and black tie.

As she studied him in turn, Zoe realized how truly cut off she was, exiled in an old world thousands of miles from her people. Achingly alone. Out of her depth. In the hands of a ruthless dictator. In a land where people lived and died on his whim.

"You are making fine progress, ah, in your recovery, Senator Laforge," he said in acceptable, but accented English, his deep voice surprisingly cordial. She met his wide smile with her own, felt his charisma enfold her, but Katherine Laforge was no stranger to powerful people. "I am glad you will soon be well," he told her. Then Saddam leaned closer, towering over the wheelchair. "Have you come to my country as my friend … or my enemy?"

Zoe's blood chilled. In one sentence Saddam Hussein dangled a choice: friendship or judgment; life or death. But Katherine Laforge had researched the dictator carefully, and Zoe had rehearsed her lines well. Drawing on that knowledge she prayed her proposals would interest him, then wet her lips, and answered Saddam.

"My experience here in your country has helped me to see more clearly Iraq's point of view," she said without evasion. "Your son's bravery in saving my life at the least makes me feel the need to offer my support to some of your causes."

She took a deep breath, continued. "Lying here as I have these last months, I've thought much of what could be done to end our political stalemate and to reestablish the friendship that once existed between our countries."

Saddam nodded, more a mere head shake than a gesture of approval, but it encouraged her to go on. "We worked with you when you fought the Iranian Islamic fundamentalists trying to overtake your country. Later you were looked upon as the most stable of countries in this area."

Zoe spread her hands imploringly. "I believe we will both agree that we need to end the animosity between our countries and move forward with a stable peace and the rebuilding of your country."

Stern eyes steeped with distrust bored into hers, but his smile never wavered. "Words," he countered, "many American politicians have said such words." When his tone hardened, the smile remained. "But words are easy. They do not lift the sanctions you Americans levy against us. Words do not purchase our oil or feed my people."

"Or fund your tanks, planes and guns," Zoe wanted to add, but she bit back such accusations. Instead, she said, "If you seek guarantees, I have none to give. I am sure you are well aware how elections work in our country. Unfortunately, being elected takes money, lots of money."

"What is that to me?" he shot back.

Zoe took a deep breath. All or nothing, she told herself. "If I become President, I will honor any agreement we come to during this meeting. After I am inaugurated, and I assure you I will be inaugurated, the sanctions could be lifted quickly." She hesitated for effect, then continued. "But any change in American policy has to be viewed as a result of positive change in your country."

Saddam's good humor died. "What does that mean?"

"Positive change," she emphasized, "like Iraq capturing Islamic terrorists, publicly displaying them, but refusing to cooperate with America until I am elected." She gave him her best smile. "I think the American people could change their views, seeing the problems that exist between our countries more as a personality clash between you and our President than fundamental differences in policy."

Zoe's heart drummed as Saddam abruptly moved behind her wheelchair, pushed it near the couch, then sat down facing her. "You would do this?" he pressed, his tone troubled. "Why would you do this?"

"Being elected takes money, lots of money," she repeated with emphasis. "You have lots of money."

For long heartbeats she held that smile. Saddam Hussein understood bribes, had used bribes effectively in the United Nations' Oil For Food Program. If Katherine Laforge received money from Saddam, she would do exactly as she promised. But any money Saddam advanced Zoe would never be deposited in the Senator's campaign war chest and this did bother Zoe, but the money was needed for her escape.

Saddam slowly stroked his bearded chin, as he considered. Then his hand dropped. "You would do this--?"

Zoe held up her hand, conscious she was interrupting him, against the warnings of the nurse. But she pressed on. "No guarantees," she emphasized decisively, "only an agreement between us with a firm understanding that it will benefit us both in days to come."

His face revealed none of his thoughts as he leaned back into the softness of the plush couch. Saddam's fingers beat an irregular rhythm against his leg as he weighed her proposal. Zoe watched his eyes, but their opaqueness gave no clues to his decision.

"You are an insightful woman, Katherine Laforge," he said finally. "Our doctors must make you well for your return to the United States." His broad lips stretched into a wide smile. "And I look forward to your Presidency."

* * * *

Zoe felt weak and hollow when the nurses returned her to her hospital room. But she was elated none-the-less.

Well, Katherine, we did it," she offered silently as they undressed her, eased her into bed. Zoe sensed Katherine's underlying disapproval of the deception, but weighed against the future, Kat's objections were trivial.

As Zoe let her tension drain away, her mind raced. The CIA had the manpower, the unlimited funds, to track her down and eliminate her. All she had were her wits and her influence in the role of Senator Laforge. And she would use her assets, as she must.

A stray thought surfaced, and Zoe eagerly seized it. Since the world believed she was the Senator, she could access funds from Senator Laforge's accounts and use what she gained as she saw fit. Zoe knew the necessary codes, but she must exercise care. She would have one opportunity to transfer funds. After that, Katherine and her staff would be alerted and change the pin numbers.

But there were other avenues as well. Zoe knew she could call on the Senator's long-term friendship with Mike Fuljenz to liquidate parts of her rare coin collection. He would do it if she asked. She was sure that no one would stop her from taking the money out of her portfolio account at Universal Coin & Bullion Co. Mike would have been aware that the Senator was supposed to be in a hospital in Iraq. And Zoe felt certain that, as Katherine's friend, Mike would wire money to any bank she requested.

First she must establish a bank account with an international bank having offices in Iraq. As soon as possible, those funds must be moved out of Iraq, channeled through offshore bank accounts accessible only by Zoe Shelly. Once that was done, she could breathe a long sigh of relief.

And it will happen, she reassured herself, and when it does, I will be free.

* * * *

Days passed, and then one day brought a team of plastic surgeons to study her, to correct the skin damage to Zoe's face and restore it in Katherine Laforge's image. But Zoe insisted on alterations, chin and cheek transplants, which could easily be removed later.

Under general anesthesia, the doctors performed the surgery in two separate sessions. Incisions began above the hairline at the temples, extending in a natural line in front of the ear and continued behind the earlobe to the lower scalp. They assured Zoe the incisions would fade rapidly, and she should suffer no discomfort from the fat and excess skin removal.

When she woke up in her room, Zoe fingered the loose bandages on her face. She fought the urge to smile for it would pull the skin I may have Katherine's face, but in the subtle differences I finally have an identity of my own.

Two days after surgery, they withdrew the drainage tubes, a simple procedure done in the privacy of her room. Sometime later the clips used on the scalp were removed. In less than a week, Dr. Ibrahim unwrapped the bandages.

"You were told to expect bruising," he reminded her, his face hovering close, "and there is some." His adoring eyes never left hers. "Do not fear.

The internal stitches will soon absorb, and the bruises will fade. Your beauty will not be marred." He grinned as he straightened. "I shall look in on my favorite patient every chance, I get."

* * * *

Zoe's battles were part of her continuing war of survival, and often the steps she had to take conflicted with that part of her that still embraced Katherine morality. It wasn't just the deceptions, and lies that bothered her, but also the harm she would eventually inflict on Katherine. To overcome these confusing feelings she would remind herself that Katherine would most likely have her killed just like she did so many times before in the laboratory. The fact that they shared the same emotions, the same memories also meant Ira was a wound that still festered.

She longed for escape from her gilded prison as much as she needed compassionate, loving arms about her. And she convinced herself that Dr. Ibrahim al-Janabi could fulfill both desires. Zoe seized every opportunity to entice him when he came to her room alone.

Her plans bore fruit. He lingered longer and longer. Finally, in the stolen moment when he kissed her, she knew he was hers.

"I must have you," he whispered in her ear. "But not here. He would know and kill us both."

"But Ira is not here," she protested. "Anyway, he no longer cares. He has another--"

"Not your husband," Ibrahim said fervently. "My President." He drew a ragged breath, as much from fear as fading passion. "If I flaunt his hospitality by being intimate with you, he would have me gelded with hot pincers, then torture me slowly, keeping me alive for days." His face pinched with deep concern. "You--Senator or not, he would simply hand over to the mob."

His voice dropped, grew conspiratorial. "We must exercise great care. There are hidden microphones and cameras in this room."

Zoe drew back hastily, her eyes widening in apprehension. "Then they will know we kissed?"

Ibrahim shook his head. "Do not fear. The video surveillance is auto-
mated. I have installed a forty-minute tape loop that records you sleeping."

Elation flooded Zoe. Through Ibrahim she now might have a way to
slip away from her hospital room unnoticed. If she somehow could elude
the armed guards in the corridors…? She laid back and sighed and thought.
"Soon she would be free."

* * * *

As each day passed Ibrahim grew increasingly enamored with his convalescing patient. His advances remained meek, lingering kisses and an
occasional intimate touch. Despite his obvious passion, fear of torture kept
him celibate.

Loneliness and isolation weighed heavily on Zoe. Day after day Ibrahim
continued to prove his faithfulness, and she allowed herself to love him. As
their relationship deepened, he grew more pliable to her pressures. More
astute and well connected than Zoe anticipated, he established an Iraqi bank
account in Katherine Laforge's name through a reputable Swiss bank. Using
his family contacts, he arranged other offshore accounts under her Shelly
alias.

One morning Zoe stood at the window, staring at the unchanging
Baghdad skyline when Hessa, her primary nurse, burst into the room.

"Good, you are dressed," she said with satisfaction. During the long
days in the hospital, she had slowly warmed to Zoe. While Hessa was openly
friendly, even considerate, they would never be friends. "He waits for you in
the courtyard."

At the hospital doorway, Hessa paused, allowed Zoe to go on alone.
Saddam Hussein waited in the garden, his stout fingers tenderly caressing a
blossom. A uniform and beret replaced the Western suit, but he offered the
same wide smile he had given her when they last parted.

"Ah, Senator," he turned, gestured, "see the blossoms wakening. Our
country is indeed a fertile land." He sighed wistfully. "But I did not ask you
here to speak of flowers and gardens. Come, sit with me."

She settled in the offered lawn chair, and let him study her face without interruption. "I see our doctors have been good to you." His opaque eyes bored into hers. "I am told your recovery is almost complete. I assume you will want to return to the United States, yes?"

"That is my hope," she answered. "But not in the way you expect." She left those thought unsaid. "I have been gone a long time. There will be much to do."

"And a campaign to run, which takes much money," he added with emphasis. "I have considered the information you forwarded to me, especially the … what do you call it? Ah, yes, biodiesel."

He waved his large hand dismissively. "No matter. My scientists can create vast algae farms in our desert areas to produce this biodiesel. I can, in turn, sell this product to other countries outside of United Nations sanctions."

His gaze softened, became expansive. "Katherine Laforge, you have done me a great service. I shall not forget it."

Zoe felt her tension fade. She allowed herself a pleased smile as she extended her hand. "To a better tomorrow."

His hand swallowed hers, but he shook it gently. "A better tomorrow for both of us." Then he grinned. "Beside the door are valises containing one-and-a-half million dollars," his grin broadened, "for your campaign…. You better go home and win that election."

* * * *

Early one morning Ibrahim barged into Zoe's room his expression grave. "We must push forward our timetable. You must escape this morning, now, or all will be lost."

She glanced at the calendar on the table beside her bed. It read March 17, 2003. "Ibrahim…," she pressed in growing alarm, "what has happened?"

"Your President Bush has given Saddam Hussein and his sons forty-eight hours to leave Iraq," he said breathlessly. "If he refuses, your President declares war."

Zoe's heart thudded hollowly in her breast. She pictured Saddam Hussein's immediate reaction, guards on her room or worse. "Yes. We must go now!"

He thrust a nurse's uniform into her hands. "Put it on. It is somewhat large, but it will have to do."

During her convalescence, Ibrahim had seen and touched almost every inch of her body. Without modesty, she stripped, and quickly donned the uniform.

"First, I must distract the guard," he insisted. "When I spill my coins, leave your room and walk in the opposite direction. Wait for me at the far door."

Zoe felt very alone with her ear pressed to the door, listing to Ibrahim's footsteps in the hallway. She glanced at the boxes, presents Saddam Hussein had sent, all of which she would leave behind without a second thought.

Palming the doorknob, she turned it slowly, silently, until she felt the latch retract. When she heard coins spill onto the floor, Zoe eased the door open, closed it silently behind her, then turned away from the guard's post and forced herself to walk unhurried down the brightly lit corridor.

Any moment she expected a shout, an order to halt, but none came. When she reached the far door, Zoe felt weak, then realized she had been holding her breath. She shook her head silently and thought, "I should know better. Only an untrained novice would be so stupid!"

Heartbeats later Ibrahim joined her. "Through here," he urged, and thrust the door wide. In an empty room, he had her change clothes again, this time into the head to toe garb of a devout Iraqi woman. Ibrahim clipped a laminated hospital badge to the front for her shawl.

"Take the main elevator down to the ground floor," he told her. "Leave by the main doorway. If you attempt other entrances, you will be stopped, questioned and exposed. Use the main door, act as if you do this every day of the year, and you will not be stopped. When you are outside, turn right and go to the curb. My car will meet you."

His hands caught her arms, pulled her to him in a long kiss. "Now go," he ordered, "and do not look back."

* * * *

Until she settled into the plush rear seat of the sleek silver Saab sedan, Zoe believed something would go wrong. That she would be captured. Her heart continued to drum wildly until Ibrahim opened the rear passenger door, and he slid in beside her. As the door closed, Bayan, their driver, eased the Saab from the curb into traffic.

Zoe twisted in the seat, met his eyes. "Why did you go through with it?"

A muscle twitched in his jaw. "Many reasons," he admitted finally, then sighed. "I love you. I love you desperately, but escaping with you meant turning my back on my family, on centuries of al-Janabi tradition."

His eyes read her disbelief, and he continued on. "Oh, I made all the plans, but in my heart, I had no intention of carrying them out. Until this morning's ultimatum."

Ibrahim laced his fingers together, brought them to his lips. "My family has great wealth, but they are not well respected. In these peaceful times we are tolerated, but...," he shook his head, "when war comes, I fear the al-Janabis will all be suspect and purged."

His gaze held hers. "And having just found you, I did not want to die needlessly."

"I do not understand," she protested. "If we are caught, you will be tried and executed for helping me escape."

He smiled grimly. "Then I die in a good cause."

* * * *

Zoe caught quick glimpses of some of Baghdad's monumental public buildings as the car snaked through traffic out of central Baghdad. The city was large, metropolitan, and with considerable charm even after years of war and turmoil. The huge double-decker bridge spanning the Tigris River, one of twelve bridges spanning the river, left her awed. Ahead, the eighteen-story Baghdad University building hovered at the river's U-bend where it snaked its way through Baghdad.

"There, on the left bank is the Republican Presidential Palace," Ibrahim pointed, almost as if they were on holiday, "and there, the Baghdad Clock

Tower standing tall above the Museum of the Leader." His lips twisted in disdain. "It details the life of Saddam Hussein for the masses."

In the rundown southeastern suburb of Baghdad, they rendezvoused with a Mercedes. Bodies resembling Zoe and Ibrahim were taken from the Mercedes' trunk and positioned on the rear seat of the silver sedan. As the other driver straightened, Bayan seized the man from behind, pressed an automatic against the skin beneath the ear.

Ibrahim leaned his face near. "Did you believe I would not sense betrayal, Yusuf?"

Wide eyes met Ibrahim's. "You make--no sense!" His features framed the question before he spoke. "I--serve you honorably. Why must you act so?"

"If you have not betrayed me, then I do it for no other reason than you are Baath," Ibrahim said coldly. "I do it because many things I confided in you, designed to test your loyalty, have surfaced through Baath contacts. You were told nothing of today, and in moments you will tell nothing."

Zoe watch Yusuf tense, his expression frantic, but the automatic kept him still. "When I am found dead to a bullet," he announced, "it will give away your plot."

"I do not think so," Ibrahim said softly. The doctor's hand lifted, a needle stabbed deep into Yusuf's neck, and a quick thumb pressed the syringe dry. "Pancuronium bromide paralyzes the entire muscle system and stops a person's breathing. I understand you will be conscious until the last. May Allah, His name be praised, have mercy on you."

Yusuf's lips framed a reply, but no sound came. Then he slumped in Bayan's hands.

"Place him in the driver's seat," Ibrahim told Bayan. "The motor must be running and the car moving when we hit it with the rocket-propelled grenades."

* * * *

From the Mercedes Zoe watched a rocket-propelled grenade punch through the Saab's rear windshield, saw the car explode in a crescendo of light and sound. Then a second grenade hit, and the gas tank exploded.

Ibrahim said nothing as he and Bayan rejoined her. He rode in stoic silence, his lips in a hard line.

"You surprise me," she said, interrupting his solitude. "You are more than you seem.'

"And you are not?" Ibrahim countered. "Perhaps there are facets of Katherine Laforge that would shock me." He sighed heavily, leaned his head back against the plush leather. "Often we do what we must and call it survival."

His comment hit far too close to home, and she did not answer. Ibrahim seemed not to notice.

"Soon we will reach a checkpoint, and we must stop," he told her. "This car has been radically altered to make a hidden compartment. The deep trunk had been shortened by some eighteen-inches, and the springs from the rear seat removed and replaced by strong flat tension bars, providing an additional six-inches of room. You must hide in there."

Zoe met his eyes without flinching. They were hard, his emotions locked away. She nodded in agreement.

When Bayan pulled into an alley, Ibrahim shifted the rear seat forward and motioned Zoe into the confining cavity. She eased herself into the narrow space, and tried to relax against the compartment's padded bottom.

Ibrahim leaned over her, brushed his lips against hers. "You will not be in here long, I promise. Most of all, no matter what, you must be silent. If not, we are all dead. Can you do this?

The coffin-like sides seem to press against her, but she nodded and echoed his words, "We do what we must and call it survival."

"Use this if you must," He said, handing her a slim automatic. "Never doubt I love you," he said, then turned away and pushed the seat back into place. She endured the darkness, heard the latch snap into place with loud finality. In the cavity Zoe concentrated on her breathing and tried not to worry about what lay ahead.

Twice more she was forced into hiding. Each time, when the bored guards found nothing of interest within the Mercedes, they waved them through the checkpoint.

As they sped south toward Basra, Bayan drummed his nicotine-stained fingers against the steering wheel in time to an Arabic tune hummed off key. Ibrahim slept against her shoulder, his soft breathing light and regular.

"I should be tired," Zoe mused, "but I am not."

After months spent in the same hospital room, she studied everything along the road. Every humble village, town, or city between Baghdad and Basra displayed larger-than-life portraits of Saddam Hussein. The huge portraits chilled her. They were vivid reminders that nowhere in this land could she run or hide and be free of Saddam. Freedom for Zoe Shelly existed only beyond Iraq's borders.

* * * *

As they drove through the desert toward Basra, Zoe moved her head as little as possible. Even in the air-conditioned Mercedes, fine air-borne desert grit became sandpaper where her robes rubbed her neck. Ahead, the road seemed to ripple in the midday heat. Dust swirled about the blacktopped surface, coating everything with a gray film. It smelled like old ashes, born from Iraq's age-old turmoil, and the rise and fall of empires.

By midday the sky congealed into a pale canopy of blue-white haze. Their Mercedes raced through a stark and brooding wasteland, which stretched for endless miles, an immense nothingness, bleak, sterile, and foreboding. Outside, the capricious winds of desolation howled, buffeting the Mercedes, swirling sand into the heavens, washing all the color from the sky.

From time to time Ibrahim spoke on his cell phone. Zoe understood none of the exchanges. When he offered no explanations, she did not press. Come what may, she had committed her life into his hands.

Toward sunset they approached an old car broken down on the road-side. A robed man standing beside it held a baby in his arms and frantically waved for them to stop.

"Stop, Bayan," Ibrahim ordered. "The child may be ill."

Seeing them braking, the man passed the baby to someone inside the car, and smiling, walked around to Bayan's side. Crouching down, he peered into the car as Bayan lowered the window. Glanced at the passengers, the white turbaned man launched into guttural Arabic Zoe could not understand. Suddenly, he brandished a rifle from beneath his robes and his other hand snaked through the open window and seized the steering wheel. Waving his rifle in the air, he yelled at them in guttural Arabic.

"He says to exit the car," Ibrahim whispered, "but to do so is death. Go!" he yelled at Bayan, "Go, Go, Go!"

Two other men with rifles climbed out of the old car as Bayan jammed his foot hard on the accelerator. Tires squealed as the Mercedes surged forward, spraying a blinding cloud of sand into the air. Thrown sideways, dragged from his feet, the robber cursed and screamed as he struggled to maintain his grip on the steering wheel and bring his rifle to bear at the same time. The Mercedes fish-tailed back and forth on the tarmac as Bayan tried to maintain control of the car with one hand and break the man's grip on the wheel with the other.

Zoe watched in horror as the robber's rifle barrel swung toward Bayan's temple. Suddenly, the small automatic Ibrahim gave her was in her hand. She fired twice. The first bullet punched into the assailant's arm; the second opened a third eye in his turbaned forehead.

When the car accelerated, the other robbers froze, then raised their rifles, and aimed at the Mercedes. But they hesitated, fearful of hitting their comrade.

With horrifying abruptness, the arms disappeared from the driver's window. Ibrahim turned in time to see the body tumbling hard upon the road. The man's head struck the 120-degree pavement, his white robe quickly dappled with large crimson spots as the corpse continued to tumble. Shots rang out as the other assailants fired repeatedly at the fleeing car, but none of the bullets found their mark.

Zoe felt a rush of exhilaration and relief as they sped away. She turned back to find Ibrahim staring at her with widened eyes. Looking down quickly, she realized the automatic was still in her hand.

"Now it is you who surprise me," he said, admiration in his voice. "I had forgotten I gave you the pistol."

She accepted his praise. "Someone I care for told me 'we do what we must, and call it survival.'

He chuckled, and his humor softened the mood. Then he sobered. "You must understand these are perilous times for my country. There is no security on the roads away from the cities, and those who travel are fair game to small village bandits." He shrugged. "These thugs are usually all related, so no one cares what family members do to strangers."

Ibrahim shook his head to banish the horrible memory. "My role is to save lives," he said softly. "When I saw the child, I reacted as a doctor. It almost got us killed." His face hardened. "I shall not be so weak again."

* * * *

Night descended quickly in the desert. Dusk deepened, and ahead, a cluster of lights pierced the dusty gloom. Bayan eased off the accelerator, cursed softly in Arabic, and then warned, "We are coming to a military checkpoint."

Ibrahim roused a dozing Zoe, handed her the forged documents he had purchased for this occasion. The papers identified her as his wife, and thankfully, by Iraqi custom, the husband spoke for the wife. If she was forced to speak, her inability to speak Arabic would doom them. But as Bayan braked the Mercedes at the checkpoint, it was too late for doubts.

As his headlights illuminated the soldiers, Bayan frowned. Many times this year he had traveled these roads, shuttling people back and forth from Baghdad to Basra. He knew what to expect, but he always worried some renegade soldiers would kill him and steal his car. His Mercedes would bring high dollars over the border in Saudi Arabia.

But Bayan's fear proved needless as a smiling guard left the sandbag-fortified redoubt, shouted his name, and added a warm greeting. With a short sigh, Bayan relaxed. He knew these guards, even had friends among them.

Zoe did not understand the exchange, but she saw Bayan offer the grinning guard a package of cigarettes, which quickly disappeared. The guard spoke again, and Bayan popped open the latch to the Mercedes' trunk.

Behind the car, soldiers combed through the suitcases and boxes in the trunk, and then joined their comrade at the window. They whispered among themselves, then Bayan's friend spoke again. Bayan chuckled, opened the glove box and passed across two more cigarette packs. At the guard's signal, Bayan left the car, pushed the bonnet lid shut, then returned to his seat. When they drove away, true night had fallen, and the dark sky was frosted by bright stars.

Ibrahim visibly relaxed once they were through the checkpoint, even allowed himself a chuckle. He twisted in the seat, drew Zoe to him, kissed her longingly.

"The soldier told Bayan it was a bad time to go to Basra," he said softly. "He warned that the Americans were going to attack again."

"But they let us go on," she wondered aloud, "Why?"

"Bayan told the guard he had no choice. These trips were how he makes his money."

Later, as they entered Basra, night shrouded Iraq's second-largest city.

"I regret you cannot see the architecture of the 'City of Sinbad' as Basra is also known," Ibrahim said, "or the wooden front doors studded with iron. They are decorated with knockers of brass shaped into the small hands of Fatima, the daughter of the Prophet Mohammed, that are said to bring blessings to those in the house."

But Zoe was too weary to care. She wanted a bath and sleep. "Will we stop somewhere in the city?"

Ibrahim nodded. He, too, was tired. "I have cousins here. But they are gone. Fled to the country because they fear the Americans will bomb Basra." He reached out, cupped Zoe's cheek with his palm. "Do not worry. I spoke to them by cell phone. They have allowed me the use of their house." He smiled reassuringly. "We will be safe there."

* * * *

Houses with overhanging balconies and projecting windows with elaborate ornaments and cupolas in the old Arabian style hugged the narrow streets in the Ashar district near Basra's bazaar. Zoe was soon lost in the twists and turns Bayan made. Eventually, he braked the Mercedes at a double gate set in a high brick wall. Stopping, he left the car, inserted a massive key in an antiquated lock, and moments later swung the gates wide enough for the Mercedes to enter. Headlights illuminated a fine imposing house fronting the tight circular driveway, something that might have been drawn from the pages of A Thousand and One Nights.

Brick walls were overlaid with mosaic tile, carved wood panels and multi-faceted glass windows surrounded a shadowy courtyard. Bayan went ahead, opening doors and turning on lights. Set in iron sconces inset into the walls, the lights flickered, giving the impression of burning candles.

Ibrahim took Zoe's hand, led her across the polished marble entranceway through the main carved-wood doors into a large reception room adorned by more carved wooden panels of intricate design and moucharabiehs, beaded wooden screens. The floor was set with low tables of inlaid wood, each surrounded by cushions, the walls hung with tapestries of gold-embroidered silk. At the upper end was a divan of alabaster, wide enough for several persons to sit upon, canopied with red satin and surmounted by ancient heraldic arms.

Ibrahim paused, gestured at the device on the red satin. "The arms of the al-Janabi family," he said, pride evident in his voice. "We are an old family," his lips twisted wryly, "even if we are not currently in favor." Then he gestured around the room, the courtyard beyond. "What you see here has been so for more years than I can remember. My uncle is an ardent traditionalist."

In the adjoining rooms, cushions were also spread, and on the terrace floor as well.

It--it is so beautiful," Zoe whispered, unwilling for her voice to spoil the moment. "I never dreamed...."

"Come," he urged, "let me show you more."

Beyond the large audience hall and reception room, a winding staircase climbed to an upper floor of spacious apartments. Beyond the tall, thin inner windows, slender white marble pillars supported a colonnade overlooking an interior courtyard and garden, dormant in its beauty, waiting for the spring's flowering.

Photographs set in ornate frames graced the wall that ascended with the winding staircase, photos of gaunt, proud men in flowing robes greeting a younger Saddam Hussein, others pictured with the old King of Iraq, British officials and officers, and a Turkish provincial governor. There were robed men before desert tents, some with modern vehicles, others with blooded Arabian horses. Others, more faded, up the stair, portrayed Nineteenth Century scenes.

Bayan brought them food, which they ate on cushions in one of the rooms adjoining the main audience hall. Simple fare, Ibrahim mused, most uncharacteristic of the meals normally served in his uncle's home. Later, as they reclined on cushions in the courtyard, surrounded by night's shadows, Ibrahim kissed her tenderly.

As his embrace grew more passionate, Zoe responded, giving herself to him with a willingness, an ardor, which surprised her. In her mind, she resisted the weakening voice of that Katherine part of her that protested her actions. She shunned it and gave herself to Ibrahim. They had what few hours remained of the night, before they must meet Wilson Lawson's boat before dawn, and she wanted that time with Ibrahim to give her a lifetime of new dreams.

* * * *

Shadowed figures like fleeting apparitions darted across the harbor dock. Crouched low the figures scanned the horizon tracking a faint object bobbing about on the whitewater of the incoming waves. As it grew larger they knew it was the dinghy from Wilson Lawson's yacht coming for them.

Zoe paused on the dock, pressing herself against a large crate. Close by, Ibrahim stood obscured by the shadows. A chapter in her life was drawing to a close, and another was beginning. Bayan had left them, intent on staying in Iraq. He and Ibrahim had parted emotionally and the doctor gave him the Mercedes as a parting gift for years of friendship and faithful service. Ibrahim had sent Zoe's message to Lawson as she requested, and she knew the friend from her youth would not fail her. More, she felt sure he would be piloting the dingy sent to retrieve them. Reassured, she stepped into the full moonlight.

Like a cowboy on a frisky horse, Lawson swayed with the motion of the dinghy in the roller-coaster swells. Salt spray from the waves' fury glistened on his cheeks, but he kept the bow pointed at the moonlight-silhouetted figures at the dock's edge.

It was a risky run. With the threat of war imminent, Iraqi forces had increased surveillance along the dock area. But it was a risk worth taking. The endless roar of the breakers dampened the high-pitched whine of the dinghy's outboard motor. Forward in the dinghy was Addas, a Basra native who fled before the 1991 war when Saddam Hussein massacred so many of the Basra Shiites. He had once worked in the harbor, and knew the docks intimately.

At the bow Addas adjusted to the dinghy's bounce and sway and scanned the dock area with binoculars. Above the harbor, a capricious moon peaked shyly though the low clouds, illuminating the waves and white breakers and the waiting fugitives. Quickly, he scanned both flanks, looking for guards. And found none.

From her vantage point on the dock, Zoe stood a good ten feet above the incoming tide, scanning the darkness for the dinghy. Poor light made it difficult to see the incoming dinghy riding the breakwater swells. Then the clouds parted and rays of moonlight illuminated Lawson's small craft on the billowing waves.

As it neared the deepwater dock, the dinghy plowed through the last of the whitewater crests, showering the crew with face-numbing salt spray. One moment large swells lifted the boat, exposing it to the constant wind, and then plummeted it back into a trough with bone-jarring force. Lawson was glad his craft was a rubber inflatable. No wooden boat could have survived the rough seas.

As the stern lifted and the propeller cleared the surface, the outboard motor whined angrily. But the drone resumed as the stern settled back in the water. With each new swell, the dinghy's four-man crew moved to counter-balance the surges and keep the craft afloat. Addas cursed in guttural Arabic as sea spray soaked him, but he held his post and continued to call out course corrections.

When they gained the dock's deep shadows, the swells eased and the dinghy made for the vertical ladder leading down to the water. As quickly as she could, Zoe descended the rusted rungs, and eager hands guided her aboard the dinghy. Ibrahim followed quickly behind her.

When they were both on board, Lawson called out, "Everyone safe?"

"Yes, go!" Zoe almost screamed, "Just go!"

Fighting the incoming tide, Lawson nosed the dinghy about. When it cleared the pilings, he gunned the outboard for the open sea and his twin-masted yacht. Amidships, Ibrahim hugged Zoe, as much for warmth as reassurance. His teeth chattered, and he trembled from the cold salt spray and the chilling wind.

On the dock, lights flashed and a bullhorn voice in Arabic ordered them to stop, to turn around, and return to the dock. Addas translated, but Lawson had no intention of obeying. At full throttle, the dinghy forced its way through the incoming waves. Zoe felt a spine-tingling elation as she embraced Ibrahim, felt his arms tighten about her in response.

Shots rang out. Bullets ripped the waves' surface near the dinghy as the soldiers search for their target. The staccato bark of heavier caliber guns drowned out smaller rifle fire, and tracers hit the waves. But they were long shots, and the dinghy proved a quickly diminishing target.

Ibrahim drew her close, kissed her, and her tears of happiness mingled with the salt spray. A lone bullet suddenly punched through an air chamber in the dinghy, and Ibrahim stiffened. Hissing air added to the cacophony of the outboard motor and gunshots, but though the craft listed, it remained afloat and droned its way seaward for the safety of the outer darkness.

Drawing her close, Ibrahim pressed salty lips to her ear. "Remember always, I love you. Now and forever."

Zoe sensed something was terribly wrong. When he slumped in her arms, she screamed his name. She shook him again and again, but he made no answer. His head fell back, and moonlight illuminated his face and the dark blood spilling from his mouth.

"No, it can't be," she cried. "Not now! I just found you."

Wild fear surged through Zoe. Vainly she sought some spark of life. But there was none. No pulse. No breath. When her brain finally registered that Ibrahim was dead, she screamed, a mindless cry of agony that rent the darkness. Tears came in a rush, her face warped by an anguish she could not contain.

Hands gripped her shoulders, but she wrenched away. Zoe clung to the lifeless body as if she could will life back into Ibrahim. He had been her anchor these past months. There for her when she needed him. Now he was gone.

Another hand gripped her shoulder. This one, more insistent, shook her, penetrated her grief. She turned to find Lawson's face near her own.

Over the roar of the outboard, he made her understand. "They will come after us in powered launches. We need all the speed we can make, and we are losing air."

Lawson shook her again. "Do you understand? We must let him go." Then, in a stronger, harsher voice, he demanded, "For us to survive, you must let him go. Now!"

Crewmen pried Zoe's hands from Ibrahim, rolled his body onto the dinghy side. Ignoring the blood, she covered his unresponsive lips with one last kiss, and then forced herself to let him go and sit back. Just let it happen. Addas gave Ibrahim a gentle shove, the body sliding over the side to be swallowed by the waves and the darkness. Gone without a trace.

New tears came, and Zoe sobbed uncontrollably. Oblivious to the final race for the yacht, she was mired in a nightmare, a hopeless maze of torment with no possible escape. Incapable of changing her future, she railed at the futility of her existence. At her pain. At life itself. At its cruelty.

But in the depths of her grief, Ibrahim spoke to her. His words echoed clearly through her mind as if she heard them with her ears. She clung to them, knowing they held the key to her future.

"We do what we must and call it survival."

Zoe clutched them to her like a talisman. Then, beyond caring, she found she had no strength left, no will to fight. With a sigh of exhaustion, she lost consciousness and collapsed to the floor of the dinghy.

* * * *

I shivered perhaps from my confusion of what Vince had narrated, or simply from watching the snow falling and blanketing the windowsills with tuffs of white. The town hall had actually gotten colder this afternoon. It was old and drafty and the semi-repaired broken window did not help. Blasts of cold air chilled the room as the big doors opened and closed letting people in and out of the auditorium.

I worried about Katherine. If she was not found by now, she might very well be frozen. With the carnage that I had seen on TV, I doubted that she would have dressed for this type of weather before escaping. If she escaped, that is.

Over the town hall's intercom, a message was announced that power lines had fallen in North Charlestown and electricity would be off for up to 4 hours while repair crews replaced the down lines.

The TV was still flickering the same footage of the campaign bus and the aftermath of the attack. While a reporter was enumerating some of the former attacks on Katherine, an older lady sitting near my table suddenly began to whisper audibly, "Oh, my god above, oh, my God; my God what evil did she do to bring down your wrath?" The woman wore a sweater that read, 'Redeemed by His Blood'. In her gnarled hands, she tightly clutched a bible. A man sat beside her, probably her husband who had bowed his head and folded his hands in prayer. He had tufted eyebrows, and thinning white hair.

As she watched the news she became more agitated and said loudly, "God has taken her for her wicked ways. Thank you Jesus."

"Amen," the man next to her said.

My eyes met hers and it seemed the auditorium had gone totally silent accept the battering of the wind against the building and her piercing voice. "She is an abomination, "she hissed. "She defiles the scripture and has brought death upon the people around her."

The air now seemed bitterly cold and all the people sitting around me were transfixed by her hissing voice as she continued to denounce Katherine as a heathen and a doomed woman. The man with her smiled and shook his head in agreement.

She appeared to sneer at us and said, "It is a bad time for her to be out in this winter snow. Maybe she has fallen through thin ice on the Connecti-cut River?" The woman stroked her bible and rolled her eyes as if possessed.

Her tone was gloating and her words incensed me as she reveled over Katherine's misfortune.

Her eyes fixed on us and her tongue flickered over her thin lips before she continued, "The scripture tells us that woman's ordained role is to be submissive to man and Laforge has rebelled against God by running for President." She paused and sort of snickered, "Her husband is dead because he did not lead his family, and he let his wife challenge her place in God's divine order. God's design for women is not to be changed by man's whim. She is to be submissive to man. It is written in 1 Corinthians 11:3"

A young man shouted over to her, "Shut the hell up, you fucking loony."

My fists were tightly clenched on my table as her caustic remarks continued.

"God flooded my soul with the message that Laforge is something evil, a heretic that has lost her way. I have felt the spirit flowing through me. God has spoken to me in dreams and told me to bring you these messages." Her companion smiled and looked at her adoringly.

As she rambled on, icy anger swept through me. Her rantings were now muffled by the protest of others who cursed her and told her to shut up.

Security personnel moved closer to her, she held the Bible up over her head with one hand and said, "The Holy Ghost will demand that you turn away from this abomination of a woman." She paused for a second, looking up at a window and then said, "Do you see Jesus' image there in the swirling snow on the window pane?"

My heartbeat was thin now, with rapid palpitation as I tried to block her irritating voice from my consciousness. Suddenly, two security officers stood in front of her. Color drained from her face and her eyes widened. Her hands tremble slightly as she reached for her glass of water. She looked up at the looming security officers and flung the glass at them. People shrieked in happiness as two burly security officers finally escorted her and her companion out of the auditorium.

My wife looked disapprovingly at me as I quietly uttered a "holy shit, amen" as the woman's voice faded into the distance.

PART EIGHT

Escape to the States

The town hall had grown considerably quieter since the incident with the strange woman wishing the wrath of God on Katherine. Beside her preaching and venomous diatribes, she had been an odd looking character. One peculiarity was her practice of closing her eyes for a period of time and then suddenly popping them open as if she was trying to catch a glimpse of her heavenly friends.

With the return of quiet, my mind struggled again over Katherine's disappearance, and I felt myself becoming increasingly agitated. My wife was reading the Boston Globe, and Tom and Vince had gone to the concession stand, while I sat staring into my empty coffee cup. Next to us a woman was cleaning the soiled table where the crazy old lady had been sitting. Just as the attendant was removing the dirty tablecloth, I stood up to stretch my cramped legs. There on the far side of the table something caught my attention. As I squinted down at its aged surface, I could clearly make out a heart with my initials and K.L. carved into it. For a moment, I was transfixed by this discovery and was gripped by some mad compulsion to stop the attendant from covering it, but I quickly regained my composure. Apparently, my demeanor did not go totally unnoticed because she looked at me with a perplexed expression as she continued to spread the tablecloth. I knew this table. It was the same one that decades ago, Katherine, and I had sat at one special night. With my mind flooding with memories. I sat back down. My fingers caressed the top of my cup while I relived that night.

It had been the annual 'Winter Wonderland' dance. A chance for every girl to wear a formal and look her best and Katherine was stunning. It was our senior year, and I was her default date to the dismay of many of the other seniors. She had temporarily broken up with her college boyfriend, and I guess she felt I was a safe date to be with on that occasion. It was during a period of time when I was very much infatuated with her.

That night I was the envy of most of the guys. She was beautiful and I was so proud to be holding her close and dancing with her. I never liked dancing that much, but that night was different. As we danced, Katherine would press against me while we moved wordlessly across the floor, swept away into our own separate worlds. Sometimes my cheek would touch her cool face and her fingertips would brush softly against my neck and shoulders producing a disquieting sensation that made my heart thump harder against my ribs. As we danced, her dress would flare out and glitter from the sparkling lights illuminating the dance floor. She was beautiful, and that night any one could have seen the wistfulness in my eyes for her.

When I was with Katherine, I felt we almost melted together. Her perfume, softness and beauty enchanted me, and I felt something that I had never felt before with any girl. I reigned in my urge to tell her my feelings, because I knew she thought we were just friends and that was why she went with me.

All I could think about every time her red lips spoke was how much I wanted to kiss them. Hanging from the entrance to the hall was mistletoe, and I kept trying to devise a way to get us under it, so I could kiss her.

I wanted to really kiss her, but as the night waned away so did my chances, and finally it was time to go. We gathered our coats and started to walk out with another couple, and just as they stepped under the mistletoe they kissed. I pounced on the situation and grabbed Katherine tightly and pressed my lips to hers. I kissed her with all the passion, I dared to display. She held me tightly at that moment and kissed me back, but then pulled away smiling coyly. She reached up and touched my nose and said, "This was fun being with you tonight. I need to help you find a girlfriend that deserves a great guy like you." Her eyebrows were knitted in curiosity as she peered up at me, and I don't remember what I replied, but I realized that she did not feel the same way I did.

Never had I hated walking Katherine home so much as I did that night. As we walked home, the sky felt huge and heavy overhead, an alien and endless canopy of sadness. Her fingers wove together with mine, and I felt her warmth, but I knew this was just friends holding hands. I tried to make small talk about the dance and who was there, but beneath it all was that crushing feeling of rejection. And I knew she didn't even realize how deep my feelings were toward her.

When we arrived at Katherine's doorstep, she thrust her face toward mine, and I found myself awkwardly kissing her once more. She held herself against me for a moment or two while her cool lips pressed against mine. Then our lips parted and she smiled sweetly up at me and whispered, "Good Night." I stood there watching her enter her house feeling the cold winter air against my moist eyes. The smell of her perfume lingered in the air around me and my lips still tasted of her lipstick. As I walked away from her house, I shivered and silently cried for the loss I had just endured.

From that night on I had never kissed her again until last night when we visited her on her campaign bus. It was a platonic kiss, but it was on my lips, and it did stir old memories. I realized that much of what I've been doing for her during this campaign was because I still had very deep feelings for her that I could not share with anyone. I loved my wife dearly, but some part of me still had these foolish feelings towards Katherine. Last night as I talked to Ira and watched my wife help Katherine touch up her hair, terrible guilt tore at my consciousness. Ira picked up a carafe of wine and poured me another glass and asked, "Can you believe your old high school friend is now running for President?" His question made me wince like I had gotten a small paper cut. I hadn't a clue of how to reply, but I did. "We all thought she was special, and I guess we were correct."

Ira spoke with a gentle curiosity that made me feel even more uncomfortable sitting with him and his wife, the probable next President of the United States.

Just as I was reminiscing that night, Vince plopped a fresh cup of coffee down in front of me along with an apple fritter and asked, "You ready to hear a bit more about her escape from Iraq?"

I looked up at him thinking that was a dumb question, but politely said, "Of course, Vince! Let's hear it."

My wife looked up from her paper and waited for him to begin.

Vince sat silent for a while and gulped down some of his coffee.

Once Ibrahim was dead she quickly returned to her self-preservation mode. They had to carry her onto the Black Phantom and into a cabin because she had lost consciousness after he was killed. Wilson was concerned that something worst was wrong with her, and that he could be in a very serious situation. But about 24 hours later with the water washing against the yacht's hull with a sibilant siren's song, she finally awoke. Oddly enough, she did not cry or act confused, but simply opened her eyes and quietly looked about the cabin. Finally, she sighed and slowly stretched her arms and legs like a cat, wincing as her left arm and hip responded with stiffness and dull pain.

That will pass, she told herself. Soon you'll be your old self. Then she grimaced, coming fully awake. "That can't happen", she declared silently, "You never were your old self. You never were Katherine Laforge."

Ignoring the pain in her hip, she pushed back the bed coverings, and slid across the silk sheets. The luxurious sensation against her bare body brought a sharp intake of breath. Kat's memories of other beds spiraled through her mind, but she purposefully held them at bay. She wanted this moment to be hers and hers alone. This moment and many others. A lifetime of them.

I am alive, she told herself as she rose from the bed. Her hand reached for the terrycloth robe draped across the foot of the bed and froze. Kat Laforge looked back at her from the full-length closet door mirror. To reassure herself, she was different, she touched the fuller cheeks, the stronger chin, which were legacies of her time in Iraq. Like the faint scars on her hip.

"I'm not Katherine Laforge," she said aloud, "no matter what my memories tell me. I am Zoe Shelly," she said, emphasizing each word, each syllable. "I am Zoe. I will be Zoe ... today, tomorrow and the day past that."

Brazenly she stood before the mirror. More gray than brown showed in the hair Katherine Laforge took such great pains to color. Her eyes traveled downward, assessing everything, missing nothing. Breasts, waist, thighs --

I've lost weight and muscle-tone, she thought with chagrin, but nothing that can't be regained.

Her thoughts drifted to her rescuer. She pictured Wilson Lawson from Kat's memories, an Inter-City black kid in her private school on special scholarship; Wilson Lawson who became a fashionable rebel when he discovered his true talent and future lay in computer science.

Time had been as kind to Wilson as it had to her. He was nearing sixty, but he had the physique of a man fifteen years younger.

Zoe knew she looked frail now, but that gaunt look would pass. How many women my age can wear a size eight dress and have it look like it really fits? She thought with some pride, even if it was borrowed from Kat's values.

Her thoughts turned again to Wilson. "He was in love with me once"-- She broke and corrected her thought, rather she said. "He was in love with Kat once."

Zoe regretted using him and realized these were also borrowed sentiments from Kat's lingering affection for Wilson, affection that time had not erased. She shook her head, took a deep breath, let it out in a prolonged sigh.

Will I ever be free of Kat and wholly Zoe? She questioned. Then another stray thought surfaced that left her even more perplexed. Do I really want to be?

* * * *

By late morning the sun crested the low clouds massed along the eastern horizon, and bathed the Gulf of Oman in golden light. From her perch near the yacht's bowsprit, Zoe closed her eyes, tilted her head back, let sea spray carried by the wind caress her face. The sensation was even more exhilarating than Kat's memories suggested. She licked her lips, reveled in the brine-sour taste on her tongue. The wind in her hair only heightened her thrill of freedom.

They ran southeast under full sail, taking advantage of the prevailing winds. The fifty-six-foot yacht was a greyhound under full sail. While she slept off the worst of her ordeal, the Black Phantom ran the gauntlet of American warships paused for war, streaked past the dangerous shallows along Saudi Arabia's western shores and rounded the Strait of Hormuz into the Gulf of Oman. Soon they would sweep past Oman's eastern tip, then catch the westerly winds and current for the run across the Arabian Sea. After that, the long run around Africa, and finally the trek up the Atlantic to the Gulf of Mexico.

Zoe's mind formed vivid images, drawn from maps and real places and all shaped from Laforge's memories. More and more she felt like a thief. "I shouldn't be here," she told the sea. "I am a mistake, a miscalculation—"

In her mind's eye, she saw the glass panel in the Lumberton lab that separated her--separated Kat from ComDefC1. In that snippet of memory, she watched it die again. Zoe understood its fears; she shared them.

"Laforge watched me die that day, or something so much like me that it really makes no difference."

She had been a tool, a weapon to be deployed. No more than that. I did what they wanted. That knowledge was plainly etched in Kat's mind. When it was my turn, with just hours to live, I wanted them to count for something.

Zoe reminded herself that she hadn't died. And because of what she was, and what she knew, there were men out there who would seek her out and try to kill her. They would keep trying until they succeeded.

"But this time I won't go meekly, like a lamb to slaughter," she promised. She ignored the favorite Albert Einstein quote in Kat's memories that challenged her resistance: Only a life lived for others is a life worthwhile.

Zoe gripped the bowsprit rail defiantly until her hands trembled from the strain. "In whatever time I have left, I want my own life, my own future," she cried. She blinked back unbidden tears. "Is--that--so--wrong?"

Gentle hands slipped around her shoulders, embraced her from behind, and a voice whispered in her ear. "I hope I can help you wash away all your pain."

She did not remember turning, but suddenly she was in Wilson's arms, chin tilted to accept his lips. Ira's image flashed through her mind, along with Kat's indignation at her weakness and her infidelity. But Zoe was only months old and lonely, lonely beyond words. She was not Kat, would never be Kat, and the sensations, the passion Wilson stirred in her at that moment drowned out all Laforge's denials.

* * * *

Anxiety plagued Zoe's slumber. In her dreams she struggled to reach the beach. Dreams became nightmares, and she ran for her life. Then she was staggering through sand and surf to where Lawson's inflatable boat waited. Those vivid images were forever etched in her memory. Zoe remembered her relief the moment she saw the dingy. Thank God Lawson had listened. Thank God he had come.

She was exhausted and out of breath when the crewmen plucked her from the waves. Zoe barely recalled the dash across the water from Al Qushlah to Lawson's yacht.

Soaked to the skin, shivering from reaction, suffering from the shock of the doctor's death, struggling with the guilt of killing with her own hands, she offered no protest when Wilson lifted her in his arms, carried her below. She had lost the will to fight. A dim memory lingered of Lawson undressing her, toweling her dry, then easing her into bed. Alone. Lawson was like that, a gentleman.

As Zoe spiraled from sleep to semi-wakefulness, her nightmares faded. A languid blissfulness replaced her anxiety, fruits of the passion she and Wilson shared. Sighing, she hugged her pillow and her eyes fluttered open.

Wilson smiled down at her as he pulled his crew-necked shirt across his broad shoulders, and let it hang outside his walking shorts. "Ah, the Lady wakes."

"Ummm--mmmm," Zoe answered dreamily, lifted her face from the pillow, and offered him a wide smile.

"From that expression I'd say the lady has no regrets."

Zoe let go of her pillow, turned over. None of us do, she mused, even Kat--in spite of all her objections. In the midst of stretching lazily, she found her voice. "You have no idea," she murmured, "no idea at all."

He sat down on the bed beside her, leaned down to brush her lips with his. His dark skin glistened in the soft lights. Her arms lifted, encircled his neck, extended the kiss, and slowly drew him to her. Zoe clung to him, pulled his strength against her. New passion stirred. She gave herself to it. And this time Kat's voice was silent.

Afterward they lay quiet in each other's arms, her cheek nestled on his chest. Wilson gently combed her hair with his fingertips. "I fell in love with you almost from the first time we met," he said quietly. "I didn't have to tell you. You knew. Did you ever wonder why?"

Zoe lifted her head, turned so that she could rest her other cheek against him. She wanted to watch his eyes. "Yes," she answered honestly. "I did wonder."

"My race meant nothing to you. You accepted me for my talents and my abilities without putting on airs." He grinned. "If anything, you were always up front and honest. Especially, about our relationship. No one else was."

She stared at him across a gulf she could never bridge. *And now everything I am, everything I appear to be--is all a lie. As much as I want you to understand, I can't share with you, the man I've just made love to, that I'm not the woman you want me to be.* Her heart caught. *Or how desperately I need you right now just to stay alive.*

Something in her expression alerted him. "You're in real trouble, aren't you?"

Genuinely concerned for him, she pushed up so she faced him. "I may have put you in terrible danger, Wil-O," she confessed, using the childhood name he and Kat shared without thinking. It was there in Laforge's memories. They shared a first kiss beneath a willow tree. "The CIA wants me dead, if they catch us together, they'll kill you, too."

For long moments he said nothing. Zoe wondered if he had been listening or just didn't believe her. Finally, he signed. "I wondered what would send Katherine Laforge running across Iraq scared of her shadow. Now I know."

She reached up, pressed his lips tenderly with her fingertips, quieting any protest he would make. "Katherine Laforge is not here," she stressed matter-of-factly. "Zoe Shelly is. You must think of me this way. You must! Even in private. If you slip at the wrong time and call me Katherine Laforge or even 'Kat,' it could betray us."

Briefly, she outlined what she must do, what she needed him to do. He listened without interruption, and then nodded. "I'll get you to Texas," he promised. "It's not as difficult as you believe. The Black Phantom can stay at sea for weeks at a time, under sail." He grinned. "And your CIA can't know where I'll put in for supplies--or when."

Wilson pulled her to him, kissed her, and she gave herself to his kiss. When he pulled back, he shook his head, regret plain in his eyes. "I have to go topside awhile. Even a captain has his duties."

* * * *

That night he held her in the darkness. "What about Ira?" he asked softly. "What happens after Texas?"

Zoe's heart froze. "You're asking things I can't answer. They will be monitoring Ira, bugging his phones, hoping I'll try to make contact." She sighed, answered him with as much truth as she could. "That goes for the Washington staff as well. I don't know whom I can trust."

He digested that, and was silent for some time. "I guessed that. I suppose at some point they'll get around to me."

"I hope not," and she meant it. "I hope that, they will never find out about you at all."

But Zoe knew that was very unlikely. If she remembered Wilson, so would Kat, eventually. Which meant, she must get to Texas and disappear before they tracked the Black Phantom into the Gulf of Mexico.

"I'd be naïve to think you have no other contacts, people to help you," he said with forced calm, "people you don't want me to know about so I can't compromise you. I won't break the law to help you, but I will bend it."

His voice hardened. "Just be careful who you trust. Especially, in the Bureaus and on the Hill. I worked for them, but I never trusted them. Not then, and especially not now."

When she said nothing, Wilson continued. "Use my communications equipment for whatever contacts you must make. I actually use it very little." He moved against her, and she realized it was a shrug. "Mostly in my business contacts, weather updates, and…," he exhaled sharply, "sports, of course. Got to follow my teams."

He pulled her against him, nuzzled her ear. "While you slept, I arranged secure com links piggy-backing the Defense Department satellite net. If they tap and attempt to trace your location," he chuckled softly, "let's just say, you won't be traced."

* * * *

Beneath a night sky dome ablaze with stars, the Black Phantom rendezvoused at sea in the Mozambique Channel with a darkened cabin cruiser out of Nosey Be, just off the northwest tip of Madagascar. Offloading provisions and water quickly, the Black Phantom's five-man crew made fast work of the storage, and the fleet twin-mastered yacht resumed its southeast heading.

From the darkened wheelhouse, Wilson pointed toward Nosey Be. "That small island boasts some of the most marvelous beaches in the world and twelve months of sunshine," he told Zoe. She could not see his face, but his tone held a half-serious note. "Perhaps one day I'll show you…"

In the darkness she snuggled against him. "Where now?"

"Around the Horn of Africa," he whispered, "and straight on 'til morning."

* * * *

She was choking. Blood filled her mouth, dribbled from her lips, stifled any scream she might have made. Pain racked her body, and she couldn't escape.

With a plea for help only her anguished eyes could express, she caught the attention of someone outside her glass prison. Across that bridge of awareness, she was at once both victim and observer, tortured and torturer.

For the love of God, help me! She cried soundlessly over and over until the words became… End this pain. If you won't save me, kill me quickly! Don't make me suffer so!

But there was no help. No mercy. Throughout the ordeal the woman watched. And Senator Laforge was that woman.

In the close darkness Zoe bolted awake, her hand at her throat. Choking. In that moment she waited for death, waited for the pain that accompanied it.

But there was no pain. And the only blood she tasted seeped from a bit lip. She shuddered. It had been so real!

Was real, she corrected herself. Again her mind replayed Katherine's memories of the death of ComDefC1 in the Lumberton lab. Or maybe it was the death of another numbered clone. There had been so many of them in the experiments that she couldn't really distinguish one from another. She just could not remember. She closed her eyes again and wondered if the daydreams she had been experiencing of moving about the old house in Houston were something more. Perhaps her mind was channeling through Katherine's. The visions were usually a collage of mundane scenes played in a staccato like fashion in her mind. She recognized the interior of the house, but strangely many things within it changed from daydream to daydream. She thought in some of these flashing scenes she had actually glimpsed newspapers that had headlined her death in Iraq. One appeared on a coffee table, and then it rose and was crumbled into a ball of paper. This was some sort of telepathic manifestation.

Zoe realized that she was very unique; she was not only a clone, but Katherine's twin. Their mental frequencies were probably the same, since they were in many ways parts of the same entity. It seemed obvious that she could wittingly or unwittingly receive images or messages that came from processes in Katherine's brain.

The mind's functions and abilities are virgin territory to scientists. A thought is a form of energy, but how that energy originates or how it is dispersed is unknown. Zoe knew that some scientists theorize thoughts enter into a global consciousness, an infinite network that is omnipotent in nature linking all humanity to God's purview. But others argue that we can actually focus thoughts like a laser beam at a particular receptive individual.

Regardless of how it works, Zoe felt she was developing the ability to receive thoughts from Katherine. Some sort of thought transference was elevated between them. Maybe because she was a special twin, her mind had developed perceptive abilities greater than a normal human. Or perhaps, since she was still an infant to the world, she had not blocked out the sixth sense that some feel lies dormant within us.

One other explanation for her assumed telepathic ability might be related to quantum entanglement, where distant objects respond immediately to changes to a related object light years away. She was cloned using quantum methods so this phenomenon might also be an answer to why she seems to now have this unique ability.

Regardless she would be patient and persistent in taking control of this new power. She promised herself to work harder at remembering the scenes in these odd daydreams. Tuning into these messages might at first be elusive, but she was sure she could learn to do it with practice.

Zoe wondered if Katherine experienced some strange sense of possession when her thoughts and visions were being hijacked. She was sure she now had more of a connection to Katherine than her creators had planned.

Suddenly cold, Zoe found her skin damp, wet with perspiration. Easing from bed, Zoe slipped into her bathrobe. Barefooted and in the dark, careful not to wake Wilson, she went up on deck.

A fresh sea breeze greeted her, toyed with her hair. Moonlight cast a silver patina across the Black Phantom's deck, and silvered the ocean whitecaps surrounding the yacht. It was serene, peaceful, but the aftermath of the nightmare left Zoe no peace. The might-have-been physicist in Katherine Laforge did not dwell on the moral implications involved in cloning, but Zoe could hardly avoid them.

Do I possess a soul? She agonized. Zoe carefully searched Kat's knowledge.

Was there a dividing line between reality and spirituality? Where is it? Her eyes widened, her thoughts raced. What if there was more stored in the brain's limbic system than just memories?

Zoe struggled to remember more. What if Limbic system also was the seat of spiritual consciousness? Would the host and its clone share a soul?

She remembered that she was created as a weapon, programmed through the training of her host, Katherine Laforge, and then became part of her fabric. She had been trained to serve a greater cause. A clone's life was finite, dedicated to the mission. A clone was not meant to outlive their mission.

"But I have survived," she said matter-of-factly. "And for good or ill, I am real." A higher power must have intervened, and that provided Zoe's existence a purpose and meaning. These thoughts gave her more hope and soothed her. If she outlived the purpose for her creation, then she was not a tool to be used and discarded. She was now God's creation.

In the moonlight, silver streaks rose from the waves in graceful arcs, hundreds of them. Her mind told her it was only fish jumping, following their natural rhythms. But a deeper part of her accepted it as a sign she had been heard.

* * * *

Zoe sat in the main cabin and pictured in her mind her alter ego. Where was Katherine Laforge? You went to ground somewhere while I was a news item, but you weren't so isolated that you are inaccessible.

She closed her eyes and try to connect again to Katherine's mind, but there was nothing but her own thoughts. The noise of her own mind was blocking any communication from Katherine's mind. She finally gave up and drank a large glass of wine and watched the waves roll about. The waves were hypnotic and suddenly she felt the visions of Katherine returning. She tried to breath normally and stay calm, so her mind would act only as a receiver to these scenes. It worked. They flowed in, scene after scene after scene. She had connected.

Katherine was in a Humvee, somewhere in some desolate place, perhaps a desert. As Zoe tried to decipher the images, she would disconnect from Katherine. But she became better at retaining the images in her mind, and she knew from the little she observed that Katherine was alive and probably hiding in the desert.

She suddenly wanted to phone Katherine, but she knew her location would be traced immediately. Something deep inside her made her want to reconnect to the whole world and feel its pulse, but that was impossible for now. In that and so many other ways she and Kat shared common traits.

* * * *

Rounding the Horn of Africa, Wilson pointed the Black Phantom north-north-west and hugged the South African coast. From Namibia's Conception Bay, he swung west-north-west across the South Atlantic on a new heading for the Brazilian coast. With good seas and favorable winds, they made the ocean crossing without incident.

Late one afternoon 200 miles off Brazil's eastern tip, the wind turned and dark angry clouds boiled out of the south, swept quickly overhead to obscure the sun. Wilson sent Zoe below for their foul weather gear and safety harnesses while he and the crew battened down the Black Phantom for the approaching storm. They barely got the sails reefed, and into their gear when the first squall hit. Huge isolated drops became sheets of rain that hammered the polished deck and crew in violent bursts.

Lightning flickered and thunder rolled, a strobe-like staccato display that highlighted the Black Phantom's bow lifting and plunging through the raging sea. A rope tore loose from a deck cleat, whipped back and forth in the frenzied wind. Disregarding Wilson's orders to stay in the lea of the wheel-house, she hooked her safety line and inched along the rail toward the flapping rope.

A huge wave caromed across the deck, just as she reached the rope. Lifted her effortlessly from her feet. Slammed her against the railing. Frantic, she clawed at the wood and steel with both hands. Zoe managed to wrap her bad arm around it and held on with all her strength as the brute force of the cascading water threatened to carry her up and over the barrier.

Poised on the brink of forever, time seemed to stop. Numbly, she stared at the frothing waves suspended above the deck, poised with an infinite patience that she could not match. Had it all come down to this? Her ordeal in Iraq. Her flight to Al Qushlah and the Black Phantom. The idyllic moments spent with Wilson. All rendered meaningless by a galvanic force of nature?

Time's bubble burst. The wave surge tore at her grip, threatened to hurl her into the churning sea. Then the safety line jerked taut. Like a hooked fish, she hung suspended between life and death. Engulfed in the wave, Zoe struggled to breathe. The safety harness straps dug cruelly into her shoulders and midriff, but it stopped her from headlong plunge overboard.

A hand seized her trailing hood, hauled her back aboard. Pulling Zoe to her feet, Wilson crushed her against him, cried in her ear against the fury of the storm, "I thought I'd lost you again."

Her tears mingled with the rain and the sea spray, and she had no voice to answer him. He led her to the hatch cover, saw her down, and sealed it behind her against the storm surge. When the storm abated and he came to her in the night, their lovemaking was frantic, desperate. Even in sleep, Zoe clung to him, to the safety he offered.

* * * *

Zoe woke with a clear mind. The long, lazy days at sea had rejuvenated her. Exercise had relieved the stiffness in her arm and done wonders to lessen the pain in her hip. The voyage had been a time of healing for both her body and her mind. And her soul--for Wilson had uncovered passion and desires Kat's memories only hinted at. Zoe now had experiences that Katherine Laforge did not possess, could never possess, new memories all her own.

With little effort she might spend the rest of her life with Wilson. But she suffered no illusions. The CIA would search until they found her or until they were satisfied Katherine Laforge's missing clone was safely dead.

But I am no longer just a clone, she affirmed. Zoe closed her eyes, pressed her fingertips to her temples, delved deep into her own mind where lies were transparent and truths were often harsh. Kat was there, and Zoe, and Kat's own memories of other clones. Multiple personalities? She chuckled. A shrink would go bananas in my mind.

Zoe managed a cleansing breath, ordered her thoughts. For good or ill, I have become a real person, she affirmed, complete with Katherine Laforge's energy, drive, and dreams.

Her emotions pulled her in different directions, but Zoe knew intuitively that when the Black Phantom reached Texas, she would board the Saturn inflatable dingy for the trek to the beach. She would wade through the surf and walk up the sand away from Wilson Lawson. It would hurt her deeply, but she would do it.

I have to find out who I am, what I am meant to be, she thought with mingled sadness and elation. Even if I throw away a chance at happiness, which may never come again.

Even now, she pictured the inevitable in her mind. Pausing just before she lost sight of the beach. Lifting one lone hand. A final goodbye to a man, who would always own a piece of her heart and soul.

* * * *

Vince's narrative was suddenly interrupted by two men flashing badges and identifying themself as FBI agents. One of the agents looked straight at me and asked me for my identification. I pulled out my wallet and handed him my driver's license. He examined it, studied my face, and handed it back. Apologetically he said, "Sorry to bother you sir, but we are trying to collect information that might help us in our investigation of the attack on Senator Katherine Laforge. Would you mind coming with us to answer a few questions?"

My wife looked at me with obvious fear in her eyes and grabbed my hand. "Agent Snyder, whatever questions you have for me, I can just as easily answer here. What I know is not any state secret." I lied straight face to them.

The two agents exchanged glances and then the older one shrugged and pulled a chair over to our table. "If it doesn't bother you, it doesn't bother me." He said smiling. The other agent remained standing with a notebook in his hand.

"How long have you been acquainted with Senator Laforge?"

I thought to myself, what an asinine question. He knows we have been acquainted all our life. "I have known Katherine, since she, and I were running around in diapers." I replied.

"Okay, but more recently when did you start working with her campaign people?"

"I am not sure if I was ever working for her campaign people. If work means getting a paycheck, I haven't been working for her at all."

"Sir, we know you have been involved in the Senator's campaign providing her research assistance and advice. We simply want to know when that all started. You were not doing anything wrong. We just want it for our records."

I sat there trying to decide whether to answer or not, and then finally concluded that it really didn't matter. I was not doing anything wrong, and I wasn't getting paid. So wasn't much I needed to fear. "I started supporting Katherine's campaign over a year ago. Just doing some basic research work for her free of political bias."

"Were you close friends with Senator Laforge?"

"A long time ago I was, but now we are just acquaintances."

"When was the last time you saw her?"

"My wife and I visited her last night at her campaign bus."

"What all did you talk about with her at last night?"

I thought about this for a few moments and then realized that what I knew could not help find her, but if I made a mistake in any of the facts that I gave them, I could find myself accused of lying to a Federal Agent.

"Agent Snyder, I worked for the government myself, as you probably know, and I realize that under section 1001 of U.S. Code Eighteen that I could be prosecuted for lying to you, if you misinterpret anything I might tell you. So let's postpone this interview until I can have a lawyer present and the interview recorded. The truth is, I am sure, I know nothing that would help you with Katherine's disappearance."

The words hung there and I saw looks of consternation from Tom and Vince.

Agent Snyder looked upset with my response, but hid it in his voice. "I am sure you are aware sir, there is a great deal of urgency involved in this investigation?"

"Yes I am, but my knowledge will be of no help in you solving this attack because we never talked politics at all. We just reminisced about years gone by, drank some wine, and my wife helped Katherine color her hair."

He looked directly at me with irritation burning in his eyes. "I can't force you to talk right now, but I can quickly get a subpoena to make you cooperate." His tone was malevolent, "We will be talking more and soon." With that, he quickly got up, sneered at me and angrily pushed his chair back under the adjacent table.

I felt a little guilty, but I knew this investigation would become big with an attack of this magnitude on a United States Senator. I needed to watch myself, and I had taken an oath that I would not divulge what I knew to anyone, and that I think included the FBI. The two FBI agents walked quickly away, and I saw the man with the notepad hurriedly scribbling something in his book. I was sure I would be seeing them again.

PART NINE

War in Iraq

The wait for word about Katherine had become intolerable, and I could feel myself becoming increasingly agitated. The scene in the auditorium had become noisier, invasive and threatening with every second that crawled by. I succumbed to taking another xanax. It might have been the second or third one, I had taken since we arrived at the auditorium. I really had loss count, but I washed the pill down with a gulp of coffee and then focused my mind on the TV's news.

CNN was taking a break from covering the Laforge story and was doing a live feed from the Tigris River in Mosul, Iraq about a downed U.S. helicopter. They were reporting that a OH-58D Kiowa Warrior helicopter, attached to the 101st Airborne Division had crashed into the river while searching for a missing soldier whose boat had capsized earlier that morning. Now members of the search team were also missing.

A stern faced commentator ended the report with the latest death toll for U.S. forces in the Iraq conflict. The count was now 513 dead, and he emphasized that the majority of these deaths happened after the President's May 1st 2003 declaration that major combat operations in Iraq were ended.

A report from a Washington correspondent stated that David Kay, the former head of the Iraq Survey Group responsible for searching for weapons of mass destruction was quoted as saying that he no longer believed stockpiles of WMDs existed in Iraq.

The sad news made my stomach ache even more from all the acid that had nothing to eat away at except my organs.

The news reminded me of how the war started on the eve of March 17the 2003, when President Bush gave Saddam Hussein and his sons 48 hours to leave Iraq or necessary military action would commence to remove them from power. One headline asserted that the United States regarded the use of force its obligation to assure its own national security and this type of action was within its sovereign authority. Buried among the myriad reports of the impending war was a report from an Iraq News agency that American CIA agents and subversive Iraqi operatives had abducted Senator Katherine Laforge and her primary physician from Ibn Sina Hospital.

The news of her escape stunned me, and I tried to imagine the impact it would have on Kat and those that were involved with operation Hulagu. She had remained secreted away from the public for months now and the possibility that her twin was now free within Iraq would be very unsettling to her. Before the day was over, the status of her escaped changed radically by a report claiming the charred bodies of Senator Laforge and her doctor had been found in the smoldering remains of their apparent escape vehicle just south of Baghdad. It did not give details of what had happened to the car. It was not known if her death was the result of an accident, CIA assassination, or by some Iraqi element that was responsible to thwart her escape.

The last report struck hard at the Senator's Houston office. Many of the campaign staff were devastated by the news and people openly cried as they listened to the report of her death. Most of them had been hoping that the campaign would take hold again and Senator Laforge would have a fair chance to win the primary. Senator Laforge's staff was sickened with the news.

For Katherine however, the demise of her twin in Iraq was a situation that would allow her to reemerge on the political horizon and attempt to rekindle her campaign. On that very day, March 18th 2003, Kat and her inner circle went about with an all day strategy meeting to plan how to introduce her back into the world.

As the plan evolved it became apparent how important it was to have Kat in Iraq as our troops moved onto Iraq soil. This would provide a way to introduce Senator Laforge back into the political landscape as a survivor who had escaped from the clutches of Saddam and the Baath party. The war and its resulting confusion would provide the perfect subterfuge for her reemergence. It was decided that as long as no contradicting reports of her twin were heard of, it would be safe to implement this operation. Senator Laforge would be fitted with the appropriate medical prosthetics, casts and makeup to appear as identical as possible to her now demised twin. Under the current state of chaos in Iraq, it would be very credible that CIA agents had abducted Kat from Ibn Sina Hospital. The report of her death by the Iraqi news would be dramatically proven false by her reemergence with her rescuers in some coalition occupied area of Iraq. It would be the perfect conclusion to her captivity and possibly give great impetus to her stagnant Presidential campaign.

As soon as the plans were conceived and agreed upon, they were immediately implemented. The next day March 19th Kat found herself wearing a full burka. The CIA agent in charge, Jim Anderson had bought it to help her conceal her identity. After an emotional filled embrace and a teary good-bye with Ira, Kat was driven to Houston's Ellington Field.

Since Operation Hulagu went awry, Kat had felt totally out of control of her life. Being sequestered at a secured location in Houston, Texas and isolated from her daughter for months had felt like imprisonment. But now with a glimmer of hope of taking back her existence, she still could not free herself of the feeling of being a minor cog of an entity that had taken on a life of its own.

Wearing the gray burka, Kat boarded a military plane that would take her to Andrews Air Force Base in Maryland. Agent Anderson accompanied Senator Laforge on the trip. At Andrews they transferred to another plane to get them to their final destination, Ali Al Salem Air Base in Kuwait.

On March 20th 2003, they arrived in Ali Al Salem Air Base. This air base affectionately called the "Rock" is located on a hill overlooking a slightly undulating stretch of desert 39 miles from the Iraqi border. The Rock's vantage point provided a panoramic view of the dun-color 120 degree arid desert plains. The base was a community of trailers, tents and some old buildings. The population of the camp had swelled from around 2,000 to the current 12,000 inhabitants. A large segment of the new population was elements of the 1st Marine Expeditionary Force that would soon be entering Iraq.

As soon as the plane taxied to its final stop, a dusty sand colored sedan pulled up alongside of it. The air-conditioned car sat on the sweltering tarmac as its two bearded occupants waited for the plane to debark. When Senator Laforge wearing her burka appeared on the steps of the plane, they quickly exited the vehicle to greet her. They were both CIA agents of Iraqi heritage; born and brought up in the windy city of Chicago. In the last three years, they had infiltrated into the social structure of the Basra posing as Shiite radicals searching for other disgruntled Shiite's. They were considered the perfect team to help Kat and Agent Anderson implement the new operation.

The two agents drove Senator Laforge and Anderson to an old concrete building a short distance from the busy airstrip. They parked in front of a masonry wall pock marked with countless bullets holes. The Iraqi's had used this building in 1991 to mass execute hundreds of Kuwaitis. The cratered wall was left as a testament to the savagery of that era.

Just as they exited the vehicle, a loud siren started to wail over the camp. The agent who had been driving the car yelled, "Incoming, take cover" and raced to the front of the building. The agent's urgency unsettled Senator Laforge and she found terror gripping her as she hobbled behind him in her bulky burka. Once inside the building, she heard the sharp crack of a missile exploding somewhere in the distance.

Her heart started to quiet as she gulped in a deep breath of air. Her nostrils were met with the musty smell of the old building penetrating through the fresh scent of pinesol used to mask the foul air in the small austere room.

Agent Anderson formally introduced Kat to the two panting CIA agents. One man was named Ahmed and the other Dawood. According to Anderson, they were perfectly fluent in Iraqi Arabic and could easily move about Basra as locals.

The four sat down at an old wooden table and Dawood offered a little contraband wine to the rest.

"We need to celebrate your arrival and the chance to work with you on this mission." Dawood said.

He continued, "Sorry for the fireworks display, but Mr. Hussein is trying to throw a little hardware at us in retaliation to our bombings in Iraq. Those were Scud missiles you just heard exploding. Not very precise, but they can do some major damage, if they hit you." He chuckled.

"We have some real work ahead of us, if this is all going to go as planned."

"I am going to give you a quick sketch of the plan, but not so much that you could give it away later. We are going to transport you into Iraq probably tomorrow morning. Ahmed and I are going to be heroes and claim we helped you escape and hid you in Basra. When we heard the Americans were nearby, we searched out friendly units and turned you over to the troops operating in that area. It will probably be the 1st Marine Expeditionary Force or some British unit. Once you are back with an American unit, you will be transported to Kuwait and Agent Anderson will be the debriefing officer."

"Before we leave here, we need to prepare you for your repatriation. Ahmed has had a lot of medical training and needs to now put your right arm in a cast and put a brace on your left leg so you will limp effectively. That cast needs to look pretty nasty by tomorrow, so we will be rubbing dirt on it and in general making it as nasty as we can. It has to look like you have been in it for a few days without proper care."

"While we talk let's get going on the cast." Ahmed interjected.

Ahmed went over to a trunk and took out a box full of bandages, gauze, plaster of Paris and other medical supplies.

"While we talk, we are going to get you physically prepared. Once the cast is on, and you are fitted with a brace on your leg, you need to get some sleep because we will be leaving early, and you have to be mentally alert to do your part."

"Sleep in your burka and no shower for you tonight. You need to stay secluded with us, and we need you a little rank when we turn you over to a military unit."

Katherine felt a keen anticipation of the inpending operation and an overriding sense of the here and now. She was also tired, but her adrenaline level was so high that she knew it would be impossible to sleep. She wanted sleep. She knew that tomorrow could be very trying and perhaps dangerous. Being rested would make her feel more secure that the operation would go well. She asked Ahmed if he had any sleeping pills, and he handed her an Ambien.

Six hours later, Senator Laforge was awakened by Ahmed. She was confused at first from the cast on her arm, her reduced mobility, and the darkness of this strange room.

She sat up and asked, "Are we ready to go?"

"No" Ahmed said.

"We must wait until we know we have a secure location near Basra to move into. Things are pretty hectic this morning. A Ch-46 chopper went down a little north of us and 16 on board are dead. Don't know what caused the crash, but 4 Americans and 12 British soldiers were killed in the crash. Saddam has also been lobbing a few missiles our way. None have hurt anybody, but the day is not over."

Dawood entered the room with a tray of food for Katherine. It contained some potent thick coffee and a few early morning bakery breads accompanied with a small jar of apricot jam.

"Thank you," Katherine replied smiling broadly.

"While you eat breakfast, we would like to give you a status report of operations going on."

"Yes, please do." Katherine said.

"First thing you need to know is that we have military forces now in Iraq. We crossed over the border early this morning. The battle strategy was changed a bit based on information that Iraqi forces had begun to threaten four oil facilities in southern Iraq. We soften the resistance along the border with very heavy artillery barrages that lasted all night and into the morning. British troops moved into the Al Faw Peninsula and are trying to secure the town of Umm Qasr. The 1st Marine Expeditionary Force is also involved in the fight for Umm Qasr. Basically all is too much in flux for us to really start our mission. So we will stay put here for a few more hours."

"When we get into position, we need it safe for you, we need confusion, but not a terribly dangerous situation where we have zero control."

Katherine could feel a new force emerging from deep inside of her consciousness. It was fear. The sounds of the tanks, APC's, trucks and jeeps rumbling about, outside her quarters heighten the reality of what she was now involved in. She could hear the chaotic racket of soldiers yelling commands and the drone of helicopters flaying the air as they sped off toward the Iraq border. This was a real war zone she was going into. A place where people kill each other and no one is really safe. The report of the morning helicopter crash, with 12 dead made it clear that death was busy this hot March morning. Imperceptibly, the tentacles of fear tighten their grip on her mind. But her fear of failing, was even more frightening to her and countered the bout of panic gnawing at her psyche.

The hours inched by as she sat there with Ahmed listing to the status updates on the command radio and mentally rehearsing what she would say to the troops when she was united with them. Noon came and went. Her anxiety seemed to increase with each second slowly ticking by. For some strange reason, her thoughts turned to ComDefC1, and she wondered if the vehicle that it had used could still be located. She contemplated the courage that her twin must have demonstrated in its escape. She wondered if ComDefC1 had begun to consider itself one of God's children or was God totally ignored.

She heard other voices in the adjoining room and a split second later Dawood stuck his head in and announced, "We are ready to go."

Those simple words and the moment triggered an incapacitating fear, but Ahmed's powerful hands helped her up and calmed her.

* * * *

Katherine looked out of the helicopter as it slowly descended into a clearing within a small date orchard near Basra, Iraq. After the chopper dropped them off, Senator Laforge, Ahmed and Dawood quickly joined a large group of refugees heading for a British checkpoint. The procession consisted of men in white shoulder-to-ankle gowns and skullcaps, men in western garb, veiled women, and children of all ages. Interspersed among them was smoke spewing dilapidated cars that inched through the crowd. Some hauled carts full of furniture, appliances, clothing, and food to support their family. Even loaded down camels, mules, and horses were scattered among the exodus from Basra.

The sights, chatter of people, the sound of the vehicles, animals and distant explosions created the semblance of some exotic movie set. The reality of where she was and what was happening almost eluded her as she melted into the scene like some movie extra quietly hobbling along. Beside her Ahmed and Dawood chatted among their selves and with other refugees in Arabic.

After about ten minutes of limping along, a heavily armed British patrol appeared moving down the road in their direction. Ahmed squeezed Katherine's hand and then suddenly released it as he darted out of line and ran toward the startled soldiers. They quickly trained their weapons on Ahmed, but he threw up his hands and yelled in English "I have a hostage for you. I can show you where Senator Laforge is." The soldiers were yelling, "Get down, get down." Ahmed fell forward on the ground and held his arms out in front of him. Two soldiers quickly moved toward him with weapons drawn. They stood over him with the muzzle of the gun just inches from his head.

"Who the bloody fuck is Senator Laforge?" one soldier yelled at him. Before Ahmed could answer, a Corporal yelled. "Where is Senator Laforge?"

Without looking up at them, Ahmed shouted, "She is in the line of refugees."

The corporal looked over at the wall of refugees just as Katherine and Dawood left it and approached them. Rifles now were pointed at them and Katherine felt a wave of fear washing over her. Dawood told Katherine. "Tell them who you are."

Katherine looked at the confused soldiers and shouted. "I am Senator Katherine Laforge. I was a prisoner here in Iraq and these two men saved my life."

In less than an hour Katherine found herself back in Ali Al Salem Air Base. This time she was given a hero's welcome. Military brass, reporters and photographers awaited her landing. As she alighted from the helicopter, a barrage of flashes warped the welcoming crowd into an eerie stuttering scene of erratic images. Behind the welcoming officers and NCOs were newsgroups shot gunning her with incessant questions. Their voices blended into the cacophony of congratulations and well wishes. Katherine slowly shuffled through the crowd shaking the out stretched hands that appeared disembodied from their owner by the blinding explosions of light from the reporter's flash. The gauntlet of well-wishers triggered sudden panic in Katherine. The crowd was more unnerving than her sojourn into Iraq had been. Part of it was her awareness that she again was Senator Katherine Laforge with a future resting on her ability to perpetuate the hoax that she had been the one hospitalized in Baghdad. The disorienting noise surrounding her enveloped her in almost a physical way. Her chest felt constricted and beads of sweat trickled down her cheeks as she smiled tiredly at those congratulating her. Through the din of noise, she could hear a man yelling at the crowd to make way for Senator Laforge. Finally, a man in civilian clothes flashed his badge and blocked the well-wishers from her as he extricated her from the partying crowd. Her savior was Jim Anderson, her primary CIA handler who was now escorting her to his office to start the debriefing process.

Katherine had rehearsed many times this debriefing back in Houston, Texas with agent Anderson. So she knew what to expect and what the right answers should be. She knew when to cry, and when to say nothing. The debriefing went as predicted and then plans were announced to the press about her return back to the states.

The events of the day had exhausted Katherine and since agent Anderson was finished with the debriefing he suggested that she take advantage of the situation and get some well needed rest before she talked to anyone else.

On the morning after her return Katherine awoke with a renewed sense of purpose. Anderson, too, had not been idle. He had assembled both a wardrobe and makeup crew to make her presentable for the morning press conference. The ordeal of her last couple days showed in the lines and hollows of her face as she addressed the waiting reporters and journalists.

"Members of the press, I am so glad to be here standing free in front of you," she began. "Just days ago I was a political prisoner in Ibn Sina Hospital." She scanned the crowd, making eye contact here and there. "I had no idea of when, or even if I would ever see my family and friends again. But at my lowest moment two brave Iraqi men came into my life." She smiled radiantly. "They became my white knights…."

Half a world away, the live coverage of Senator Laforge's news confe-rence from Iraq was carried by all the American networks.

"I cannot thank them or put into words the gratitude I have for these two Iraqi gentlemen who risked their life for mine," Katherine's voice cracked, and she paused to regain her composure. "But their bravery and perseverance made it possible for my appearance here today." She sighed, offered an apologetic head shake. "As much as I would like to provide details behind my escape, they must remain secret to protect the lives of those who assisted in my escape and still remain a part of Saddam's regime."

"One day…," Katherine cleared her throat, "after the defeat of the cur-rent regime and the successful formation of a new government, perhaps then the details can be revealed." One television camera tracked in on Senator Laforge, and her eyes glistened with tears. "It is unfortunate that the savagery of Saddam's regime prevents me from naming these true heroes, the brave ones who saved my life." Katherine's tired face grew sad. "But they know who they are, and how grateful I am to them."

On the podium, Katherine paused again. "Originally I went to Iraq in an attempt to negotiate a diplomatic solution to the problems facing two great nations." Her face hardened. "Instead I ended up in a hospital. My inability to alter the course of the war leaves me with a terrible nagging feeling of failure. But I cannot change what has already happened."

"What I can do is learn what war is like by experiencing it firsthand. When I return to the States and my Texas hometown, I want to be able to provide the citizens a real understanding of what is going on in Iraq. To that end, I have elected to return to Iraq on a fact-finding mission for a short duration. I will be embedded with the First Marine Division and members of my staff will soon join me."

"Tomorrow I will fly to Basra to link up with the Marines." Her eyes scanned the suddenly-quiet room. "This decision has been made with my family's knowledge, and we have agreed it is a sacrifice I should make." She sighed heavily, gripped the podium with both hands. "I hope this expe-rience will give me the wisdom needed to wisely make those difficult decisions of sending troops into armed conflict against people who seek our destruction."

A smattering of applause answered her, but Katherine went on unperturbed. "I further hope that you all will focus on this war and contribute in whatever way you can to try and win it as soon as possible." With a ghost of a smile, she stepped away from the podium. "I regret time permits only a few questions."

In the sudden bedlam, she pointed at the first of the journalists, and then raised her hands for silence. From the back of the room Anderson offered a grudging smile. "She's good," he mumbled to himself in spite of his bias against women politicians. "She could make a decent President ... if she lives that long."

The next morning she was introduced to Bakr, an Iraqi translator and CIA operative. He had operated in Iraq for almost a decade and was very versed in the culture and tribal rivalry that was so much a part of Iraq's political fabric. Around his neck he wore a silver Allah pendent and a piece of Bedouin jewelry with a cylindrical "du'a" containing tiny paper prayers believed to ward off misfortune, sickness and death.

In March 21, 2003 Katherine was back in Iraq viewing a convulsing dark cloud crawling across the afternoon sky. It appeared supported by columns of black smoke and flickering red flames roiling up from burning oil fields. Even the sun hid behind this evil tapestry, blocking its view of hell's specters spreading death and misery across the besieged city of Basra.

An exodus of soot smeared refugees inched along the ruptured highway leading from Sinbad's fabled birthplace. Snaking past them was Senator Laforge's entourage. She had just returned from the carnage unfolding on the thousand yard bridge spanning the Shatt Al Arab waterway. Iraqi militiamen and Baath Party loyalists hiding in mud huts on the far side of the bridge were firing indiscriminately at the escaping Iraqis. Bloated bodies of men, women and children littered the bridge, a macabre warning to those still attempting flight from the city. In an attempt to hinder the attacks, British troops would sporadically fire at buildings on the opposite side suspected of harboring snipers.

Senator Laforge's caravan of Humvees came to a stop at the security checkpoint manned by Irish Guards. They parked near the makeshift checkpoint providing her the advantage of being able to observe the unending task of searching the stream of refugees fleeing the carnage in Basra. The conditions in the city were bad. Water and food was scarce, and electricity unavailable. No one was starving yet, but supplies were running very low."

From behind a wall of crates an Irish officer accompanied by a Sergeant appeared and strolled up to her vehicle. The officer saluted Major Holland, the Senator's escort and introduced himself, "Captain Finnegan, Desert Rats, Seventh Armored Division."

"How is the situation here, Captain?" Katherine asked.

"It is a nightmare, Senator. We don't know who's a bloody fighter and who's a civilian. They all look the same."

Peering over a pile of sandbags, a young Irish soldier excitedly shouted to a comrade. "It's a bleedin' diplomat!"

"If you please, Private," Captain Finnegan snapped at the soldier.

The Captain resumed, "Senator, We are happy to have you here, and I will be glad to answer any questions you have."

Katherine smiled and said, "Captain, I am just here to observe, not to interfere with your mission."

A woman in a drab gray burka was next in line at the checkpoint. She looked tired, tense and frightened. Her face, streaked with dust and dirt, belied her real age. She balanced a baby on her hip as two female guards quickly frisk her for weapons and other contraband.

The renewed thud of Artillery exploding somewhere off in the distance and blaring sirens from the city reminded Kat of the real danger she faced. Her left arm was still in a cast and a metal brace was taped to her left leg. . She could not allow her disabilities to impair her ability to move about or burden those traveling with her. Even with these handicaps, she was still quite agile. Getting in and out of the Humvee was a minor challenge, but was diminished because the doors had been removed to make escape easier if the vehicle came under fire. Her ability to adapt to a combat environment was very important. She had never been in a real war environment. How would she comport herself? Could she deal with the gore of war? Could she cope with the lack of privacy and the hygiene challenge?

Suddenly there was a flurry of movement as a staff sergeant, near the Humvee yelled, "Scud attack." A collective frenzy of hands and arms flailed about as marines held their breath and grabbed for their alien-looking chemical mask. The chaotic spectacle emanating from this unseen evil force locked faces in rigidity as all struggled to find refuge within their mask before touched by this invisible force of death. Within seconds Katherine had secured her mask and had pulled up her chemical protection suit.

Katherine's baptism of wearing the protective gear was harrowing. It was like some smothering dream. She felt she was suffocating and feared it was from being exposed to the deadly gas. Through the misty panes of the mask, she searched the smoke filled sky for falling birds and the ground for any mist floating about. The stifling Iraqi heat added to the terrifying experience. Inside the mask perspiration drenched her face and fear gripped her as she tried to assure herself that it was the heat and not some deadly gas that caused the flood of dampness and the panic she felt. She fought this ghostly menace that seemed to invade her mind with confusion and sap strength from her body. This was war and even the air became a weapon that could kill with paralyzing suddenness. She felt her entire existence focused on making it to the All Clear.

Peering from the protective mask, Kat observed the huddled troops, all waiting for that all-important "All Clear." There was an attempt of false bravado as muffled jokes and nervous laughs resonated from behind the façade of the mask. War quickly teaches a somber awareness of our mortality. Most who have descended into the world of death and carnage emerge scarred, and perpetually haunted by memories of those swallowed by the vortex of destruction. Some, however, find combat an elixir and relish the battlefield and its stimulation of the senses.

The cry of "All clear," echoed up and down the convoy and sweat streaked faces emerged from behind masks. Some looked shaken, some angry, some relieved and some oddly exhilarated with their experience with the darkness and savagery of war.

Kat tore off the mask and took a deep breath of the tepid Iraqi air. The smell of smoke, sweat, exhaust and a panoply of other odors engaged her senses. Off in the distance a herd of camels bellowed and bleated as they enjoyed the hot afternoon totally oblivious to the evil embracing the desert. Kat wiped the sweat from her face and savored the warm breeze caressing her face.

Their convoy finally stopped north of Basra and Katherine was able to stretch her legs or at least one of her legs. She was tired, drained from the heat and her legs ached from being cramped in the Humvee for so long. Katherine met up with her aide, Paul Shermer, and realizing how pathetic she looked, joked, "What do you think the chances are of taking a shower tonight?"

"The closest thing to a shower you're going to get tonight is handy wipes and maybe some drips from a bottle of water, unless it rains." Paul quipped. The attempt at humor was welcomed because the fear of a potential gas attack was still paramount in her mind. She worried what would happen if she was asleep, sick, or going to the bathroom and a scud attacked occurred. She knew she would be nervously studying the actions of troops and no longer simply relying on hearing the ominous cry of "Gas Attack" to warn her of danger.

She was adapting to the rigors of war and to the same discomforts experienced by the troops waging the battles. She had learned to accept that sand and the sun were inescapable perils that could easily incapacitate or kill. The tepid air was always infused with sand that entered the nose, ears, filled your pores, dried your face and abraded the eyes. Even wearing goggles would not completely protect the eyes from the sand. When it did enter an eye, its sharp jagged edges felt like flecks of broken glass, scraping and scratching, impairing vision and sometime causing extreme pain. On days when swirling sand thickened the air, your lungs would ache and spasm with retching coughs. And then there was the sun. It beats down on you incessantly, devouring your strength and sucking the moisture from you like an omnipotent vampire. Your tongue thickens in your saliva-less mouth and your throat becomes raw from the heat and grit.

Katherine feared not so much the suns damage to her body, but more its debilitating effects within her mind. The blistering sun could invade the brain and elusively alter its mental state. If you were one of the unlucky, it could fill your mind with hallucinations, confusion, disorientation and bizarre visions that virtually incapacitated you. For some, the sun's sapping strength would make them nauseous and drop them to their knees vomiting and defecating uncontrollably. These basic elements of existence in Iraq could be as deadly as the actions of the Republican Guard, Fedayeen or other armed Iraqis.

The whirlwind of events and the relentlessness of the Marines awed Senator Laforge. The 1st Marine Expeditionary Force pressed forward up Highway 7 toward An Nasiriyah leaving the besieged city of Basra in the hands of the British troops. Iraq roiled with battles. The port city of Umm Qasr was still showing resistance to the British and even though 8 thousand Iraqi troops surrendered, the Fedayeen and other irregular military elements continued to mount pitched battles against the Coalition. A primary goal in the Basra area and Al Faw peninsula was to prevent the destruction of the oil fields. Major General Mathis, the 1st Division Commander was given this mission and his troops quickly seized Az Zubayr Oil fields and others that dotted the landscape around Basra. Only a handful were set on fire by the Iraqi military before the Coalition troops took full control of them. It was only the third day of the war and the Coalition troops had met little resistance to their blitzkrieg into Iraq.

March 23, 2003

In the early morning calmness of March 23, 2003 morning Senator Laforge sipped coffee and munched on a chocolate-covered oatmeal cookie from her MRE as they called the dehydrated Meal-Ready-to-Eat. She listened to the chatter coming from the radio and the distant echoing of muezzins chanting from the minarets of mosques calling believers to morning prayer. Anytime you are near a town or city and the weather is calm, the early morning or evening call to prayer can be clearly heard in the quiet desert. It becomes as expected and natural as the rising and setting of the sun.

The atmosphere was tense this morning. Something was different than the normal minutiae of survival of scanning the surrounding for hostilities and checking equipment for readiness. Senator Laforge asked Lance Corporal Parkers, "What's going on?"

He said that some army unit has been ambushed up ahead in An Nasiriyah and a rescue attempt was in process, but things were very sketchy.

They had assigned their Task Force Tarawa to the mission of aiding the army unit and securing An Nasiriyah.

Senator Laforge asked a Captain for more details of what had happened. The Captain was intently monitoring radio transmissions from the units engaging the enemy at the ambush site.

She caught bits and pieces of the transmission and from it, she discerned that it was a supply convoy from the 507th Maintenance Company that had made a disastrous wrong turn.

Thirty-three soldiers and 18 vehicles led by Captain King mistakenly missed a left turn at an intersection and continued across a bridge spanning the Euphrates River. They entered An Nasiriyah, a city of 400,000 swarming with Fedayeen and Iraqi irregulars. As the Army unit tried to retreat out of the city, they were attacked by heavily armed Iraqis. An innocent wrong turn brought them to the mouth of Hell. A virtual hail of bullets rained down on the unit as it desperately tried to maneuver through the morning shadows and dusty streets of An Nasiriyah back to the bridge. The bloody chaos fragmented the convoy even more as the soldier fought back against Iraqis firing at them from all directions. Some of the soldiers were hit by the torrent of bullets. Rivulets of sweat streaked the pale ashen faces of the wounded, as they fended off darkening thoughts of dying. Survival was the only thing that mattered now. They fought on with no time to tend the wounded or mourn the fallen. Stark fear of a waiting death drove them on.

As the vehicles weaved through the gauntlet of barricades, exploding RPGs, hail of bullets, menacing tanks and truckloads of attacking Fedayeens, the casualties mounted. Vehicles crashed into obstacles, some exploded from RPG hits and some were crippled from the withering firepower of the Iraqi force. The unit continued to fight and miraculously the lead three vehicles led by Captain King finally escaped the city. They drove south of the city and encountered the Marine's 8th Tank Battalion, Task Force Tarawa. Once briefed of the situation, the marines immediately dispatched an element up Highway 8 to reinforce the remaining 27 soldiers. The marines first came upon a group of ten soldiers of the 507th, firing from behind five of the disabled vehicles at an advancing Iraqi element. The men led by SGT Rose were a ghastly sight with blood caked hands and eyes blazing from death's beckoning. The Tarawa unit joined the fight and quickly routed the enemy. SGT Rose's element had half of its men wounded, some hit multiple times. They had escaped the labyrinth of hell with their life, but its horror would surely haunt them forever. Seventeen more of the soldiers were still fighting with Iraqis on the streets of An Nasiriyah. Before the marines could reach them, they were killed or captured by the enemy. The entire battle had gone on for around an hour. At the end only sixteen soldiers escaped the day's carnage. Eleven soldiers were killed in the battle and another seven captured by the Iraqis. Many of those that did escape were severely wounded.

Senator Laforge was sickened by the news of the event. She bit down on her parched lips to stem their quivering. Her emotions had to stay hidden. If a tear glisten in her eye, over an event like this, the media would pounce on her like hyenas as an indication of her weakness.

The simple accidental turn by the supply unit had sparked euphoria for the Iraqi forces. For the Iraqis, the battle had become a rallying point. The dark event provided a tsunami of optimism for war skeptics and was celebrated by war protesters with the enthusiasm of zealous cheerleaders.

The three women from the supply unit, the battle and its aftermath became media fodder for days. For Katherine, March 23 dragged on as units from the 2nd Marine Expeditionary Brigade and Marine Task Force Tarawa pushed deeper into An Nasiriyah. Their mission was to secure two bridges that would help the Coalition troops cross the Euphrates River on their march to Baghdad. Heavy resistance confronted them as they entered an Nasiriyah and it became the bloodiest battle of the campaign.

After digesting the grim news of the battle in An Nasiriyah, Colonel Joe W. Dowdy, commander of Regimental Command Team 1 of the 1st Marine Division considered his alternatives. With the new problem of pouring rain and the resulting sludge filled streets in many of the side roads, there were few choices. Colonel Dowdy decided to rip through the center of An Nasiriyah, on a dangerous stretch of road nicknamed "Ambush Alley" after the infamous 1993 deadly firefight in Mogadishu.

Katherine was nervous about charging through An Nasiriyah, to say the least. Paul informed her of Colonel Dowdy's decision and then helped Kat gather her belongings. Gathering her things wasn't the hard part for Kat - she only had a few notebooks and pens aside from her rucksack of essentials. Suddenly, she was thinking about her family, about Lyndsey and Ira. She realized that she was now – in effect – going in to combat. Not only was she traveling around Iraq with Marines, she might actually now be shot at. She also realized that there was thousands of women and children now in harms way in the town of An Nasriyah. She felt a bit selfish worrying about herself, but before she could ponder it further, Kat was whisked off in an armored Humvee, and they were on their way to, and hopefully through, An Nasriyah.

Everyone deals with fear differently. Some block it out by talking to others about inane subjects, their favorite singer, TV Show or sexual conquests. Then there are the quiets ones who sit and sort of hallucinate about the impending battle. They envision their death in horrible permutations. They see their limbs ripped off and lying on the ground with white bone protruding from the carrion. Grotesque visions of their entrails bursting from their abdomen and blood spurting from severed arteries play out in their mind. Even the shrieks of their own pain vividly echo in their minds. Katherine, luckily, had not been fully exposed to the horrors of war to be plagued with these demons.

The first part of the battle Senator Laforge witnessed was the bombardment of An Nasriyah. The attack was intense. Thousands of rounds, like specters swarming to their prey, streaked northward toward the city of four hundred thousand, their incessant wavering whine reminded all of their ominous mission. Kat could hear the constant whine of the projectiles zooming high overhead and their distant thud as they slammed into their targets.

As she drove by a battery of artillery, she watched the howitzers spastically jerk and belch out tongues of flame as they spat out their lethal packages. The stillness of the afternoon air and the intensity of the firing produced a thick gray fog that shrouded the howitzers. Wispy tentacles of smoke gave the illusion of some ethereal veil embracing the men manning the guns as they faded in and out like dull gray apparitions.

As they approached the city, its stench bespoke its years of neglect under Saddam's regime. Fecal odors rose up from the oozing puddles of sewage that flooded the city's main intersections. Rows of one and two story mud huts and cinder block houses dotted a landscape filled with miles of dirt roads. Dowdy led them through the bowels of the city. However, he didn't take any chances. The possibility of plain-clothed Fedayeen insurgents attacking as they passed through the city was a dilemma he wanted to prevent. At strategic points in the city, Dowdy had Marines dismount to watch out for surprise attacks. Scattered shots rang out from over the cement rooftops, and the Marines quickly returned fire and put down any resistance. It disheartened Senator Laforge and the Marines to pass through the city and see bodies of civilians and fellow Marines strewn about in charred heaps along the dusty road. For safe measure, the Marines fired rocket-assisted projectiles, or RAP rounds, into the heart of the town.

The Fedayeen, Saddam's loyalists, used tactics that defied our military rules of engagement. Iraqi militiamen would wave white flags of surrender, then as U.S. forces approached, suddenly open fire. Other Iraqi guerillas dressed as civilians would hide behind women and children as they fired knowing that U. S. Marines would not dare fire back into crowds of civilians.

The massive convoy of amphibious assault vehicles, medvacs, army tractors, trailers and Humvees came to a grinding halt. There was confusion about unconfirmed firefights ahead. A wounded Marine was in bandages, still awaiting a medvac that was supposed to come and take him away. As questions arose, Iraqi citizens came out from behind their small shops, houses, and narrow, dingy alleys to view the monolith that was the convoy of RCT-1, standing in the middle of the road like an elephant in a nomad's tent. Some of the men laughed, pointed and gawked. A Marine stood atop an Amtrac (amphibious assault vehicle) and pointed his M-16 at a group of men to warn them from getting too close. Finally, word broke that the medvac had arrived, and after it whisked the wounded Marine away, the convoy resumed its trek.

The images of the battle in An Nasiriyah were still vivid in Kat's mind when they finally arrived at their next resting point. She had seen Amtracs ripped apart from large explosions with Marines inside, and bloodied uniforms littering the road. She recalled a lieutenant from Lima company dismount his vehicle and placed a white cloth over the body of a fallen soldier. Katherine wondered if that soldier was married and how devastated his wife would be. How soon would she hear the grim news of his death from a military official expressing his regrets? Katherine considered the possible scenario for just a moment and shook her head to try to rid herself of the morbid picture. She knew she would forever remember the price of war, and revere the men and woman who were willing to pay that price.

A few miles out of An Nasiriyah the convoy was greeted by smiling farmers and children lining the road waving. A man stooped with his spine bent into a permanent calcified arch shook his cane at the convoy and striking young women hiding behind swaying trees waved demurely at the marines. The last hours had been a trip into madness. It started with running a gauntlet through a city of 400,000 as an invisible enemy fired RPGs and bullets into the convoy hoping to kill Americans. But now just a few miles outside the city, it was as if they were part of the rose bowl parade. In the new calm of this trek she felt safe and weariness overtook her. Her eyes glazed over, flickered a few times and her mind shut down.

Katherine's head bobbed about as she dozed in the backseat of the Humvee. Suddenly, she awoke as the vehicle violently bounced about. The noise of the convoy echoed in her ears as she squinted into the glare of the late morning sun. Through her obscured vision a surreal image emerged. Outside, the road was strewn with mangled remains of Iraqi fighters. Some were indistinguishable as humans; just reddish lumps of carrion oozing onto the asphalt. Many corpses had been mashed by 70-ton tanks that had found the road impassable without running over them. On either side of the highway, the landscape was blanketed with bodies sprawled in every direction. Between some of the bodies were shimmering puddles of a thick bloody stew congealing in the sun. Swirling around the corpses were black swarms of flies enjoying their bounty of carrion.

She strained to hear, above the rumble of the convoy, the expected crack of enemy fire, but heard only the occasional chirps of birds. The battleground maintained an eerie reverent silence for the fallen Iraqi soldiers.

Katherine looked out into the madness and felt fear and a burning sensation deep in her stomach. Bakr observed her confusion and pulled out his bottle of arrack and offered it to her. Katherine omitted a simple "Jesus yes" and grasped the bottle, quickly taking a drink of the liquor. The mind and soul lack the capacity to process the emotions to deal with horror of this magnitude. Demonic visions like these warp and muffle sensibilities like the distorted rattling of a speaker as it tries to output sound beyond its ability. The nightmarish spectacle reminded Katherine of the scene from "Hotel Rawanda" where Paul Rusesabagina finds himself driving over the hacked to death bodies of his fellow Tutsi on a foggy dark night as he tried to return to his hotel.

Katherine handed the bottle of arrack back to Bakr and thanked him.

"Evil rises up from the dead." He said. "What did you say?" Katherine asked.

Bakr repeated himself, "Evil rises up from the dead. The families and friends of those five hundred soldiers will seek revenge and more will die. It is the way things are here in Iraq."

"It is the way we all are." Katherine replied.

"Maybe, but here we forget and forgive very slowly."

Lush trees lined the road outside and the nightmarish scene disappeared as if someone had flipped a channel from a horror movie to an exotic travel show. But the blood-streaked tires on the vehicles were vivid reminders of the carnage they had just driven through.

"I am afraid that America is about to find that freedom in Iraq is like opening the gates to a lion's cage. We are a country of caged people and without the fear of Saddam and the Baath party, Iraq will go insane."

"I would think Iraq has leaders that will take over once Saddam is gone."

Bakr's voice was quiet and sad, "Saddam kept the criminals off the street, and he outlawed radical religious groups. Now Iran and Syria will operate freely inside our country."

He took another sip of arrack and washed it over his stained teeth. For a few long seconds, he sat quietly looking out the window at the barefoot children running alongside the noisy convoy.

"Iblis will take advantage of the confusion and death that surrounds the Iraqi people and his evil will embrace them like the swirling sands of a sandstorm."

"What is Iblis?" Kat asked.

"Iblis is the name Islam gives to the devil. Iblis will temp the spiritually weak and many will follow his directions and more blood will flow. Insanity will prevail with Sunni's killing Shiites and Shiites killing Sunni's."

Katherine took one more sip of arrack and closed her eyes again, but the scene stayed vivid in her mind. She had come to realize that war was a nightmare kingdom deep in the darkest forest of man's insanity. Katherine had experienced the smell of cordite, blood and the stench of rotting flesh riding upon God's scorching breeze. Here was a land where trees and grass shriveled and died from man's evil leaving withered trunks with gnarled branches veiled in gray mist. A dominion whose streams became rivulets of slime, shit and blood winding through a netherworld that stretches out its tentacles to all of humanity. This was Katherine's awakening that war is the collision of our world with another that moves in dark shadows.

This savagery was not a horror movie, it was real life, nor was its God's will that we slaughtered one another. Something else sparked this. Something that mutates the soul and consciousness to the point where the spread of misery and death is as fulfilling as the rapture of one's first love. Kindness and mercy becomes Evil's abomination. This evil spirit spreads like some loathsome cancer ravenous for new souls and minds. Its sacrament is spilled blood of the living. Katherine knew from her Catholic upbringing that only one demonic spirit strives for the death of all mankind and that is Sorat who is more destructive than Satan or Lucifer. In his world all that once was held sacred falls like dust as Hell metamorphoses into a heaven of darkness here on earth. Blood and gore become the nourishment of Sorat's being. A part of her fought to believe that evil is an entity that has substance or is real, but then why does man kill one another? It was a question she could not answer.

The next day Kat found herself heading north of An Nasiriyah on Route 7 shrouded by orange dust. Gale force winds pick up the rusty dirt and pummeled anything in its path. The ferocity of the swirling sand would make your face and hands tingle or often sting from its impact. The whole train of vehicles was blanketed in thick orange dust that made it nearly impossible to see. The reduced visibility forced the convoy to move at what seemed like a snail's pace. Occasionally, the dust thinned and they got a glimpse of reality.

But what they saw didn't seem real. Corpses along the desert road, flashes of light as radio propelled grenades sparked in the distance, burned out vehicles and the fleeting sketch of an animal or person silhouetted against the curtain of orange.

As the storm approached, the swirling orange sky darkened until blackness swallowed everything.

Kat could tell that some of the Marines felt fear for the first time in the campaign. It was probably the perception that God had now joined forces with the Iraqis plunging day into total darkness with a howling sandstorm of biblical proportions. The slow going of the convoy had given these Marines more time to contemplate their tenuous situation. Their defenses were seriously affected by the storm, and they felt more vulnerable to attacks from the elite Republican Guard and Iraqi irregulars. The convoy started receiving 122 mm Katyusha rockets and heavy artillery, but the Iraqis overlooked that the marines counter battery radar, U-2, and EP-3 aircraft with guided munitions system were unhampered by the storm. The unit Kat was with quickly targeted the Iraqi's positions and obliterated them.

As they rumbled through one small village, a young man stepped out from behind a tree and leveled a weapon at the Convoy. Before anyone could respond, a burst of light accompanied by a loud boom signaled a RPG's blast. A building behind the convoy exploded from its impact and several Marines leapt down from their Amtracs to engage the gunman. Shots rained down from Iraqi gunmen hiding behind the rooftop parapets of cement buildings lining the road. The pandemonium of gunfire and explosions intensified, as more Marines joined their comrades in battle. Then incredibly the buildings, rifle flashes and explosions faded from view as the storm worsen leaving only the cacophony of noises signifying the battle. For a short while more, shots were fired blindly until a sergeant ordered his crew to cease-fire and move out. As they loaded into their vehicles, AK-47 rounds continued to whiz overhead and ricochete off the cement walls, but the Iraqis were also firing blindly.

There were rumors that up to five hundred plain-clothed Fedayeens were mingling with the townspeople in Ash Shatrah and preparing to attack the convoy. But the raging storm that once had disturbed the marines now seemed to be a neutral menace making combat equally as difficult for either side. They were battling a common enemy, as well as each other.

The weather deteriorated further with strong winds blowing in from changing directions. Rain mingled with the dust, creating thick mud that stuck to anything it touched. Men took shifts, standing outside to man their observation posts and then retreating into their vehicles to steal a moment of warmth and reprieve from the incessant wind. Weariness plagued many marines as they shivered in the cold. A few still wondered what advantages if any. the Fedayeen could gain from this storm. This was their backyard and surely they were more experienced in how to utilize a sandstorm to their advantage. The Fedayeen were thick-skinned and better able to brave the nasty weather, a Marine claim. Kat couldn't help but grin, when she heard another Marine reply, "They may have thick skin, but ours is thicker. We're Marines Goddamn it!"

Along with the winds of the dust storm came the clattering of helicopter blades. Two CH-46s swooped down to carry off the wounded. The evacuees were not only Marines, but also Iraqi civilians and enemy combatants. It amazed Kat that this sanity and humanity were displayed in the hell of war. Outside, Marines joined up with the evacuation crew to load the wounded into the helicopters.

As the convoy crawled further north, a Humvee pulled over to inspect a wrecked car burning on the side of the road. A line of bullet holes stretched across the driver's door. Dangling from its shattered front windows were bloodied bodies, unmistakably dead. One corpse was completely missing its head with the black hole of the trachea leering out from between the shoulders like an eye. A coating of sand plastered their bloodied clothes and the vehicle's roof. The winds had been very active indicating the killings were recent or the vehicle would have been coated with inches of sand. Kat had never seen anything as gruesome so close. She averted her eyes, but the image floated about in her mind. She violently shook her head, but the vision remained accompanied by an ominous stillness that swallowed all sounds except the light howling of the wind and sand.

The marines exited their Humvee and cautiously approached the smoking vehicle. Something important or someone breathing was still in it.

Whatever sat inside the car was apparently more horrific than even the corpses hanging from its windows. Because as the marines reached it, one of them started gagging and then stooped over vomiting. Kat could taste the bile in the back of her throat as the sounds of him gagging filled the silence. A tall marine of Chinese heritage quickly shattered the vehicle's rear window with a jack handle. Just then sand swirled around the vehicle, veiling the activity momentarily. When it subsided, the Marine was holding in his arms a little girl, dressed in white with the severed head of a woman taped to her torso. He was yelling to another marine to cut the tape securing the head to her body. The second marine tried to cut the tape, but the girl struggled to escape them and shrieked in terror.

Kat could not sit as a spectator any longer in the Humvee. The girl's screams and shrieks were tearing her heart out. Kat's eyes were glazed with tears, and she grabbed Bakr's hand and said, "Please come with me and tell that little girl that we are here to help her."

Kat sort of skipped with her leg in the brace over to the side of the car and asked Bakr to tell the girl that they wanted to help her. Bakr tried to comfort the girl, but her shrieks were so loud that she probably could not hear what he was saying. Bakr told Katherine that the girl was saying, "Please don't kill me. Please don't kill me. I want to live. Allah please don't let them kill me."

Katherine tried to get closer to the girl without getting kicked by her flaying legs. She was motioning to the girl with her hands and her mouth to relax and Bakr was talking to her in Arabic trying to comfort her. Suddenly, the severed head broke loose from the tape and fell to the ground. It rocked back and forth between the two marines helping the girl. Katherine yelled at them, "Move her away from the head. She is terrified. Move her away." Just them, the girl kicked one marine in the face making him loose his grip. She fell from his arms and sprinted away screaming something in Arabic. She headed toward some houses set back off of the road trailed by the four marines closing in on her. Then it came to an end, as a single shot cracked in the distance and the girl's head burst open with blood and brains spraying out of the back as she skidded to a stop on her face. The deadly silence swept back again as everything just stopped. Katherine stood transfixed, as the girl just laid there with a tiny fountain of blood barely visible spilling her life in to the dirt. Katherine's eyes narrowed their arc of vision until only the girl's body was visible. She started to hobble to where the girl was laying, but immediately tripped over rubble. Paul grabbed her as she teetered and his strong arms steadied her. He pulled her upright and yelled to her over the staccato of the marines' firing machine gun cover fire for their retreat.

"It's over Katherine. She is dead and we must get out of here immediately. The next bullet might be for you or for me." Katherine realized Paul was right, that there was nothing she could do for the girl now. "Let me help you back to the Humvee." Paul added. Bakr appeared at her side and put his arm around her also and the two of them helped her back to the Humvee. The four marines that had tried to save the girl cautiously retreated back to their vehicle while scanning the terrain for any sign of the sniper. No gun smoke or movement could be seem in the houses lining the road, but somewhere within them the girl's murderer hid.

In the Humvee, Kat still shaken asked Bakr, " Why did they do this to the girl? Why were they so cruel to her?

Bakr looked at Katherine. He saw the anger, confusion and pain in her eyes. He wanted to comfort her, but what could he say that could make her understand the chasm between the Sunnis and the Shiites. "Katherine some Sunnis believe that Shiites are infidels, and that Allah desires them killed. Bakr's disgust was evident and in his lap his large hands were clenched into fists. Many Mullahs actually claim 'He who kills even one unbeliever…shall be rewarded by Allah.'"

"So this is Sunni killing Shiite? I still do not understand why they would be so cruel to even a little girl." Katherine replied.

"The subject is very unpalatable to me Katherine, but I will tell you what I think. Many of my Muslim brothers have been surrounded by this darkness of death, hate and revenge for so long that when they kill an unbeliever their gloom is brighten by the agony they inflict on their victim. The kaafir's life is now more miserable than theirs and that is uplifting to them even euphoric. They are convinced that this bloodletting pleases Allah and endears them to him."

The Iranians have a saying 'Saints fly only in the eyes of their disciples.' In America, those 'saints' would be called sociopaths and locked in institutions, here they are called martyrs. These bandits of life feel no more sympathy slicing open the throat of a child or woman than squashing a roach. They are void of soul."

There was a disturbing moment of silence and Katherine search for something to say to Bakr, but he broke the silence and continued. "I use to detest that Irish politician Connor Cruise O'Brian because he said, 'A Westerner who claims to admire Muslim society, while still adhering to Western values, is either a hypocrite or an ignoramus, or a bit of both … Arab and Muslim society is sick, and has been sick for a long time.' When I see what we do to each other in the name of Islam, I can understand why O'Brian said that."

"As Muslims we must rid ourselves of those abominations that destroy Islam and turn it into a religion of death."

"War is horror, but it is even worst when people kill others because they are told that their God wants them to. Muslims are taught, 'Doubt is the key to knowledge,' but they fear to question these calls to kill. Why would a God, the only God need mere mortals to do His killings?"

"Some have told me that at first their mind goes in circles thinking and rethinking their killing of a kaafir. They may have killed at first out of fear of Allah, but soon it becomes their addiction. While you will have insomnia from this and awake from sleep touched by her spirit, her killers will be immune from her visitations because they no longer serve Allah, but instead Iblis. The Prophet said that Allah does not allow those to enter Paradise until they believe, and you cannot believe until you love one another."

On the dawn of March 27, 2003, a bright sun bleached away the red haze that had hidden the sky for the previous days. Kat accompanied by Bakr and Paul sat at the back of amtrac shaded by a canvas canopy. They were sipping coffee and discussing the tactical situation that had developed. Nearby, Colonel Dowdy stood with some of his staff looking over a map in a plastic sleeve. He looked bleary-eyed and weary. The conflict and his unit's casualties bothered him immensely. Kat wondered how does a commander diminish the feeling of guilt when their decisions or indecision bring death to their followers. She wondered how President Kennedy felt when his vacillation on the promised support for the bay of pig invasion into Cuba resulted in 68 killed on the beaches and over a thousand captured by the Castro forces. How did Clinton feel when his siege on the Waco Texas religious compound turned into a burning inferno killing 76 innocent women and children? How did Abraham Lincoln, the Great Emancipator, feel when he received a congratulatory letter after Christmas from, Brigadier-General, H. H. Sibley stating, "I have the honor to inform you that the thirty-eight Indians and half-breeds ordered by you for execution were hung yesterday at Mankato at 10 a.m. Everything went off quietly and the other prisoners are well secured." Kat remembered it was the largest mass execution in American History. She wondered if she could prevent herself from being manipulated into similar contemptible situations if she was elected. Her thoughts were interrupted when Bakr informed her that they were invited by Colonel Mayers to accompany him to a small Shiite village close by. His battalion was heading to secure a small intersection where Route 7 met 17. Mayers planned to use Route 17, which ran west of Route 1, as a short-cut to shuttle supplies back and forth to the division. Traveling up Route 7 they approached a small town. Kat was surprised at the starkness of this village, which was completely devoid of commercial buildings. It consisted of mud huts and open pits for bathrooms very much resembling a movie set of some African village. Slits were cut into the side of the huts to serve as windows. Primitive as it appeared, it did enjoy the luxury of electricity evidenced by a single power line snaking down the road through the town. Suddenly, a rocket propelled grenade shot out of one of the mud huts. It was a futile gesture because the convoy of tanks could have pulverized this town in minutes. Some Marines immediately dismounted and took up position to fire on the sniper. But before another shot was fired, a red Vespa with a young man on it sped away from the hut where the round was fired and was quickly out of sight.

The Marines decided to search the village for others and started to enter a hut when a toothless white-haired man, apparently the elder of the village, emerged. He carried the Koran in his right hand and uttered a "As-Salaam Alaikum" greeting to the soldiers advancing toward him. Bakr heard the greeting and responded with a "alikom elsalam." The old man appeared to be a Shiite mullah. To the dismay of the marines, people began to exit the huts and clamored around the old man chattering to each other. The situation had an air of foreboding. Something about the village just made it feel sinister, like you were in some horror movie like "The night of the living dead" where the villagers would all attack with open mouths and bite into your throats. But nothing like that happened, and with the help of Bakr and another translator, they concluded that this was not a threatening situation, but simply an isolated act of defiance by a single person. The Mullah claimed that the only guns his people owned were for hunting and that the people of the village just wanted peace. Bakr did not really believe the man, but this desolate Shiite town really posed no imminent threat so the Marines moved further up Route 7.

The convoy rested awhile, it was a much-needed break for Katherine. Her cast was an irritant to her, and it was still difficult for her to move around. The stop lasted for several days. Longer than anyone, including Kat had expected. It had evolved into what was referred to as an "operational pause." CENTCOM had ordered it insisting that some of the battalions needed to refuel. The pause in fighting was quickly portrayed by the media as a sign that the campaign was going bad. Some commentators claimed it looked like the Fedayeen and other Iraqi fighters had weakened or perhaps stopped the push to Baghdad. Cynical military analyst wasted no time in interpreting the pause as signs of weakness, questionable command decisions or lack of resources. A few days later the pause ended and the campaign continued toward Baghdad.

March 29th a new darkness was thrust upon survival in Iraq. The first suicide bomber attacked and killed four U.S. Soldiers. It was reported that at a check point near Najaf a taxi driver beckoned four soldiers to his cab and then detonated a bomb killing himself and the unsuspecting soldiers. Iraqi's media described the suicide bombers as a martyr.

The attack reminded Senator Laforge of her talk with Bakr about Iblis and her muddled thoughts of how evil must exist as some entity that fills the atmosphere with venomous seduction. An energy that can possess a person just as love can seize our being. These suicide bombers were the new permutation of evil where man gives himself as a weapon to kill other humans. Her belief in the existence of these powers was something as frightening to her as the probability that this entity also shared our world. She wondered if she was just a foolish superstitious woman, believing in this Deity of darkness named Sorat, or was she aware of something others weren't. If she was right, then these suicide bombers were the embodiment of the type of carnage that this destroyer of mankind desires. Sorat was a malignant fallen spirit that stripped humans of their souls, egos and all goodness. He could make horrible acts virtually impossible to eradicate because people would become unable to recognize their actions as evil. Above all she wondered how could one induce another to become a suicide bomber for some God mission whose purpose is to kill innocent people and blow yourself apart? How can the human mind become so clouded and susceptible to such evil and debasing acts? These questions bored into her mind, but no answer revealed itself.

On the morning of March 30, Senator Laforge was listening to the English version of Radio Baghdad with Paul and Bakr. The Iraqi Information Minister al-Sahaf started the news with an important announcement. He reported that the Iraqi Revolutionary Command Council had made an important announcement that he would report on after he gave an overview of the status of the war. Baghdad Bob, as he was known to the troops started his overview of the war, "Americans are now in disarray. They are again in the dirt in the desert. They will try to enter Baghdad, and I think this is where their graveyard will be. Their objective is to get to the outskirts of Baghdad. So be it. We will see how the issue will turn out when they come to Baghdad. We are determined to defeat them and destroy them on the walls of our capital, as we are determined to destroy their miserable armies in every Muslim spot. Iraq will spread them even more and chop them up. The Iraqi troops and the Iraqi fighters are in control of all the places, as we have witnessed. They are retreating on all fronts. Their military effort is a subject of laughter throughout the world. No big change in that. The imperialist invading U.S. and British forces are like a snake that slithers all over the place, but that doesn't control anything." Then Baghdad Bob paused for a moment and informed his audience that he would now give important news from the Revolutionary Command Council, "A bounty of one million American dollars will be paid to any fighters or heroic sons of the Iraqi tribes who successfully captures or executes the American Senator Katherine Laforge. She has been found guilty of being a spy for the Americans and Israelis and of blasphemous statements against Islam. Katherine winced at this. Paul said, "This death sentence will probably help you in the polls as long as it goes no further than rhetoric. Just about anything Al-Sahaf says is bullshit. Like his statement, "They are trapped in Umm Qasr. They are trapped near Basra. They are trapped near Nasiriyah. They are trapped near Najaf. They are trapped everywhere." Paul laughed. "The guy is a loony toon!"

On April 1, Senator Laforge and her entourage joined Regimental Combat Team 7, 3rd Battalion, 4th Marines. She joined them as they rumbled toward the city of Ad Diwaniyah. Ad Diwaniyah was an important city situated in a riverine area about 20 miles west of a channel of the Euphrates River and about a hundred miles south of Baghdad. The city was reputed to be a command headquarters and stronghold of Fedayeen fighters.

As they approached Ad Diwaniyah, a city of half a million, tanks began being shot at by rocket-propelled grenades fired from behind some palm trees in front of an apartment complex. The attacks were more of an annoyance than a threat to the convoy, and the tanks continued to move until they reached a high mound from where they overlooked the enemy positions in the palm groves. Fedayeen fighters were hiding in "berms", crude holes dug out with bulldozers, where they fire and then take cover, hoping to conceal their location. Soon, like fireworks, sniper fire began to erupt from behind city buildings. Tanks replied with their .50-caliber weapons. Above the din of combat noises, many Iraqi civilians ignored the fighting and continued to mill around or go about their routine business.

Suddenly, they were mired in traffic, unable to move and as Katherine glanced out the window she saw an Iraqi woman waving at them with one hand while motioning desperately with the other to her mouth, begging for food.

Images or chaos passed before them in a flurry. A large city bus whipped around the traffic circle at high speed provoking concern and apprehension among the Marines. Tanks fired 120 mm shells into a factory. Eight men dressed in black, darted frantically from house to house. The Iraqi soldiers hiding in the berms began to sporadically expose themselves as they fired at the marines -one here, one there. Almost instantly Marine marksmen positioned on tanks facing the berm shot them. In the end the few Iraqi survivors waved white flags to surrender. Caches of weapons, including RPG's and other explosives were recovered from their fighting positions.

That evening Senator Laforge found a brief reprieve from the day's events listening to some very welcomed news. On BBC, Voice of America, FOX, and CNN the amazing rescue of PFC Jessica Lynch was retold with varying details. She had been taken hostage in the ambush of the 507th Maintenance Division a few days earlier. Conflicting tales surrounded her initial capture and now the rescue. Some said one of the ambushed sergeants jumped from his Humvee disregarding Iraqi gunfire to help PFC Lynch escape into his vehicle. Others claimed that PFC Lynch had resisted her attackers by unleashing hundreds of rounds of bullets from her M-16 rifle at them. Yet others reported that her weapon had jammed making her unable to defend herself. Even her wounds were reported differently by competing media outlets. Some claimed she had been shot, and another stated that she had been stabbed. Regardless of the terrible reporting by the media, her rescue was reason to celebrate.

The unit Katherine was now with headed toward the Tigris River, to cross a bridge at a juncture before meeting with RCT-1 on Route 7. Katherine's SUV weaved in and out of the long convoy of vehicles heading toward the city of An Nu'maniyah. This town was about 90 miles south of Baghdad. The approach to the city had been mostly uneventful. Many Iraqis stood on the side of the road and yelled Baghdad, Baghdad. Katherine felt that the Iraqi people often treated the marines as liberators instead of conquerors. If was very common to have people stop what they were doing and wave at us or give us a thumbs up. Iraqi children would salute the men in the convoy. Ten miles outside of An Nu'maniyah, they did engage a small force of dug in Iraqis who tried to stall the advancing convoy, but were quickly defeated.

The change of scenery was dramatic as they neared An Nu'maniyah. The new vista consisted of lush greens and palm groves spreading out into the fields surrounding the road leading to the town. The military used loudspeakers in the city to seek cooperation from the locals, but fighting raged regardless. Over forty tanks were involved in battles around the city and explosions could be heard throughout the day. Some factories and military training facilities were destroyed and continued to burn throughout the night. Numerous Iraqi armored vehicles and artillery pieces were also destroyed or captured. Katherine heard that about fifty Iraqi soldiers and fourteen Baath officials surrendered during the battles. In general, the residents seemed very cooperative, prompted probably by not wanting their homes, schools and Mosques destroyed. By the end of the day, RCT-5 crossed the bridge over the Tigris as they had hoped.

The next day the sprint toward Baghdad continued. RCT-5 commander got an order from Major General Mattis: "Go heavy kinetic all the way to Baghdad." With these orders, Colonel Dunford moved onto Route 6 and headed toward Baghdad. They did not have villagers lining the road cheering them on, but instead were fired at by Iraqis hiding in fields, behind buildings, and in the woods lining the road. There was much more resistance along Route 6. Another tactic used by the Iraqis was setting fire to trenches filled with kerosene or crude oil. This tactic blackened the sky and made driving a little more hazardous, but was of little consequence to their march to Baghdad.

The new pace of the campaign plus the heighten concern about gas attacks as they grew closer to Baghdad tired Kat considerably. She had also been in the same outfit for several days, and was conscious of how rank she had become. She supposed it should not bother her because this is a war zone, but it did, and it concerned her even more that it did. Kat was not as talkative as usual and Bakr could sense a slight tension in the silence. He tried to strike up a conversation with Kat, but at first she was unresponsive. "Bakr, these last few days have been life altering to me. It makes me ashamed that as humans we continue going about killing each other. We are still some primitive being going about destroying, killing raping and enslaving each other, just as we did thousands of years ago. It seems the one advance, we have accomplished is making killing as natural, unemotional and unmemorable as a bowel movement." Kat said.

"War and death affect all who experience it firsthand. You will make a much better President from what you have encountered here." Bakr replied.

"I certainly won't forget what I have seen here. The smell of death will never leave me. Its odor is a part of war that will linger with me, along with the visions of the many dead, I have witnessed."

In the distance you could hear the occasional sound of wolves and other wild dogs howling.

They raced through Al' Aziziyah and arrive at Tuwayhah, where the Marines took some heavy casualties. The fighting was fierce. They passed wrecked and burning Iraqi T-55s, T-62s, trucks and fuelers along the highway. Fedayeen fighters had cut fire trenches at intersections, filled them with oil, and lit them, to try and make movement more difficult. Columns of smoke rose above the city, but they did not really hamper the marines nor the CH-46s that swooped in to evacuate the wounded. At a field shock-trauma hospital, Kat saw a Marine sitting in a pool of his own blood. The man had not said anything about the seriousness of his condition, until he nearly fainted, and doctors rushed to help him up. They asked why he remained silent. He replied that the others were hurt far worse than he was.

The night of April 7th was alive with the sounds and visions of war. High in the Baghdad sky ghostly flares slowly descended. Their eerie light casting shadowy silhouettes of blacken war machines across the vista. Swirling smoke from the fires in Baghdad coalesced into an undulating glowing canopy rippling with flashing red lines from the tracers and artillery rounds slicing through it. This menacing thunderhead was like a black hole swallowing all light, even the dancing flares dropping from the sky. From within its darkness the dull thud of bombs reverberated as if a monstrous giant was stomping through the city.

It was rumored that the next day the marines escorting Kat would attempt to enter Southeast Baghdad by crossing the Diyala river. Baghdad was surrounded by coalition troops. They flowed around the outskirts of the city like the swirling waters of a flood; poking and prodding the city's perimeter for any openings. Some defenses had already crumbled and through them rumbled a tidal wave of armor and troops.

Kat felt emotions welling up inside her that she wanted to contain. The calm of the night had freed her mind from the constant thought of survival. A bottle of arrack with Bakr and her aide Paul Shermer had greatly diminished the effects of battle induce adrenaline that had masked much of the horrors of war. Now, unwelcomed visions entered her mind. She thought of where she was in Iraq. Wasn't this roughly the area where ComDefC1 was purportedly destroyed? The relief she had once felt about her twin's demise was gone and in its place was sadness. Seeing violent death first hand had softened the callousness she had once held. Haunting her now were the eternal stares of the blacken corpses entombed in the vehicle graveyard along Route 7. Who were all those people? Why do we do this to each other? Her emotions had to be contained. There was no one she could confine in about the emptiness she felt.

Katherine had come to view members of the military as the noblest Americans. They joined as innocent young men and women and slowly metamorphosed into the modern day warrior. Regardless of the rhetoric aimed at them, they are the saviors of our way of life. It is their blind faith in our nation and their unwavering perseverance in their missions that keeps our country a superpower. Although the blood and horror of combat quickly ebbs away their youthful immortality and innocence, a new reverence of life takes its place. Daily survival became God's gift and living takes on a much greater meaning.

In the early morning mist of April 8th the marines from RCT-5 rumbled toward the Diyala River. Their mission was to take control of Baghdad's Rasheed Airport. The route to the river was a macabre scene of rotting bodies littering the road juxtaposed to buildings festooned in colored lights casting carnival glows over old men sipping coffee. Katherine was surprised at the lack of panic displayed by civilians. If this scene was unfolding on the outskirts of Washington D.C. and hundreds of thousands of Islamic jihadists were encircling the burning capital and blasting it with rockets, mortars and slaying infidels, civilians would not be nonchalantly sipping coffee as they rumbled by. The outskirts would be deserted or hopefully a bastion of resistance. But here in Iraq, as the Coalition tanks and armor lumbered toward the Diyala River, people just watched, waved or quietly went about their business.

Katherine was closer than ever to the real action. The Marines a short distance from the Diyala River set up a temporary command post and this would become her vantage point for the upcoming battle. Katherine could feel the earth shake as sixty-seven tons Abrams tanks clanked by flattening anything in their path. As they neared the river's edge their co axial machine guns roared into action spewing out deadly burst of bullets across the Diayala River.

The north side of the river was heavily defended by Republican Guards, irregular forces, and foreign jidhadist. They fought from behind two story homes and small stores lining the river's edge. Some darted back and forth from date tree to date tree firing wildly at the marines on the south side of the river. They used mortars, artillery, RPGs, rifles and even donkey carts mounted with a crude rocket launcher to engage the marines.

Exploding artillery and cannon rounds shrouded the north side of the river with dark plumes of smoke. Massive displays of Marine firepower obliterated trees and buildings on the heavily defended far side. The Iraqi show of force was quickly decimated. By the afternoon of the 8th many marines were on the north side of the bridge and setting up a new perimeter.

The onslaught of fire either killed or caused members of the Republican Guard to retreat deeper into Baghdad. From within Baghdad Iraqis fired artillery at the marines crossing the Diyala River. Two marines were killed, but their death did not prevent the completion of the floating bridge and repairing a bridge bombed previously by the Iraqis to hinder entrance into the city.

It was strange being a part of this historic moment with troops that soon would attack Baghdad. The visions of Hulagu's army encircling the city centuries ago came to her mind. The similarities of that event and operation Enduring Freedom were many. The Shiites were remembered for assisting Hulagu's entry into the city and much help was given by the Shiites in this campaign. If Saddam Hussein had just left Iraq the war probably would have never happened and in 1258 if the caliph had left Baghdad and surrendered the city bloodshed would have been averted.

They rumbled into Baghdad at last with RCT-5 near the Dyala River. Artillery shells fire back at the military encampment while RCT-1 and RCT-7 charge into the center of the city. For days, precision-guided bombs from U.S. aircraft had pounded the city, weakening the Republic Guard strongholds and probably sparing many lives that would have been otherwise lost.

The various regiments engaged in a number of scattered firefights, but the most poignant and symbolic victory for the Coalition forces came on April 10. On this day the military seized Saddam's family palace-compound without a fight. The troops halted at Firdos Square. There, a six-meter high metal statue of Saddam Hussein with his arm upraised loomed above the traffic circle. His stance was reminiscent of Stalin, ruling with an iron fist. This is the man, Kat reminded herself, who would be Nebuchadnezzar, a man with an ego and ambition virtually unrivaled in the Middle East. This is the man who through intimidation was able to bring together the Sunnis and Shiites and breakdown many of the tribal customs. But some felt his evil surpassed his good and were glad to be rid of him.

Firdos Square was crowded with Iraqis that were attempting to knock over the statue of Saddam Hussein. A tank crew decided to help them and hooked two cables to the neck of the statue. The other ends of the cables were attached to a M-88 tank retriever. To the cheers and applause of the gathering Iraqis in the street -- and broadcast around the world -- the tank pulled away, toppling the statue of Saddam Hussein to the ground, in a moment that resonated with as much poignancy as the toppling of the Berlin Wall. Iraqi men quickly dragged Saddam's head along the street, with men and boys slapping it with their shoes. A man yelled, "Damn you, Saddam! Go to hell! Damn you, Saddam! Go to hell!"

A field hospital set up in one of the more secure areas near downtown Baghdad was staffed by both coalition and Iraqi doctors. It was one of the few positive happenings among many negatives that Baghdad could be proud of. Most of the patients were children and mothers. To insure media attention, the Iraqi medical staff had somehow convinced members of the Iraqi's Symphony Orchestra to visit and perform a few pieces. The military wanted to present a picture of normalcy, cooperation and promise for the visiting reporters, upper brass and politicians. They had even set up a table loaded with a selection of Iraqi dishes to cater to the dignitaries visiting the field hospital. On it was al maskoof a fresh water fish from the Tigris river, hummus, baba ganoush, tabbouleh, bamieh, Kubba, and the famous Iraqi kabab. They even had kubba hamiz, a famous Iraqi dish consisting of minced meat and minced rice stuffed with meat and spices, all in tomato sauce with chick peas, turnips, rice and other vegetables. They had a delicious dessert called min alsama, which Iraqis claimed is prepared only in their country. Kat's favorite was the Iraqi pickles made from cucumbers fermented in date vinegar and stuffed with parsley and garlic. While people mingled and sampled the epicurean delights, the music of Amr Diab played in the background. His songs were big hits in Iraq. They were mostly love songs that sounded very contemporary with a middle east flair. Bakr told Kat that Amr Diab was one of the biggest super stars in Iraq. Kat visited the field hospital section where the kids were being treated. After Amr's beautiful song called "Wahshteny" ended, some musicians from the Iraqi's Symphony Orchestra played "My Country," which brought tears to many in the mingling crowd. It is an intense haunting song that talks about reuniting everyone and healing wounds. It is a beautiful piece that ends with "Oh my beloved Iraq." being repeated.

As Senator Laforge with Bakr's help, talked to some of the wounded children, an Iraqi gentleman in a hospital smock walked toward her smiling broadly.

Bakr noticed him also and stepped out to greet him. "Is-salaamu alee-kum," Bakr offered. The gentleman glanced at Bakr quizzically and quickly replied, "Wa-aleekum is-salaam"

Paul had noticed his blood stained smock and guessed he was a doctor wanting to talk to them. In these trauma centers, doctors were like angels who volunteered their services and performed miracles with limited equip-ment and drugs. Paul sympathized with them and respected their devotion. "May I help you sir?" Bakr asked the Iraqi man. The doctor asked Bakr if that was Senator Laforge, he was accompanying.

Bakr answered in the affirmative.

Katherine glanced at him and he smiled broadly. In broken English, but very understandable he congratulated her on her escape and how wonderful she looked since he last saw her having plastic surgery at Ibn Sina Hospital. "You look much different than what I would have expected," he said. "But you have healed well Senator Laforge." Katherine felt herself go weak and without words as she realized who this man was, and what he was talking about.

"Do you remember me, Senator Laforge?" The man asked.

Katherine hesitated for what seemed like an eternity before she responded. "I have gone through a lot in the last few months and really do not remember …."

The doctor cut her off and said, "I will help you remember. Let me show you something to help you." He reached behind his back and struggled for a moment with something. Paul leaned toward Katherine to ask her who he was just as the Doctor's hand came back in view holding a gleaming pistol . Katherine froze as the man, with his smile stretched taunt across his face, stood there pointing the gun at her.

"Senator Katherine you are a deceiving American whore." For a moment longer the man stood there lost in his own world and then suddenly he yelled, "Allahu akbar!" — "God is great!"

Katherine found herself slammed to the ground as an explosion deafened the world around her. She thudded against the floor, her head snapping back hitting the tarmac hard. Blood sprayed into the air and fell like rain on her face soaking into her blouse. On the ground a puddle of blood widened. She could faintly hear people through the ringing in her ears, but her vision was just a red haze. Her head throbbed and she reached up blindly to it and felt her blood soaked hair. When she withdrew her hand, pieces of bloodied brain tissue was stuck to it.

Katherine tried her voice and a yell poured from her mouth. To her it sounded muffled and distant. She twisted her head and immediately felt gushers of warm blood hitting her face, and she knew she was dying. Somewhere in the fog of fear and the ringing in her ears she faintly heard Paul tell her, "Katherine lay still!"

She could feel her heart frantically beating to pump the blood through her body, and she wondered how much longer she would last. She wished she had spent more time with Ira and Lyndsey. There were many things she would love to say to them if they were by her side. The thought of dying, being forever extinct while the world kept spinning disturbed her even more. Kat did not want to die! She gasped another breath of tepid air into her lungs and felt her body quiver. It was then that she realized that she had also soiled herself, but it meant nothing to her as she laid still on the blood soaked ground. The next breath of air was the only thing that mattered to her now. Paul was there again and he was wiping her face with a wet rag. The gusher of blood had somehow stopped spraying on her face and as Paul wiped around her eyes the world came back into view for Katherine. She could see a surrounding crowd staring down at her and inches away a man sprawled on the ground with a smile spread across his face. In the middle of his forehead was a dark hole with blood trickling from it into the widening pool beneath the two of them. Paul and Bakr lifted Katherine from the floor while a squad of marines secured the position pushing back the onlookers.

"Katherine we need to leave, now." Bakr shouted in her ear.

Kat heard him and asked, "How bad am I?"

Bakr told her "You just have a bump on the head, and he is dead. Paul shot him before he could shoot you. But you need to get out of here before you are killed."

* * * *

That was Katherine's last day in Iraq. Within hours of that incident, she had been flown out of Baghdad on route to Houston, Texas. It was a time to celebrate for many of us who were behind her candidacy. When the news of her return flashed across the TV screens, millions waited to see how the government would receive her. She had broken some antiquated laws and some of her distracters were hoping that, they would fine her and remove her from office. Following her was also her death sentence that now was publicized even more due to the failed assassination attempt in Baghdad. The bounty was a lot that Saddam Hussein had placed on her head, and she was sure that others would be very interested in earning the million American dollars. Her return was going to be a big time for the media.

I heard a few gasp in the auditorium and looked up to see that everyone was staring at the television screens. A flurry of trumpets played introducing breaking news and then Senator Laforge's face flash on the screen.

PART TEN

Senator Laforge is Found

"We have come to be one of the worst ruled, one of the most completely controlled and dominated Governments in the civilized world no longer a Government by free opinion, no longer a Government by conviction and the vote of the majority, but a Government by the opinion and duress of a small group of dominant men". ~ Woodrow Wilson

I could feel my eyes fill with tears as the announcement was made that Senator Katherine Laforge had been located. In my heart, I had hoped that, she would survive. This was what I had prayed for, but then I wondered how she was. Suddenly, I realized that the damn news had not even said if she was alive or not. Someone did some channel searching and another broadcast came on and a few more details were revealed. She was alive. "Thank you Jesus." I had said then. She was tough and I just had a confident feeling that she was alive and well. She was destined to be President, I felt. Any woman who can traipse around a raging war zone and survive some crazy Iraqi doctor trying to assassinate her has her shit together. I remembered when she had returned from Iraq, she was so far more determined than I had ever imagined she would be. She had seen the carnage of war and smelled the stench of death first hand. She was invigorated with a new sense of direction and immediately went to work implementing plans to bring to the attention of the American public her views that our dependence on oil was the cause of this war and would result in many more violent confrontations as oil became less plentiful and needed by even more countries. Her exuberance was even undaunted by the plague of anti Laforge protests that she immediately encountered.

I had received an invitation from her campaign manager to attend her arrival ceremony at Andrews Air force Base. My wife and I were very honored to be on that special list of guests that was handpicked by Katherine and her staff. However, things were still confusing, and I was not even sure, if I should let Tom or Lance know that she was on her way home. Stacie and I just claimed we were going to visit friends back in Maryland and more or less that was true. A story a bit vague, but something most appeared to believe.

At Andrews Air Force Base, Senator Laforge and her entourage were welcomed by her new campaign manager, Frank Payne. Frank had been a long-time supporter of Senator Laforge and very instrumental in her previous Senatorial win. His acceptance in running her campaign was a huge relief to Kat. He had put her campaign back on track and actually turned the Iraq trip from a negative into a very big political plus. He was a very political savvy and effective manager that made things happen. He had just recently married a beautiful woman named, Diane Gager. She was a librarian back in his hometown.

Military security, a part of the 89th Air Wing had let a few Laforge well-wishers, and journalist into the reserved area for the plane. Mr. Payne hoped that most of them could be quickly skirted allowing the Senator's entourage to quickly escape to the waiting limousine.

The cheers and shouts of supporters and constant flashes of the photographers greeted the Senator as she debarked from the plane. She felt good to be back home again. For a woman who had been away for months she looked quite refreshed and energized.

Senator Laforge looked out at the group of people in the welcoming party and waved her hand for silence. As soon as the group settled down Kat started to deliver her speech.

"I want to thank all of you for coming out to welcome me home. It is a great relief to be standing on American soil again, with the ability to travel around without the constant threat of a bomb, mortar round, or sniper wielding instant death." Cameras snapped and a rumble of claps and cheers emanated from the crowd.

Senator Laforge continued, "I will remember my past few weeks with the troops as an unforgettable chapter in my life, where I observed heroism being displayed daily and witnessed the devotion, bravery, skill and professionalism that is the distinguishing characteristics of our troops. I want to express my sincere gratitude and admiration to all the brave American troops, who made my survival and ability to return back to the United States a reality. These are the men and women, who sacrifice over and over to make America and the entire world a more secure and humane place to live. The history of the war on terror will be filled with the stories of heroics of our troops who helped liberate one of the most important countries in the Middle East from the grips of a tyrant who victimized his own citizens and supported terrorism against others."

Katherine stopped and motioned to the troops who stood guarding the perimeter of the hanger. "These are our troops, they are great men and women who are not only subjected to the sacrifice of being away from their families, the constant threat of a suicidal enemy, but the belittling and chiding of elitist pundits here at home."

The well wishers all stood and cheered at this statement. Once the noise subsided, Katherine continued. "On my way back home I read about the President's visit to the USS Abraham Lincoln to express his gratitude to the sailors for a job well done. The President's visit to the Lincoln was a proper and fitting compliment to the Sailors and troops who are so deserving of our gratitude. The message was all, but loss by some very biased commentating degrading the President's tail-hook landing as an overpriced photo opportunity done to simply gander publicity. Let us not forget that four years ago the naval destroyer USS Briscoe, its command and sailors were appropriated as part of the ostentatious burial at sea of the civilian JFK junior. It is the acts of these selfless individuals in our arm forces that allow elitists the liberty to create royalty out of fantasy and with impunity belittle the acts of those who give the ultimate sacrifice to maintain our way of life." This statement evoked more applause.

Katherine had to motion for silence, so she could continue. "My exposure to the realities of war, the smell of death, the constant fear of impending doom and the disturbing lack of appreciation by so many of our citizens and Iraqis for the sacrifice of our soldiers galvanized my views even more that we must find ways to wean ourselves from the need to maintain relations with countries whose government or citizens seek our destruction. We as a country must strive to make our country energy self-reliant, so bowing to foreign powers will no longer be a necessity." Katherine stopped and took a sip of water.

"After witnessing a nation at war, I look forward to the challenge of leading this country into a more secure existence where the savagery of people in distant lands will not affect the lives of our citizens. I hope that the horrors that I witnessed in Iraq will make me stronger and more driven to solve the staggering problems of our country's addiction to foreign oil and our abusive antiquated tax system. We need a cure for our OPEC dependence before we are destroyed by the weight of this huge tax on our economy, and we need a new tax system that taxes all, but does not subject us to abuse and intrusion into our lives. It is time we put aside our trivial pursuits and calmly, confidently begin to find our bearings, correct our mistakes, and take aim at our most pressing national goals: energy self reliance and a fairer tax system."

"Ladies and Gentlemen, Thank you again for welcoming me back."

Smiling and waving at her admirers, Katherine Laforge was ushered out of the hanger to an awaiting limo.

Now it would be family time for a day or two, a time to reconnect with her husband, daughter and even her four cats. She looked forward to seeing them and her friends in Houston, Texas. She knew in just a couple of days she would be back in Washington answering lots of questions about lots of issues. A day she did not look forward to.

As Senator Laforge's motorcade crept down the exit road from Houston International Airport, hundreds of protesters, including some carrying flag-draped coffins, lined the streets chanting and yelling obscenities at her as she drove by. The protest was the largest ever staged against her. She felt confused by their blatant hatred and anger that they demonstrated toward her. The protest included stilt-walkers, drummers, people with painted faces, placard waving teenagers, groups of students holding banners against the WTO, the Iraq War and even the existence of Senator Laforge. Some signs showed pictures of Senator Laforge with a bull's eye on her head, and some proclaimed her a hate monger and religious bigot. Behind all the hate and outrage a carnival atmosphere prevailed with protestors drinking beer, getting high and challenging one another to be the most obnoxious.

Senator Laforge's motorcade emerged from the protesters splattered with various colored paints, vegetables, eggs and other debris. Kat was unscathed, but perplexed over this mob of hatred.

Frank Payne recognized Kat's utter confusion and her disbelief that she had been in a country torn apart by war and now in her own country, she was again threatened by those who disliked her or those who idolized others who professed their dislike for her. As they drove south on 59, Frank Payne told Senator Laforge that her husband and daughter were waiting at the Lancaster Hotel to reunite. It would be impossible to go home now because another group of protestors had converged in front of her house. Police in riot gear who had erected steel barriers protected her house and her neighbor's residences. The police were on one side of the barrier and the protesters milled about on the other side. They consisted of boisterous teenagers and some college students who were on edge. A small number of older political activists participated and tried to maintain a calm.

About 30 minutes after Kat landed in Houston, police were reporting a segment of the protest group were hurling sticks and bottles over the steel barrier. After police arrested a protester in front of their "fence line," a fight broke out. The individual had damaged a car and tried to start a fire. In protest of the arrest, the crowd surged causing the police to use pepper spray and rubber bullets to disperse them. The Houston police provided the protestors with a degree of freedom to express themselves, but many of them were intent on causing property damage and the inability of others to use the street.

As her limousine glided along the freeway toward downtown Houston, mental images of the angry protestors, her cheering supporters and her Iraqi experiences tumbled about in her mind. It was a darkness she wanted to leave behind her. The anticipation of seeing her husband and daughter make her even more restive. As they exited onto McKinney Street, familiar sights welcomed her back. A huge sign advertising "The Trip to Bountiful" starring Jean Stapleton at the Alley Theatre till May 10th caught her eye. This was the Houston theater district, where she had visited often to enjoy a play, ballet, symphony or an opera with her family. The sight of the Hobby Center, Alley Theatre, the soaring Chase Tower and familiar sidewalks unimpeded by protestors or her supporters calmed her. She actually felt a refreshing sense of anonymity envelope her. The limo turned right at Texas Ave and pulled up to the entrance of a 13 story European looking hotel replete with multinational flags and distinctive burgundy awnings. She looked out the limo's window at the Lancaster Hotel's stately brass and beveled-glass front doors, somewhat hoping to see her husband and daughter, but only a smiling doorman awaited her.

Within seconds of the limo parking, two more men appeared at the hotel's entrance. One was a sharply uniformed valet who immediately took care of the Senator's luggage and the other man was Mr. Murry the hotel's concierge. With a welcoming smile, Mr. Murry said, "I am here to make your stay at the Lancaster Hotel a pleasant one. He offered Senator Laforge his card. Your family is anxiously waiting for you in the presidential suite. He continued, "Anything I can do to make your stay more comfortable at the Lancaster, please call me. I will be most happy to assist you." He pointed to across the foyer, "That is the elevator to the Presidential Suite. I think you will find some very excited people waiting for you there."

Frank escorted her as she rode the elevator to the 12th floor of the Lancaster. "Frank, do you think they are going to recognize me when they see me?" Frank did not reply, but just looked at her inquisitively and smiled. While in Iraq her hair had become a silvery gray and the CIA agents insisted she maintain the disheveled look until she returned back to the states. Without access to a beauty parlor, that was easy to do. She did not feel like the elegant Senator that she was when she started her campaign.

The elevator door opened and Frank still smiling at Kat said, "They will know you! See you tomorrow morning."

Outside the presidential suite, Senator Laforge uttered one deep shuddering breath as she quelled her anxiety and then knocked softly on the huge oak door. Almost instantly she heard the click of the latch and the door swung open. Ira and Lyndsey stood in the doorway, their beaming faces assured her that she was recognizable. The second she stepped into the room, she was locked in Ira's embrace. On her back, she felt the caress of her daughter's hands and heard Lyndsey murmur "I'm so happy you're back mom." This was the moment she had longed for, the feel of her husband's arms around her, to see the smile of her daughter, and to hear their voices. She trembled uncontrollably as Ira kissed her neck. For a long moment, they stood locked together, and then she broke away from her husband's passionate embrace and looked down into her daughter's tear-filled eyes. She pulled Lyndsey towards her, brushed a stray lock of hair from her moist eyes and gently kissed her. She felt beautiful again and loved.

It was a fantastic feeling being home the first night. She listened to Lyndsey telling her all that she had missed while away. For a few minutes, she played with their cats that Lyndsey had smuggled into the room. Later she talked to Ira about how much she had missed him and some of the tragedy, she had witnessed in Iraq. The conversation was difficult at times and Kat told him they would talk about it later. She felt a bit guilty that she was now safe with her family, and for those that she had become so much a part of were still in harm's way. She prayed that they would stay safe and make it home alive. She had developed a great empathy for the frightening emotions that our soldiers live with as they perform under the constant threat of death that plagues their every moment. She knew this experience would never go away, it would be in her memories and heart for the rest of her life.

The day quickly faded away and Senator Laforge welcomed the first night in bed with her husband after almost two months of separation.

At 8 am the following morning Katherine sat in a large overstuffed chair in the living room of her Suite and looked out over the city of Houston. She felt rested and hoped she could get a good day of work toward moving her campaign forward. The city spreading out in front of her reminded her that Houston, the onetime capital of the oil empire was still a giant in the energy game. It was still a major hub for the energy barons boasting headquarters for billion dollar companies like Halliburton, Shell Oil, and Conoco. According to the morning paper's headlines, her return coincided with Houston annual Offshore Technology Convention with seventy five thousand attendees. She hoped that Houston and Texas would embrace the needed changes to maintain their roles in the pageant of history as energy leaders.

She glanced at the paper, while she nursed a cup of coffee. The major stories were about the execution of Roger Vaughn, for a 1991 robbery and slaying, the blight of prostitution in the Houston neighborhood just off the Southwest Freeway, protecting Baghdad University from attacks by rebels and an article comparing the insurgency in Iraq to the bloodletting period following the end of the Civil War. This article intrigued her. It chronicled the anniversary of the May 8th, 1865, raid on a Georgia storehouse by a band of four hundred former confederate soldiers. The raiders carried away or destroyed all the contents of the depot. The post Civil War years deteriorated into widespread riots, looting, gang arsons, group beatings and killings of Yankee collaborators. There was a disturbingly similar parallel to the mayhem now happening in occupied Iraq. Rampant crime didn't exist in Saddam's era nor did it in the pre Civil War south. But the dissolution of the governments and armies of the vanquished triggered a period of bloody mayhem following both wars. A year after the end of the civil war, the headlines continued to emphasize the terrible atrocities, robberies, rapes, lynchings, and murders spreading across the south just as the media now focuses on the hideous acts of post war Iraq. The civil war insurgents evolved as the Ku Klux Klan. In its infancy it was a harmless fraternal organization, but quickly became the invisible army of the white south that eventually became notorious for its public hangings, shootings, lashings, rapes, acid brandings, and castrations. The similarities between the two insurgencies were many, hiding behind mask, preying upon civilians, and using religious scripture to justify their actions. The post civil war insurgency went on for many years. Katherine wondered how long and bloody the Iraq's insurgency would be, but her thoughts were interrupted by Ira as he entered the room and planted a kiss on her neck.

"Good morning, Sweetheart!" He murmured.

"This is a good morning!" Katherine turned her head and met his eyes.

"I am anxious to get the show on the road. Frank should be here by now shouldn't he?

"He is on the way up now." Ira responded.

Just as Katherine got up to get herself another cup of coffee, the doorbell rang.

It was Frank. The three of them got comfortable in the living room with coffee and pastries as Katherine started to outline the day's business.

"Before we hit the campaign trail, I would like to visit with some of the most knowledgeable and respected individuals on the subject of alternative energy. I think you should contact those who could help our cause and invite them to visit with us here in Houston or in Washington. Let them know we would even be amendable to visit them, if they cannot get away. It would be nice to see a larger variety of alternative energy implementations anyway."

Frank Payne responded, "Well, I am glad you feel that way, because I just happen to have a gentleman from your home state that I think can answer many of our questions on one form of alternative energy, biodiesel."

"And who is that?"

"Professor Briggs from the University of New Hampshire. He is a researcher that has written an insightful paper called 'Wide Scale Biodiesel Production from Algae,' it seems to be a serious roadmap on how our foreign oil habit can be kicked by biodiesel produced from Algae."

"Have you read his study?" Katherine asked.

"Yes I have and I was very impressed with it. I have also researched him on the Internet and found his ideas are quoted by various groups involved in biodiesel and alternative energy." Payne replied.

"So when do we meet him?"

"Well, it just so happens he is here in the Lancaster for the day. So what about meeting him for a discussion over late lunch?" Payne answered.

"Good that will give us time to go over a few other candidates that I want us to meet and get them behind our team. I have read about a woman named Judy Treichel with the Nevada Nuclear Waste Task Force. She seems to be a well known authority on the problems with nuclear waste disposal and for years she has represented those opposing Yucca Mountain as a national waste dump for everyone's radioactive garbage." Katherine made a note before she continued.

"I would also like to get together with Congressman Nick Lampson. He shares our desires to become less dependent on foreign oil. He has some great plans for getting farmers being paid not to produce certain crops to have them grow soybeans or other biodiesel yielding crops. We need to nail down a meeting with him to view his Safuel facility here in Houston. It is supposed to be a much safer version of biodiesel." Katherine quipped.

The meeting dragged on for another hour and finally Senator Laforge suggested they quit for the morning and work on their individual list of experts in the alternative energy and National Sales Tax areas. They would reconvene for a late lunch in the Lancaster restaurant at 2 pm with Professor Briggs and Congressman Nick Lampson.

Kat's list of experts and political allies in the energy or tax policies grew longer and longer. Their names made her feel more confident that her priorities were correct. She had found political allies on her National Sales Tax agenda in all political parties. The need now was to create a grass-roots galvanization of citizens that pressure their elected representatives in Congress to support the National Sales Tax issue.

At 2 p.m. precisely, Kat, Ira and Frank walked into the Lancaster restaurant. The place was empty except for a young man sipping coffee on the far wall. The trio sat down in a large booth, ordered some coffee and patiently waited for the arrival of the professor and Congressman Lampson. While waiting, they exchanged lists of the experts they had culled to assist them in the energy and tax issues. Before anyone could discuss the list, Nick Lampson appeared at the entrance. His eyes immediately locked on their party and a smile lit up his face as he approached their table. He had served as a Texas Congressman since 1997 and had a strong background in biology. Kat had heard his reputation as a man of character and conviction, which were the type of leaders she hoped to use to bridge the chasm between Republicans and Democrats. She was looking for leaders who were uniters, not dividers.

Ten minutes passed and Kat was now chiding Frank that his expert did not seem to know how to tell time. While they were waiting, Ira was fielding calls from various news organizations that wanted quotes and interviews with the Senator. As he got off the last call, he said to Katherine that it would be better if he returned to their room and provided the press with some news coverage of her return. The constant phone calls would be a distraction during their business with Lampson and Briggs, and it was equally important that they maintain a good rapport with the press.

After Ira left the restaurant, other individuals entered, but they were groups or couples who did not seem to be looking for anyone. Kat saw Frank's eyes lock on to something behind her. He murmured quietly, "We have company, I think." A young man in his twenties moved to the table and asked if this was Senator Laforge's table? "Who are you?" Frank replied.

"I am professor Briggs." Kat realized he was the young man they had seen sitting alone when they first entered.

Frank stood and welcomed Briggs to the table. "Is this seat okay?" Briggs asked motioning to a seat opposite the Senator.

"Of course." Senator Laforge quickly replied.

Once they were all seated, Senator Laforge commented to Professor Briggs, "I had never expected a professor so young. And I am sure you were looking for a Katherine Laforge that looked a bit closer to the person in the campaign posters. I have to apologize that I have not had time to transform myself into her, since I returned from Iraq."

"I hope you are enjoying your stay here at the Lancaster." Kat said rhetorically, "You know that Mr. Payne asked you here to give your perspective of the biodiesel's chance of being our replacement for overseas petroleum imports. Will it really work? So, please tell me all about biodiesel produced by algae." Katherine queried as she smiled at Briggs.

Briggs leaned over the table and said, "I hope that what I have to tell you will be something that you can see as a major answer to our energy dilemma. I have great faith in it as a way to end our reliance on foreign oil, but I know many will argue against this solution for various political reasons. Basically, Senator, biodiesel produced from algae is the most economical and self sustaining solution available for producing a replacement for foreign oil. It can be produced on land that is of no value for food crops so it doesn't affect food production and their prices. It is fast growing and needs very little care. It can help decrease our co2 problem and its production can actually be tied into absorbing the co2 created from coal burning power plants." Mr. Briggs took a sip of his coffee and met Katherine's stare.

"How much better is it from the other options we have to create biodiesel?" Katherine asked.

"Well compared to other alternatives that are currently being used to produce biodiesel, algae makes them all look ridiculous. For example, soybean is the most commonly used plant to make biodiesel and it only produces 40 gallons of biodiesel per acre per year. You have an algae farm in west Texas right now that can produce twenty thousand gallons per acre per year, which obviously makes it a much better way to produce biodiesel. Senator, literally and figuratively biodiesel from algae is the mother lode of green fuels."

Frank Payne asked, "How much do you think it would cost to create enough production facilities to replace or seriously reduce the use of foreign oil?"

Professor Briggs looked pensive and then said, "It would be a few hundred billion dollars to get this method of fuel production up and running to the point it could completely replace our need for foreign oil.

"You are saying that could completely replace our foreign import of oil?" Lampson asked.

"Absolutely! The cost would be less, if we created more facilities like Glen Kertz's place, near El Paso. His facility is the one that I mentioned produces 20 thousand gallons per acre per year using a vertical system, which grows the algae in long rows of moving plastic bags. The bags are transparent so this method exposes the algae to more sunlight and allows for greater production than simply using the surface of the pond."

Biodiesel from algae is probably the best possible candidate to replace fossil fuels as our primary transportation energy source. And that's because it is a renewable fuel that can replace petro-diesel in current engines and transported and sold using today's infrastructure, if Big Oil companies allowed it. A few fuel stations are making biodiesel available to consumers, and more and more large transportation fleets use a proportion of biodiesel to fulfill their fuel needs.

Lampson questioned him about the scale of some of the various production facilities? Are you familiar with Kent Batman's biodiesel facility in Hardin County, Texas that makes his fuel from rice bran, sunflower seeds, flax and cottonseed?

"No, I am not." Replied Briggs.

"Well, really my question is how difficult is it getting EPA approval for these small refineries?"

Frank answered for him, "From my experience, the EPA can be a major obstacle to biodiesel producers. It appears that the tentacles of Big Oil have reached out and complicated approvals to where they are virtually impossible unless you have tremendous legal and financial resources. Things will get even tighter, because some Big Oil lobbyist are proposing laws to prohibit even those who make biodiesel for their own use from used cooking oil."

The discussion of various alternative energy methods continued for about another hour and then Briggs excused himself, because of another engagement. Lampson also decided it was time to leave so only Katherine and Frank were left there sipping coffee.

Almost as soon as Briggs and Lampson exited the restaurant, a man with a briefcase walked toward their table. He was a rotund, pale face man in his fifties. Smiling broadly he exclaimed, "Senator Laforge!" in a tone as if they were old friends. Katherine could not recognize him, but his demeanor appeared harmless. Frank Payne stood up and said, "Hello, I am Frank Payne the Senator's campaign manager. I am sorry, but I don't believe I recognize you."

"That is understandable, Mr. Payne, because until today, I have never had the privileged of meeting you or Senator Laforge. We do however move in the same circles, and I am very impressed with the verve of the Senator's campaign. My name is Donald Hill, and I wanted to chat with the two of you about your campaign and see if I could be of some assistance. I represent some very influential people with great financial means who would very much like to see Senator Laforge elected. I hope you can give me the courtesy of a few minutes to express my clients concerns and offer."

Frank hesitated and then beckoned Mr. Hill to sit down. "So who do you represent, Mr. Hill?"

He pulled up a chair and sat down opposite Katherine and placed his pudgy hands on the table's surface. A contemplative look replaced the smile, and he replied, "Well, I represent various companies involved in the energy industry. I guess you could call me a career lobbyist. I know some look down at my profession, but I think you both would agree that we are as instrumental in making laws and keeping those big government wheels turning as most elected officials. Anyway, I think I have the ability to give your campaign one hell of a cash infusion." He declared with a toothy smile.

"What part of the energy industry are you with?" Katherine asked.

"Good question." Hill cleared his throat, "I think I have read that you call it Big Oil. I represent most of the biggest producers of petroleum products being sold here in America. In the 2000 election, Senator, one of my clients contributed more than four million dollars to help worthy individuals get elected."

"Mr. Hill, I am sure you are aware of my desires of cutting our shackles to foreign oil, and I know you realize I have voted against every bill providing your associates with the roughly $113 billion in yearly federal subsidies. So why would you think I could or would accept any funds from those that get rich from us being dependent on foreign oil?"

"Senator, Senator, we see the same things, but just from different perspectives. My clients would love to be in the alternative energy business, but they have stockholders to appease, serious obligations to leaders in many countries and billions invested in a business that is making more money than it has ever made. So why would they do something to kill the golden goose?"

"The golden goose cannot live much longer, and while it does it is robbing Americans of their money. And you didn't answer my question why you would be here talking to me about supporting my campaign."

"Well Senator, we think it would look good for our industry's image to put a few millions into your bid for the presidency. A woman running for President backed by Big Oil would say we are working out our differences. It would be good for both of us, and frankly Senator your vision of making any dent in our market share is hopeless. We have your colleagues promoting worthless alternative energy programs that are so ineffective that they will do nothing more than anger consumers. We have helped promote methods like the production of biodiesel from soybeans and ethanol from corn, which is about as effective as attempting to cut down a forest with a plastic knife."

"Mr. Hill, I'm totally aware of the futility of our current programs, but my administration would produce biodiesel from algae that is absolutely doable and financially feasible. We will also promote the use of solar and wind to produce electricity."

"That is a great plan, but by the time you could get elected and get anyone to even listen to your ideas my colleagues will have the price of diesel so high that no one will own or want to buy a diesel vehicle. The market will just be a bunch of big rig redneck truckers who will just keep buying our product because we won't let biodiesel into our pumps. And as far as wind turbines and solar energy goes, we have enough members of congress on our side to stop any projects that we want killed. Look at the Cape Cod wind energy project our friends in high places have totally stopped. The truth is Senator you will have to work with congressional members like that. Power hungry pompous blowhards that don't do shit for their constituents, but with our money keep getting re-elected."

"So, Senator your election would not hurt us at all because we have so many friends in congress that your pet bills would not pass unless we approve them."

A red faced Frank Payne pointedly said, "Mr. Hill, I am sure you already know that Senator Laforge could not accept any contributions from your group, so we really are just wasting each other's time. I do thank you for your candor, but we both know we have nothing in common and any association with your companies would hurt our campaign. So, Mr. Hill I think our conversation is over." Frank stood up to bid Mr. Hill good-bye.

Mr. Hill stayed seated momentarily and then with a wry smile began to rise, "Frank, Katherine, I think you need to think more about this because you are dealing with an industry that has more money than most countries and supports enough of congress that your interference is not just a threat to profits, but also to your national power structure. I am sure you have read the story of Pinocchio. Remember wicked Honest John and his companion Gideon, who work for the evil puppeteer, Stromboli. Well, you have many Honest Johns and Gideons in your midst so be careful or Stromboli will be pulling your strings for free."

With that he picked up his briefcase and walked toward the exit. At the exit, he turned, waved and mouthed "See you soon!" and then exited.

"That was an interesting meeting," Katherine said. "What in the hell did he mean by his Pinocchio statement?"

"He means to divide us and make us paranoid. Between threats, telling us how hopeless our cause is and planting the seed of distrust between all of us in hopes of destroying us."

"So Frank, was this just a chance to threaten us before we get things rolling or do you think they actually thought we would be interested in their offers?"

"I think it was both. But the whole thing is more of a threat than anything else. Katherine, enough talk. This is your first day back, go upstairs and spend some time with Ira and your daughter. Tomorrow is another day and we will do better if we have some time to digest some of what we have discussed."

"And I am sure you need to spend some quality time on the phone with your new wife." Katherine said as she winked at Frank.

She felt a bit of relief as she stood in front of her hotel room door. It was her first day back working on her campaign, and she saw a ray of hope again. She opened the door and walked into her suite. She froze as she saw a blond hair woman standing over her husband holding a pair of pointed scissors. Their eyes met and Katherine tried to rush to her, but her braced leg prevented any speed. Suddenly, Ira said "It's time for you to start looking Presidential. I called Felicia and begged her to come and get you looking like your old self again."

"Felicia, I'm shocked to see you. How have you been?"

"Well, Senator, I think it's more like what has been happening in your life. My life has changed a bit since I last saw you. I now have my own hair salon in Beaumont, Texas called Felicia's Studio West, and I am doing quite well."

"That's fantastic, Felicia. I always thought you would have your own place. This is wonderful that you came. Do you think you can really salvage any of this rat's nest?" Katherine tousled her hair with her hand.

"Senator, your husband asked me to come here and give you a makeover and that is what I intend to do. When we are done, you will look beautiful and very Presidential."

"I think you have the makings of a politician, with big promises like that."

"Katherine, sit down and relax," Ira said, "and let her get going so she can get home before midnight."

"I am so excited to help you, Senator." Felicia smiled as she unfolded a smock to cover Katherine. "Since the last time I cut your hair, I have been worrying about you. I can't imagine how hard it was for you in Iraq. Now, please sit back and close your eyes, while I work."

Katherine obliged, and as she relaxed, she thought how wonderful it was to have a husband so thoughtful to have arranged for her favorite hair stylist, Felicia to come to the hotel to give her a makeover. She loved him.

The next few weeks were a flurry of meetings with various groups. Katherine met with congressional groups, grass roots organizations, union representatives and others that could give her a better vision of the direction she needed to take to get elected. During the same period, Ira had commissioned a ghostwriter to draft her book detailing her Iraq experiences. She now had the fun of constantly recording tapes of her experiences for the book while trying to assemble a campaign team that exuded confidence and professionalism. But all this was necessary if she wanted to win the election.

Finally, the real campaign trips began. Frank Payne had scheduled Kat to appear on July 15th at a very interesting event in Round Rock, Texas. It was the start of the Dell-Winston Solar Car Challenge, a 1500-mile race with competitors from Colorado, New York, Indiana, Mississippi and Mexico. The Round Rock, Texas to Cocoa Beach, Florida race is unique, because the solar powered cars are designed, constructed and driven by high school students. It's a great spotlight on renewable energy and helps educate the public to the potential of solar power. It was an event that expressed Senator Laforge's deep-seated belief, that the sun could provide much of our energy needs.

On a warm overcast Tuesday morning, Senator Laforge was introduced to a frantic Danny Lantrip and Keith Reese who were busy trying to assure that the Houston, Mississippi team was up to the challenge. Kat's campaign manager had read about their team's inspiring accomplishments and had relayed the Senator's admiration of their successes. Her pro solar power stand won her a personal invitation to accompany their team on the race circuit.

An odd looking vehicle stood In front of her, stretching out about seventeen feet and standing four feet high. Perched on top was a six-foot wide solar panel resembling a magic cape flowing out behind the seven hundred pound car. The solar vehicle was named Sundancer, and was the car that all the other teams would target to beat. At its controls sat Cody Spenser, who would drive it the first leg of the race.

The threat of Claudette, a category 1 hurricane swirling off the Texas coast had intensified the normal race jitters. The news had reported that its 80-mile an hour winds had spawned dangerous waterspouts in the choppy waters near Galveston. The National Hurricane Center (NHC) was predicting five to eight inches of rain in affected areas. Another looming problem for the race, was a huge dust cloud from the Sahara Desert that was hovering over Texas causing hazy skies. The dust cloud was driven by the same easterly trade wind that carried Claudette to the Texas coast. These two phenomena had the potential of shutting down the Dell-Winston Solar Car Challenge. For the time being, however the treat had energized the event, increasing the level of excitement for the teams and viewers.

A team of 8 students headed by Mandy Davis raced Sundancer. The team consisted of four girls Mandy, Sherrie Springer, Jessica Sykes, Angel Kilgore and four boys Justin Black, Jesse Lal, Matt Mangrum, and Cody Spenser. The students, this morning, were all on edge. This event marked the pinnacle of their life and each felt their share of competitive anxiety. Much could happen in this eight-day odyssey giving any of the four competing vehicles a chance to beat them. The Solar Stealth from Columbus, Indiana and the Sol Machine V from Newburgh, New York, however, were their biggest concerns. They felt that these machines had superior design and posed their biggest threat.

Kat was feeling troubled also. Recently, she had started receiving disturbing "Hello Kat" phone calls and then silence. They always registered private on her caller ID. The voice was always a woman, and she thought it was the same voice each time. No threat, just a simple 'Hello Kat' and then silence. That horrible sensation in her stomach was back. Maybe it was the call, or maybe it was a fear that she was exposing others to something more than they had bargained for when they invited her to their race. The rhetoric and protest against her were becoming much more hostile as her campaign gained momentum and her views taken more seriously by voters. She hoped her presence at this student event would not be marred by protest or worst. This was their event and she wanted to be as inconspicuous as possible, just another spectator.

Despite the menacing hurricane and the Sahara Dust Cloud darkening the Texas sky, a large crowd had gathered waiting for the race to begin. Sundancer would start the event. At precisely 9 AM, the green flag descended and Sundancer whined away from the starting line. Its destination was Palestine, Texas 161 miles away. Fifteen minutes later, all five solar cars were scurrying along 79 to Route 84. People lined the route to see these apparitions of the future. Some resembled a Jetson bubble car while others had the alien look of a Star War's creation. But these vehicles were real, not movie props or inventions of big industry, but the realizations of teenagers unfettered by the politics of profit. Their creations were a window into a tomorrow of new energy innovation.

Senator Laforge and Frank Payne in their rented Honda Hybrid joined the caravan of vehicles trailing the five solar cars buzzing down Route 79. Local news crews lined the road reporting the minute-to-minute action of the event and describing in detail the solar cars and the teams behind them. The five schools and 50 students plus involved in the event provided many interesting stories showcasing education and youth with character. For the national networks, with their penchant for the morose, good news is not news and their school related news of the day became the death of a sixteen-year-old Dallas, Texas high school student who shot and killed himself on campus.

The competition was fierce, with each team trying to log as many miles as possible in the shortest amount of time. The Sundancer struggled to maintain its lead position and behind them the Solar Stealth followed like a foreboding shadow. The day was hot and the small cockpits were stifling under the Texas sun. By mid afternoon, with miles and miles behind them, the perspiring drivers with their eyes stinging from sweat had the town of Palestine, Texas finally in view. As the sun-powered vehicles whizzed into town, they were welcomed by curious looks and excited kids who were enthralled to see these colorful strange contraptions.

After 161 sweltering miles, the evening's top priority for the exhausted team members was the removal of sweat soak clothes, refreshing showers, meals, and rest. For some, sleep would elude them as they lay in bed, eyes wide open speculating on their team's probable placement and watching a swollen orange moon creeping slowly across their window. Tuesday's results would not be announced until the following morning at 8 AM, when the judges would report their observations and any penalty miles assessed against a team for infractions of race rules.

The same night, Senator Laforge was taking in the quaintness of the Wiffletree Inn. Frank Payne picked this lodging because it was famous for its ghostly apparitions. The low orange moon cast another dimension of eeriness to the two-story house built in 1911. The ghost haunting 1001 N. Sycamore Street was said to have appeared as a filmy apparition descending the staircase and expressing itself with a tirade of door slamming upstairs. Frank did not believe in ghosts, but found the stories entertaining. What he really liked was the Wiffletree's promise of a homemade breakfast of eggs benedict, freshly baked bread and coffee.

Senator Laforge looked forward to a relaxing shower, meal and hopefully good news on her campaign progress. She was not particularly thrilled that she was staying in the only haunted Bed and Breakfast in Palestine, Texas. Her main goal was to stay focused on the immediate problems and the progress of her campaign.

Frank Payne did have some good news for her, but along with it a bit of bad news. The good news was private citizen contributions to her campaign were drastically up. Her campaign coffers were also receiving money from alternative energy companies that would benefit from her election. Contributions now totaled in the millions yet trailed her opponents. The best news was that Libertarians were seeing her as the most viable candidate representing their views of the two major parties.

"Now the bad news!" Frank Payne grimaced as he spoke. "A large protest by "Citizens Against Sales Tax" led by some big name Hollywood stars have planned to stage a protest in Macon, Mississippi on Saturday. The latest we have on it is that pro oil and nuclear energy groups are being bussed in also.

Large donations from oil industry, nuclear energy companies, lawyer associations and the Hollywood crowd are providing a media blitz about how your sale's tax will ravish many businesses that survive solely because of special tax breaks. Hollywood claims that their industry will suffer immensely because movie tickets will cost more and movies will be more expensive to produce because of loss tax breaks.

It is really sad that the greed of a handful of Hollywood elitist would trash an event that these kids have put so much into and their communities have supported so well.

Well, that is four days away. I want to get more information on it before we make any decisions.

Wednesday morning a ground mist hovered over the Palestine High School's parking lot. It rippled like a ghostly veil around the shimmering metallic vehicles. By 8 am the five solar cars were joined by their respective teams. Some members busied themselves wiping away the tiny crystal like droplets that sparkled on the solar panels. Others just gazed attentively at the assembled judges. Wispy tendrils of mist spiraled about them, as they anxiously waited for the results of the previous day's race, Finally, the presiding judge held a list in his hand and asked for everyone's attention. An instant hush fell over the group. The judge glared down at the list and started reading what everyone had been waiting to hear. The results of yesterday's race are as follows: Fifth place position. "Chamizal Solar Car Team." In fourth place was the Colorado team "Sunshine Mountain Traveler."

Now the knots in the stomach of the Houston team were tightening. They knew that the race had to have been tight, and they could really be in virtually any of the remaining positions.

The Judge read off, "Third place is "Hudson Valley Solar Car Team"
Now it was between Houston and their archrival the "Solar Stealth"
Who would be read next….?

The judge looked up at the teams and announced that the two remaining spots were only less then eighteen miles apart in their overall score. A very close race at this point. Another long pause as he looked out at the competitors. "Ladies and Gentlemen second place goes to Solar Stealth."

The ecstatic yelling of the Houston team drowned out the announcement that they were now in first position.

By 9 am, the sun had melted away the mist and Sundancer stood waiting for the fall of the green flag to start the race. The solar cars would race from Palestine, Texas to Natchitoches, Louisiana a 171 miles journey. They would follow US 84 and pass through the towns of Maydelle, Rusk, Reklaw, Mount Enterprise, and two towns Tex Ritter immortalized, Timpson and Tenaha, Texas in his 1950 song "Tenaha, Timpson, Bobo, and Blair" . At Tenaha, Texas they would cross over the Sabine River and be in the Pelican state about halfway to Natchitoches.

After the last vehicle disappeared from sight, Senator Laforge and Frank Payne hurried back to the parking lot for their rented car. They would be trailing the Houston Team and wanted to be as close to the Sundancer as possible. Just as Senator Laforge reached the gate of the lot, her cell phone rang. She looked at it with a bit of trepidation and was relieved when she saw that the call registered a real number. The call was from Las Vegas. Senator Laforge snapped the phone opened and gave an inviting "Hello"

"Hello Senator, this is Judy Treichel with the 'Nevada Nuclear Waste Task Force', we met a few weeks back!"

"Yes, Judy. It is so good to hear from you again."

"You asked me to keep you informed on any news about nuclear waste issues. Well, I think today's dismissal of a ten billion dollar lawsuit for the Paducah, Kentucky uranium plant workers meets that criteria."

"What is the story behind the lawsuit?" The Senator asked.

"The workers who were exposed to plutonium at the Paducah plant filed a lawsuit back in 1999 to compensate them for their health problems and for management's decision to expose them without warning to much more radioactive material, plutonium and neptunium. Former plant operators, Lockheed Martin and Union Carbide Corp., as well as General Electric Co. were also named in the suit."

"Judy, are you saying it was all dismissed?"

"Oh yes! The U.S. District Judge ruled the plant operators were exempt from any liability because they are protected by the 1957 Price-Anderson Act that limits the liability of private operators of nuclear facilities 'in the event of a nuclear related incident.' It is a protected industry unlike any other."

"That is awful!" Exclaimed Senator Laforge.

"Until you see places like Paducah, Kentucky or Hanford Washington, Senator, it would be hard for you to imagine how nuclear waste can affect a community. It is an industry that preys on the poor and communities that offer little else for employment."

"Judy, I will be visiting both those sites to get a first hand view of what is going on."

"Well Senator, there is one more thing that is happening at Paducah. Yesterday a 110 million dollar Health Protection Program was announced with fanfare giving out a few hundred thousand to stricken workers with chronic beryllium disease. I think this was supposed to diffuse the rejection of the ten billion dollar lawsuit."

Senator Laforge stopped listening to Judy and gazed dumbfounded at her car. She stood there for a long moment with the phone pressed against her ear. She heard Judy ask if she was still there. Senator Laforge mumbled to Judy, "I need to go." And without waiting for a response hung up.

In front of her was her rented car with the tires flattened and shredded. Red graffiti was scrawled across the side of the car. It read "Rich man's whore go back to NH. We don't want you." On the other side of the car, someone had scribbled, "'live free or die' needs to be 'live our way or die.'"

Beneath the car was a cardboard box that had been crushed by the weight of the car as it descended onto its rims. The box had a blackish red stain around its bottom. Frank Payne stopped Senator Laforge from getting any closer to the car. He grabbed her arm and hurriedly escorted her out of the parking lot. In an excited voice, he told her that he needed to call the police, and that she needed to call for another rental.

They waited outside the lot for the police. Within a couple of minutes the wailing siren of the approaching patrol car could be heard over the sound of the traffic. Just as the blinking lights became visible a car quickly exited from the lot with four men. Frank Payne noticed that all of them were looking away from him. He immediately felt a tinge of suspicion, as the car sped away he squinted at its license plate. There wasn't one, just an empty frame. The car turned the corner and was out of sight. The patrol car screeched to a halt in front of the entrance and abruptly the shrill siren went silent. Two police officers clamored out of the car and walked briskly over to the Senator and Mr. Payne as staring, unspeaking bystanders gathered on the other side of the road.

"Are you the people who just called in a complaint?" The tall officer questioned.

"Yes we are!" Offered Mr. Payne.

"Well I'm Sergeant Sandford and this is my partner officer Niven. What's the problem here?"

Senator Laforge stepped forward and offered her hand and said, "I'm Senator Laforge and this is my campaign manager Frank Payne. The problem sir is that our rented vehicle has been trashed by vandals."

Sergeant Sandford looked at Senator Laforge inquisitively and said, "I'm not much on politics Ma'am so could I see some ID real quick, so I know you two are who you say you are?"

"Sure officer here is my driver's license. Frank, give him yours, so we can get this over with quick."

Sergeant Sandford looked at her license and her senate pass and smiled at her as he handed them back and said, "No offense, I hope Ma'am, just always need to know who we are dealing with! Don't you all go around with a bunch of secret service agents?"

"Well, I wish that was so, but as you can see it is just the two of us." The Senator quipped.

"Yes Ma'am, well let's go look at the car."

Frank Payne interjected, "Officer, there is a box under the car and something is leaking from it. I think it would be safer for everyone if you got someone down here to check and see if it might be a bomb."

"You really think someone would do something like that to the Senator?" Officer Niven asked wide-eyed.

"Oh yes, there are a lot of powerful people hating Senator Laforge who would love to see her seriously harmed." Senator Laforge interrupted Frank Payne with:

"Officer, what Frank means is a lot of people would like to see me dead. Not hurt, but dead! I would not want others to be harmed, so it is best that you get someone down here to look into this incident."

"Okay Senator! Let me call it in, and we will cordon off this place until we find out what it is. A bit drastic, but better safe than sorry, as they say."

While Sergeant Sandford called in for assistance, Frank Payne gave a more detailed account of what he had seen to Officer Niven. He told him of his suspicions of the car driving away. Unfortunately, he was not sure of the car's make or its color. It could have been black, dark blue, dark green or a dark shade of gray.

As they went over the event and waited for more police, two more cars pulled up; one was another Honda Hybrid rental and the other an older Chevy used to escort the delivery driver back to the agency.

Frank Payne asked the police sergeant if they could leave and have an associate pick up their belongings after the police checked out the car. Sergeant Sandford drawled, "I guess it is okay. You need to keep in touch with us. We got your cell phone numbers, and if we need you, we will call you."

Frank Payne slipped behind the wheel of the Honda Hybrid and Katherine slid into the passenger seat. They sat quiet for about a mile, listening to the news, the quiet hum of the engine and contemplating what had happened. The quiet was interrupted by a call from Danny Lantrip. He had noticed that they were not in the caravan of cars that were following the Sundancer and wondered if they were lost. Frank filled Mr. Lantrip in on the incident. Danny Lantrip prophesized that it was just some drunken pranksters leaning toward another candidate who did it.

"Well, I hope you are right. How is Sundancer doing now?"

"We have had problems. We had some electrical difficulties, probably due to the dew this morning and that set us back a bit, and then we had a bad incident on a straight away where we were going to attempt a pass. The Sundancer was given a signal to pass just as an 18-wheeler came zooming by. If the driver and others had not been observant, we would have had a major incident, but the correction was made, and now we will just suffer some big penalty tomorrow at the announcements."

"The weather is predicting showers on the race route. Hope you miss them." Frank said.

"Well if they come, they will affect all of the teams because we are still pretty close to each other."

"We will catch up to you soon, I expect probably in Tenaha, Texas. See you soon." Frank said as he hung up the phone.

Kat was scribbling some notes and was lost in her own thoughts.

"You know Kat we really need to get more security for you. There have been just too many strange incidents happening lately. I am not trying to scare you, but many candidates in the last few elections have been shot or killed."

"I know!" Senator Laforge replied looking up from her notes.

"Well Senator I don't want some Travis Bickle gunning for you. Did you know that movie Taxi Driver wasn't just fantasy, it was based on the guy Arthur Bremer who shot and paralyzed George Wallace during his Presidential campaign?"

Frank did not wait for a reply.

"I am just trying to make a point. Let's not forget Robert Kennedy was shot dead in a kitchen on his campaign and Reagan, and Ford both were used for target practice by some angry citizens. I think we have to hire some bodyguards for you until you get secret service support."

"Okay, Frank! When we get back to Houston let's do it."

Frank was quiet for a long moment and then said, "I was thinking they can get going on hiring right now back at headquarters. I am sure Ira would be glad to handle it."

"I guess on days like today it would have been very nice." The Senator replied.

Frank didn't answer, he just fixed his eyes on the long black ribbon of asphalt stretched out ahead of them bordered by swaying pines. The wind had picked up and dead leafs and debris swirled like tiny whirlwinds across the road. Katherine slipped down deeper into her seat and closed her eyes for a few minutes of rest. Frank turned on the radio to a local am station and listened to the news. The major headline was about the mysterious death of Dr. David Kelly, who was found dead on July 18. He had recently testified at the British Parliament's Foreign Affairs Committee that he saw Iraq's nuclear capabilities more of a spin of fabricated information than reality. The statements made by Dr. Kelly were refuted and ridiculed by officials. Their explanation of his death was the result of suicide according to the official version, but the whispered story was murder. It was rumored that Kelly was silenced to prevent him from embarrassing powerful members of the British Parliament.

Frank tried to relax as he watched the center markers on the road stretch out like a dotted line flashing in the afternoon sun. The gnarled trees that grew among the tall pines fascinated him, their wavering bare branches appeared to reach out beckoning at him as he drove by them. Exhaustion was overtaking Frank just as the sound of the Senator's cell phone lifted his mental fog.

Katherine opened her eyes and fumbled for the cell phone on the console. It was a Texas number that displayed. She didn't recognize it, but took the call anyway. She voiced a weak, "Hello!" A booming voice came back, "Is this Senator Laforge?"

"Yes it is." Kat replied.

"Well this is Sergeant Sandford. Got some info on your earlier incident."

"I am glad to hear that." Katherine replied, sitting up in the seat.

"Well Senator, the good news was there was no bomb in the box. What was in there was a bizarre layout of cat parts."

"Cat parts?" Katherine echoed.

"Yup, looks like someone took the time to cut up a cat or two and use some of the bones to write the word "KAT." They also left a cat's head in the box. I guess it is really just some sicko who was trying to scare you. Could have been kids also."

"God, that is horrible. So you have no idea of who might have done it?" Katherine asked.

"Well not yet, but we are checking it out more to see if any locals are talking about it. Besides that, we do not have much more to go on, unless someone reports a missing cat or something like that. Sorry!" Sergeant Sandford apologized.

"I understand. Well thank you for calling us with the news, Sergeant. If anything else comes up, please keep us in the loop."

Katherine exchanged goodbyes and settled back into her seat again. "Well, that is another mystery, I bet will never be solved."

Frank glanced over at Katherine and saw that she had already closed her eyes. With them still closed Katherine said, "Frank, I think we should cut this trip short before that protest in Macon, Mississippi. I won't feel right having my presence interfering in this race and causing such a tremendous expense to that little town. Macon is only about two thousand people, so I think the plan should be we leave this race at Houston, Mississippi right after I deliver my speech. Okay with you?"

"No problems here, Senator. I think that is the best way to handle this nasty situation. Those protesters will still create a bit of a ruckus in Macon, but a lot less if you are not there."

Senator Laforge responded, "We need to get back to the give and take settings of town meetings, late night TV, and the standard fair of speaking engagements. Two things I want to do is visit some electric coops on our way back and then visit that area in Galveston where they are building the "Galveston Offshore Wind" farm."

"That is something I would love to see also. I think I read that they are planning to have 50 wind turbines installed, generating about 150 megawatts, or enough power to supply 45,000 homes." Frank said.

"Yes that is what I read. So how about making plans for us to visit it as soon as we get back to the Houston area." Senator Laforge said.

The third day of the race would start in Houston, Mississippi, the home-town of the Sundancer and its team. On the morning of July 19th Senator Laforge addressed the event's crowd. It was a proud occasion for the locals; their team had won the race in previous years and this fact filled the townsfolk with pride.

After being introduced by the Mayor of the town and quieting the ap-plauding followers of these solar car teams, Senator Laforge expressed to the audience her genuine surprise at the dynamics of the race. She said, "When I was invited to this event, I had no idea of the education and excitement that this race generates. It is easy to become enamored with these vehicles of the future and this unique group of young men and women. What these students from Mississippi, Colorado, Indiana, New York and Mexico have demonstrated in the last three days is harnessing solar energy is a reality that big industry needs to embrace." The Senator paused for a moment as the audience applauded, and then she continued, "If the federal government will not see the benefit of this plentiful energy source, than the states need to create their own energy plans to replace the soot belching coal power plants and dangerous nuclear power plants with biodiesel, wind, solar, and wave power."

Senator Laforge waited for the applause to die down and then said, "This will be my last day with the race. Late this afternoon, I will be flying to meet with community leaders in Buzzard Bay, MA. to learn firsthand the complications of cleaning up large oil spills. Buzzard Bay has become another disaster of Big Oil and another reason why imported oil needs to cease. The cleanup has already cost 2 billion dollars.

While I have your attention, I wanted to take a couple minutes of your time and give you a little more of my campaign concerns. Freeing us from our addiction to foreign oil is one of my primary goals and the actions of these wonderful dedicated young men and women prove that the answers to our energy crisis are not that far away. This group of students has harnessed the sun's energy to power their solar vehicles to speeds of up to 65 miles per hour. These young men and women should not just be seen as racers of solar cars, but as national champions who are helping to usher in a new era of power. If big business would follow their lead, we could prevent wars being fought for the dwindling supply of oil, because we would be using solar power, wind power or the movement of ocean waves. We would not have to have refineries belching out tons of pollutants into the air you and I breath. You would not be worrying about petroleum products seeping into your water table like what has happened in New Hampshire and Vermont. With solar energy you could eliminate devastating oil spills like the Exxon Valdez or the Buzzard Bay tragedies. Alternative energies are here today, and you need to send a message to your representatives to promote and embrace this change, or you should vote them out. Your actions in this matter do not simply create cleaner energy, they also eliminate the need of our men and women to fight wars over yesterday's energy source and big business's greed. Energy self sufficiency would prevent members of this community from dying in some foreign land for a cause that you have the power to eliminate."

Senator Laforge thanked the crowd for listening to her comments. She hoped some had embraced her message and would become a part of the solution. Suddenly, a roar went up as the next leg of the race started. Down

Main Street this fleet of alien looking vehicles whizzed by the applauding and shouting onlookers. These flying saucers and manta ray looking vehicles awed the onlookers and enchanted the young.

As Katherine watched the vehicles zoom down the road, Frank handed her an envelope. On the outside it read "Private for Katherine Laforge" She unfolded its content and suddenly the roar of the crowd dissipated and only the pounding of her heart was audible. The single sheath of paper was a missing children's flyer with a crudely altered picture of her daughter added to it. It was a recently taken photograph of her Lyndsey leaving school with friends. A message scrawled with a black marker read, "Let's hope your sweet Lyndsey is not one of the 2,300 children that disappear everyday in the good old USA! It could happen so easy!"

She stared down at the flyer as a maelstrom of emotions swirled through her mind. Anger, fear, hate, confusion, sadness all boiled into an overpowering rage. She wanted to turn and run from this horrifying nightmare, but another voice in her told her she could not. Even with this new darkness closing in on her, she had to continue her quest for the presidency. She tried to catch her breath and gulped in air. The air suddenly felt cold and stunk of a freshly lit match or perhaps the stench of a solar car battery. Inside her head she was screaming.

Katherine turned to Frank, handed him the paper and blurted out that he would have to cover her while she called her daughter. Her voice sounded almost controlled, but her eyes exposed her fear. Payne said, "Katherine you need to call her." As he glanced at the cryptic message on the flyer, he added, "We need to get more protection for her, Ira, and all of us."

Katherine meekly shook her head in agreement and walked back to their vehicle. She turned on the engine and felt the cool air from the conditioner hitting her in the face. She pulled out her cell phone and dialed her daughter's phone number.

It rang and rang again. No answer. Finally, the voice mail picked up and Lyndsey's recording played. Katherine waited till the beep and started her message. "Lyndsey, as soon as you get my message, call me. This is very important and I must talk to you. Have your dad call me too. Remember this is important, call me right off, or you are grounded forever. I love you."

She hung up the phone and thought for a second. That was a dumb message "I'll ground you forever!" She hoped Lyndsey would get her message soon and call her. She was not sure what she wanted to tell her, but she really wanted to hear her voice and make sure she was safe. She dialed Ira and listened as the phone rang over and over with no answer. On the forth ring she heard a call coming in on her phone, and she switched over to take it. "Hi mom, what's up?" the voice said.

She closed her eyes and breathed a sigh of relief. "Honey, I was just calling you to see what you were doing and if everything is all right. Can a mom do that?"

"Of course mom, but nothing is going on accept you know the same old stuff. I am getting ready to go to the mall, okay?"

"Yes!" Katherine replied.

"You sound a lot happier today." Lyndsey said.

"What do you mean,' I sound a lot happier today?' Why do you say that?"

"Mom you were just about crying last night when you were talking to me. I know when you are getting ready to cry. You even made me cry when you talked about all the things we did when I was little. You made me remember what a great mom I have!"

Kat didn't say anything. She just sat there frozen in confusion. She was sure she knew what this meant, but she could not talk to Lyndsey about it.

"Mom, are you there?"

"Yes sweetie I am, but what you just said, took my breath away."

"Mom, you are not going to cry again are you?"

"No Lyndsey, I'm not. But, I do want you to be more careful of what you do and who you talk to. You know a lot of people don't like me, like you do, and I don't want some crazy to take their dislike of me, out on you. I am going to get a couple handsome guys to hang out with you to make sure no one hurts my baby, okay?"

"You mean guards, mom?"

"Yes, I'm sorry. But they will be cool and fun to be with and that is the end of this discussion."

"Mom, I am fine. I don't need guards."

"Like I said 'End of discussion.' And under the current situation I have to by law."

"Mom!"

"Lyndsey, tell your dad to call me as soon as you see him."

Katherine could see Frank looking inquisitively at her, and she knew she had to cut the conversation short.

"Lyndsey, I love you. Please don't make this hard. It is for your best interest, and they might be fun. I'll talk to you soon. Be good."

Katherine heard a grumbled "Love you too mom!" as she hung up.

The next few days passed without incident and then about eleven days later Katherine was on her way back to Houston from Galveston, Texas. She had gone there to see firsthand about the proposed wind power project. It was another announced event that was going to be a question and answer session with the contractors, officials and the citizens of Galveston, TX.

The event was successful and very informative. As she sat in her car parked on the Galveston Ferry, she called Danny Lantrip, to congratulate him on the Sundancer's win of the Dell-Winston Solar Car Challenge. She had been following the race and was elated to read that they had won it once again. She wished she could have been there to see Cody Spenser, Mandy Davis, Matt, Sherrie and the rest of the crew at Cocoa Beach Florida receive their trophy, but she was coming to realize that politics can be very dirty and dangerous.

Before Lantrip could even answer the call, a swarm of police converged on a vehicle that was parked near hers. The driver, an individual with Middle Eastern features looked stunned as the wall of police surged toward him. The police were yelling at him in English and in Arabic to raise his arms, but he did not comply, and suddenly he was on the ground wiggling about like a beached fish. He had just been hit with fifty thousand volts from a taser. Agents were on him immediately cuffing his flaying hands behind him. Senator Laforge found herself surrounded also and was quickly led off of the ferry.

"What is going on?" Senator Laforge asked.

"Possible explosive in his car." The agent replied.

Senator Laforge felt a coldness embrace her, but she was use to this type of fear, and she quickly controlled it. The ferry now was swarming with agents, and they quickly removed all of the passengers from it.

Four hours later she sat in the Galveston Police Station watching a monitor in front of her that displayed a dark haired young man sitting alone at a table in the interrogation room. An officer in a rumpled suit moved into camera view and positioned himself in a chair directly across from the shackled suspect. Frank Payne gestured at the monitor and in a whispery voice, informed Katherine that the interrogating officer was Detective Green. The sound of rustling papers could be heard over the monitor as Detective Green nonchalantly thumbed through the contents of a bulging folder. The young man didn't bother to look up as his interrogator flicked on a tape recorder. Detective Green scowled hard at the man shackled to the chair and cleared his throat, but no greetings were exchanged. Finally, Detective Green opens with, "Abu Mujahed, that is your name correct?"

Abu replied, "Yes!"

Detective Green continued, "I got a big problem. I got fifteen or so witnesses to the incident, but the accounts don't all line up. So what say I add your account to the pile."

"OK!" Abu said.

Looking down at the file, Detective Green asked, "Yesterday, were you on the Galveston-Bolivar Ferry at about 3:15 P.M?

Abu weakly, "Yes."

What were you doing there?

Abu was still not looking at Detective Green, "I was returning home from Galveston."

"What was in your trunk and in the boxes in the back seat?" Abu did not immediately reply.

Detective Green waited for about 30 seconds and then said, "Let me help you. It was a few hundred pounds of explosives."

Abu smugly replied. "The car was not mine. I didn't know anything about explosives in it."

"Whose car was it?

Abu did not reply.

"Did you steal it?"

Abu sat silent. Detective Green looked down at his notes and said. "Abu, I bet this will come as a surprise to you, but a woman reported that car stolen ten days ago. Just before it was stolen, she had gotten the oil changed. When they change oil, those Jiffy Lube people record the current mileage on the car. So we know that someone had this car for ten days and only drove about 30 miles. And coincidently, the nice lady and the people at Jiffy Lube claim they didn't notice 450 pounds of explosives in her car that morning."

Abu crossed his arms in front of him, but did not say anything.

Detective Green continued. "Abu, we know all about you. You fought with the Taliban in Afghanistan. You went to school in Pakistan. You held the position of Chief of the Talibs in your hometown in Afghanistan. You use to go around and whip and beat women that you felt were breaking the Taliban's Islamic laws."

Abu glared at Detective Green, "I did the work of Allah. I made sure women followed the rules of Islam and loved Allah and stayed obedient to their father and husband. I was a policeman just like you."

The reply seemed to confuse Detective Green for a moment. "Abu, I do not go about hanging girls because I catch them dancing."

Abu leaned over the table and glared, "You are right Detective, and that is why your country is full of whores and men who have no respect for women. You know nothing about our customs and how we respect and protect our women. Those women I punished violated Islamic laws and deserved Allah's punishment. I was admired and loved by my people as a devout Muslim. Who admires you?"

Abu's caustic question hung in the air.

Senator Laforge followed the interrogation intently on the monitor. She wondered if this man had really tried to kill her or was it a mere coincidence that she was on the ferry he had planned to blow up. As she watched the proceedings on the monitor, she flipped through a dossier containing background material on the suspect. Some of it was startling. There was a photograph of seven very young women hanging in some kind of ware-house. Abu posed for the camera near one woman who looked like her spinal cord had been severed and the weight of her body had grotesquely elongated her neck. In the background a group of Taliban soldiers were visible, but appeared disinterested in the hanging.

The photograph was attached to a transcript from a previous interrogation of Abu. It read like a page from a horror novel.

Agent Collings: What are you doing in this picture?

Abu: We are hanging the condemned.

Agent Collings: What was their crime?

Abu: They violated Islamic laws.

Agent Collings: What did they do?

Abu: They violated Islamic laws and the decree of the Taliban.

Agent Collings: What specific crimes?

Abu: They were repeatedly caught listening and dancing to western music. They were viewed by three Taliban mullahs who testified against them. They disgraced their families with their action and were uncontrollable.

Agent Collings: How old were they?

Abu: I do not remember?

Agent Collings: Were they 50 years old or more like fifteen years old?

Abu: They were fourteen or fifteen, but they had violated Islamic laws and disrespected the village clerics.

Agent Collings: Did you enjoy punishing them?

Abu: Yes, they violated Islamic laws, and I felt very special that Allah had chosen me to carry out His will. One of my proudest moments was when I succeeded in hanging those seven whores even while the Americans were bombing our village. I found pleasure in doing Allah's bidding watching the condemn strangle in their noose, surrendering their life to Allah. I was one of Allah's chosen and my obedience to His will was my duty. You are an unbeliever and cannot understand.

Agent Collings: How long did it take to hang seven girls?

Abu: I had soldiers that helped me carry out the sentences. Taliban Soldiers would place a rope noose around their neck and another soldier would tighten it and lift her to the top of a barrel. After I gave the order to kick the barrels out from under them, the girls would take a minute to maybe five minutes before they accepted Allah's will and hung quietly.

Agent Collings: Abu, you must have been very important in your village. How many offenders of Allah did you hang?

Abu: I am not sure. Maybe 80 or 90. I don't remember.

Senator Laforge turned back to the picture and stared at the image of the seven young girls hanging. The thought of their suffering made Katherine's neck muscles bulge wire tight and her face turn scarlet with anger and disgust. The smiling Abu posing proudly beneath them taunted her even more.

Senator Laforge returned her gaze to the monitor and Detective Green's interrogation of Abu. She had never seen this individual before, but now felt that it was not a coincidence that she happened to be on the same ferry that he was attempting to blow up.

Detective Green had recovered from Abu's personal insults and was pressing him about his feeling on women in general.

"Who is the lady you live with when you are in Florida?" Detective Green asks.

Abu sat quiet at first and then replied, "You already know who she is. Why do you ask such dumb questions? She is a dumb American woman who just needs a man."

"So there is really nothing between you?"

"She has learned obedience from me, and I have taught her much about the Koran. But she is a dumb woman. She takes care of my house and I feed and clothe her."

"Do you know Detective Green what Ali, Mohammed's cousin and fourth Caliph said about women?"

Detective Green displayed great interest on his face and replied, "No"

"He was a great leader of Islam, and he is quoted as saying, 'The entire woman is evil and what is worse is that it is a necessary evil! ... You should never ask a woman her advice because her advice is worthless. Hide them so that they cannot see other men! ... Do not spend too much time in their company for they will lead you to your downfall! ... Men, never ever obey your women. Never let them advise you on any matter concerning your daily life ... They have three qualities worthy of an unbeliever: they complain of being oppressed when in fact it is they who oppress; they take solemn oaths and at the same time lie; they make a show of refusing the advances of men when in fact, they long for them ardently. Let us implore God's help to escape their sorcery.'"

"Do you agree with Ali?" Abu questioned smugly.

Detective Green exclaimed. "I am impressed that you have memorized his words so thoroughly. You must have been a very good student of Islam."

For the first time, Abu's face beamed. "I studied in Pakistan and in Afghanistan. I am a very devout Muslim."

Detective Green asked, "With your excellent memory, it should be easy to remember who helped you with all those explosives for the car. Was it the lady you lived with in Florida?"

Abu just sat there and did not reply.

"You are right about what Ali said about women. They cannot be trusted. Your girlfriend is talking all about your plans to agents in Florida. She claims you had plans to kill a few non-believers in Florida also. She told them you were going to use sarin gas in aerosol dispensers to kill visitors at the amusement park. When was that going to happen?"

Abu sat impassive.

Detective Green continued, "Your girlfriend, Lisa, said she had undergone a double mastectomy, and you had bought her some new silicone prosthesis to wear when you two go out in public or for special occasions. That was loving of you!

Abu did not respond.

"We checked those prosthesis you bought Lisa. They were very interesting."

Detective Green looked at Abu questionably.

Abu looked away from Detective Green and shifted in his seat.

Then Abu just closed his eyes and lowered his head as if he was dozing.

Green slapped his hand down on the table and said, "Instead of silicone, they were filled with Sarin gas. That is pretty slick!"

Abu didn't jump, or respond at all, he just sat there with his eyes closed.

"What guard would ever ask a woman to see her breast prosthesis? That is really class! You could get into anywhere with those." Detective Green paused again, but Abu did not respond.

"Good thing they didn't leak or goodbye girlfriend. I think you should know that Lisa is a little angry with you now. I think she feels used."

"Fuck you and fuck her. She is fucking American shit like you." Abu spat out.

Abu's plan to use sarin gas shocked Senator Laforge. She was well aware of what sarin gas could do and remembered the terror she felt when she thought she was going to be exposed to it in Iraq. Part of her fear was the fact that it is so difficult to detect. It is odorless and colorless, yet deadly if inhaled, absorbed through the eyes or skin. An amount equivalent to the size of a grain of sand could kill a child. It can kill within minutes of exposure. A horrible death of drooling, double vision, vomiting, troubled breathing, and finally affixation. She clearly understood why Sarin Gas was one of the terrorist's preferred weapons – feared, undetectable, deadly and relatively cheap to manufacture. It is a clear liquid that can easily be disguised as a bottle of water and carried in plain view of security. Antidote is available, but death usually occurs before it can be administered.

Senator Laforge cringed at the thought of how horrible a sarin attack on an amusement park would be. It would affect the country in much the same way as the 9/11 attacks. The number of casualties would be less, but the psychological effect would be just as dramatic. The visitors would be lulled into feeling secure and would never expect anything wrong until it was too late. Senator Laforge thought of the mad melee that would follow in the crowds at the park once they were aware that they were being attacked by sarin nerve gas. Some would die from suffocation, and many more from being crushed at the turnstiles as the panicked park goers rushed to leave the area. Others would be crippled or badly injured in the stampede. The carnage would spill out onto the roads as panic-stricken drivers trying to escape the park littered the roads with their abandoned wrecked cars and the dead. It would be a devastating attack.

* * * *

While Katherine thumbed through the files on Abu, two FBI agents came over to her. The two introduced themselves as Special Agent Nelson and Plouffe. With a congenial smile, Special Agent Nelson said, "Sorry about the interruptions in your plans today. We are grateful that it worked out as well as it did. Mr. Mujahed is one little terrorist that we have been following for months. Guys like him crave a big name for themselves, which makes them attempt to create tremendous devastation."

"Well I do commend you for your quick control of the situation." Katherine replied.

"Senator Laforge, if you would honor us with your presence, we would love to chat more with you on these subjects. I think you will find it very interesting. We can take you and Mr. Payne back to your car, which is waiting for you at the ferry parking lot. What do you say?"

Senator Laforge replaced Abu's files back into the folder and handed them to Agent Nelson. "I think we would like that, and you have piqued my interest."

Once in the Agent's car, Plouffe turned his head back to face Katherine in the back seat. He said, "Senator, we were going to meet with you soon to go over terrorist operations, but this incident moved the timetable up a bit. So if you do not mind we would like to give you a run down now of some of the actions and activities that we are monitoring."

"Yes, after this event, I am certainly interested in knowing how wide spread these types of activity really are." Katherine responded.

"Well Senator, I guess we will start with some facts you probably already know like al-Qa'eda's "modus operandi is to have multiple attack plans in the works simultaneously and to have cells in place to conduct them. These terrorist operations could be launched by al-Qa'eda cells already in place in major cities in America, Europe or the Middle East." Plouffe took a sip of a diet soda.

Special Agent Nelson interjected, "Small towns and buildings may be just as attractive targets to a terrorist as larger ones. For example, if the point is to make people lose confidence in their water supply, you can create terror in a smaller water system just as effectively as in a big one. The point is not necessarily to kill large numbers of people, but to frighten, panic and create distrust in the government. Just two weeks ago we stopped an attack on the Los Angeles water system. An operative going by the name of Khalid rented a dilapidated house in South Central Los Angeles and had lived there for over a year waiting for his call to action. He is from one of the numerous terrorist cells operating in LA. His function was to attack the water supply in the Watts district of LA. He had attached a feeder pipe to his water line in his house and pressurized it with a pump. The feeder pipe contained ricin, a deadly poison, he would pump into the water line. Others sharing this waterline would then be exposed to the poison. The Watts area of LA was selected because the water lines in many of the houses are exposed and easy to access to alter them for this purpose. More importantly al-Qa'eda hoped to create racial strife leading to riots that would kill more people and paralyze the city with problems. They had hoped they could escalate this situation into something like the 1965 riots that lasted 6 days and left 34 dead and thousands injured."

"How did you stop this attack?" questioned Katherine.

"We were very lucky. It is very difficult to spot a minor drop in pressure that could be the start of a backflow attack. But Khalid was such a lousy plumber that he let water drip down into the apartment below. The tenant of course complained to the manager. When they investigated the drip, Khalid was not at home, but his device was set up with the ricin ready to go with another full container of it sitting next to the feed pipe. Police were notified and we stepped in. Never did get to interrogate him however, because when we attempted to arrest him, he darted out into traffic and was hit and killed by a school bus."

"So stopping that attack was just pure luck?" Payne asked.

"I am afraid so." Agent Nelson replied. "When someone is attempting to contaminate small water lines, it is very hard to detect. Things have changed a bit with some utility companies in the frequency of their pressure checks, but such a small drop-off would probably still go unnoticed."

"I never read anything about this attack. When did it happen?" Katherine asked.

"Well that is one of those situations where we decided to keep it quiet. A little article about how Khalid died was in the paper, but the rest we never released to the media. The fact is that many attacks by terrorist are kept from the media because that is one way to reduce the effects of an attack or an attempted attack. They want to create terror, fear and confusion among us, so not reporting an incident diffuses it to a large degree. I am sure you have read about the forest fires that have ravaged Colorado, California, and Texas. Well, many of them have been set by various terrorist cells to prove how defenseless we are in stopping them. And they are right, we are stretched thin. The arsons are not reported unless we catch the perpetrator, even if we do receive claims by terrorist cells that they did it. "

Agent Plouffe added, "Senator, we have reason to believe that there are cells that are planning to plant explosives in hospitals, movie theaters, and at high school sporting events. But we have very little we can do to stop such attacks. We don't know if the information we receive is simply misinformation to keep us busy chasing shadows or something that is a real threat. We think that it is about half and half and that much of these operations will be carried out by some groups when they are ordered to proceed."

"Do we know who these terrorists are, or where they operate?" Katherine asked.

"We think we know who some are, but unfortunately they often live in communities that are very hostile to government agencies and see our investigations as simply harassment of Middle Easterners. Some of these operatives have lived in a community for years and are not viewed by their neighbors as threats or anyone who would ever have a darker side. It is a very difficult job trying to weed out terrorist from law abiding Middle Eastern immigrants." Plouffe responded.

They had arrived at Katherine's abandoned car.

"Well here we are. I hope we have given you a bit more of an idea of what you are getting yourself involved in as President. We would be glad to keep you up to date on new activities that we are monitoring if we are given the authorization. By the way, Senator, I come from Bethlehem, New Hampshire, right up the road from your home town,." Nelson stated.

"I thought I detected a bit of New England in you. Well please feel free to contact me with anything you have about these terrorist situations."

"We will Senator, and be careful out there. We don't want to read about you in our files as some terrorist target. Enjoyed talking to you."

Katherine and Payne hurried over to their vehicle and felt the cool night air blowing in on them from the bay. The day had been another long day that had gone much different than planned. Frank wanted to call his wife the minute he got in the car and apologize for not answering his cell the last few hours. He wanted to tell her he was okay. It would be a little pass her bedtime, but he knew she would be glad to hear from him and perhaps a little pissed off. He dialed Diane's number and waited for her to pick up. It rang multiple times and then the answering machine came on. He started to close his phone, just as he heard her excited voice. "Frank, don't hang up. I'm here."

"Hi Diane."

"Where have you been all day? I have been calling you for hours."

"I'm sorry sweetie, but we had a major security issue, and I was not able to contact you until now. Is everything okay with you?"

"Well, if you are okay then yes everything is wonderful. I got something very special to tell you."

"Okay! Tell me."

"We are going to have a baby, Frank"

"Diane, did I hear you right? Did you say we are going to have a baby?"

"Yes, I found out late today and have been trying to call you to let you know, but of course you can't answer your damn phone. Are you happy?"

"Christ yes, I'm happy. I am going to have to talk to the Senator to give me a couple days off so we can celebrate."

Frank held the phone to his chest and said to Katherine, "I'm going to be a dad in a few months."

"That should be just about inauguration time. We will hopefully have a lot to celebrate." Katherine quipped.

As Frank chatted with his wife, Katherine reminisced about when she found herself pregnant at the age of 43. It had scared her, but now she was grateful that it did happen. She probably was a better mom at 44, then she would have been in her twenties or thirties even. Having a baby is just so much more sacred as you mature. Her mind jumped to the trip they would be taking to Roscoe, Texas the next day. It tired her even thinking about the drive, but maybe in the morning after a couple hours of sleep it would seem better.

When Frank hung up he was still elated. Being a father was something he really looked forward to.

The trip to Roscoe, Texas started at 7 am at Houston's Hobby Airport with a flight to Abilene, Texas Regional Airport. On this trip they decided to have Jannie Venter a former deputy sheriff, turned campaign worker, accompanied them to do the driving and to watch over their rented car. Venter's driving would also provide Katherine and Frank a bit more time to get some rest after the exhausting events at the Galveston ferry. They had not yet incorporated their new hired security people into their campaign trips, so he was also going to act in that capacity.

Roscoe was a small farm town with a population of about 1,300 west of Sweetwater near Interstate 20. Sweetwater was located in what West Texans affectionately call the "Big Country." It had already made a name for itself as the hub of wind energy development and now a few miles away Roscoe was having its reincarnation as a town that was the heart of one of the biggest wind farms in the nation, if not the world. Katherine was proud that her state had become a leader in wind energy in such a short period of time. Texas had led the country in the oil business, and now it was leading in the wind power arena.

Entering Roscoe was like stepping into a photo of the past and having details from days gone by transformed into a shimmering scene of a new beginning. The glistening white towers stretching 400 feet into the constantly moving air virtually erased the inscrutable blurs of deserted buildings that grayed the landscape. Just a short distance into town Sparky's Café beckoned with its reborn veneer and cluster of vehicles sparkling in the late morning sun. It was one of the few businesses still opened in Roscoe after Interstate 20 was built, and the town lost its precious traffic and slowly wilted. The majority of the buildings on Broadway were boarded up with plywood. As they pulled up to the parking area in front of Sparky's, they spotted Mr. Etheredge sitting in his open-top jeep. He had told them, "Just look for a man with one arm sitting in a canary yellow vehicle and that will be me."

Standing next to the yellow jeep was another gentleman.

Venter drove the car behind the jeep and the Senator and Frank Payne exited. Mr. Etheredge jumped out of his jeep and strode over toward Katherine. In a soft Texas accent he said? "Senator Laforge? I am Cliff Etheredge and this is my son David. Would you like to sit down and grab a cup of coffee while we give you some background on our wind farm?"

Katherine smiled and shook her head yes. She introduced her campaign manager as they walked into the café.

A hostess met them as they entered and asked, "Y'all want a booth or a table?"

Mr. Etheredge replied, "Let's have a booth."

"Right over thar, Cliff, go ahead on", She directed.

They sat down in a red vinyl booth and Katherine took in the west Texas ambiance of the café.

"Here is the menu. If you are hungry, the pancakes are great here. That is, if you like having a late breakfast." Cliff offered.

"Thanks, Mr. Etheredge, that does sound good. We took a short flight to Abilene and drove the rest of the way, so we never really stopped to eat. Breakfast does sound great."

"Senator, please call me Cliff, you make me feel a heck of a lot older than I am when you call me Mr. Etheredge."

"Okay Cliff and the same for you. Call me Katherine please."

Everyone had read the menu and a smiling waitress offered, "Y'all want some hot coffee? I'm fixin some fresh?"

The waitress looked at Katherine and said, "Senator, I just want to tell yew that since Cliff got things goin' richeer in Roscoe, jist about everyone now is walkin' in tall cotton. We all luv him."

Katherine could sense the reverence that the people held for Cliff Etheredge. A few people had looked his way and slightly nodded their head, but respected him enough to not interrupt his meeting.

"Cliff, how did this wind farm business get started here in Roscoe?" Frank asked.

"Well, I was just riding around near another wind farm not to far from Roscoe and started wondering if that could be our solution to our problems.

So I started investigating and asking questions. From everything I read and learned, it just seemed Roscoe would be a prime spot for a wind farm. We have a perpetual wind of about 17 or 18 miles per hour blowing across our farm land, and I thought instead of just letting it dry up our land, we could put the wind to work."

Dave Etheredge interjected, "Dad introduced the idea to local land owners and organized them into a group with a common goal called 'Wind Works.' Then he went hunting for investors and was lucky to find a company call Airtricity, out of Dublin Ireland. They are spending more than a billion dollars installing the wind turbines. We plan to eventually have about 640 windmills."

"And that will produce enough electricity for over a quarter of a million households and pay some very decent royalties to a few hundred of my neighbors here in Roscoe." Cliff added looking straight at Katherine.

A smiling waitress appeared at the table and asked, "Y'all want anuther cup o' coffee?"

Once cups were refilled, Katherine said, "Cliff, beside the obvious benefit of the additional electrical resources, how else has it benefited the area?

"Well we have a lot of farmers and townsfolk that now have an additional income that they did not have and that makes for a pretty happy community compared to before when the town was struggling to just stay alive. We are attracting new people to our area now. My own son decided to come back to his hometown to live, once this business got going." Cliff said with a smile as he glanced at David.

"The participating landowners are getting royalties of five thousand to fifteen thousand dollars per year for their leases to the wind farm. We have friends that are…

Katherine all of a sudden felt a chill and the hair on the nape of her neck tingled. Something was happening, but she was not sure what it was. Cliff's words went unheard as she tried to control her loudly beating heart. Then the phone rang. It sounded abnormally loud, erasing Cliff's voice completely. She clumsily reached for it and instinctively knew the call was something special.

"She said hello into the receiver as the faces of those at the table came back into view. She smiled apologetically at them and said, "I need to take this." And stood up to leave the table. Katherine walked out of the café and stood in the breezy air. "Who is this?" she said into her phone. For a couple seconds, there was no reply and then a woman's voice replied, a voice she had heard before "Hello Katherine, this is Zoe."

"Zoe?" Katherine repeated confused.

"Yes, your twin. I am not dead. We are still connected. Maybe I am connected more to you then you are to me, but we are still one, just in two different bodies."

Katherine held the phone to her mouth, but she was speechless. Was this a cruel joke? She knew it wasn't, not with the hair on the back of her neck standing straight up even before the call came. She had sensed the call, or maybe she had felt some sort of connection between the two of them even before Zoe had made the call.

"Why are you calling yourself Zoe?" Katherine asked and then felt stupid for asking such a foolish question.

"I needed a name and that was one, we used to like, remember? Are you upset that I still exist?"

Katherine's stomach knotted as the full recognition of what was happening registered in her mind.

"Oh God no. I really had hoped you would survive. But it is so unbelievable. It was you that called Lyndsey a while back wasn't it?"

"I called her because", Zoe's voice broke and Katherine could hear the anguish in it. Because I am as much her mother as you are Katherine, and you know that. My life was your life, and it is hard to erase it from my mind."

"How did you get here?" Katherine whispered into the phone.

"That is not important now. I am calling you because you are in danger. You are being followed."

"What?" Katherine scanned the parking lot, but the only person she saw was Venter sitting in their vehicle. He nodded at her as her eyes for a second locked onto his.

"There are two men who were at the airport when you arrived who have continually been following you since you rented the car. They were watching you through binoculars while they sat in their car. One of them has been driving back and forth pass the café while you were in there. I am not sure where the other one is."

"You are here also watching me?"

"Katherine we cannot spend time talking about that now. Go back inside the café and be careful."

Zoe abruptly hung up and Katherine stood for moment milling over the situation. She looked up and down Broadway, but really didn't see anything suspicious. She realized that she had to return to her meeting inside the café, but first, she went over to Venter and told him that a reliable informant had just told her they were being watched.

"Just someone trying to get dirt on you, Senator." Venter offered.

"You are probably right", Katherine responded as she walked to the café's entrance.

When she approached their table, she could hear Cliff giving some specs on the wind turbines.

"Each one of the turbines reach up about 400 feet topped with a carbon-fiber propeller that spans another one hundred and fifty feet. The sound the propeller makes is a whoosh sound similar to the sound a wave makes. Senator everything okay?"

Katherine smiled and said, "Yes everything is fine just some important issues I had to take care of. I see you all are finished eating. Should we visit the wind farm now?"

"Katherine, you didn't finish," Cliff protested.

"That's fine. It's cold now and I am really not that hungry. Let me take care of this bill and then let's visit the site."

"Senator let me take care of the bill. This is my treat. We invited you here."

"Mr. Etheredge you better just let her take care of it. She is the government and when the government offers you something for free without red tape, you better take it. You are not going to win, I know her." Frank Payne joked.

"Well, okay, then I will get the next meal." Cliff said.

Katherine leaned over to Cliff and said, "Does this buy me a ride in your yellow jeep?"

"Darn right it does. It would be my pleasure to have you ride with me. The jeep might not be the most comfortable vehicle in the world, but it makes it easier to see around the town as we take the tour.

As Katherine climbed into the jeep she saw the sign hanging off the glove box that read 'Get In - Sit down - Shut up - Hold on'. Cliff smiled at her and said, "Senators are exempt from those rules. Okay?"

Katherine smiled and looked back to see if any other cars beside her rented one were following them. She saw nothing that looked suspicious and Frank and Cliff's son David riding with Venter did make her feel a bit more secure. Their presence, however, did not lessen the anxiety welling up inside her.

"So what are you going to show me first?" Katherine asked.

"Well as you can see this town looks like it was close to being a ghost town before this wind power project got started. Now we have some new places opening up and people actually coming here to live and work. That is very satisfying to me to know that we are giving life back to Roscoe. You can see poking up all over the horizon the wind turbines. Those white giants have become Roscoe's salvation. Now we have nearly 400 property owners benefiting financially from the wind turbines, and they are still left with the land to farm cotton. Not a bad deal!"

The rumble of a garbage truck thrummed through the jeep as it passed them making its morning rounds. Behind it another vehicle followed with two men gawking at the jeep.

"Are those friends of yours Cliff?" Katherine asked motioning to the passing car.

"Nope, could be workers, tourist or just friends of friends. Like I said we are growing, and we have people moving in now instead of out." Cliff smiled with a bit of pride in his voice.

Katherine's concern about those two men was interrupted by Cliff.

"Just three years ago, no one could've imagined this. What has happened is absolutely unbelievable. I think all of us who use to curse the wind, now loves it."

Katherine took in the majestic white towers that jutted up over the landscape, and as she turned her head, she glanced out of the corner of her eye behind them. A feeling of relief washed over her as she saw that only her rented car was trailing them.

"The royalty payments from the wind turbines are probably going to be more dependable than the money we earn from the cotton crops. It has certainly given many of us a greater sense of economic security. In Roscoe, right now, with so many of us over 55 this money sort of becomes our retirement fund."

Enjoying the warm breeze blowing through her hair, Katherine said, "Cliff, Roscoe should be proud of what it has accomplished."

For a few seconds quiet filled the air and Katherine could hear the faint rhythmic swoosh of the wind turbines.

"Not many people realize that my little town of Roscoe will produce more electrical energy from wind than most countries, but I hope that, we can promote that and get on the map for pioneering this change in energy production. We hope to open a Wind Energy Visitor's center here in Roscoe, and coax cars off the interstate to come and visit us. The new direction Roscoe is heading makes us all excited and proud of its accomplishments. We recognize it will change our town and a lot of us are very proud to be associated with all of this."

Cliff coughed a bit and then continued,

"To many communities, the wind farms have become like the oil boom we once experienced decades ago. But growth is going to stop if we don't get government support for the creation of better transmission lines from West Texas to the East. We need a way to transmit the electricity we generate across the state to areas that lack the resource we have. We are trying to get legislature passed to invest $6.4 billion into new transmission lines, which would last 50 years, and would reduce power prices by more than $3 billion a year. That is a great deal for our state where in two years we earn the money back in savings and at the same time reduce greenhouse gases."

"Cliff, you are right. It would be great to power more homes and businesses with solar and wind energy, so your group being a little vocal about it, hopefully will wake up politicians and the PUC to provide the infrastructure needed. They don't want to be the reason why a backlog of wind energy projects sit idle here in Texas when we so desperately need new energy resources."

Cliff pulled the jeep off of the main road and drove up to a parking area near one of the wind turbines. "Are you ready to take a look at these beauties?"

"Absolutely, It will be nice to get out and walk around a bit." Katherine's rented car swung into the parking lot right behind them. Frank and David climb out into the late afternoon sunlight. David walked over to join his father. Frank stood by the car for a couple moments busy talking on the phone. He continued his conversation as he drew near to Katherine, she could tell he was talking to his wife. He hung up the phone and said, "So Katherine are we going to take a walk around?"

"Yes, I think that would be very informative and give you a chance to talk to your wife about that new baby. We are going to go ahead, and you take a few minutes and do what you need to make her feel okay. Catch up with us as soon as you are done."

"Katherine, Diane is fine. Just a bit confused as to when I will see her again!"

"You tell her soon. Once we leave here, you need to go home for a weekend and see her. That is an order." Katherine said sternly with a smile.

"Okay, if you say so. She will be happy to hear that. Just give me a couple minutes and I will be with you."

Katherine, Cliff and David started hiking over to the base of the first tower and Katherine asked."

"David can you take a picture of Cliff and me with a wind turbine in the background?"

David happily obliged taking a series of pictures of his father and Katherine posing with the wind turbines glistening in the background. The wind was a little stronger than usual and Katherine's hair kept blowing over her face, but he was sure he took some good ones that she would like.

Katherine commented, "The sound of the props turning are actually very soothing and probably even more soothing to anyone making a few thousand dollars for just harnessing the wind."

They moved up the row of towers that cast eerie gray shadows across the late afternoon landscape. Cliff was going to meet one of the engineers just up ahead and show her some of the inner workings of the turbine.

Frank had not returned yet, and she was a little perplexed with his personal business interfering in the tour of the site that Cliff was providing.

Her phone rang and at first she did not recognize the number. It was Diane. She took the call knowing that she was going to be thanked for giving Frank a weekend off.

"Hello, Diane."

"Senator, what is wrong with Frank?" A frantic Diane blurted out.

"Whoa, Diane what is wrong?"

"He was talking to me, and then he was not, but his phone was still on, and I could hear something horrible." She said in little gasps.

"Well, Diane we are just up ahead of him looking at some wind turbines, and we will walk back and find him for you."

"I am afraid. The sounds I thought I heard were something like him gasping or gurgling, and I thought I heard a voice whisper 'die bastard'. When he wouldn't say anything to me, I hung up and tried calling him back a few times, and he never answered the phone" She said in a very emotionally choked up voice.

"Diane, calm down and we are going back to find him. We will call you right back okay?"

Katherine really did not wait for a reply, but hung up and called Venter, "Jannie, listen up. We need you to come and get us. Bring your gun and be careful. Something bad might have happened to Frank."

"Katherine, you stay on the phone with me. I am coming right now, and I am being careful. What am I looking for?"

Adrenalin surged into Katherine's veins and fear tightened its cold fingers around her heart. "You're looking for Frank," she said hurriedly, "and be careful because I am afraid it might be those two, I mentioned to you earlier behind this."

"I was the only car in the parking lot, so I doubt that anyone else is here other than those who work here. You are with Mr. Etheridge, and his son?"

"Yes, I am."

"I think you need to start coming back toward the parking area, so I can cover you better. Right now you are too far away for me to be very helpful, if someone tries to attack you."

Katherine motioned to Cliff and his son to come with her. They wore that 'what in the Hell look' on their face as they tried to figure out what was going on.

Suddenly, Venter voice boomed across the cotton field. "Katherine I found him. You stay there. No, Jesus Christ, you need to go back to the car. You need to get back there fast."

Katherine started to come to where Venter stood, but he waved her away, and started coming toward her with his gun drawn. "Move Senator. All of you get back into the car. Just listen to me."

David and Cliff grabbed Katherine and Cliff said, "I think you better listen to him Senator. He looks very serious."

The three of them quickly moved back toward the rented car with Venter dashing behind them with his gun at the ready. Katherine strained to control the awakening fear coursing through her. Her senses intensified, and exaggerated everything around her. The crush of the grass underfoot sounded like sticks cracking in two and the blood pulsing through her veins became so loud that it blocked the swoosh of the turbine's propellers. The comforting breeze blowing against her face, now felt like some crushing evil entity.

Their heavy breathing punctuated the stillness, as they reached the car. Without hesitation, they clamored into its safety. Venter arrived and quickly slid behind the wheel. The car roared with power almost the instant he closed its door. Venter threw it into reverse and gravel flew in all directions as he quickly backed up.

It was late afternoon and the highway was now far more congested. Venter raced along an open stretch of blacktop and the parking lot fell away "Jannie, what is going on?" Katherine asked feeling her heart beating erratically.

"Someone killed Frank." Venter said matter-of-factly and without waiting for a response he barked" Mr. Etheredge, can you call the police for me?"

Katherine sat in stunned disbelief as Venter swung the car into the passing lane.

David Etheredge pulled his cell phone out of his pocket and said, "I'll call them. What is the message?"

"Just give them the address of where we just came from and tell them there was a killing there. Tell them it was an attempt on Senator Laforge's life"

Just then Katherine's phone rang. It was Diane. Katherine hesitantly answered it. In her mind she tried to think of what she should say. She knew that she could not yet tell her what had happened. "Hello Diane, I don't have an answer for you yet. Give me a few more minutes and I promise I will call you back." Her stomach turned as she spoke these words. How could she tell Diane that her husband was dead?

"Please tell me that Frank is okay! Why can't he talk to me?"

"Diane, I just do not know what is going on yet. I am as confused as you. I just don't know anything concrete yet. Please give us a few more minutes. We do have a situation here and the police are on the way. I promise, I will call you, as soon as I know what the situation really is."

"What do you mean situation?"

"Diane, I have to talk to the police now. I have to hang up." Katherine felt so guilty lying to Diane, but at the same time she wanted to know more about Frank's death before she told her about it.

Katherine sat motionless for a moment and then exhaled the breath she had been holding since she had hung up the phone and willed herself to stop trembling. Now her fear was diluted by rage and anger. Her mind envisioned what probably happened, and what she supposed had been planned for her, if Venter had not been there. The mental images were pornographic in their violence. Thankfully, her thoughts were punctuated by the wobbling wail of nearing police sirens. In front of her, she could see the police cars charging down the highway.

Venter abruptly pulled the car over to the side and barked out that they were returning to the scene with the police. He shot the car across the road and idled it, waiting for the police to pass them. At the same time, he kept up a constant conversation with the police on his cell phone. Three police cars tore by and Venter eased the car back onto the highway and raced after their flashing red lights.

By the time they got back to the site, and waited for the police to secure it, the moon had replaced the sun. Katherine tried not to think about this new horror, and instead focused on the darkening sky and the eerie shadows cast by the white towers over the gray landscape. She needed some distraction to ward off her tears and suppress the building anger roiling within her. Clutching at her fragile sanity she reminded herself that she was running for President of the United States, and she had to appear strong. But that was not how she really felt, under the pretense of strength was a feeling of abject helplessness accompanied by a numbness that slithered into her along with a sense of a tangible evil pervading the air about her. Somehow Hell had crashed into her life again.

Finally, three police officers came to her car and asked Katherine, if she would accompany them to where the body laid. Katherine struggled to suppress her tears as she climbed out of the vehicle. Once outside, her confidence disintegrated even more, and she found her hands shaking and cold sweat oozing from her brow. She closed her eyes tightly, hoping to squeeze away the confusion and fear that tore like talons at her stomach. Somewhere in the swaying cotton fields a dog howled mournfully.

For a moment she just continued to stand there, as if paralyzed, and then her eyes opened, and she breathed deeply of the night air. An officer's voice penetrated the silence and asked Katherine if she was okay. She uttered a barely audible yes, and then started to walk falteringly with them to Frank's corpse.

The walk seemed to go on for an interminable time. Above, the moon sailed through the black clouds illuminating the wind farm with quivering shadows. As she walked, Katherine began to delude herself that she was simply experiencing a terrible nightmare and that when she awoke, Frank would be there smiling.

She just had to let this nightmare play out, and all would be okay.

Suddenly, they stopped and the scent of death and blood assailed her nostrils. She knew it was not a nightmare, you wake from, but one of those nightmares you live within. As she looked down at the form in front of her all the doubts and fears rushed back into her being.

There propped up against its base was the body of Frank Payne. His blood soaked clothes glisten under the full moon as blood still oozed from his slit throat. A note hung from a knife stabbed deep into his face. Senator Laforge was overcome with anger, remorse, and revulsion as she stared at the gristly sight of her brutally murdered campaign manager. She stared in absolute horror at the gruesome scene. An officer's voice finally broke her fixation. "Senator, is this Frank Payne?" He quietly asked nodding at the corpse.

She did not reply, perhaps from her confusion, she was still trying to comprehend his question. A sliver of the moon's illumination washed over the form on the ground, and it was enough to spotlight the familiar hair now matted with blood and the face twisted in shock.

"Yes, it is Mr. Payne." Katherine said in a barely discernable whisper. In her mind the questions raced, why did they kill him? She reached for the note. But an officer grabbed her arm and stopped her.

"Sorry Senator, until the FBI gets here no one can touch anything. I can tell you this, however, the note is a threat against you. If you are ready, I can take you back to the car and get you back to the station." The officer said in an apologetic voice, while he gently held her arm.

As Katherine started the walk back to the car her stomach churned, and she staggered to her knees vomiting uncontrollably. She kneeled there gasping for air trying to compose herself as the three officers watched helplessly as she continued to dry heave. Finally, her stomach stopped convulsing, and she regained her composure. She defiantly wiped the spittle from her face, but could feel the acid still burning in her throat and mouth.

She got back to her feet, and like in a trance slowing started toward the car. It was now time to do what she could put off no longer. With a fog of tears burning her eyes, she opened her cell phone and dialed Frank's wife, Diane.

* * * *

The town hall was filling up once again. After the announcement, that Senator Laforge was found, many of the town folks decided to return. The town hall was where the action would be. In fact, it was already happening. A large number of armed police and plain-clothes security personnel had arrived and appeared to be taking up positions within the auditorium. I hoped this was a good sign.

I assumed Katherine had been found alive, and was still going to come here. It sounded crazy, but then why else would they have all this security here. Some of the guards were speaking to the people sitting at the VIP table. One of the women sitting there was Frank's very pregnant wife, Diane. Apparently, she still supported her deceased husband's dreams. Others seated with her were party officials and community leaders. I had also noticed at a table, near the rear of the auditorium, sat the numismatist, Mike Fuljenz with some of his associates. He had been an unwavering supporter and friend of Katherine's during many of her ordeals. Many out-of-towners had come to this town hall meeting because it had been heralded as one of her most important campaign events, and because it was held in her hometown.

Witnessing this army of security brightened our day. My wife, Tom, and Vince exuded excitement from this turn of events. It was an odd thing to be thinking about, but even the fact that Katherine had gotten this far in her campaign was still hard for me to comprehend.

PART ELEVEN

The Speech

O utside the town hall was still terribly cold and windy. The sky was a deadly gray with an occasional streak of light cutting through the gloom. Everyone appeared to be in a perpetual state of alert as they waited for word of Senator Laforge's expected arrival.

I was still thinking about how Katherine was able to cope with the death of Frank Payne. I remember reading that a common mode of coping with death is denial, but for Katherine that was an impossible luxury. She had to suppress her grief and quickly dispel any disbelief, anger or confusion over Frank's death. Her ambitions dictated that she deal with death quickly and differently and reject denial and accept his passing.

Besides accepting his demise, Katherine had the immediate problem of finding someone to fill his position. That would be difficult, because Frank had taken over the day-to-day control of Katherine's campaign, and his no-nonsense style had made a huge impact on her rising popularity numbers. Katherine had told me once that, "Frank was fearless, and understood how all the different parts of a campaign needed to come together. He was part teacher, part manager." His replacement would have a very difficult task.

Frank was someone who made things happen from his forceful manner, and inspired fierce loyalty among aides. Once Katherine came back from Iraq, he had people flocking back to her campaign to work for him. But now he was gone.

I remember the days directly following Frank's death that there was a great out pouring of anger by people expressing their feelings about his murder. People were outraged at the brutality of the crime and many could not comprehend that this was a deliberate act by those opposing Katherine's political platform.

The funeral was a portrait of grief and shock. The specter of murder loomed over the already grim occasion, as throngs of mourners converged at Frank's final resting place. His funeral was covered by all the major networks and workers in offices, barrooms, stores, and beauty shops paused their workday to tune into a piece of history in the making.

The hundreds of mourners attending Frank's funeral, heard his grieving parents Nancy and Nicholas, and his pregnant wife Diane, speak of their grief. Their words had individuals from all backgrounds, wiping their eyes and holding their mouths. Sorrow and anger were present in equal measure.

When a flock of doves were released into the sky, Frank's mother wept openly. Balloons were also released as a symbol of peace and hope for the future, and as a sign of the community's support for the family, said Frank's dad.

The graveside service was even more emotional. It had poured just before Frank's casket was lowered into the ground and now the gravestones glisten from the falling rain. A softer rain now washed away the gloom of the day and hid tears that oozed from swollen eyes.

When it was over, Frank Payne's graveside service had been a somber affair buffeted by gusts of wind that wisped away the sound of sobs and occasional curses like some supernatural censor.

Escorted by her husband, Katherine hastened back to their limousine. Ira, holding an umbrella, tried to shield Katherine, but the wind-driven rain still sprayed her face with droplets that helped conceal her tears.

By the time Frank Payne's casket rested at the bottom of the grave, his family, friends and other mourners were back in the sanctuary of their vehicles. But even buffered by metal doors and thick glass windows, a coldness apart from the weather permeated the air of all who had attended the service. Not from the rain or the gray skies swirling over the cemetery. Something spiritual. No one was free of it.

It affected Katherine deeply. Perhaps it emanated from the sadness of the shattered dreams Frank's death had caused. Or the spreading poison against the murderer festering in the minds of those who loved Frank.

Inside the Senator's limousine, Ira tried to console Katherine while they waited for Pamela Tutton. Pamela had been Frank Payne's right hand political strategist and had accompanied the Laforges to the funeral. Ira held Katherine tightly, but his actions seemed in vain as her body continued to convulse in silent weeping. Here in his arms she could grieve safely without fear of exposure or ridicule from the media. The flowing tears were a needed catharsis for the raging emotions she had stifled since Frank had been so brutally murdered. His gaping throat wound, the knife buried deep in his face, and all that blood was a nauseating vision that haunted her.

For the last few days, bitter grief had gripped Katherine. In her tired, agitated state she struggled to suppress an unendurable nightmare of Frank's restless spirit attempting to escape from his fresh grave. A damp place that grew darker and more permanent as each shovel of dirt and clay blanketed his casket.

Ira held Katherine tightly and whispered, "Sweetheart, you need to get control of yourself. Pamela will be here shortly. You must be strong. It is time to think of the living, of those Frank's murderers are trying to quiet."

Katherine shuddered. When she answered, her voice was little more than a whimper. "You're right." She shook her head contritely. "But, I feel so guilty that he died for something I started."

"Frank died for what he believed in," Ira retorted. "He was not doing this just for you. Honey, you were often marching to his orders. He set the tempo of this race and certainly after all that has happened to both of you, he was well aware of the dangers that hound you. You need to remember that, if what you were doing was not working, you wouldn't be a threat to them. What you are saying and doing is scaring the shit out of someone, and that means you probably do have a chance to win."

Katherine managed a calming breath. Looking out a side window of the limousine she blinked through a mist of tears. Suddenly, she saw another face looking back, a face fuller, younger with hair flaying the air as the tempestuous weather flung it about. The rain had become a downpour again, and it thundered on the roof of the limousine. Katherine stoically forced her thoughts away from the lingering image of Frank Payne's mutilation and the horrible note left pin to his face. The vulgar harsh note that warned, "QUIT THE CAMPAIGN, BITCH. OR NEXT TIME THIS WILL BE YOU."

Kat's reddened eyes tightened as her resolve hardened. Ira kissed her gently on a moist cheek as Pamela Tutton rapped on the limousine's window. He released the door's lock and a feminine voice greeted them, "I hope I didn't delay you too long?"

"Get in out of the wind and rain," Kat urged, "before you soak all of us."

Pamela stepped into the limousine, closed her dripping umbrella as she slipped into the plush seat opposite Katherine and Ira. A Secret Service agent peered in the open door, shielded any avalanche of rain with his umbrella, and tersely gave Katherine a status update before he closed the door behind Pamela.

Katherine had always applauded Frank's choice for his assistant. The petite blond had a reputation for tenacity and perseverance and already had established a remarkably successful career of enviable accomplishments: a former news co-anchor for a major cable network, a successful lobbyist, and a rising name in political circles.

"I thought I was accustomed to rain," Pamela fumed, brushing her sleeves vigorously, scattering stray droplets from the fabric. "In Seattle we have more rainy days than sunny ones," she quipped, "but this is a deluge! There's no way to stay the least bit dry in this downpour."

In spite of her depression, Katherine laughed softly at Pamela's remark. Then Kat's thoughts ran on to the days ahead. If she and Pamela worked well together, could they be the sparks to ignite the campaign?

The limousine lingered just long enough for the Secret Service agents to take their position and give the all clear for the return trip to the hotel. Against the gentle acceleration, Pamela's head turned and her blue-eyes locked with Katherine's.

"Senator, I need to tell you -- I admired Frank, and I felt privileged to work with and learn from him. More, I want to make those who killed him pay, and the best way to do that is not let them win." A look of determination hardened her attractive face. "I hope I have read you correctly, Senator, that we are going to press forward regardless of this tragedy. Frank would want you to press on with the campaign so those bastards won't win."

"Thanks for your candor," Katherine managed in a broken voice. "You have a big job ahead as my campaign manager. Frank had been a master strategist who understood and mastered the nuances of Washington's political scene. His job was not an easy one, but I do have confidence that you can handle it equally as well."

"I'm sure you understand," Ira broke in, "with Frank's death, we can expect more such attacks if we continue the campaign?" He paused, let his warning penetrate, and then added. "You understand the danger to you?"

Pamela nodded. "I understand the risks involved, sir. But I won't let acts of terror from faceless cowards stop what we have begun. Yes, I don't want to die like Frank, but I also won't be bullied by these bastards." She paused, scanned their expressions. "Excuse my strong language! It bluntly expresses my feelings." She folded her hands in her lap. "And speaking of being blunt -- if you, and I are to build a strong relationship, it must be built on trust. You, Senator, must know what I think, where I stand. Which means being brutally open, can we agree on that?"

Katherine did not hesitate. "Yes, I believe we can."

Pamela twisted in the seat to face Katherine and Ira. "Senator, you are inherently a play-by-the-rules person with a magnetism that communicates well to audiences. They sense your sincerity and dedication to your ideals. They can see you are as dedicated to the voters as you proclaim, and they respond well to you. That is your strength. Do you agree?"

Katherine sighed, nodded. "Yes, I hope it is. Who do you think is behind Frank's murder?"

Pamela's expression did not change, but a sudden tension radiated from her. "Oh! Senator, that is the sixty-four thousand dollar question. Unfortunately, it could be any one of many enemies your campaign has produced. First, I thought it was Big Oil. Because of the note and where Frank was killed. But killing him there at the wind farm, just as well served those at the IRS, the tax attorneys and accountants while casting the blame on some other groups."

Pamela smiled frostily. "But you certainly cannot exclude Big Oil as being responsible for his death. Your proposals on alternative energy could affect their profit margin, and that threat alone is reason enough to suspect them. Worse, they fear the American people. Critics have said – 'Where the American people go, so goes the world.'"

She paused, looking for understanding in Katherine's eyes. When she found it, she plunged on. "That statement may or may not be true," Pamela affirmed, "but the major oil interests can't afford to take the chance. In their minds anyone who can fire up the American people against them, make the public buy into your brand of progress, is too great a threat to discount, to underestimate."

Knowing how to play an audience, Pamela paused, and then plunged on. "You want to know why? Because right now the United States has the level of technology to produce and support alternate fuels as a major source of energy. It's just that the American people don't understand the possibility. Not yet. But, if your campaign catches fire, the people will. That's why your enemies want you quieted. This is where they do want to kill the messenger"

Ira glanced at Pamela and added, "Well, unfortunately our enemies are not just the oil cartels and major oil players. They are all the companies, which support the oil-related world market. Worse, most of Congress has been bought one way or another by oil companies. We've come to an era where you cannot find a member of the house or senate that is not receiving major contributions from oil interests. The oil industry has become American's shadow government complete with free use of our arm forces to protect its products and profits. Our service men and women die to protect their profits, and billions in tax dollars are used to support their industry." He sighed heavily. "The simple truth is--to stay elected today, you have to coddle oil and be their lackey."

"It is a very gloomy assessment of our government's marriage to Big Oil," Katherine offered, "but as repugnant as it sounds, it is where we are today."

Pamela ran her fingers through rain-dampened hair as she nodded. "I would better describe it as our government's capitulation to Big Oil. If they need the strength of our arm forces, tax dollars and the blood of our soldiers to stay in business, then this is an industry that should be nationalized."

Katherine shook her head. "That will not happen. But if we can support those alternative energy companies that can free us from Big Oil control, then their power will wane as fuel costs begin to drop."

"Frank's death was some sort of coordinated attack," Pamela warned. "The power to the security cameras on the towers was killed just before he was murdered." She paused, continued thoughtfully. "What you need to ask yourselves is this -- why go after a candidate's campaign manager rather than eliminate the person who threatened them?"

The question caught Katherine off guard. "I really just felt they thought we would just cave in and go away, and Frank was accessible."

"Let me tell you why," Pamela pounced like a cat after a mouse. "Because you're news. Kill a campaign manager and the public's interest wanes after a few front-page days. But assassinating an American Senator has much longer lasting and far reaching repercussions."

A quick hush answered Pamela. She let Katherine and Ira digest the idea, before she plunged on. "What we need to do immediately is augment our security with people outside the Secret Service. It looks like all the agents assigned to us are borrowed Treasury agents who previously worked with the IRS criminal investigation bureau."

Her penetrating gaze searched their faces. "I seriously doubt that any of them would be willing to take a bullet for any of us. Especially if they feel your national sales tax would eliminate or curtail the current scope of the Internal Revenue Service. They would probably do little to protect you from your enemies. You can bet they worry that their jobs would be eliminated if your national sales tax replaces income tax." She smiled frostily. "Plus I bet they are hounded and chided by other IRS agents for being on this detail."

Ira twisted in his seat and stared out the back windshield at the trailing escort car. "Yes, I think it is time to find our own security people," he agreed angrily. "Don't look now, but we got guys sleeping on the job in our rear escort vehicle."

"We need them to understand that the IRS will not disappear," Katherine said. "Only its collection focus will change. It will become the agency delegated to collect sales tax." Katherine nodded at her own logic. "I am sure there will be work for all of the fulltime IRS employees."

"I agree," Pamela said. "The problem lies with the greedy tax attorneys and accountants who are creating this distortion of what we are trying to accomplish."

"I think it's time to approach and sound out our agents about what a national sales tax means to them," Katherine said. "Hopefully some of it will get back to others in their agency."

As the limousine sped down the freeway, a hush fell over the three. It did not last long. "None of us are immune to assassination," Pamela said. "Think how assassinating a controversial American Senator would appeal to extremist groups. They know it would buy them respect from other American political groups, be celebrated by executives in Big Oil and cursed only by the mainstream public. Think of the bragging rights their act would give them!"

Katherine's eyes widened. "It is disgusting and frightening, but so very real. But I do wonder how they would expect to get away with such blatant…?"

"Oh it's possible," Pamela interrupted, "probably the actual killers would be disposed of immediately or die in the attack to prevent them from talking. If it was some radical fringe group, they would take total credit for the attack without divulging where the funding came from. There are so many powerful people that have selfish reasons to kill us, it would be virtually impossible to figure out who hated us the most. Whoever it was would make the chain of evidence stretch so far and in so many directions that it would be impossible to know who really was behind it all." She shrugged. "For those at the top it would continue to be business as usual. They would face only a slim chance of discovery. But, with you dead, any threat your election posed to their bottom line would be over."

Katherine pinched her lower lip thoughtfully. "You do argue a strong case," she admitted.

"There are also other points to consider," Pamela offered, "but they need to be discussed in detail." She leaned back in her seat. "Which can wait until we reach the hotel. Yes?"

* * * *

In a common room of their hotel suite Katherine and Ira listened to Pamela Tutton's recommendations. As Pamela detailed the expertise they needed for their new bodyguard detail, Kat thought immediately of Jim Anderson, her CIA contact in Iraq. Excusing herself from the discussions, she went to the bedroom, and called a special number from her cell phone.

"Katherine, it's good to hear your voice," Jim said immediately, and his voice sounded genuine. "I'm not sure what prompted this contact, but I will hazard a guess you somehow need my help."

"Yes, I'm sorry, but I do hope you can help me, Jim."

"Is it about the latest smear story about your old school buddy claiming he rescued you from Iraq a few days before we did?"

Katherine did not respond for a very long second "What are you talking about, Jim?"

"Well, it seems that a guy named Wilson something claims he picked you up in Iraq and sailed you all the way back to Galveston Texas. And to make it juicer, he claims you two were hot lovers?" Jim chuckled on the other end.

"Jesus, that is not funny," Katherine exclaimed, "That is a major problem."

"No, not really. There are thousands of people who saw you on television and in person in Iraq during the same time he is claiming you were sun bathing on his yacht and having a little extramarital affair."

"Was his name Wilson Lawson?" Katherine asked.

"I believe it was, yes, that was it. Do you know who he is?" Jim asked.

"Yes, he was a guy that I knew as a kid and kept in contact with my entire life. He was the only black man in Charlestown, New Hampshire, probably in the entire county. He was a great guy so, please don't let anything really bad happen to him. Can money take care of this problem?" Katherine asked.

"Don't worry. We will take care of the problem, and Katherine, you know better than to ever suggest money as a solution. If you were not with him, which you could not have been. Then he is just lying and that can be addressed. So if the problem wasn't Wilson Lawson, what is it?"

"Wow, under these new circumstances this really sounds odd, but I need men I can trust," she told him without evasion, "men who can remain cool in dangerous situations. Most of all, men who will remain loyal."

"Tell me more," he encouraged. "What is your reason behind this?"

When she started, the words came in a rush. Jim Anderson listened quietly, interrupting only for additional details on specific points and situations. Strangely, when it was all said, she felt cleansed, almost as if she had confessed before a priest. And that seemed almost poignant. Short of dropping out of the campaign, she could expect no absolution.

"You have pen and paper?" he shot back. "Your man is Joshua Fitzhume. Ex-military, ex-Company, soldier of fortune, mercenary, and the best damn recruiter I've ever met. We use his services when the Company can't officially get involved. If he stalls you, have him phone me. He has my number. Now, do you feel any better?"

"Yes, it looks like you are again my savior! And thank you." Katherine responded.

"Be safe, Katherine." The phone went dead.

Good God, she thought as she hung up the phone. This is a real war where I need my own private army just to survive. She pushed the absurdity aside and made the call, left the requested message, and waited for Fitzhume to contact her.

When she returned to the suite area, Ira and Pamela were still discussing options. "A large bus would be safer than a limo or car," he agreed. "I'm thinking of a commercial bus shell that's been converted into a corporate coach. Marathon Coach has a manufacturing facility in Coburg, Oregon, and…."

They looked up as Katherine stepped into the suite's common room. Ira turned to include her in the discussion.

"I have an announcement. You ready for it?" Katherine paused and the room went silent. "The news media is reporting that an old acquaintance of mine is currently claiming he saved me from Iraq the same time that I was traipsing around the desert with the troops. And to make it a little seedier, he claims we were lovers." Katherine announced.

"Jesus Christ!" Ira exclaimed. "Who in the hell is this bastard?"

"It's Wilson Lawson." Katherine responded.

"Wilson? Wilson Lawson! I can't believe it. We were supposed to be friends. Why would he be claiming this? Let's get in contact with him and find out from his own mouth what this is all about", Ira ranted, "Someone must have paid him, or he has gone nuts."

"No, we are not going to contact him. I was told by reliable sources that the problem is being taken care of, and I pray that is true. Until I hear different, we do nothing. And our only reply about this to the media is it is a fabrication, by an old acquaintance that is sometimes delusional. That will be our only comment about this subject." Katherine said determinedly.

"That is all I know, and I do not want to waste time talking about it. What were you all working on when I interrupted you?"

"We were talking about using a motor home as our mobile campaign office." Pamela replied.

Ira added, "Marathon Coach up in Coburg, Oregon produces lots of the touring buses for celebrities and corporate use, so I'm sure they could take care of our needs. Marathon could also take care of the modifications Pamela wants, like special plating on the sides and shielded motor, fuel tank, and chassis areas."

Like a touring rock star, Katherine thought derisively. But she bit back the retort. The danger they faced was real. With a smile she said, "Ira, this is your baby, you get something that we can live in the next few months and conduct our campaign from. I will leave buying the bus to you, because I am sure you have a better grasp of what these things are than any of us have. Pamela, let's talk about the security measures, we need to implement and the number of men we need to augment our Secret Service team…."

* * * *

With the news media's insatiable hunger for mistakes, gossip, and innuendo, Pamela was able to insure a large media response for all of Katherine's scheduled campaign stops. Every media name wanted to be the first with new dirt on the Wilson Lawson story or the reported Saddam Hussein million dollars contribution to Katherine.

Pamela continued with Frank's basic plan of having Katherine visit various alternative energy producers. The morbid desire of the news people to learn more about Katherine gossip paid great dividends as Katherine's visits created headlines, wherever she went, promoting solutions to a runaway oil juggernaut. Feeding on the controversy, reporters and cameramen swarmed about her. Their attention gave local, regional, and national coverage to her denunciation of Big Oil's resistance to change and their manipulation of solutions to make change appear hopeless.

Capitalizing on the national publicity opportunity, Marathon Coach took up Ira's challenge. The Coburg plant worked around-the-clock to outfit and deliver the forty-five-foot Laforge campaign bus, the outside shell airbrushed with a huge American flag and Katherine's smiling portrait, within record-breaking days. Ira and some of the new security team picked up the brand-new coach, drove south, and met the Laforge campaign team in Texas. Then on to Deming, New Mexico, where the Senator was scheduled to view a solar energy joint pilot project.

As they drove, the Laforge team relaxed in new plush easy chairs, part of the luxury accommodations provided by Marathon. In route Pamela discussed their itinerary.

"The National Nuclear Security Administration's Sandia National Laboratories had teamed with Stirling Energy Systems, Inc. to build a 300 megawatt solar farm," she said. "It produces power for two hundred-forty thousand homes. They want you, Senator, to visit the facility, study their methods, and review the data they have gathered."

Katherine sat back thoughtfully in her seat. "How many more sites like this are there?"

Pamela smiled. "I must admit, I am not sure. But if you look at our proposed campaign schedule, you'll see we are going to visit quite a few of them across the country." She pushed the ambitious campaign schedule to Kat. "National coverage will help your campaign and also promote public awareness of the projects. I think that's what's called a win-win situation."

"I have one other idea that I hope you will like." Pamela added. "I want to express the cost of these alternative energy projects in relation to the money spent daily on the war. I want to coin a name for it like the new

'Laforge war cost yardstick' or for short the 'LWCY scale' We are spending roughly 200 million to 275 million per day in Iraq on our war efforts. Whenever we discuss the cost of a alternative energy project, we will make sure the public realizes how much just a few days of war expenses could buy us in terms of solving our energy problems."

"I think that is an excellent idea", Katherine said, "Certainly, one that will make us a little more hated, but what the heck, let's go for it."

It was the first light of dawn, and Katherine had already been awake at least an hour. She had been gazing out at the barren, but beautiful landscape along Interstate 10 a few miles east of the New Mexico border. She liked watching the break of dawn. Seeing the glimmer of headlights streaking by with their autonomous travelers. It was her time of solitude to plan, to contemplate, and gather strength. But it was often a time when thoughts of her daughter crept into her mind and her eyes would well up. She grabbed one of her many reports to focus on to turn the vision of her daughter to a fading shadow in her mind. She hated not being with Lyndsey, but it was a necessary sacrifice, if she wanted to continue with her quest for the presidency. But it was the one thing that would shatter her heart into a million pieces. Her darkest fear was that her enemies would kill Lyndsey, just to keep things at a status quo and to keep their billions rolling in.

Swaying just slightly with the motion of the moving bus, Katherine lifted her face to the hot shower spray hoping it would wash away the images of the day and her new reality. But no amount of water could change the fact that this campaign was no longer just a race for the Presidency. It was war, and a fight for her life.

"Land of Enchantment" is what the welcoming signs read as you enter New Mexico on Interstate 10. But the state did not seem that welcoming as the bus creaked and swayed from 50 mile an hour wind gust. The swirling dust was so thick that the sun was just a dim glow in the grit filled sky. It reminded Katherine of her stay in Iraq. The bus pushed on and finally the winds subsided just outside of Deming, New Mexico. A town shadowed by the rugged rocky Florida Mountains. Deming was a railroad town that funnels trains laden with coal to power plants located out in the steaming desert. Just south of Deming the terrain was a jumble of volcanic rocks resembling a scene from the Flintstones. Suddenly, the prehistoric landscape evolved into a futuristic sea of solar panels shimmering brightly in the New Mexico sun.

A welcoming committee met them at the gate. "Senator Laforge, I want to welcome you and your guests to the world's largest solar farm!" boomed the deep voice of Mr. Carson greeting Senator Laforge and her entourage at the visitor's gate. His words rode on a rushing roar of applause from the gathering that her visit had attracted.

"Mr. Carson, we are so excited to see this fabulous installation," Senator Laforge shouted back, "It looks like those solar panels go on forever. How large is this solar farm?"

As Mr. Carson nodded to the Mayor of Deming who had accompanied Katherine, he said proudly, "Well the site covers about 3,200 acres of New Mexico desert. I know it looks like just rows of dark glass out there, but 300 megawatts of electricity pour out of these babies. That is enough electricity to power a quarter million homes. And I don't mind bragging that we are 60 times bigger than our largest rival located in the Bavaria region of Germany."

"How much did this facility cost?" Katherine pressed.

"Well, Ma'am, I've read the newspapers about you and prepared for that question using your war cost yardstick. This place cost about the equivalent of 6 days of war expenses in Iraq or in dollars, one point five billion."

Katherine nodded. "Your company is doing what this country needs."

"Here in New Mexico we consider 'sun rays' as one of our natural resources, Senator, and we have a lot of it." His eyes squinted through heavy-duty sunglasses. "Your state has oil, West Virginia has coal, and we have sunshine. We are proud to be leading the way in this industry and contributing some small part in reducing our country's fossil fuel dependence."

The group was winding its way down an avenue of Solar Panels, and Katherine was enjoying the caress of the dry warm wind blowing in the desert. She asked Mr. Carson, "Are the winds normally blowing like this?"

"Oh, yes, Deming is definitely a windy town." Mr. Carson replied.

"Is it strong enough for powering wind turbines?" Pamela asked.

"Certainly, but geothermal would be a better natural resource to develop here in conjunction with solar," he confided, "There are a few wind turbines around here now, and I'm sure someone will eventually build a wind farm here! Senator, my company is dedicated to providing cheaper sustainable energy, that is ecologically safer, and non-destructive to the earth. We are in direct competition with the old fossil energy companies, and I do mean old fossils. We pride ourselves that our energy sources are not only cleaner, but also far safer for the crews that bring the power to the people. Our power sources do not expose employees to cave-ins, black lung disease, or require soldiers to die to prop up some oil producing foreign regime lining Big Oil's pockets."

Katherine felt suddenly disconnected from the discussion. Carson's words melted into the warm wind unheard as she tried to comprehend what she saw before her. It was a strong Déjà vu feeling that took hold of her. A hand-written cardboard sign taped to a post read "We love you, Katherine," but this was not the first time she had seen it. This sign had been a fragment of a dream she had experienced early in the morning. She had seen a woman's hand scrawl the message across the cardboard. The same hand then taped a coin to where the dot of the 'I' was. She recognized the handwriting. It was hers and the coin was an ancient Hulagu coin. She knew that Zoe had somehow placed it there. Why she had dreamt it was a bigger mystery. In some unexplainable way, there was still some mysterious connection between Katherine and her twin.

Ira put his hand on her shoulder and asked, "Katherine, are you okay?"

Katherine said nothing, only nodded absently still gazing at the sign. Ira sensing a problem announced to Carson, "I think Katherine is feeling the sun just a little too much, and I need to get her back in the shade." Her face was pale, but she snapped out of her trance and protested ending the tour of the facility.

"Mr. Carson this is just one of those things I live with, and I assure you that I am fine. I just had a momentary bout of nausea, and it is gone. So let's continue with our tour. What new developments do we see on the solar energy horizon?" Katherine asked.

"Well, Senator, to righteously answer that question we do need to go back to my air conditioned office. I have a presentation of the future of the solar industry and great visuals on the new technology." He motioned them back to the control office. "Senator, we are at the threshold of the solar energy era. Our technology today is equivalent to what the computer industry was when they marketed those old floppy drive computers, people use to rave about back in the eighties. Our current solar panels convert less than 20 percent of the sun's energy to electricity, and our nemesis harp on how inefficient that is, but we are rapidly advancing this infant technology faster than the advances of most other industries. For example, we now have methods of using the solar arrays' excess energy to power large compressors that squeeze huge volumes of air into underground caverns. When there is no sun, the compressed air is released to turn the turbines that generate the electricity. Another method being used is called concentrated solar power. It consists of mirrors focusing sunlight onto a pipe filled with a liquid to create steam to power a turbine that generates electricity. The hot liquid heats molten salt, which has great heat retention qualities. The super heated salt is later used to create steam to power the turbines."

Carson's explanation sounded more like a badly skipping CD than anything comprehensible to Katherine. Only some of his words were heard as her mind kept struggling with the sign, she had just left and her dream from the morning. How could she have dreamt of the note and the Hulagu coin before she had physically seen them?

"I think this is all very wonderful and certainly a promise of a much better future," Katherine said, hoping her remarks had some bearing to what Mr. Carson had been talking about. She realized that she had probably appeared very preoccupied and felt this was time for one of those little speeches previously prepared for these occasions. Katherine looked past Mr. Carson and started. "I think everyone in the alternative energy industries realize that they can reduce foreign oil dependencies to zero, if we can simply prevent Big Oil from derailing these programs. Being an energy self sustaining country offers other major benefits. It lowers global tension and the huge military expense Big Oil requires of our country for it to find and transport the oil from the many countries that would like to see us destroyed. Our massive trade deficit would be greatly reduced and greenhouse gases would be slashed. Domestically more jobs would be created in emerging energy sectors, than loss from the oil industry. This is a new era that can reshape the power bases of the world. As countries become energy self sufficient, some will find this as a strength that they can exert on countries that have fallen behind in the energy race, like us. They can deny access to the antiquated oil reserves or destroy them with little effect to their own energy needs. Countries such as ours could become powerless to lesser countries that desired to cripple us by denial of energy. Unfortunately, we are not far from that possible scenario. We need draconian change in the source of the energy we use. But only you can make that happen, because Congress only marches to the order of the titans of Big Oil."

For a few moments Katherine forgot about the note, the Hulagu coin and glowed from the raucous applause she was receiving from her speech. She looked out into the crowd and smiled as a feeling of warmth of their acceptance embraced her. The sea of placards waved about over their heads, and suddenly a woman toward the back came into view. Her eyes locked onto Katherine's, and Kat felt momentarily transfixed. It was that same feeling she had experienced back in Lumberton, Texas when ComDef1's pleading eyes stared at her through the laboratory's observation glass as it died. Then a placard rose up in front of the woman's face, and she vanished. Katherine watched the spot, but when the wavering placards parted, the woman was no longer there.

A reporter shouted at her, "Senator Laforge, what are you going to do about the immigration problem we suffer with here in New Mexico?"

Katherine heard the question and snapped to her senses. Her face was drained of color, but she turned bravely to the reporter and said. "My immigration solution is tied to my National Sales Tax proposal. If we adopt the National Sales Tax, everything anyone buys in America will be taxed. That would apply to all people physically here in our country. Illegal aliens would be paying the same tax that their neighbor with a social security card pays. Their tax-free wages will no longer be an incentive to come here or an unfair advantage over law abiding American workers. Now regardless of how you obtained your money, you are going to be taxed when you buy something with it. Since people earn money simply to exchange for goods and services, a new non evasive, easy to implement method will solve many of our immigration problems and underground economy issues. Millions of people who do not pay taxes at all, now will pay their fair share once my plan becomes law. Even the petty pickpocket will pay taxes on what he steals and the maid who you occasionally employ will pay her fair share. The street corner drug dealer flashing his roll of cash will pay his fair share of taxes for his gold chains, spinning hubcaps and baggy pants. No more citizens being fined, harassed or imprisoned for not understanding complex taxation codes where even educated tax lawyers disagree on their interpretation. Our current system is abusive, invasive, complicated and one that makes criminals out of many citizens because of its complexities and unforgiving nature. My new National Sales Tax will solve the majority of our immigration problems and make April the 15th, Freedom Day."

Through the roar of clapping and chanting "Katherine for President" she could hear Pamela telling the press no more questions would be entertained. Katherine stood there waving and smiling at the adoring crowd and then felt one of her secret service agents nudge her forward. She turned to Mr. Carson and thanked him for his time and praised him again, and then she and Ira started down the corridor lined by security agents and police. A corridor cut though the middle of her supporters by arm linked men in uniforms winding right up to the steps of her awaiting campaign bus. Katherine started moving down it, smiling and shaking some hands. A few yards from the bus a little girl stood smiling excitedly on the sideline and reached out her hand to Katherine. "Ms Laforge, don't forget your coin. Don't you want it?" The little girl yelled.

Katherine looked at the coin. It was a Hulagu coin. She stooped over to speak to the little girl and get a closer look at it, but an agent interrupted and told her that he should take it from the little girl. Another agent kept pushing Katherine down the corridor. Katherine shouted out to the little girl, "Thank you! Where did you get it?"

"A lady asked me to give it to you," the girl yelled back, "Do you like it?"

"Yes!" she instinctively replied as she felt her stomach churn as the secret service agents helped her up the steps to the campaign bus.

Once the door to the bus closed, Ira looked at her quizzingly, "What in the hell was going on out there?" Katherine looked at him and Pamela standing next to him and replied, "I don't know. I thought I saw someone

I knew for a second, but I am not sure who I thought it was, and then that note that was there with the coin. I dreamed about it early this morning."

Ira glance at her questionably then reached out to hug her. "Katherine, I want you to go to bed now. Get some rest. This has been a very hard day. Hot sun. Tons of pressure on you. No wonder you feel confused and see some simple coincidence a supernatural event."

Katherine pushed away from him and glared up at him. "This was not my imagination. I am not going to bed yet. I need to do some research, eat and then go to bed maybe." She sighed heavily, " Don't doubt me. I need your support."

Ira stood there wordlessly looking at Katherine. Only the sound of the motor broke the silence. No one said anything, and Katherine turned around and strode back to her desk where the Hulagu coin sat.

That night, before she went to sleep, she gave instructions to a guard to wake her at 4 am, if she was not already awake. She had read numerous studies on the web about dream recall. Some people have less of a barrier between states of sleep and wakefulness and pass between them easier. These people have excellent dream recall. Even better is the group of people who go back to sleep after they are awoken in the morning. These dreams experienced during this period are recalled even more vividly. If dreams are truly triggered by events and experiences, Katherine wondered if she was sharing Zoe's experiences and seeing them in her dreams. Or was it more like Zoe had the ability to dream within Katherine's consciousness when she was in a dream state? The constant hum of the tires and the mild sway of the bus soon lulled Katherine to sleep.

A secret service agent holding a cup of steaming coffee hesitantly touched Katherine's shoulder and softly said, "Senator, it is 4 am, time to get up. I have a cup of coffee here."

Katherine peered at him between squinted eyes and said, "Thank you. Just give me a minute. I am awake." The guard placed the coffee on the nightstand and left the bedroom. Katherine quizzed her mind, but this morning there was nothing. She laid back down and tried to fall asleep again, but it didn't work. Soon it was 6 a.m., and she really did have to get up and start her daily ritual.

Katherine read her email as she sipped her coffee. No one brought up yesterday's events, and that pleased her. Pamela on the other side of the desk reading her email suddenly glanced over to Katherine. "Do you have an official piece of email from the Senate Sergeant of Arms?"

Katherine looked back through her in-box and exclaimed. "Yes, I do." When she opened it, the message read, "We will be calling you this morning at 8 a.m. Please take our call. Your humbled colleagues."

Pamela said, "This did come from the Senate, I'm sure it was not really from the Senate Sergeant of Arms, but someone had access to his email. We need to take this call. Let the Secret Service set up a trace on the incoming calls and see who these fans might be?"

The clock's hands slowly moved as if time was about to grind to a halt, then suddenly a phone rang. It was Ira's cell phone. Secret Service agents hustled around attaching a tap to it and putting it on a powered speaker device.

Katherine said, "Hello!"

A raspy voice greeted Katherine over the phone's speaker. "Good Afternoon, Katherine! It is so nice of you to take our call. My colleagues and I were concerned that your scheduling and security issues might prevent this little chat." Another voice as equally as raspy interjected, "Katherine, we are five here and the call is untraceable, so we intend to be quite candid with you. I hope you will take what we say seriously and understand that we are very concerned about the noise you have been making about some of our most loyal supporters and your future."

"Who would these supporters be?" Katherine asked, her controlled voice neutral.

"Senator, I think you know that we cannot divulge names in this conversation. So let's not waste each other's time with such foolish questions," one of the voices replied. "It was so unfortunate about Mr. Payne. Our condolences, but it is somewhat understandable since you have attacked so many patriotic and influential citizens."

Katherine interjected, "Mr. Payne's murder was our 9/11, and we will not rest till those who are responsible are punished."

"Of course, that is admirable of you Katherine'" taunted one of the voices. "But let's talk about some particular issues, so we can make things easier and safer for everyone. We need you to cease your negative rhetoric about Big Oil and start talking about a long term phasing in of alternative energy. This will give these pillars of our economy time to make the transition without the terrible financial loss your current actions promise."

"But that would mean we would have to provide military support for Saudi Arabia, Iraq and continue to buy oil from countries like Iran and Venezuela who would like to see us annihilated." Katherine shot back.

"That is true, but if we radically decrease the oil we buy from these countries, they will either raise our prices or cease selling to us altogether. In either case our industries and economy will starve the same way a piglet does without its momma. In fact, Katherine, an upset momma pig will eat its young, and that is not much different than what we face with these countries selling us oil. We have to continue to buy their oil, plain and simple."

The deep gravely voice broke in again, "Katherine, you think you are some sort of a savior with all kinds of solutions for what some call our oil addiction. But look at your own state and all the dimwitted assholes with trucks, four wheelers and SUVs. What have you done there in Texas? Your own goddamn state produces more pollution than the next three combined. It's your own constituents that have perpetuated this problem, if you want to call it a problem."

Another voice blared from the speaker, "What I think my colleague is trying to make you understand, is that we all keep abreast of the energy situation and as bad as you portray it – it is what most of us find most beneficial to those of us who actually make things happen in this country. Katherine, you know in Rome the peasants could go to the Coliseum and watch the killings for free. You know why the Roman senate did that? That is just a rhetorical question… They did it to keep the peasants content."

"Today we use TV to keep our masses content and occupied. They are so busy following who is fucking whom that they don't have time or the inclination to question what really is happening around them. They are like sheep. Make up a law and they will follow it without question. Have some pathetic celebrity speak for us, and we got half the country thinking it's a revelation from God. Don't be naïve, Katherine, we make laws and make things happen for those who count, and those who make sure we get elected. The old 'support your constituents shit' is just crap for the naive. We need to keep the peasants happy, but just a few crumbs does it, and you can dictate to them what happy is. Do you understand, Katherine?"

"Yes, I understand you," Katherine replied, "It also makes me ashamed that I am one of you, if in fact you are Senators. And you are right, I am naïve. I never thought I would have colleagues who would be as despicable as you seem to be."

"Oh my, Katherine, how can you run a country if you've got your head in the sand and don't understand how things really operate?"

"Hell, that is not having your head in the sand," another voice broke in, "That's having your head up your ass." A chorus of laughter joined him.

Ira slammed his hand on the desk and blurted out, "That's it. We are not going to listen to anymore insults. If you have something to say – say it, or we are going to hang up!"

The laughter subsided and someone ventured, "Well, you are right. We have things to attend to, so let's get on with what we contacted you for. We want you to change your rhetoric about Big Oil. You will receive some informational material about oil's future, and you should study it well and quote from it for now on. We need to get this all turned around, Katherine, or we are going to lose control of some very angry citizens who see you unfortunately as the enemy. These are individuals who are bad luck to those who won't be their friend. It just seems that bad things start to happen to those people who cross them. They get sad and commit suicide, don't pay attention and have accidents – bad things like that. Katherine, you don't want to live like this. Hell, you riding around in that big old bus, you never know when you might expose yourself to one of those random bullets from some crazy redneck hunters, and all kinds of road hazards. But that is the kind of powerful bad luck, we are talking about. Bad luck that even happens to other family members. If I had a sweet little daughter like your Lyndsey, I sure would be more careful who I pissed off."

"You bastards," Katherine shouted at the phone. She heard a few chuckles at her outburst and then someone said, "We will call you again, Katherine. Bye!" The phone went dead.

* * * *

The Secret Service was able to trace the call to a home in Oakland California where the occupants were on vacation. There in Oakland, two Secret Service Agents listened to the approaching fire engines while they sat in their car facing the house as flames devoured it.

And Katherine knew that even if evidence was there, enough money had been paid to enough people that nothing would ever come of the investigation.

The next few days Katherine was consumed by a whirlwind of campaign stops at electric co-ops, town hall meetings, green energy groups, solar battery companies, tax reformers and the like. Every morning the same old ritual was repeated, eating a continental breakfast while reading the glut of emails consisting of praise, campaign pledges, and the usual diet of hate mail. And every morning as the miles sped by, Pamela, Katherine and Ira would work at composing responses for questions expected at their next campaign stop. For Katherine the day started even earlier, she would get up at 4 am and then try to go back to sleep, in an attempt to experience another dream of an event that she would live. But her dream theory appeared flawed since no new dream brought her visions of her twin's actions.

About eleven am on a Wednesday the daily humdrum was replaced with the excitement of visiting her eccentric old friend, Dick Montgomery, a pioneer biodiesel entrepreneur. Ira had developed the friendship in college and the relationship with Montgomery had endured ever since. He had a reputation as a hard man to work with, but Katherine always respected his logic and ability to get things done. Dick Montgomery was tall with that Marlboro man look, minus the cigarette dangling from his lips. He had always fascinated Katherine because he was that type of individual who could teach himself anything.

*****

As the doors of the campaign bus opened, the sounds of classical music mixed with the drone of the crowd met Katherine's ears. She smiled as Dick Montgomery strutted up to her, and she instinctively embraced him. It had been months, since she had last visited with him and there was much to discuss. "Well, I am delighted that you found my endeavor here interesting enough for you to visit me in this official way. We are one of the leading biodiesel production centers in the country, at least from the standpoint of making it from algae."

Montgomery gestured to the large covered containers behind him. "What we grow in these vats is the most serious contender to Big Oil's hold on the economy."

"Well, I have been briefed quite a bit about biodiesel made from algae from Professor Bob Briggs, but this is the first time I've visited a facility that actually produces it." Senator Laforge said.

Handing Katherine a brochure, Montgomery said, "Let me give you a few numbers about biodiesel and what is currently happening with it. It is all there in that pamphlet, but I want to emphasis some of them personally. There is a lot of hype about biodiesel, but the government has approached it in a way that tells me they want it to fail miserably."

"Why do you say that?" Pamela pressed Mr. Montgomery.

"Because we would need to produce 140 billion gallons of biodiesel to replace all petroleum-based transportation fuel in the U.S. The problem is we would need about three billion acres of fertile cropland to produce that amount with soybeans, but we only have 434 million acres of cropland in the entire country. So no way will that work. You only get 40 gallons of biodiesel out of an acre of soybeans a year, but biodiesel produced from algae gives you between ten to fifteen thousand gallons per year per acre. And you don't need to use cropland. The barren dessert or some rocky terrain are just as effective when biodiesel is produced from algae."

"Why aren't we using algae to produce biodiesel?" Katherine asked loud enough for the press to hear the question.

"I think members of the government for their own selfish reasons promote solutions that they know will fail so Big Oil will continue to back them for reelection." Montgomery said, "Or you have a Senate and House full of incompetents. Perhaps a bit of both. The sad thing is people are dying because of their incompetence and misuse of their office. They are not serving the interest of the people of this country, but only their own greedy desires."

"I understand your frustration, and I hope I will have some success in changing the way we do business," Katherine said, "Certainly we should remove government subsidies that help the most profitable companies make even more profit."

"Senator, if we could just get congress out of Big Oil's pockets, we could replace all petroleum transportation fuels with biodiesel from algae at a cost of $308 billion, which is less than we will spend on blowing up Iraq in a couple years of war."

Katherine asked, "How much land would it take to create enough algae farms to produce 140 billion gallons of biodiesel"

"At current yields, Senator, we believe we need a total of fifteen thousand square miles. These farms would be spread across the country in locations like the Salton Sea in the Sonoran desert. The wonderful thing about this solution to our energy needs is that the land we need for these algae farms doesn't compete with farmland used to grow food crops. We have at least 400 thousand square miles of desert spread across our country. And we have marshlands and many other acceptable sites that could be set aside to build algae farms. So the 15,000 square miles needed is easy to find in areas that do not interfere with other uses," Mr. Montgomery responded.

Katherine looked at the massive bubble topped transparent vats that spread out before her. She watched a mechanical skimmer in the vat closest to her slowly move through the greenish goop. The slimy globs of green coat the skimmer and leave behind an eddy of greenish opaque liquid that will quickly grow new algae. Things that looked like transparent bags of pea soup hung from hundreds of racks. Her stare did not go unnoticed.

"Those are two different ways to grow the algae. There are other ways, but these are the two, we are experimenting the most with. This Senator, is our country's energy future. That is if we can get a foot hole in the diesel market, before Big Oil drives diesel prices so high that consumers stop buying diesel vehicles."

"Do you thing that is a possibility?" Katherine asked.

"If you are asking me about the threat to destroy the diesel market, the answer is yes. Ever since the possibility of diesel being a replacement for gasoline, diesel prices suddenly shot up above the price of gas and stayed there. Big Oil is trying to prevent the distribution of biodiesel in their company's pumps. They are trying to buy out anyone making biodiesel and then closing the operation. They do not want it to succeed, period."

Montgomery took a frustrated breath, and released it noisily.

"Algae frightens them because it not only provides a way to cheaply produce biodiesel, but its starches can be used to create ethanol. The protein refuse from the algae becomes high-grade food for livestock. We are talking about the most common plants on earth that just happen to voraciously consume CO_2 like a pig eating slop from a trough. That means it isn't only a source to produce various fuels, but also a way to mitigate our CO_2 problem. Power Plants using coal can feed their carbon dioxide exhaust into these algae nurseries, which devour it and hasten their growth. Beside feeding the algae, it reduces the carbon dioxide emissions by about eighty percent."

"Some other companies have set up algae farms that clean the coal's emissions and produce additional fuel for the power plant. This makes it even more cost effective. The coal industry view us as friends. For the coal industry, this has become a profitable way of handling their emission problems."

Montgomery gestured expressively, "But there is friction. Right now biofuels are getting a bad reputation because the industry is using food crops to produce biodiesel. Corn prices are shooting up along with soybean products. Like I said before, I feel this is a concerted attempt to destroy the public faith in Biodiesel and ethanol."

"Senator, my company has arrived at a historical moment where we have the potential to make a contribution to society that most of us only dream about. This is the most natural solution to our energy crisis where a miniscule plant captures light and turns it into energy by photosynthesis."

After an intense tour around the algae farm, they rode their golf carts back to the front gate of the facility to answer questions from supporters and the press. An office trailer was set up near the gate with a deck facing the crowd. The deck was covered with political signs, banners, balloons and a podium. As Katherine's Secret Service agents helped her up the stairs of the platform, Mr. Montgomery smiled at her and said, "I hope you can take a moment to welcome my son, Jack, back from Iraq."

Katherine paused and smiled before moving up to the podium. "Yes, of course, Dick. Bring him up here, and I would love to introduce him to the public." Looking out at the crowd, she announced, "Please give my good friend's son 'Jack Montgomery' a hero's welcome. He has just come back from Iraq and is here with us today. Let's hear it for him."

An energizing applause spread through the crowd. The clapping, whistles and cheers grew louder as the trailer's front door swung open. A young man in an electric wheelchair exited the door and whined toward the podium. Most of his hair was missing and a shiny reddish indentation marked his gaunt face where an eye had once been. His nose was just a knot of red grizzle above a hideously deformed mouth missing any real lips. He wore a tee shirt that exposed a bluish red knob where once an arm had been. The remaining arm and hand, scarred and pock marked, was busy moving the controls of the wheelchair. The silence that gripped the crowd was punctuated by gasps and signs as the young man rolled into view. Two scaly red, stumps protruded out from under the bottom of his Army tee shirt where his legs should have been. They were lumpy knobs of flesh that resembled heads of cauliflower that had turned a bright purplish red color. Katherine was stunned and stood there motionless. The young man let go of the controls and raised his only hand to his face. He held a cupped hand in a salute over his eyeless socket for a moment and then reached out to shake Katherine's hand as his broken mouth emitted a slurred welcome, "We hope you win, Senator Laforge." The young man's one eye locked on Katherine's face. Behind him, Mr. Montgomery's tears welled up and his body shuttered from his emotions. Katherine felt panic swell through her as she realized her shock had been obvious to her friend Dick.

"Senator, this is what Big Oil did for my son and my family," Montgomery said hesitantly as he tried to retain his composure. He wiped away spittle from his son's mouth and paused for a moment. That is when Katherine realized that the hushed silenced was begging her to speak.

"I am so sorry you were wounded." Katherine said quietly as she still held his gnarled hand. The cameras zoomed in on the son, father and Senator Laforge and recorded a moment that would replay on TV for nights to come. Katherine floundering for words said, "Our country owes you for your courage and sacrifice, and I am proud to know you and your father. It is men like you that keep this country free. We all owe you a debt of gratitude."

Dick Montgomery emotionally said, "He's my son, my hero and my miracle." The crowd responded with a standing ovation that did not cease until Mr. Montgomery signaled to them to stop. Then he took the mike and in a very controlled voice expressed more of his bitterness, "I just want to say, that Goddamn greed, excuse me, was the cause of this. If those bastards running those companies felt any allegiance to our country, as my son did, if they had been willing to sacrifice just a little profit to solve our energy problems, my son would not have sacrificed all that he did to insure Big Oil can make its 20 billion a quarter profit."

Leaning into the mike, he continued, "They have billions to solve our energy problems, but they make more money, more profits, when oil is scarce, and wars are fought to increase its price. They grow richer off the spilled blood of our sons, daughters, fathers and mothers. Yes, I am very angry. Very disgusted at these people whose ghoulish greed has hurt my son so badly." He rubbed away unashamed tears and paused for a moment. "That is all I guess I want to say, other than making sure the press realize that Senator Laforge did not know about my feelings or my son's wounds. My son and I will do as much as we possibly can with our biodiesel farm to end this tyranny of Big Oil over us." He turned to Katherine who was still speechless and handed her the microphone. The crowd again roared uncontrollably.

Katherine stepped closer to the lectern and said, "This is truly a moment I never envisioned. I think Mr. Montgomery has said what a lot of people feel. When you feel taken for granted, unappreciated and just part of a large plan to insure a company's bulging profit, you have reason to be angry. I am sure, I will get heat about this day from the press and oil lobbies, but it gives me hope when I realize others feel as I do. It hurts and angers me to see my friend struggling with what fate delivered."

Katherine glanced over at Pamela. She was signaling that time was up. "I need to open this meeting to any questions now, but I do have one more belief, I want to share with you. Our future rest with people like you and pioneers like Mr. Montgomery and his son to make the changes and sacrifices necessary to deliver us from Big Oil's grip and make our country energy self efficient."

That evening, as they drove toward Retledge, Missouri, Katherine contemplated the day's events. She could see in her mind the twisted face of Jack Montgomery and tried to imagine the horror he had gone through. How broken emotionally was his father? This was a young man who was once a ladies' man, – but now? She took an Ambien with some tea and looked at the pile of snail mail that had been opened and stacked on her desk. In front of the pile was a booklet about the future of Big Oil. This was the document her earlier call had mentioned. She thumbed through it, and then tossed it aside realizing whatever they would have liked her to not say she had probably already done it earlier this afternoon at Mr. Montgomery's biodiesel facility.

Partially lulled by the hum of the bus and from just being exhausted, she soon fell asleep in her chair. At about two in the morning a frantic Ira awoke her. "We are changing some of our plans," he announced to her in a whispered voice. "We are going to Alaska instead of Missouri."

Katherine blinked her eyes clearing sleep from her brain. She could hear sirens in the background, and the bus was stopped. "Why? What has happened?"

"We need to change our itinerary because it looks like we have pissed someone off a bit more. Our bus has been shot at and your bed has a couple bullet holes in it."

Katherine was wide-awake now. She looked at Ira and said, " I guess it's lucky that we were too tired to sleep in it."

"Perhaps, but now we are going to count on more than luck. We are going to add a little more armor to this house on wheels before we use it anymore for our campaign and maybe change the interior around a bit. The improvements will be done while we are in Alaska. It should be ready when we get back. Anyway, I think you will enjoy our next stop. It is Chena Hot

Springs Resort in Alaska. Doesn't that sound romantic?" Before she could respond, Secret Service agents walked in and announced that they were ready to go to the airport.

* * * *

Alaska's mid-summer sun hung low against the horizon as the vintage twin-engined Beechcraft began its final approach to the Chena Hot Springs Resort airstrip. As the plane descended, Katherine Laforge studied what she could see of the shadowed valley. Cradled comfortably amid surrounding birch and aspen, the 3500-foot dirt runway might have been a giant charm bracelet stretched taut over the landscape, the attendant lodge, outbuildings, greenhouse, ice museum, and other buildings, its many myriad charms.

This junket north had been a patchwork of long flights and delays, but Pamela Tutton assured her what she found at Chena would be worth the break in her normal campaign schedule. She hoped so. In any event she was here, and Katherine intended to make the most of it. Her advance team had arrived early, was already on the ground and waiting at the airstrip with Gwen Holdmann, a mechanical engineer and the Chena project director.

As Katherine climbed from the Beechcraft's cabin, Gwen Holdmann stepped forward, greeted her with a contagious smile. At first glance the Senator liked what she saw. Blond-haired and pony-tailed, the trim Holdman wore jeans and sweatshirt and fit the professional dog musher profile her background claimed. Holdmann came to Alaska as a hydropower consultant four years earlier with her husband and stayed because of the resort's geothermal potential.

"What makes Chena Hot Springs Resort so important?" Katherine asked bluntly as she rode with Holdmann to the resort's well-appointed lodge. "There are other geo-thermal projects out there."

Gwen smiled. "They said you were straight to the point. I like that." She drew a deep breath, marshalling her thoughts. "Alaska is an oil-producing state, yet we're worried about our energy costs. Let me tell you why. Because we have some of the highest electric power costs in the United States. Rural residents typically spend twenty-five percent or more of their income on utilities, well above the national average of eight point six percent."

She pointed southwest. "Fairbanks is some sixty miles in that direction, which places Chena some thirty-two miles from the nearest electrical grid. Until recently, the resort spent a thousand dollars a day on diesel fuel just to supply its electrical power. Now our facility is Alaska's first geothermal plant, and it is producing electricity from lower temperature water than any plant in the world. We've reduced the cost of energy here from thirty cents per kilowatt to only five cents. And the cool thing about this…," as she began many sentences, "what we've done can be duplicated. We feel we just need to show how it works, and other companies will pick up on it."

"How is this really different…?" Katherine pressed.

"Its effective use of the lower water temperature," Gwen summed up. "Many researchers have concluded there is no way to generate power out of lower temperature water, that anything less than 230 degrees Fahrenheit is too marginal for an alternative energy source." She grinned broadly. "But we make it work with a four- to five-year payback on capital expenditures. And if we can, other sites with similar conditions in the lower forty-eight states can as well."

Katherine echoed Gwen's enthusiastic grin. "Show me."

* * * *

Sprawled on the floor of Chena's vast hanger-like building, the power plant throbbed with sound, its great whine like a harnessed jet engine, reverberating incessantly from metal walls in a discordant symphony. Gwen Holdmann pointed at the apparatus's center.

"Refrigerant blasts through the turbine at 1000 mph," she explained, shouting to be heard. "Water at 165-degrees Fahrenheit is pumped from our 700-ft deep production into the walls of the evaporator, which heats the refrigerant within, vaporizing it. That vapor is then expended supersonically through the turbine, rotating the blades at 13,500 rpm, which causes the generator to turn at 3600 rpm, producing electricity. Water at 40-degrees

Fahrenheit is pumped from a shallow well into a condenser, which returns the refrigerant to liquid form, which is then pumped back into the evaporator to continue the cycle."

Katherine nodded pensively. "And the electricity that is produced…?"

"Our two 299-kilowatt modules produce enough power to supply the entire resort," Gwen said proudly, "with enough surplus to power an old electrolyzer we have. With it up and running, we should be able to produce enough hydrogen gas to run the resort's vehicles. It's ambitious, but if it doesn't work out, we will power the vehicles with biodiesel and blend the hydrogen gas with propane for cooking, displacing fossil fuel as a source. That will save the resort about $10,000 a year. But that's in the future. Blending the gasses is a work in progress."

Gwen's smile widened. "But there's more to see."

She led Katherine to the far end of the runway, near the Ice Museum, to a metal tubing framework, covered with two layers of polyethylene inflated with air to retain its geothermal heating, and introduced Rusty Foreaker, the greenhouse manager.

"We bypass Alaska's short growing season in the greenhouse using hydroponics," Rusty said proudly. "Half of our 4300-square–foot facility is devoted to producing seven vegetable varieties, and our first crop produced 6,500 pounds of tomatoes in four months. They were used in the resort's restaurant. The other half has space and shelving for two thousand heads of lettuce. We also are working with the University of Alaska Fairbanks on other varieties, such as green beans, squash, herbs, cucumbers, bell peppers, strawberries, and other varieties. Some are experimental; some are for the restaurant." He gestured expansively at the neat rows. "Without geothermal heating, it would be cost prohibitive to do what we've done."

"What Randy's not saying, is a direct heating system links all forty-six Chena buildings," Gwen added. "This gives us an annual savings of $300,000. Thanks to hot water running through the radiant flooring and heat exchangers, the main greenhouse remains 78-degrees Fahrenheit when the outside temperature dip to minus 50-degrees Fahrenheit."

From the toasty greenhouse, Gwen led her inside the heavy wooden doors of the Ice Museum into a constant twenty-one-degree Fahrenheit chill where the resort's owner, Bernie Karl, awaited them.

"This is the largest ice structure in the world," Bernie said proudly. "The wall to your right is built from 2500-pound ice blocks, harvested from the lake last year. The wall on the left is lined with custom tools. Here Heather Brice, a four-time world champion ice carver, and her husband create ice sculptures while tourists and resort guests watch."

"The museum is kept frozen by an absorption chilling system," Gwen explained, "using a concept that's been around since the mid-19th Century. "Absorption chillers take advantage of a temperature differential rather than a mechanical compressor to create refrigeration. Using an ammonia-water absorption cycle to chill brine circulating in the air handler behind the museum, we generate fifteen tons of refrigeration daily at a cost of $12. Fuel for the traditional compression system ran about $200 per day."

"It's the coldest building ever to be kept refrigerated by an absorption chiller," Bernie said, "and the only one to do it with geothermal energy."

That night Ira and Katherine enjoyed a suite in the Moose Lodge. This was the first time in months that they stayed in something other than their campaign bus. This ad hoc trip happened without the cheering swarms of people, or waving placards, and that was a relief to Katherine. She had not realized how wonderful and refreshing a quiet night could feel. The day was even more relaxing because only two news reporters were invited to accompany Senator Laforge on this impromptu trip.

In the morning, an angry looking Pamela handed Katherine a copy of an email. Katherine quickly read it and shrugged her shoulder. The message read:

"Hello, Katherine. That was quite a production you and Mr. Montgomery put on for your captive audience. Unfortunately, since you are such a slow learner. We feel we need to speed up your education. Talk to you soon."

Words spilled out of Katherine's mouth in some incoherent jumble, but then a calm took hold of her. Outside the sun turned a dusky rose as blue sky erased the darkness. Ira held Katherine without speaking.

Ira consoled Katherine and reminded her that they were supposed to be taking a break at the Chena Moose Lodge, not working. He told her, "This is something you, and I need to recharge, so please kick back a little and relax. If anyone is going to hurt us here, they have to realize, that they will be noticed in a town this small so far out in the wilderness. I think we need to kick back and let the Secret Service and our bodyguards do their job while you enjoy a nice sauna. What do you say to that?"

Katherine looked at him and said slowly, "Okay!"

The next two days proved uneventful. Katherine had time to catch up on the news, do some research, plan and correspond with various friends and associates that had been long overdue. The last night before they were to leave, the people at Moose Lodge put on a huge feast in Katherine's honor. She was touched by their generosity and sincerity in expressing their support for her. After the meal and wine, she didn't need an Ambien, but only the embrace of her bed to put her to sleep.

In the middle of the night she awoke from a horrible dream or perhaps a nightmare where she saw two men being shot. They were frantically running, but behind them, almost in slow motion, she could see bullets slicing through the air. Suddenly, the bullets punched into their skulls and fountains of blood sprayed out as they tumbled hard onto a concrete surface. Then she felt like she was floating closer to the bodies. In the dream, she hovered above them, and watched the puddles of blood spread out until they became one large red pool. Submerged in the pool of blood, a dislodged eyeball appeared to stare back. Wisps of smoke drifted hazily through the scene of the expanding pool of blood until suddenly a woman's foot materialized at its edge. That was all she could recall.

Katherine sat up in her bed and sweat beaded up on her forehead even thought the room was cool in the Alaskan night. She glanced at the time. It was 4:40 AM. The dream shook her because it seemed so real, but she was still sitting in her bed with Ira snoring next to her. She felt this was another one of those dreams, but she could not see the faces of the men that had been shot. Was she seeing something that was going to happen? Or something that had already happened, or was it simply a dream brought on by the drinks and the realization that tomorrow she would be back campaigning. She was excited, yet so afraid because she did not understand what these dreams were, if they were anything. She was tempted to wake Ira and tell him about this experience, but she knew the last time he thought she was nuts. At that moment, she didn't give a damn; she shook him and he bolted up out of the bed like a madman. "What is it?" Ira demanded.

"Get back in bed, and I will tell you." Katherine replied. He slid back under the covers and asked again, "So okay! What is it?"

"I think someone has just been killed or is going to be killed very soon. It is not us, but two men. I saw it in a very weird and vivid dream. I felt like I was there. I could see things in such vivid detail. There was an eye in a puddle of blood, and I remember that it looked almost yellow. I can still see the bodies falling and sort of tumbling onto concrete."

Ira grimaced, "Katherine you just had a nightmare." He reached over and hugged her. "Come on, lay back down and let me hold you."

Katherine shook her head sadly. "I didn't think you would believe me, but I wanted to tell someone I could trust that wouldn't think I was a raving lunatic. I am sure there is something to all of this, and I think we will find out about this one very soon."

Morning was just a few ticks away so neither of them really went back to sleep, but just laid there in the quiet of the night thinking.

* * * *

When the private plane touched down at the Devil Lake's Airport in North Dakota, a contingent from Katherine's staff met them with the big campaign bus. The trip to Alaska had been beneficial. Besides making her feel a little more rested and more focused on her campaign, she had come to accept that her political platform was truly a threat to some. She also had realized that these powers had become a scourge to the American way. Their greed makes it impossible for them to fix themselves. She remembered the famous quote by Edmund Burke that "All that is necessary for the triumph of evil is for good men to do nothing." She realized that billions of dollars in profits is incentive enough for the greedy to feel it necessary to eliminate her so the public will forget her crusade. Their biggest fear is that somehow the public will put enough pressure on Congress to actually take actions that will steer our country in a direction that makes it energy self reliant.

As she boarded her bus, her staff welcomed her back with smiles, hugs and handshakes. The sight of her special security contingent supplemented by Secret Service agents gave her an even stronger sense of well-being. Quickly, they got settled in the revamped bus as it slowly rolled across the tarmac and headed toward the US-281 freeway. Turtle Mountain Community College was only an hour and a half drive from the airport. As they drove north on US-281, her odd dream kept resurfacing in her thoughts. She even felt her visions of the two dead men had taken on more clarity. She asked to see all the morning newspapers and looked for any news of double murder, but found nothing. She was sure the dream was significant. She was sure it was something that would happen or something that had happened, but knew she was unable to really prove that to anyone.

Katherine Laforge's campaign caravan entered the drive leading to the Turtle Mountain Community College's administrative building. Its windows gleamed like the facets of a diamond from the bright North Dakota sunlight. The blinding radiance, once just a natural phenomenon, was now a security concern. They would want Katherine to stay in her vehicle until agents could clearly see the windows. Now a shadow, an obscured window, or a strange face in the crowd might unnerve Katherine or her entourage. No attacks or real threats had happened lately, but everyone felt something bad was imminent.

While Katherine's entourage waited in the vehicles, a reception party stood patiently on the wide steps. Excited students lined the walks, hoping for a glimpse of the Presidential contender and interspersed among them were television cameras and journalists.

In methodical manner Katherine's bodyguards and Secret Service men, scrutinized the location, spoke briefly with members of the reception committee, and then voiced the all clear in their radio microphones. As Katherine descended the bus steps, she could feel fear creeping through her being again, but she hid it. An attractive raven-haired woman with high cheekbones whispering of her Native American ancestry stepped forward with a wide smile and outstretched hand.

"Welcome to Turtle Mountain Community College, Senator. I'm Kris Delorme, project manager here at TMCC."

Answering the brilliant smile with one of her own, Katherine let herself be drawn forward with her husband Ira right behind her. A cheer roared from the onlookers, her name a continuous chant that made further introductions impossible. The celebrity welcome was one that would have been intoxicating to Katherine a month ago, but now it was just part of a nerve-jangling commitment. Katherine waved back while the reception committee led her up a short flight of steps and into the glass-domed TMCC Administration Building. As the doors closed behind them, the chanting muted, but was still audible. A feeling of security enveloped her again.

"Your visit has made the students very excited and enthusiastic," Kris Delorme said approvingly. "And I might add, many of our students are old enough to vote."

Ira chuckled. "We appreciate their interest. My wife needs every vote, she can get, if she is to win."

"But she will, I feel certain," Kris pressed, then speaking to Senator Laforge, she grew serious. "We've read your views, and I like your push for alternative energy sources and environmental concerns." Her dark eyes reflected her passion. "If we don't save America for tomorrow, who will?"

Then others closed in around them, and Katherine was whisked away to meet the TMCC faculty. She endured countless introductions and a cursory tour of the campus before finding herself with Kris once more in the north campus facility. "Celebrity status must be quite trying, I'm sure," Kris said with an impish grin as she ushered the Senator into the project director's office.

Katherine brushed back an errant curl and sighed. "It does have its moments."

Pamela Tutton, part of the entourage asked, "May, I call you Kris?" and continued at Kris' nod. "We would love to see your Green Energy projects including your implementation of geothermal heating and cooling in buildings, electric floor heating, the straw bale building, and your wind turbine. Regretfully our time here is limited, so we need to economize what we have. Can you show us some of these energy projects in operation?"

Kris nodded. "Well, first let me tell you about our geothermal heating system. Regretfully there is not much of the system, I can show you other than its pump stations, valves, piping, and the buildings in which the flow pipes are embedded. We have very cold winters here in North Dakota, so we looked for the most efficient and economic way to provide heat. This is a system where we take advantage of the earth's ability to store vast amounts of heat in the soil. Ground-source heat pumps use twenty-five percent to seventy-five percent less electricity and have a lifespan of twenty to thirty years." She smiled broadly. "These systems pay for themselves in two to ten years and reduce fossil fuel consumption while producing no harmful emissions."

Katherine held up a hand. "Do I understand correctly that it is used for both heating and cooling?"

"Absolutely! A series of valves can switch it from the hot or cold side. For cooling, heat from the building is transferred to a heat transfer unit that takes advantage of the natural coolness of earth a few hundred feet below. The earth itself does the cooling. This is a far more economical and efficient process than current conventional systems. Even the displaced heat from the system is put to good use by helping heat the building's hot water supply."

She glanced smiling at Katherine, her entourage and the reporters. "What we end up with is a very cost efficient and environmentally safe HVAC system."

As a couple of reporters raised their hands to get Ms. Delorme attention, Pamela smiled and admonished them to wait until the tour's completion to present questions. She then turned to Kris, "Now tell us about the Straw Bale Building?"

"That is it over there." Kris pointed to a large square building on the other side of the common. "The eighteen-hundred-square-foot building was completely built for $255,000 and is used for various classes, project meetings, and weekend program activities."

"So the cost of creating this building is roughly what we spend on the war in Iraq in less then 2 minutes." Katherine interjected speaking directly to the accompanying press. "Let me reiterate, this structure cost less than what we spend in two minutes in Iraq to help secure oil reserves." With that Katherine turned back to her hostess.

Kris led Katherine and her entourage to a large square building set behind a wooden fence. An exposed-beam porch sheltered its entrance. Stopping in front of it, Kris said, "At first glance the building appears very normal, but if you look at the window insets and the thickness of the walls near doorways it becomes obvious that this construction is different. Sandwiched between the exterior wood panels and interior plastered walls are stacked bales of hay. These are grown and baled right here on campus. The resulting thickness of the walls provide high insulation protection from our frigid North Dakota Weather. We save about sixty percent in construction cost, and we end up with a much more efficient building for our climate."

Just as Katherine turned to speak to Kris, blinding flashes of light washed over her. She stood transfixed trying to gain her composure like a deer caught in bright headlights. The hairs on the back of her neck stood erect as a chill rushed up her spine. Suddenly, a hand shot out towards Katherine.

Katherine felt the hand tightening on her arm and Pamela's voice telling her, "It's just the network photographers. It's okay!"

Katherine's gazed turned to Pamela with eyes still displaying fear. "I'm sorry, but those flashes are unnerving after you've been shot at a few times. I'm sorry I acted so stunned"

Pamela stepped in front of Katherine and exhorted the reporters and their crew to step back and give the Senator and Ms. Delorme enough room to conduct the tour. Security men came forward to enforce Pamela's request.

"Yes, please give us some room!" Kris urged, "I have more to show and explain about this building. I would like to point out these features while we tour it. First," she said, pointing to the floor, "it has radiant floor heating. We also are using LED lighting in entrances and bathrooms, with compact fluorescent lighting in the classroom. The roof consists of structurally insulated panels capped by a metal roof and solar panels." She paused, gestured at the surrounding walls. "And we are proud to say it is all state-of-the-art and built largely by volunteers."

"I am very impressed with what I see, and what you describe." Katherine exclaimed, "Your project is certainly evidence that we have many ways to make more effective use of our resources and save on fossil fuel."

"Impressive," Pamela said approvingly, "and especially the fact that you have taken such great strides to make Turtle Mountain almost self-sufficient."

"It's part of our Chippewa cultural heritage," Kris replied. "Our ancestors did not believe in wasting the natural resources available to them, and we carry on that belief. For us, self-sufficiency is not a goal, it's a driving force."

She continued, "Since North Dakota's wind energy potential is among the greatest in the United States, our choice of taking advantage of it to provide electrical power coincides with our cultural beliefs and desire for independence."

"Then incorporating a wind turbine to establish energy independence," Katherine pressed, "is as much an expression of the Band's cultural beliefs as it is an economic goal?"

Kris nodded approvingly. "Yes to both. Our wind turbine reduces the electric utility cost for our 145,000-square-foot main campus by fifty percent. It also serves as an educational tool for both environmental and pre-engineering programs."

"Did you receive any of DOE's two million dollars allocated for these purposes?" Katherine asked.

"DOE grants provided about 80 percent of the cost." Kris responded. Senator Laforge placed her hand on Kris's shoulder and spoke directly to the press, "Again I just want to make it crystal clear that our government's two million set aside for all these types of projects equals the cost of about 12 minutes of our war in Iraq. A war that helps Big Oil provide our country with today's oil, but offers nothing to solve America's future energy needs. TMCC project does. Even this miniscule amount of government money will provide energy to the citizens of this community for years to come and have minimal environmental impact."

With that parting shot, the tour caravanned to a spot just outside of Belcourt, North Dakota. High on a tree-covered ridge, the sun glittered off the wind turbine's silver blades rotating quietly in the breeze. A sickening feeling swept through Katherine as the visions of Frank Payne's murder at the Texas wind farm once more filled her mind. They came to a parking area and Katherine and her entourage exited their vehicles. Rejoining Kris Delorme was a welcomed diversion for Katherine to help block her thoughts of Frank. They all began the climb up the ridge to a better observation point of the wind turbine. Now she could hear the steady 'phfoop ... phfoop ... phfoop' noise of the turning propellers. She looked about and she could see her security agents scanning the distant ridges and slopes. She realized that this was a perfect spot for an assassin to kill her. The embankment she was climbing framed her perfectly for anyone with a long-range rifle, like the one that had pierced holes in her bus. There was nowhere to hide on this barren slope. She had to face this hazard bravely, and accept whatever might happen. Halfway up the slope was a wooden pole fence and Katherine braced herself against it and watched the wind turbine's huge three-bladed array rotate in the stiff breeze. She knew film crews were angling to record her profile against the wind turbine's tower, and she accommodated them. With her hair flying in the breeze she turned toward Kris Delorme and said. "I am impressed."

Katherine glanced back at the whirling blades. "With more of these…?"

Kris seized the cue. "Oh yes, Senator, it's been estimated that North Dakota's wind energy alone could provide forty-five percent of the United States' electrical needs. Add to that the accompanying reduction of fossil fuel use, CO_2 emissions, and acid rain. I think that this is certainly part of our country's solution to provide sustainable energy."

A strange thought ran through Katherine's mind, and she chuckled. At Kris's questioning glance, Katherine spoke softly, her words only for Kris' ears. "Don Quixote tilted windmills. I'm embracing them."

A stiff breeze carried away their soft laughter as Pamela announced to the press. "The Senator is now ready to entertain questions about her energy platform."

Immediately, a hand shot up from a reporter who had been at numerous stops. "Senator, do you feel the murder of Dick Montgomery was a result of his out-spoken support for your bio diesel platform?"

Katherine felt her stomach tightening. She felt broad sided. She paused for a moment to gather her thoughts and said, "I was unaware of this tragedy. Mr. Montgomery was a friend and speculation on his death is not something I will do."

"Senator, while you were on your way to this installation, his body was discovered by his employees. It was floating in one of his algae ponds. His throat had been slit. He left behind a suicide note denouncing his stand on bio diesel and you. Would you care to comment?"

Katherine glared at the reporter and said, "I will not even attempt to answer a question so morose, and that I know nothing about. Mr. Montgomery was a dear friend, and my heart goes out to his family."

Katherine signaled to a different reporter, and a Mr. Burns asked, "Senator, in Jeremiah 10:13, it is stated that God brings out the wind from His storehouses. Do you think it is blasphemous that we do not use this gift of energy that he apparently provides for us?"

Katherine paused smiling and replied, "Mr. Burns, if that is true, I pray that He blesses those like Kris, who have had the wisdom to recognize his gift of wind energy. And I think if God was to see anyone as blasphemous it would be the titans of Big Oil, coal and nuclear energy industries for the terrible carnage they have done to his creation. Have you ever seem the destroyed mountaintops of West Virginia from the coal industry? Or wondered how the nuclear energy industry plans to dispose of their dangerous spent fuel? Well, sir, they do not have a working plan, and it appears they really don't care as long as they can make a profit today."

Fifteen minutes zoomed by as Katherine fielded the questions. Finally, they were back on the campaign bus on route to the next stop. Her overwhelming feeling of relief was like what the final winner of a Russian roulette tournament would experience. Now they were heading to Rutledge Missouri, to visit a place called "Dancing Rabbit Ecovillage." As she sat on the couch next to Ira, the events of the day flitted through her mind. She wondered what had happened to Dick Montgomery, and if she had not visited him would he still be alive? Even these tragedies and her returning cloud of guilt no longer kept her awake and quickly her head rolled onto her husband's shoulder, and she was asleep.

At about two in the morning Katherine awoke. She was alone on the couch now, covered with a blanket. The wheels of the bus were a steady comforting drone, but Katherine was wide-awake. She had been dreaming about death. Perhaps brought on from thoughts about Frank Payne or Dick Montgomery. Out the window, the sky was clear and Katherine could see the bright moon floating swollen in the night's darkness. She looked at it transfixed and fantasized, that it was like an orb that beckoned the dying from darkness into its brilliance like the flames draw moths. She hoped that if her death came at night, it would be one like tonight with a moon blazing, with its rays cutting through the darkness to guide her home. Immortality was not a delusion she entertained. She realized that death was real and only its moment was unknown. The threats, the constant fear of imminent death was so menacing it often numbed Katherine. It was terrifying to wake up each morning and wonder if death was but a few moments away, lurking somewhere out there as innocuous and natural as air. She accepted she was at the apex of her life with death hovering around it, in all its permutations, accident, sickness, and murder. Death she could not defeat, but she could and would resist her assassins. Time was precious now. Katherine knew she had to stay composed and consciously face the inevitable, if she wanted her final chapter to be one of accomplishments and greatness.

Katherine wanted to accept the inevitable so she could be free to focus on her fight for the presidency and perhaps to be the catalyst in freeing her country from the grips of Big Oil, foreign powers, and invasive taxation. Sleep overtook her again, and she slept fitfully until a flood of rose roiled across the early morning sky.

Ira was already up and had a report for Katherine along with a steaming cup of coffee and a bagel. The report was about the death of Dick Montgomery. It stated that at about 2 am the day after her visit, three employees were checking a malfunction on a skimmer in one of the Algae ponds and discovered Mr. Montgomery in it with his throat torn open, but still alive. His body was twitching with his legs flaying the water. He had appeared to be trying to pull himself up onto the pond's skimmer. His shoulders were jerking back as he futilely struggled in agony. A suicide note was found, but authorities believed it was written by someone else and then given to him to sign. His wife and disabled son both rebuked the assertion that he had taken his own life. And to complicate the suicide claim, no knife or object was found to explain how he could have slit his own throat. Two other bodies were found outside, on the concrete parking lot. They were two unidentified men with gunshot wounds to the back of their heads. One of the men's ocular prosthetic was found nearby in a pool of blood. It was not known if their murder was related to Mr. Montgomery's death, but there was a great deal of suspicion that they were.

The passage about the two men shot to death made Katherine almost drop her coffee. She was sure that they were the two men in her dream. The ocular prosthetic must have been the eye she had seen in her dream. She had thought it was a real eye, but it could have easily been a prosthetic. It was probably dislodged by the impact of the bullet or the fall to the concrete.

Before she could really digest this news, Ira handed her another note that stated, "Katherine, we hope the new lesson helped you understand our commitment. The interference in the lesson did upset some of our friends, and they feel that the next lesson needs to be your final one." It was signed, "Your Colleagues."

The note's ominous tone made her want to scream in anger. She pushed it away and fought to control her thoughts. She felt a furious rage building inside of her. Ira massaged her shoulders and offered, "Honey, we have security, and they all know about these new threats. They are working on finding out who is behind it and providing even additional support for your protection. Katherine, the one silver lining in all this is the media and public have turned their eyes on to you. Your message may now get heard."

Ira's words were prophetic because change did occur to the point where Dick Montgomery's murder appeared to have altered physics. Time seemed to accelerate and now a month became a week and a week a day. Time had collapsed into some tightening vortex that shrunk the hours as the day unwound. The murder of Dick Montgomery galvanized the public and drew people to Katherine's cause. It was stronger than anything she had ever done intentionally to win voters. It seemed odd that the murder of a single man would polarize people more than the deaths of all the soldiers in Iraq, but war is too big and abstract for most to comprehend. Dick Montgomery's death was easy to imagine with all its horror and pain, but the death of a soldier couched in some obscured casualty count does not evoke the same emotions. Especially, when written in some anesthetized fashion. Iraq's deaths are relegated as filler paragraphs stuck between hemorrhoid ointment ads and half-page reports of some star's traumatic experience when changing her hair color.

Katherine's staff realized that this murder had done just the opposite of what their adversaries had hoped it would accomplish. It did not derail the campaign. Instead the tragedy pummeled it forward, making its numbers swell exponentially at a velocity that made the race inescapable for Katherine. It now controlled her, consumed her time and demanded her loyalty. She was its face, its voice, but no longer its captain.

* * * *

Suddenly, Father Grudzinsk interrupted the narration of Katherine's campaigning. He crooned into his wireless mike, "Ladies and Gentlemen, I have exciting news for all. Senator Laforge has been found." Yelling, whistling and applauding reverberated through the town hall. Father Grudzinsk just held the mike helplessly in his hand waiting for the bedlam to end. When it did, he said, "Senator Laforge is now on her way into the town hall and wishes to speak to all of us. I hope that after the horrific morning she endured, we can all agree to give her the courtesy of listening to her without interruptions or harassment. She has seen enough evil for one day, and it is time for her to experience the love of neighbors and friends again."

"Hey, we have freedom of speech!" The proclamation floated weakly from some man's mouth sitting with some out-of-towners. In response, a burly man shot up out of his chair. I recognized him as one of the Porter boys; a long time Charlestown local. He turned to face where the comment had come from and glared at a group of men whose faces took on that 'Oh Lord, I shit my pants' look.

In a crusty New England voice the Porter boy growled, "Now you listen flatlander—you have no business bein' hearyah whatsoevah! And if you dayah open your mouth", he says lifting one of his big fist, "I'll knock the bejesus outa you and taint no one will stop me. Heyah?" He glowered at them for a second, and then a thunderous applause went up with a few "Damn flatlanders" tossed in. Porter sat back down and Father Grudzinsk said, "Let's keep it civilized in here, now." He actually sounded a bit bemused.

Father Grudzinsk's announcement made my eyes tear up and my throat constrict. I felt my wife squeeze my hand, and I realized that my emotions were visible. I didn't care. I loved Katherine, I loved what she had become, that she was my friend and even more what she had done for me. I felt so sorry for her and so terribly angry. It felt as if this day was some strange dream where all our lives had been sucked into this old town hall and stitched together into some mysterious web.

All of this bothered me even more because, Katherine was a woman who was good and truly wanted to do good things for all. I also knew that the war and the deaths of so many of her associates had made her question her faith and religious beliefs. One thing for sure she saw evil differently than ever before. The night before all this happened, when I was visiting her, the subject of good and evil came up and Katherine was very vocal about it. It had been a subject mentioned in many of her emails to me. Katherine had said that her view was not something she could go public with, without being ridiculed, so she shared it with only those she most trusted. Katherine believed that evil was like the air we breathe, an entity that surrounds us waiting for a chance to invade our consciousness and then spread like a cancer. She saw evil as a darkness that invades our souls, when we are weak or have lost empathy for others. Once it has entered our being, it thrashes about in our mind taunting us to do its bidding. Its messages often gnawing at our consciousness as thoughts that drive us to destroy or hurt even the ones we love most. Katherine had gone so far as to believe that this entity could actually be the manifestation of Sorat, the rarely spoke of spirit of evil that some theologians say is part of a trinity with Satan and Lucifer.

Talking to Katherine about evil and faceless entities who do not want our soul, but instead our very extinction was unnerving. Remembering that she said "Sorat waits for that day of storm, of blacken clouds, of lost ways before he flashes his shadowy image across your path. And then if you succumb, he becomes you." That thought made me shutter because today was such a day.

The main door to the auditorium opened and about a dozen armed state troopers entered. Following them was Katherine escorted with more state troopers and some of the town's deputies. She appeared unhurt, but she looked so much older than she had from the night before. She looked dazed and I wondered if she should be here at all. A thin smile seemed to faintly flicker on her face, but other than that she appeared grimly expressionless.

As she moved toward the stage in the auditorium, Father Grudzinsk started his introduction, but no one listened. All eyes were on her as she strode to the stage. Those of us who really knew her probably all wanted to rush to her and hug her and give her our condolences. When I looked passed her, I saw plenty of teary eyes. There were so many of us who were saddened by the events of this morning.

Katherine climbed the few steps to the stage and Father Grudzinsk embraced her as they stood by the podium. He blessed her, and then walked to the side of the stage where two state troopers stood with their hands resting on their pistol grips.

In silence, Katherine gazed out at the audience, her eyes flitting back and forth over those who gazed up at her. The only sound was the light murmur of the camera crews and hushed voices of TV reporters as they shared this event with their viewers. Katherine poured a glass of water from a pitcher sitting at the podium and gulped it down.

Suddenly, Katherine spoke, "Thank you, for being here today," her voice seemed distant as it floated out to replace the quiet of the room. Outside the wind battered the windows on the north side and dark clouds skittered across the afternoon sky. Katherine continued, "After the tragic events of this morning, it is very uplifting to feel the warmth and generosity from my friends, wonderful supporters and my former neighbors here in Charlestown. I am sure all of you know that today was a day of horror for me. A part of me was stolen; my husband and some of my dearest friends have been taken from me. They were people I loved. People who had been in my life intimately, and who's memories I will always cherish. It was also a bad day for you because today they stole from you the hopes and dreams that change was imminent." Katherine stopped and took a drink of water. Her last words had been broken with emotions.

She looked hesitantly out at the audience and said, "I realize that you would like all the details about the attacks of this morning, but that is something I just cannot talk about right now. The major news channels and papers, however, will certainly provide all of you the details, gore and analysis for the next few days. I had come here intending to discuss our involvement in Iraq, but these morning events changed my priorities, and now while I have the courage and your interest, I wish to talk to you from my heart about America."

"I have been involved in politics for most of my adult life and have always been proud that I was member of congress. This morning's murderous attacks have shaken that view considerably. Those events brought me to the realization that we are a country that has evolved from a democracy into a plutocracy, a government where a select group of the wealthy decide and shape the laws of our nation through the subservience and obedience of many of my colleagues in the House and Senate. This I am sure sounds like the raving of a lunatic, or at least the venting of an angry old lady, but before you jump to conclusions, hear me out."

A few sighs and murmurs rippled through the audience, but no one said anything discernable. While Katherine paused for a second, the reporters were busy rephrasing and repackaging her words in their whispery voices.

She cleared her voice and continued, "How has this happened? Well, we as citizens have become complacent and left the decision making entirely to our elected officials. Unfortunately, for many at Capitol Hill the power they wield is so exhilarating that to keep it, they prostitute their integrity for a handful of dollars they know will come if they stay in lockstep to Big Oil's agenda and a few other powers. One of my most esteemed colleagues, Ron Paul once quoted that 'Political power must be fiercely constrained by the American people.' Today, his sage advice appears prophetic because we have basically become a serfdom under the boot of those wealthy individuals who sinisterly dictate the direction of our country to the very Representatives and Senators you elected to look out for your welfare. And we meekly accept this as our destiny and offer no resistance."

Senator Laforge looked angry now as she spoke. "We are a country that places our soldiers in harm's way to support hated totalitarian regimes, so Big Oil can maintain their sources for crude and ensure billion dollar profits. We watch our government launch programs to produce alternative energy from the least efficient methods known, while creating obstacles for those methods that are the most promising. How can they do this, you ask? Because we let them. Did your Representative promote the creation of biodiesel from soybeans instead of algae or block the import of inexpensive Brazilian ethanol with punishing tariffs. Did your Representative support the production of ethanol from corn instead of sugarcane? If the answer is yes to those questions, then your concerns, your welfare, and your future are of little interest to them because they voted to protect Big Oil's interest not yours."

Katherine paused for a moment and took another sip of her water. Outside the clouds continue to churn in the sky with billowing gray chunks drifting lower. Looking a bit pensive at the podium, she wet her lips and then began to speak into the microphone once more.

"We have a bureaucracy that has created an entire library of books to regulate and hold you accountable on how you pay your taxes, complete with severe penalties including prison if you misunderstand any of the rules buried in those millions of pages. But these same bureaucrats cannot put forth viable alternative energy programs that end our dependence on foreign oil. You need to question their sincerity. Are their failing alternative energy programs a result of their utter ignorance, or the consequence of their subjugation to Big Oil? Ladies and gentlemen, we need change. And that needed change won't come from the cronies in Washington D.C., but from you electing new Representatives that have enough integrity and backbone to support your views and look out for your welfare. It is time that you begin to hold your Representatives accountable for the way they vote, and what they accomplish. They need to be voting for laws that make positive change toward moving away from foreign oil and replacing our abusive complicated and unfair tax system with a national sales tax. They need to be serving you. Your elected officials are your civil servants, not the lords of a fiefdom. Today we have a government full of elitists who view the citizens as vassals of their dominion."

"Once again, let me reiterate. The rhetoric, legislation, and empty promises of government and its elected leaders will not bring about the necessary changes. For these changes to happen, each and every one of you must make it your responsibility to demand that your Representatives make energy independence from foreign oil and a national sales tax their top priority. This, ladies and gentlemen, is your responsibility. Will you do this?"

A huge applause exploded from the auditorium with foot stomping and whistling. I wondered if maybe she had touched a nerve and her speech would be this miracle that would cause these necessary changes. The noise was so great that a few icicles fell from the windows during this applause. Katherine appeared to smile from the exuberance of their applauding and then as the noise subsided, she continued.

"This message that I bring to you today triggered the murder of Ira, my husband, Frank Payne, my former campaign manager, Mr. Montgomery a bio diesel pioneer and dear friend and unfortunately many others. I hope you won't let them die in vain. Even if they succeed in killing me, please take up the cause and help us as a country, once again become a great nation. I pray that you will do the right thing and fight on. This country bled to be a nation of the people, by the people, and for the people. We need to embrace and honor those principles once again."

"That is all I have to say other than Thank you for your support. I love all of you." Katherine turned and the state troopers standing on the stage converged on her, and escorted her down the stairs and into the applauding crowd. I thought I could see the sparkle of tears on Katherine's cheeks, but she still appeared to exude a smile to her friends and supporters as she was hustled to the rear door of the auditorium.

PART TWELVE

Assassination Attempt

High over the pastoral town a slate gray sky spread like an endless canopy. Ragged edges of thinning clouds glowed as the sun's rays burned through them. Deep within me, a similar glow flickered and radiated through the darkness of my subconscious. But questions plagued my mind. Ghost and shadows of the past continued to emerge from the secrets, and memories that Stacie, Tom, Vince, and I revisited so passionately earlier this morning. The rustic beauty of this austere New England town etched in pearly winter monotones lost a bit of its serenity from the dark secrets that had marred the day.

The conclusion to the morning attack was far from being perfect, but the Senator's survival from assassination and her appearance made me feel proud to be her friend. In fact, I felt exhilarated from the excitement even as questions gnawed at my mind. A part of my exuberance came from the fervor of the Laforge supporters lining the street, waving placates and hastily made signs. Their passion created waves of emotions that soared to new heights as the town folks reveled in the success of their favorite daughter. Their cheers and chants drowned out the cold wind and their passion dulled the cold.

Stacie held my arm tightly as we stood there observing the events. Vince with his duct taped pants and Tom shaking from the cold stood close by sharing yet another moment together. Out of the corner of my eye, I noticed a police officer coming toward us, and I grew tense as he neared where we stood. Immediately, a wave of anxiety flooded my being. I heard Vince rhetorically ask, "What in the hell is going on now?"

The officer addressed the four of us and asked if we would come with him.

Stacie quickly asked, "What is this about?"

"I am not really sure. I was just asked to escort you to the Senator's limousine, Ma'am. Other than that, no one told me anything more." The officer replied.

All of us? Stacie asked.

"Yes, all of you, is what I was told."

We all stood there mute for a long moment and then Vince said, "Hell, let's go!"

The officer led us to a waiting patrol car and we all packed ourselves into it. I think all of us were very excited about being invited to visit the Senator. I know I was. The patrol car circled around the block to the back of the Senator's motorcade. We pulled up alongside a couple men dressed in long heavy coats with radio headsets over their ears. They greeted us and motioned us out of the patrol car. The tallest of the men offered his hand to me and told me he was happy to meet friends of the Senator. He said, "The Senator thinks highly of you, and is looking forward to seeing you." He opened the door to the limousine and asked us all to enter and get comfortable. We did as he asked and climbed into the limo. After everyone was in, he poked his head in and said, "We are going to drive to the town hall and the Senator will enter the limo there. She felt it would be easier to have all of you riding in the limo before we got there and less obvious to the public about your impromptu meeting with her. I hope you understand her concerns and are not offended. Please accept our hospitality, relax, take a drink from the bar or watch the TV until we get to the Town Hall."

We sat for about five minutes talking, then the crackling of the driver's two-way-radio was heard, giving him the go ahead. Outside a woman rushed to the limo as a guard opened a door for her. It was Pamela Tutton. She was a little out of breath as she climbed in and sat beside Vince facing me. As the driver revved-up the limo, she quickly introduced herself to us. The conversation was cut short when a man outside signaled to her, and we started to slowly move down the road escorted by police contingents in front and back. Through the limo's windows, we watched throngs of people, lining the streets yelling and cheering for the Senator. The glass was one way, so we were unseen. The limo inched its way toward the town hall's steps. From my advantage point, I could clearly see the Senator shaking hands with her supporters. The Senator inched her way toward the limousine and then suddenly a guard opened our door to let her inside. Senator Laforge backed into the limo still waving and smiling at the throngs of people as guards and police moved in to separate the well-wishers from her.

TV cameras focused on the Senator and followed her every move.

The Senator slid into the limo seat where her campaign manager, Pamela, and Vince sat. She looked tired, but a smile flicker across her face, as she got comfortable on the leather seats. As the limo door closed, it immediately began to inch forward into the road lined with an ecstatic crowd. Inside, the mood was not quite as cheery, as we each quietly expressed our condolence to the Senator over her loss of Ira and members of her staff. Her eyes had hollowness to them, yet she still seemed defiant and very much in control. Other than a smile or a perfunctory "Thank you!" to our voiced concerns, our physical presence was virtually not acknowledged by her. She seemed to be in her own world staring blankly out into space. She sighed and closed her eyes while she quietly asked if she could just have a minute to gather her thoughts. Without waiting for an answer, Pamela came to her rescue and reminded us of the terrible day the Senator had endured.

It was an uncomfortable situation sitting there with the Senator. We had dissected her life for most of the day and we all felt a bit guilty now sitting with her.

She looked at us and said, "I owe all of you my gratitude for having been such good friends to me this last couple of years. I wanted to thank you personally for your friendship, and your faith. I hope that somehow in the future I can repay you. I also want to explain just what has been going on in my life and how you have all been a part of it. I am sure you have many questions about what happened this morning. After all that has occurred, I feel I really owe you an explanation."

Her statement had piqued all of our interest and we all sat there waiting. There was a bit of electricity that sort of rippled through my body. I could feel the anticipation that we all shared.

Vince interjected, "Senator, this has been a long, hard day for you. Are you sure you want to talk to us now?"

"Oh yes!" She replied, "It is very important to discuss these events with you. I feel it is my obligation to tell you what has transpired over the last couple years. If you remember, I told you that just knowing me might pose a danger to you. Well, that statement now appears true, as you can quite well see. If you have the time, let's just ride around a few minutes and talk. What I have to say might relieve some of your concerns and help you avoid problems in the future. If any of you do not want to stay, I will have my driver take you to your car immediately."

Silence hung in the air for a long moment and then Tom answered for all of us, "Senator, I am sure none of us want to go home before we get to hear what you have to say."

"Okay", the Senator smiled, "I need to go way back and explain 'operation Hulagu' that I mentioned to all of you when we first talked. Operation Hulagu was a covert program to create very sophisticated replicates of selected individuals for various purposes. I was one of the individuals that was selected to be replicated. I like to think that my replication was to help bring about peaceful resolution to some of our world problems."

The Senator paused briefly to collect her thoughts and then continued. " I was selected to be the first person replicated and my replica was named ComDefC1. It was designed to have 72-hour life span. Her longevity was carefully tested many times in the laboratory and our calculations had proven accurate every time. Repeatedly, her death would happen within minutes of the predicted time. It is hard to explain how I felt seeing this living replica of me dying over and over again. Scientifically we had succeeded in duplicating what some might call 'the miracle of life,' but I was not prepared for the emotional side of being spawned and witnessing myself repeatedly destroyed. To me this was as traumatic as cutting off my arms or legs."

Katherine paused again her eyes glisten with tears. "I was taught to think of her as a transient physical extension to my own being, but in my mind, she was me. She was my physical, mental and emotional mirror image."

The Senator bit her lip and looked down. All of our eyes were on the Senator.

She squeezed her hands tightly and continued. "We never anticipated what would happen when we employed her in the field. ComDefC1 was an extension of me. When I was told she had failed her mission, and she had failed to expire after the 72-hour window, I was filled with mixed emotions. First I was actually happy, even ecstatic over her survival, but then fear set in, and I was afraid of what it meant. I knew how hard I would fight to stay alive, and I knew she had my drive and would do the same."

Absentmindedly, Katherine curled her silver hair between her fingers.

"This situation made it necessary for the CIA to hide me away for the remainder of the time she continued to live so publicly. When I received the news that she had disappeared from the hospital in Iraq and the news that it was believed she had been killed in a car bombing, I was relieved that I could resume my life again."

Katherine paused, "The CIA kept me in hiding for a couple more days, and then it was decided to move me to Iraq and have me found by agents in Basra. It was important to have me found in Iraq to convince the media that I had been there all along. Well, you know I was found and what happened after."

The Senator hunched forward and paused while rubbing her knee. Tom took the occasion to tell the Senator that he had read her book on her experiences in Operation Iraqi Freedom. The Senator looked at Tom and flashed him a smile.

"Thank you, Tom. One thing that was not included in that book was how I was almost killed by a doctor, a plastic surgeon, who thought he recognized me as his former patient at Ibn Sina Hospital in Baghdad. He intended to kill me, but luckily one of my aides shot him before he shot me. That was my first encounter with people trying to kill me. Since then I have carried a loaded pistol virtually at all times."

"Kat, can I ask another question?" Tom Asked

The Senator looked up, surprised and nodded.

"Did you know then that she was alive?"

The Senator looked at Tom and shook her head, no and continued. "I certainly had doubts and a very strong feeling something was amiss. I definitely believed there was a chance she was alive, but I hoped I was wrong, or that she would look so different that we could both exist without affecting the other."

"No definitive proof of her existence was immediately found, and I began to feel a bit more secure, but then another problem surfaced. My twin had absconded with about a million dollars given to her by Saddam Hussein. This money was supposed to have been for my Presidential run in exchange for currying favors for Hussein, if I was elected. When, I resurfaced, he put a hit out on me. Also at that time, the CIA blocked my access to all information about ongoing research into cloning and made it amply clear that I was to talk to no one about the project. The laboratory in Lumberton, Texas was quickly dismantled and the property sold. Now a big white house sits where the old entrance shack, use to be. No one with the CIA would talk to me anymore. I was a persona non grata. But regardless, I still knew the experiments were continuing."

Katherine shook her head forlornly and said, "My dear friends, they are still experimenting with quantum cloning. Apparently, once they realized how to prolong life longer, more Senators were enlisted into the program. I don't know how they were convinced to join, but they did, and now we have a very clandestine fraternal order of Senators that have active twins."

"Are you saying they only enlisted Senators into the program?" I asked incredulously.

"Yes," Katherine responded, "The CIA was interested in gaining control of one of our existing legislative branches. They wanted to have more control of government policies and officials. They also were disgusted with congressional interference in their covert operations. Senators were the perfect congressional members to control, since they can stay in office indefinitely making it the most powerful governmental branch. It was the perfect power base to infiltrate."

Vince looked astonished and asked, "Are you saying, our current Senators are not who they appear to be?"

Katherine looked grimly, "No, I am not saying all of them have been compromised, but quite a few have been. Some were already obligated to the CIA and continued to cast votes in the CIA's favor to insure certain skeletons remained buried and others were so corrupt within their own power circles that they had no desire to cede power to the CIA. But the younger, hungry naïve Senators could be enlisted."

"So how many have been cloned?" Vince asked.

"I don't really know," Katherine replied, "but I do know that the last cloning project number before I was cut from the program was ComDefC28."

"Jesus, this is insane. Are you sure this is happening? Do you have proof?" Tom asked in disbelief.

Pamela Tutton answered Tom, "We have proof, but it cannot be used. Who would we go to? Those who are behind this program are covert CIA operatives aligned with powerful individuals outside the government. They have such powerful media control, that the only news the public ever knows is the truth that is created for them. Perception Management and Public Relation companies spew out all kinds of truths for the public's consumption, and that is what the public is given and accepts as the truth. This new order views the public as the worker ants of the new society. They see them as expendable, easy to manipulate, great cannon fodder, and an excellent tax base to support their projects. We live in sort of a virtual world, where much of what happens is fabricated to support what powerful elements of society want us to perceive. Even the most obvious truths are often warped into absurdities by reporting the contrived news from so many media outlets that eventually it becomes the undisputed truth. Often there is not an iota of truth in these fabricated stories. News reporting using perception management has become a type of psychological means to insure that people view things properly."

Katherine interrupted, "Who would believe a ridiculous story about members of the CIA and powerful outsiders trying to take over the Senate? No one would believe it. Here you are sitting with me, someone who has been involved in this program, and no media outlet ever recognized or brought up the question that perhaps there were two of me. When Wilson Lawson tried to tell the truth, he was labeled psychotic, a liar, a publicity hound and a greedy son-of-a-bitch for selling his bullshit story to the tabloids. No one can intercede and stop this, because it isn't happening."

I felt noxious as her words sank in. If this is real, there is little we can do. We cannot have a Salem witch-hunt of cloned Senators. Just thinking about how preposterous this all sounded made me feel helpless. This was probably how Giordano Bruno felt when he tried to convince the inquisition that earth was not the center of the Universe and then was subsequently burned at the stake for heresy. Now we simply use political correctness to obscure truths and stifle dissent. Who wants to be labeled a heretic by the Grand Inquisitor of the new politically correct doctrine?

Katherine apologetically said, "The simple fact is what you know, or what they might think you know could complicate your life or even hurt you. You must not speak to anyone of this. If you do, I am sure you will be visited by someone to help you forget what you know."

I looked at Stacie in disbelief that this was happening. I felt guilty that I had gotten her involved in this mess. Her face was one of shock and fear.

"Do you still want to hear about what happened this morning?" Katherine asked glancing at all of this.

We all still wanted to know more.

Katherine continued, "Once I was back in the states, I began to have a vague feeling of being watched. Then one day a letter was returned to me that had been mailed to a person that I had known, but who had been dead for years. At first, I thought I was losing my mind. Why would I have written to a person I knew was dead? I opened the letter and read the content. Immediately, I knew I had not written it. Thoughts that I had buried deep in my mind were revealed in the letter. Scenes were described from a dream that I had as a young girl. It contained things that only ComDefC1, or I could have known.

A month or so later, I received a call on my cell phone from a woman who identified herself as Zoe. The voice on the other end was my own. It was my twin, I was talking to. I was speechless and she said very little other than "Congratulations Kat on your campaign. I truly hope all goes well in your election bid." There had not been much to the conversation and a few days later I questioned myself, if it had just been my imagination. I almost wrote the call off as some sort of daydream, but then I received another call and after that they continued right up until just a couple days ago. They were never threatening. She never said much other than informing me that she was alive, and that she was watching what I was doing. One time, I asked her if she wanted anything from me, and she simply said to live in peace and not worry about anyone trying to kill or capture her. I tried to tell her I had little control over that, but we were disconnected before I could finish my sentence."

Katherine popped open a can of Moxie from the limo's bar and drank a swallow straight from the can and then continued, "I no longer considered Zoe as an adversary, but more of a daughter to me, my offspring. I had become emotionally attached to her and looked forward to hearing her voice reassuring me that she was well. I definitely felt she was really a part of me, and I could not bear the thought of her being killed."

The Senator's voice broke here, and she stopped to recover her composure. Talking about this after having lost her husband and some of her closest friends must have been very hard for her emotionally. The Senator moved an open hand to her eyes and covered them momentarily. When she removed her hand, she let out a loud sigh and then continued.

"I will spare telling you all about my campaign and the multitude of protests that have been orchestrated against me. I am sure you have read all you want to know about that from papers, magazines and the Internet. What I want to tell you now, you are not going to find about from anywhere else, but here in this limo. This, of course cannot go any further then the walls of this limousine."

The Senator paused and looked inquisitively at us for our response. We all of course agreed and for a second or so the Senator scanned our faces. Then her eyes lost their focus as she started to recount the morning attack on her campaign bus. Her voice was almost a whisper as she spoke.

"This morning as we drove down Route 12 from Bellows Falls, a 2001 Toyota SUV Sequoia came roaring around us. After it passed, it swung in front of us fishtailing back and forth. It quickly decelerated causing my driver 'Jim' to apply the brakes hard. While Jim was trying to keep control of the Bus, the Sequoia's hatchback window suddenly retracted and two shotguns protruded from its darkened interior. I could see the faint silhouette of two men aiming the shotguns at the front of our bus. The flash of the muzzles lit up the rear of the SUV as both shotguns fired simultaneously. The blast of buckshots from the two shotguns slammed into the windshield exploding it into a million pieces. Shards of glass along with buck shots punctured holes all over the driver's pit. The dense cluster of shotgun pellets and intense shower of broken glass ripped into Jim, my driver. They continued to fire and Jim's face was virtually pulverized, but a part of him still instinctively tried to stop the bus. The suddenness of the braking caused the bus to career across the highway and smash into a snow bank. The impact of the crash heaved Jim's body forward over the steering wheel leaving him hanging lifeless out the front windshield."

"The blast of the shotguns and the crash woke all of us that were not already up. Ira rushed out of our bedroom into the sitting area of the bus and realized what was going on. Everyone was now in the main living area except me. I was standing in the corridor holding on to the doorframe to keep my balance."

"The first salvo of shots had been intentionally aimed at my driver, and he had been hit numerous times. More men had started to shoot at the bus with automatic rifles and pistols. They shot the tires to pieces preventing us from even trying to escape. There was a constant crackle of gunfire and holes from armor piercing bullets began to appear all over the exit side of the bus. An icy certainty of death crept over me as I envisioned their stalking eyes calmly aiming their rifles at my head. Each flash of their guns punctuating the night's darkness magnified this terror even more. My mind almost closed down as I fixated on these unseen grotesque monsters shooting at us. My brain churned for a way to escape, but there was none."

"The gunmen tried to open the front door, but couldn't pry it open. They apparently used a grenade on the handle, pulled the pin and ran away. The device exploded blowing the door off and buckling the doorframe. The front of the bus filled with swirling smoke and then the darkness was sliced by steadily moving flashes of an automatic weapon. My bodyguard, Steven, began to fire at the muzzle flashes, and they abruptly stopped. Another attacker emerged through the smoke, and was shot numerous times. He staggered forward a couple steps and crumpled to the floor dead."

"Bullets from the others, outside were raking the side of the bus and Roger, another body guard, and my husband, Ira were both shot. Steven tried to shoot the lights out in our cabin, so they could not see us, but he was hit almost as soon as he started firing. None of my bodyguards were dead, but then another man made it on the bus holding a semi-automatic pistol. He moved up to Steven and fired it point blank at his face. Steven had raised his hand as if to stop the bullet, but it sliced through his hand shattering his wrist and ripped into his body shattering more bones before it finally smashed into the floor beside him."

"The scene was surreal. The killer fired so close that the hot air and the particles of gunpowder blew across Steven's face as the first bullet was shot. Blood and pieces of Steven's flesh sprayed across my face and the chair behind me. The man shot Steven again, and this time the bullet smashed into his upper jaw and exploded out of his cranium. The shooter was probably using hollow point rounds because the bullet did tremendous damage, leaving a gaping hole in the back of Steven's head. Those visions of him dying will never leave me. They were horrible."

"Roger took aim at this bastard and shot him in the chest, but the bullet did not kill him, just knocked him down. The guy fell on the other side of Steven's body, which prevented Roger from shooting him. I pulled myself out of my trance, and I grabbed my pistol from my holster and shot at him numerous times. His body jerked each time I hit him. The fear was still there, but now I felt anger and that primitive desire to survive. I had just killed a man who was trying to kill me and my mind now went into a mode of survival. I was now in a cold homicidal rage."

"Roger was hit again by a bullet from those shooting at us from outside, and this one killed him. You could see the flashes of the muzzles outside as they shot at us in the bus. I crawled over to Ira, who was bleeding profusely and tried to pull him to safety. Just then another man climbed up the bus's twisted stairs and saw us trying to move across the floor. Ira was on top of me and the shooter just pointed his pistol at him and shot Ira killing him. I was helpless and he shot Ira again and this bullet also struck my side splitting it open. It turned out to be only a flesh wound that did little damage other than terrify me. I knew I was dead. I could not defend myself, because my pistol was empty."

"I glanced up at the bastard as he walked over to me. He had spittle flying from his smiling mouth, and he said 'Senator you are yesterday's history.' He pointed the gun at my face, and I could see his right eye looking directly at me over the sights of the pistol. My gaze was locked onto his eyes that seemed to glow with the delight of my helplessness. He sort of laughed as he pointed the barrel straight at my temple and then his squinting right eye erupted with a shower of blood spewing out all over me. My ears rang from the discharge of a gun close by that had just sent a bullet ripping through his head. His arms jerked up to his face and the pistol fell from his hand. For a moment his body sort of swayed above me with blood gushing out over his face, washing the snow from his moustache. Then noiselessly he crumpled lifeless to the floor a couple of feet from me. At the top of the steps was Hulagu, Zoe Shelly, ComDefC1 or whatever you want to call her. She was shot and bleeding profusely, but she walked over towards me and knelt down in the blood pooling around Ira. I was immobilized in fear. It was like the feeling you have in a nightmare as you try to wake yourself to stop the horror, but you can't. I was frozen and could not even utter a sound, but just waited for her to put the muzzle of the gun to my head and splatter my brains all over the floor. She was now there, kneeling beside us and all I could see was her pants soaking up Ira's blood. It seemed like an eternity, and then I felt the weight of Ira being removed. She had grabbed Ira by the shoulders and pulled him off of me. "They are all dead." She quietly said. I flipped around and sat up as she lowered Ira's limp body back into my lap. I pulled Ira close to me holding his head to my chest as my own body convulsed with fear and emotions. I found myself gasping for breath and my eyes closed tightly to hide my tears. It was a moment that was filled with a thousand emotions. When I opened my eyes her face was only inches away nuzzled in Ira's hair. Her exhaling breath caused strands of Ira's hair to flitter across my face. I had never been this close to her. And now she was mourning Ira's death, kissing his cheek and stroking his hair as I held him in my arms. My heart was heavy with sorrow, but still raced with fear. I feared her. I still felt she might shoot me at any moment, but her gun rested on the floor in the ever-widening pool of blood. I held Ira even tighter as if his closeness protected me from her. And perhaps it did. My eyes looked into her face, and I could see tears trickling down her cheek. She kissed his lips, caressed his face and began to weep."

"The night was calm now. No gunshots. No bullets whizzing by, just the quiet whisper of the winter wind blowing through the holes and broken windows of the bus. The loudest sound now was our breathing, soft sobs and the occasional rustling of paper skittering across the floor."

"My eyes swept over my likeness, inches from me. Her jacket hung heavy with blood, a mixture of hers and Ira's. Her presence diminished my emotional pain. The agony of his lost she shared with me as we sat there with Ira's lifeless body. In her mind, held in a parasitic grip, were my memories of Ira. Those memories reached out like tentacles and touched her every thought. To her, Ira was as much her husband as he was mine. She was finally touching the man whose memories had plagued her mind for months. The man that her mind had told her was her life, which she remembered nights of passion with and a thousand life's adventures. Now he would always stay a dream to her because tonight his life was reduced to nothing, but a memory to both of us."

"I heard the silence broken by my voice. It was me speaking and the sound of my voice, our voice startled her. I had looked into her eyes and said I know how much you must love him, and I know you are thinking of all the yesterdays that were good ones and even perhaps some of the bad ones because that is what is in my mind. I am sorry for the emptiness you must feel now. It is the same kind of emptiness that tears at my heart. She did not reply, but just stared at me. I lowered my eyes ashamed of having tried to presume the pain she felt. Her eyes were a mirror into my soul and their glance made me fear what I might see of myself within them. They cut through me, knowing everything about me, every secret, and every possible lie hidden deep within my memories."

"My body shivered from the cold or my emotions and my tremors caught her attention, and she asked quietly 'Are you shot?'"

"I raised my head and look at her again and said. 'Yes, but not bad! But what about you? Your jacket is soaked in blood.'"

"'I think I am going to die this time.' She replied and actually smiled at me."

"Her words made me feel sick. I felt guilty and wanted to say something that would purge the remorse I was consumed in, but I could not think of one word to say to her."

"I finally blurted out, 'Let me get you to a doctor.'"

"'Christ no! If you took me to a doctor I would either be killed or locked up until I did die.'"

"'They do not have to know who you are.' I said to her pleadingly."

"'I look like you and after these killings, every doctor in the area will be contacted for anyone with bullet wounds. There is no way I could get medical help without being captured or killed by the CIA. It is foolish to talk about this, and I know you know that. Do you still want to be President?'

"'After this, I am not sure.' I responded."

"'You do. I know you do, and we must leave here now or your chances will be destroyed. We cannot be found together.'"

"I looked at her and started to protest, but stopped as she pulled Ira from me and laid him down on the floor. She stood up and said, 'Please come with me.'"

"'Where are we going?' I asked."

"'Trust me. I just want to be with you now. I know and you know you want to be with me when I die this time. You have always been there to comfort me when I died. This time I need you more than ever. Please help me.'"

"I wanted to be with her. She was a part of me that was missing, and I reached out to touch her."

"She had lost a lot of blood and was very weak. 'Call me Zoe.' She said to me."

"'It makes me feel real. I tried to live a life of my own, but all your memories haunted me, and I could not escape from being you,' she said."

"She was like a part of me, even then as she helped to save me, Zoe thought how to prevent anyone from knowing about her and the program that created her."

"She told me. 'We have to get away from this bus because my car is parked down the road, and if it is discovered, then everyone would know about the program.'"

"I realized she was right and helped her stand up. Her jacket was soaked with blood and some was crystallizing into the fabric from the cold. We moved away from Ira's body to the destroyed entrance to the bus. I jumped down first and helped her climb down from the mangled doorway. Gingerly, we hobbled over to her car parked about 100 feet behind the bus. I helped her into the passenger seat. The car was still warm inside. Zoe had apparently just driven up, jumped out, and shot her way into the melee."

* * * *

Inside the limousine my wife openly sobbed and tears burned in my eyes as well. Katherine paused for a minute and wiped her eyes and took another sip of her Moxie. She took a couple of shuttering breaths and then continued, "What had just happened felt like an eternity, but in ticks of the clock it all transpired in a mere four or five minutes. Eight people had been killed and two wounded in that short time."

"Zoe was slumped in the passenger seat like a bloody immobile lump of flesh as we drove along Route 12. She told me to just drive around with her for a while. She just wanted me to talk to her."

"'No one should ever know that I was here.' Zoe cautioned me."

'You should just tell people you ran away from the bus to save yourself.' Zoe offered.'

'You must stay with me till I die and destroy any proof I was ever here. I have a five-gallon can of gas in the trunk. Use it to cremate me and to destroy this car.'

"I was speechless for a moment. I had not thought of this problem and the thought of burning her body bothered me immensely."

"She painfully reached over, and touched me and said, 'You must!'"

"I glanced over at her and quietly agreed that I would do as she requested."

"A mile or so north on Route 12, I drove the car off of the highway and parked it behind an old barn. She just wanted to be with me for her remaining time. I reached over and held her. It was like holding a dying daughter to me. I felt terribly emotional as I felt her trembling body in my arms. I told her how I wished we could have known each other better. She replied that she had been happy for the few months of life that she had been given. Zoe knew this would be the last time she would be created, and she feared her end."

"'You know that there are others like me now?' She whispered."

"'I thought there was, but I am not part of the program anymore,' I replied."

"She looked up at me inquisitively and said, 'They are preparing one of us to run for President, and it isn't me.'"

"'Who is it?'"

"'Katherine, I hurt. There are all kinds of voices talking in my head right now. Mentally, I am linked with all the others of my kind and their thoughts become maddening sometimes.'"

"She took in deep breaths and said, 'He is a young junior Senator, and they want him to win. And they will make sure he does.'"

"Zoe coughed and I wiped the blood from her lips".

"'Am I human?' She asked."

"'You are as human as I am.' I told her. Her question made me feel like I was outside of my own body holding myself as I died. My body shook with the grief I felt for her. She was me and she did things that I could not believe I would have ever been able to do. Her bravery in saving my life made me feel sick to my stomach, now that she was dying. I told her how proud I was of all she had accomplished, which was the truth. She was laboring to breath, and I swear I felt her spirit, yes her soul preparing to leave her bleeding body. I truly hope that she was as real as I was and if there is a God, that she is given the reward and the peace she deserves for being a woman that was the epitome of good."

The Senator bit her lip to restrain her emotions that had consumed her and an uncomfortable silence hung over all of us. Stacie was squeezing my hand tightly, and I knew that there would be tears in her eyes. But she was not alone, sadness showed on all of our faces.

The Senator cleared her throat and continued.

"Zoe's eyes seem to stare unseeing into nowhere. I held her hand while I talked to her and stroked her fingers. Her head tipped downward and she spoke of my mother. She asked, 'Will mother know me? I have had so many thoughts of her. So many memories of her. I hope….' Her voice trailed off with her thoughts, but I told her that mother was as much hers as mine, and she would love both of us the same."

"'Be a good mother to Lyndsey.' Zoe whispered."

"She moaned and added in a raspy voice, 'I never got to touch her or kiss her, but I felt so much love for her. She is a wonderful daughter. I loved her!'"

Katherine brushed away a tear and continued, "I think Zoe was now at that point in dying where she felt no pain. Some point between living and the final darkness of death. An instant where all your moments of life pour from your subconscious and converge into one whirlwind of memories ascending with your soul into heaven or some other dimension. I hoped she was enjoying a kaleidoscope of these visions of the life she had been a part of. While I listened to her sporadic breathing, I wondered if I would think of the same things when I die."

"I sat next to her, and her clenched left hand rested limply in my lap. I talked to her quietly about our life. A life that we had shared as one. I don't know if she heard what I spoke of, but I felt and hoped it comforted her in some way. She never said anything more to me, and finally I felt her slump into my arms and her breathing stop. I felt her pulse and realized she was dead. I removed her hand from my lap and something fell from it. I turned on the dome light and saw a gold coin on the floor. I picked it up. It was still warm from her grasp. It was one of the most precious coins I had owned when she sold them. She must have been handing it over to me as she was dying. I put it in my pocket. It was now priceless."

"I kissed her on her forehead and tore myself out of the car. Here I was, unable to return the compassion, mercy and love, she had shown me, a person, who she must have believed wished her dead. Zoe had sacrificed herself for me, and I will never really know why. I feel I could have saved her, if I could have gotten her medical attention, but that was an impossibility."

Katherine fell silent again and her body quivered from emotions. I realized then, how much she had loved Zoe. My wife said, "Katherine, maybe you should stop. You don't need to torture yourself with this."

Katherine bit her lip and said, "No, I need to tell you the rest. When she died, I felt in my heart that the earth should have stopped with her death, but the world kept right on going uncaring and untouched by this tragedy I had just witnessed. A part of me felt that tonight we had reunited once again, and Zoe, and I had metamorphed back into one entity. It was almost like we had cheated death."

"I hated what I had to do next. I pulled out a five-gallon container of gas from the trunk and sprinkled its contents over the seats and Zoe's lifeless body. I dribbled a trail of gas out of the car door and along the snow covered ground for about fifteen feet. The gas was quickly evaporating into the snow, and I worried I would not be able to light it. I took my empty pistol and chambered one shot. I held it close to the snow and fired. The muzzle flash ignited the gas and the blaze wiggled along the path back to the car. Suddenly, the car burst into a ball of fire. This was Zoe's funeral pyre. She had lived only a few ticks of eternity's clock, and now she was returning back to the cosmic realm from where she had come. I had hoped she would have lived forever, but now she was simply gases and ashes that would flutter over the white snow and become earth once more."

"My back was against a cold biting wind piercing through my jacket, but in front of me the terrific heat from the fire blew against my face. The bright flames dazzled my eyes, and I could hear the pyre crackling as it consumed the car and my twin. The fury of the fire belched up churning clouds of smoke, and somewhere in that swirling darkness my memories and perhaps a piece of my soul floated high up into the ebony winter night. It was all a dantesque dream that I was living. A nightmarish hell that made me want to scream. A whiff of the pungent smoke hit my nostrils, and I realized that part of the smell is the flesh of my double burning violently in this fire of death. Each breath of winter air carried the scent of her death, which will haunt my memories forever."

"Tires popped from the heat and the windshield of the car exploded. I listened intently for ghostly whispers from my twin. The heat and smoke from the fire snaked its way through the branches of the nearby trees and suddenly an avalanche of snow cascaded to the ground. The snow sizzled in the roaring fire making white clouds, but the fury of the fire won and its flames leapt into the sky again."

"I turned from the roaring fire and started to run down the road we came in on. I was about a quarter of a mile from Route 12. I found myself in pain, and gasping after just a hundred feet or so. It was very dark and I found myself stumbling as I ran over the snow-covered road. I could still smell the smoke from the fire as I reached the highway. My throat and lungs were burning from my run and the cold air I was breathing. Once on the highway, I ran north going even further away from my bus and the car burning. I saw car lights coming toward me, and at first, I feared it might be someone else trying to kill me. I quickly scurried over a snow bank and crouched shivering behind it. I waited, hoping that I had not been seen. It felt like an eternity, but finally the roar of a vehicle zooming by broke the silence of the night. I stayed hidden for about 30 seconds more before I ventured my head up over the snow bank. Down the road, I could see the faint glimmer of taillights fading into the distance, so I climbed back over the snow bank. I struggled on for about three minutes more on Route 12 until another side road came into view. I could see a darkened barn just a short distance down the road, and I panted toward it. I wanted someplace out of the wind and snow. My lungs burned from the run and my bruised ribs throbbed from the shot, but I felt I was now temporarily safe."

"I had to stop and think for a bit to sort out what I was going to do, and what I was going to say. Then the shock of Ira's death and the others hit me, and I felt like I should take my own life. I threw up in the hay there on the barn floor and continued lying there almost paralyzed from what had happened. Some of it I was not sure had even happened anymore. It just seemed to be a nightmare or a hallucination of some sort. But as the cold bit into my face and hands, my senses returned, and I knew I was now truly alone as Zoe had been except for you my friends. My husband was gone and I was not sure if I should go on anymore, but then I thought about Zoe taking her life to save mine and about my daughter. I realized that I had to go on, and I had to try and now be the epitome of good as she was as an honor to her sacrifice. So I went back to the road and flagged down a car that brought me to the police and after a quick bandage job they begrudgingly brought me to the town hall. I wanted to thank all those who supported me and to deliver my message. Because the only way we can win this fight is electing new Senators and changing the laws that allow Senators to hold power forever."

"Just you all knowing this makes me feel a bit better about Zoe. I hope you will also remember her in your prayers. I just cannot express to you how much I really loved her. The longer she stayed alive, the more my love and admiration grew for her."

Pamela Tutton interrupted Katherine and reminded her that they had to return to the police.

"Pamela is right, we did promise the police to go over everything, as soon as I was done with some personal matters You four were those matters." The Senator tapped on the glass partition and the limo pulled over to the side of the road. Behind them a police cruiser with blinking lights pulled up beside us and stopped. Two officers sat in the black and white cruiser. I suddenly realized that we were now in south Charlestown a short distance from where the attack had occurred earlier this morning. Police cars lined the road and in the distance I could see her campaign bus, with police milling around it.

Senator Laforge reached out her hand to shake ours and to bid us good night. Stacie and I said good-bye to Kat. Stacie kissed her on her cheek one last time. Katherine apologized again and said, "With the number of enemies, I've accumulated, it's impossible to know who was trying to kill me. Big Oil, CIA agents, Saddam's agents, tax fanatics or some other psychotics."

In a low-pitched voice she added, "I do sincerely hope we get to see each other again."

A behemoth police officer pulled opened her door and she and Pamela alighted and climbed into the waiting cruiser.

I glanced out the door and a dull metal object in the snow caught my attention. It looked like a Hulagu coin lying there outside the door. Did Katherine drop it? I just had a glimpse of it before our limo door was closed, and we pulled away. But that is what fixed in my mind. I glanced out the window, but I could see only the swirling snow, the waving police officer and Katherine's vehicle returning to the stricken campaign bus still stuck in the embankment.

Her departure had been rather sudden; we really didn't have much time to say good-bye. There was now an uncomfortable silence between the four of us.

The limousine drove down Main Street stopping at each parking place where we had left our cars earlier that morning and each of us said good-bye to the driver and exited out into the cold.

When we came to where my car was parked, we said our goodbyes. Something new was nagging at my consciousness about today. At first, I couldn't figure out what it was that was bothering me. But as I inched my car out of the snow, it struck me. Katherine's hair had been virtually white. I distinctly remember her twisting it between her fingers as she sat in front of me on the bus.

It was much lighter than the salt and pepper hair that I remembered from the night before when my wife helped her color it even darker.

I looked at my wife and asked, "Did you notice anything different about Katherine than how she looked last night?"

Stacie looked at me oddly and said that she had not. I reminded her of how Katherine's hair had looked when we left her the night before. "Why would it be so white today?" I questioned.

She looked at me strangely and said, "Sometimes when a person gets very scared their hair turns white. She also might have just decided to wash the color out and be her natural self. What is bothering you?"

I didn't reply, but doubts were growing about what was real and what was not. Or was I just being paranoid?

Since that traumatic day, strange and disquieting thoughts continue to plague me. Maybe it is just my doubting nature, but the image of Kat's face with her white hair does not easily fade from my memory. Perhaps her hair getting wet from the snow washed the color out or maybe the grayness of her hair was the results of poor lighting in the limo, but I do wonder. I have many thoughts about that day wandering through my mind. I admit that I want to believe all she said, but I am sure there is something more to Katherine's story than we know. There may not be, but part of me won't bury those doubts.

I guess to 'keep the peace' and perhaps my life, I must repress these things inside. But I can't do it forever. Sooner or later, I will have to let it out; otherwise, I will drive myself to insanity. If I could say what I need to say, you may think I am a terrible person. You may think that I am simply trying to confuse.

In all honesty, I am trying to tell you the truth, and whether or not you can accept it, is your choice. I know she said that this secret group is enlisting other Senators and in particular junior Senators, with one chosen to become President, but that logically couldn't happen. They would have to convince the public to vote for an inexperienced junior Senator without a power base and no amount of perception management could accomplish that. Senior statesmen would never support the election of a junior Senator. And where would they raise the money? Wall Street would not gamble on a powerless junior Senator. It is inconceivable. But then I also doubt that major contributors like Big Oil or Wall Street would embrace their nemesis, Katherine.

Her story of destroying the car and her twin's body with fire also bothered me. A shell of a burnt out car was found close to Route 12, but not any human remains. I suppose it is possible that wolves, dogs or wild hogs hauled it away and ate what was left, but where would the bones be? Maybe deep in the Connecticut River.

I really feel lost sometimes. Now I won't go into all the details I am referring to, but certain people reading this will understand exactly what I am talking about. So was it Katherine or her twin that told us her story? Was it just a way to confuse us because she is their chosen one?

'Truth, like light, blinds. Falsehood, on the contrary, is a beautiful twilight that enhances every object.' I have always liked Albert Camus' quote and in this context it is so apropos.

I know some people do see things that are not real, like long-dead relatives or faces changing before their eyes. But, I am not like that, I just have doubts.

But I no longer doubt Sorat's existence. I have come to believe he is that evil conduit who invades our being and mutates our soul to the point that spreading misery and death becomes as fulfilling as the rapture of one's first love.

Since my wife and friends don't share my concerns about that infamous Sunday, I find it more comfortable keeping my views to myself.

I wish I had never said anything to Stacie about Katherine's hair. I don't want her to think I am some sort of psychotic. Even when we socialize with my old friends, I feel a keen sense of dread and anxiety as soon as Senator

Laforge's name comes up. When it does, I just sit there quiet, saying nothing, but just rocking in my chair, looking out my window and savoring the knowledge that only I have of that day.

To sin by silence when they should protest makes cowards of men.
~ Abraham Lincoln

About the Author

David Hearne is a former military officer who has been involved in the IT Industry for the last 20 years. His last book was a 500-page book called "Enable Command Performance". This was an exhaustive and comprehensive reference to the Enable Procedural language, a scintillating read for the Dilbert crowd. He also has written numerous articles on technology and interviewed its luminaries like Ted Wait the founder of Gateway 2000 Computers, Heidi Roizen the founder of T/Maker and a Vice President of Apple Computer.

He now lives in Southeast Texas with his wife and daughter.

www.ingramcontent.com/pod-product-compliance
Lightning Source LLC
Chambersburg PA
CBHW071529260626
47170CB00002B/567